What the critics are saying:

"The third book in the Deep Is The Night series is well worth the wait...Agnew ties up loose ends from her wonderful series with a good mixture of humor, mystery and of course, hot sex. I can't wait to see what she comes up with next." ~ *Romantic Times Book Club Magazine*

"*Deep is the Night - Haunted Souls* is a hot little number with quite a punch...The danger and suspense in *Deep is the Night - Haunted Souls* will have readers quickly reading to get to the end." ~ *Fallen Angel Reviews*

"As usual, Ms. Agnew treats the reader to a suspenseful ride and certainly an excellently written conclusion to what is a great series... Deep is the Night: Haunted Souls belongs on my keeper shelf, along with the other two titles in this series. I definitely recommend it." ~ *Just Erotic Romance Reviews*

Haunted Souls
Deep Is The Night

Denise A. Agnew

HAUNTED SOULS
An Ellora's Cave Publication, March 2005

Ellora's Cave Publishing, Inc.
1337 Commerce Drive Suite #13
Stow, Ohio 44224

ISBN #1419950150

Edited by: *Martha Punches*
Cover art by: *Syneca*

Warning:

The following material contains graphic sexual content meant for mature readers. *Deep Is The Night: Hauted Souls* has been rated *E–rotic* by a minimum of three independent reviewers.

Ellora's Cave Publishing offers three levels of Romantica™ reading entertainment: S (S-ensuous), E (E-rotic), and X (X-treme).

S-*ensuous* love scenes are explicit and leave nothing to the imagination.

E-*rotic* love scenes are explicit, leave nothing to the imagination, and are high in volume per the overall word count. In addition, some E-rated titles might contain fantasy material that some readers find objectionable, such as bondage, submission, same sex encounters, forced seductions, etc. E-rated titles are the most graphic titles we carry; it is common, for instance, for an author to use words such as "fucking", "cock", "pussy", etc., within their work of literature.

X-*treme* titles differ from E-rated titles only in plot premise and storyline execution. Unlike E-rated titles, stories designated with the letter X tend to contain controversial subject matter not for the faint of heart.

Also by Denise A. Agnew:

Haunted Souls

Deep Is The Night

Prologue
Pine Forest, Colorado

They must all die.

When Halloween comes, my energy will be fiercest. I will be invincible.

As a swirling draft leaked through a crack in the broken tomb, the ancient one drank in the cold night air. Despite a weakened body, the old vampire's anger rose high. With a groan he lay back on the stone floor near a wooden coffin long ago starting to disintegrate. Ah, but he loved the old, the forbidden, the gloom surrounding him in the crypt. The place didn't possess the heavy pall of the tunnels, the delicious sickness he craved so much. No, all that lingered here was the reality of death, the inevitability for all but the undead.

He would have to be satisfied.

No one would look for him here. This long-forgotten crypt resided in the desolate area not far from Pine Forest. Well-hidden, surrounded by bushes and trees, the stonework neglected and weathered, this sanctuary would serve as safe shelter. Few people probably even knew this crypt existed.

A day had passed since his last encounter with the group of meddlesome, hateful mortals and the immortal Irish pup, Ronan Kieran. Closing his eyes, the ancient one replayed in his mind the mistakes he'd made. He cursed that a thousand years of experience had broken down under mortal will. Energy had drained from him fighting the mortals' combined psychic energy fields. He'd underestimated Ronan Kieran's will, but more than that, he underestimated the power the group could generate between them.

An ache built inside him as he thought of Erin's betrayal. She didn't want him and didn't recognize her reincarnation as his beloved Dasoria. He had one alternative. No longer would he indulge her, no longer would he spare her. Lachlan, her lover, would die with her when the time came, and suffer a fate far more horrible than they could imagine. Her new friends, Micky Gunn and Jared Thornton, would also suffer before succumbing to his wrath.

He planned and plotted, his desires hotter and stronger with each passing hour. Once he regained his strength, he would return to the tunnels under the Gunn Inn and make an alliance with the malevolent energy residing there. He'd sensed the power, far older than himself, would enhance and compliment his own desires. He wondered if other vampires had wandered the tunnels and discovered what he now understood. This town seeped with evil, with darkness so dominant no mortal could guard against it in the end.

The ancient one understood he must be careful when dealing with the strange energy, for shadows invaded the tunnels under the Gunn Inn, more hate-filled and growing with each minute. Sentient, the darkness felt stronger and more defined as fear multiplied in Pine Forest. Whenever an act filled with dislike and pain, hatred and dread entered the mind of someone in Pine Forest, the evil drew upon it, added to it, and fed it in an ever-increasing circle.

When Halloween came, all putrefying emotions would gather and wicked entities would join. Nothing could stop the most horrible strength on earth.

Few people could imagine the entity. As it invaded their dreams at night, it came cloaked in recognizable forms. The missing child, the missing spouse, the horrible monster chasing them in the night. Because it lived in the tunnels, it became one with the earth, penetrating the ground people walked upon and absorbing their doubt and trepidation with every step. Soon all the signs would be there, a total accumulated from more than a century of continual strife and discontent. The sleepy little town sat upon a boiling wound. Blood flowed from the cut, the hurt inflicted upon it by human nature and excessive greed.

On Halloween, the inequity of the ages would merge with the ancient one to become one horrible power.

The Final Darkness.

Chapter One
Pine Forest, Colorado
St. Bartholomew's Catholic Church
The central graveyard

"Give me your money, bitch."

Clarissa Gaines' heart stopped and her breathing ceased.

At least that's what it felt like as a dark form stepped out from behind a crypt and into her path. She took a step back as the man leveled a gun on her, his black-gloved hand steady.

A tremor ran over her body as dread froze her blood. Icy wind blew across the graveyard, rustling the pine trees into a chilling whisper. The last rays of sunlight were swallowed by encroaching clouds. Shadows swept across the gravestones, darkening their gray faces. Cold seemed to encroach on the churchyard and blanket her soul.

Night came and apparently so did the neighborhood kooks.

Or the serial killer haunting this town.

Seconds drew out as she took in the horror caricature. Dressed like a pirate of old, the tall man's swirling cape, tall boots, and feathered hat would have looked dashing at any other time. The Freddy Kruger *Nightmare on Elm Street* mask ruined the effect.

He moved a step closer and she flinched. "I said, give me your money."

Guttural and determined, his request sounded more than dead serious.

Good deal, Clarissa. Go ahead and prove your friends right. Put yourself one step into Pine Forest and get dead.

Her brain kicked in and she took a deep breath to steady herself. She hitched her camera case higher on her left shoulder. Licking her dry lips, she tried to piece together a coherent sentence. "I only have a couple of dollars."

The man snorted and waved the weapon back and forth. "You're lying. What's in your fanny pack?"

"Driver's license, tissues—"

"Take it off and give it to me."

She unclipped the fanny pack and started to hold it toward him. He stepped forward and snatched it. The movement wrenched her right ring finger, the fanny pack strap catching on her large citrine ring. Pain stabbed through her hand. He grabbed her right forearm in a harsh, bruising grip.

She gasped. "Let me go!"

He yanked and she stumbled into him. The man smelled of sweat and whiskey. She wrinkled her nose in disgust. "You're askin' for it, bitch. What if I give *you* some?"

She pulled back from his revolting stench and he let her go.

Before she could blink he slapped her across the face. Sharp pain stabbed her jaw as she fell backwards and dropped like a rock. Her camera case went flying.

Dizziness assaulted Clarissa as she lay on her back. Stunned, she couldn't gather her foggy thoughts except for one. She must escape. She struggled to sit upright, one hand to her bruised face. If she'd expected to find death in a graveyard, it hadn't been at the hands of a pistol-welding pirate with no sense of humor. The bastard was definitely not playing trick or treat.

What she saw next defied logic and sanity.

A brown-cloaked form materialized with an audible pop behind and to the right of the pirate. The pirate flinched. Breathless and beyond surprised, Clarissa didn't budge.

Before the pirate could make another movement, the large cloaked form clamped one hand on the pirate's neck and whirled him around. The Freddy Kruger wannabe dropped her fanny pack and it landed a short distance away.

"What the—?" The pirate tried to bring up his weapon.

The cloaked form wrenched the gun from the man's hand and jammed the barrel against the pirate's throat. The pirate's hat landed in the snow. Greasy dark hair hung lank around the purse-snatcher's head.

"This is my territory." Harsh, husky, and vibrant with an Irish accent, the deep voice issuing from the cloaked stranger sent a strange shiver over her skin. "And you are bloody well trespassing."

His territory? Oh, shit. She'd stepped from one fire into another. Maybe if she tiptoed away neither man would miss her.

She saw the pirate's Adam's apple bob up and down. "I didn't—I didn't know—"

"You ought to feckin' know," the cloaked man said, his tone unforgiving and hard.

"Please, let me go." The pirate's voice wobbled. "Please. I won't ever come back."

Incredibly, the cloaked figure lifted the purse-snatcher by the shirt collar. The pirate's legs dangled and kicked in the air as he started to choke and gasp.

She could barely see the cloaked man's face in the encroaching night, but his voice, inflexible and determined, told all. "Never, ever treat a woman that way. If you come near her again, I will break every bone in your body. If I hear you've mistreated or tried to rob *anyone*, I will hunt you down and kill you myself."

Somehow, the cloaked figure's words sounded old-fashioned, the inflection tinted with centuries of understanding. The vibrancy, the sheer assurance in his tone guaranteed severe punishment to anyone who defied him.

Clarissa shivered with reaction, her heart pounding and her fingers trembling as she reached for her camera case.

"Is that understood?" the cloaked form asked.

The pirate made a choking noise and rasped, "Yeah. Whatever you want. I'll do anything you want."

The cloaked man tossed the pirate aside. A screech left the pirate's throat as he sailed into the air and landed on his back just short of a gravestone. Whimpering in fear, the man scrambled to his feet and ran.

Sunlight shifted as it dipped between parting clouds, then descended behind the mountains, casting deeper darkness across the area. Renewed apprehension gathered inside her as a cold lump grew in her stomach. Her ring finger throbbed and so did the rest of her body. A strange disorientation plagued her, as if she'd stepped into a surreal dream.

In a blink of an eye the remaining man yanked off his cloak and it landed at his feet. Her savior turned and started toward her. She scrambled to her feet, ready to flee if the man made one suspicious gesture.

His gaze flared yellow, as penetrating and abrupt as cat eyes in a dark room. Her heart leapt with unholy fear, her muscles strung taut. His long legs ate up ground, and although self-preservation told her to retreat, she found she couldn't move.

Common sense made her struggle against the fear holding her in place. Suddenly a voice whispered in her mind. *You are safe. There is no need to fear me.*

Despite the reassurance, her anxiety grew. *I must be losing my mind. He can't be in my mind. He can't be.* Her entire body trembled.

He appeared one hundred percent capable of ripping a person to pieces. Evening meshed with the stranger, as if he belonged to the night more than the day. His open long black leather coat, black sweater and black jeans made him a part of the shadows. Why on earth would he wear a cloak over that gorgeous leather jacket?

Impressions assaulted her like a gale, knocking her breath from her lungs for the second time in a few minutes. His visage defined hard, rugged masculinity to perfection. If anyone asked her what made him handsome, she would say his intenseness, the undeniable heat in those searching, searing eyes.

As a photographer she appreciated the surreal scene of a menacing stranger stark against gravestones. As a woman, she drank in the most incredible man she'd ever seen.

His shaggy chocolate, collar-length hair ruffled in the breeze. Sooty, dense lashes framed obsidian dark eyes that sparked with golden fire. In profile his nose seemed almost perfect, a compliment to his high cheekbones. His sideburns lined all the way down his jaw and to his chin in a close-clipped beard, turning cinnamon at his mustache and chin.

She would love to photograph him.

Clarissa snapped out of her thrall, her voice whispery. "Thank you."

His attention dropped to her lips, his warm gaze a physical caress along first her upper, then lower lip. When he didn't answer, she wondered about the sanity of waiting for him to speak. Anxiety twisted in her stomach.

Finally she heard his rusted, husky voice. "Do not be afraid."

As rich and full as one glance from his glorious, thickly lashed eyes, the stranger's tone trapped her in place like a rabbit under the hunt. Maybe he lured victims with the liquid, soothing tone wrapped around a dangerous, telltale rumble. She cursed her defenselessness and his ability to see her apprehension.

When he stopped a short distance from her, the man's gaze played over her features then down the length of her red wool peacoat. His unswerving assessment warmed her entire body with strange flutters of attraction.

He had to be at least six-four, his shoulders wide, his chest broad. She allowed her imagination to conjure a fleeting fantasy about the body he owned under all those clothes.

Without a doubt the mystery man would be built like a god. She visualized taut muscle under smooth skin, dark hair sprinkling over hard pecs and a muscled stomach. And further down his manly attributes would be large to fit the rest of him.

Untamed sensation hit her in the stomach, a powerful and stunning craving. She felt hot and needy, itching for his touch.

As she looked up into his eyes, she noticed a stunning firelight in the center. Gold melded with rich, deep mahogany. As the light swirled and tumbled, so did her equilibrium. Her knees felt unsteady and she couldn't look away. Yellow flecks swirled in his irises, spinning with the intensity of a hurricane, and she felt weightless.

"Your eyes," she whispered in amazement. "How...?"

He blinked and the strange light went out. Maybe the face slap the pirate had given her rattled her more than she thought.

He studied her intensely. "You're hurt."

Clarissa swallowed hard. "No, not really." She cleared her throat and gathered strength. "I'm fine."

He traced her jaw with his index finger and the sensual touch made her shiver. He tilted her chin up so she fell into the depths of his eyes. Her heart fluttered and a warm rush filled cold places in her body. A sense of unreality overcame her; she couldn't be certain this was happening.

"You'll have a bruise here in the morning." He shook his head, his eyes filled with anger. "You shouldn't be here without a chaperone."

Indignation removed her strange malaise. "Chaperone? What century are you living in? I can go where I please, thank you very much."

His gaze simmered with annoyance. "You misunderstand me. I imagine you can take care of yourself under normal circumstances. Haven't you heard about the serial killer? No woman is safe alone in this town at any time. Neither day nor night is a haven. You should leave here and not come back."

His patronizing tone cut through the heady attraction. "Now wait a minute, I'm doing a job here."

"Reporter?"

"No." She hefted the camera case. "I'm a writer. I take photographs for my books. I came out here to take maybe two pictures very quickly. I wasn't out of the car more than five minutes when that jerk showed up."

His gaze intensified. She tried to remember the last time a man enveloped her with his attention as if he found her fascinating, and she couldn't. Not with the single-minded attention of a man sexually entranced and worried for her well-being at the same time. It was a heady sensation having this man's full attention locked onto her like a heat-seeking missile.

"Are your books worth losing your life?" he asked, his voice a husky whisper.

"Of course not." Curiosity made her change the subject. "Who *are* you?"

"Ronan Kieran." The name rolled off his tongue with that distinctive lilt.

"You're Irish."

"Yes." His gaze danced over her face with red-hot appreciation. "And your name?"

"Clarissa Gaines. I've written several books on haunted areas."

"Some places are quaint. Some places are old. Pine Forest is the most haunted place on earth," he said.

She couldn't help but smile. "That's for sure." She put out her hand to shake his. "Thank you again. You may have saved my life."

"It was all my pleasure."

He clasped her hand and brought it to his lips for an old-fashioned kiss. Startled, she squashed a gasp of surprise. Although she'd seen him lift a man with one arm, his grip remained gentle with her. In fact, as he released her, his fingers drew over hers with sensual exploration.

She inhaled, her breath a little sharp as a twirl of sensation traveled up her arm and landed in her lower belly. *Wow. Could a man get any sexier than this?*

A smile curved one corner of his mouth for a second, almost as if…as if he knew what she'd been thinking. "Why did you come here if you know there is a serial killer lurking and that this whole town is haunted?"

She smiled. "I grew up here."

One of his eyebrows quirked upward. "Interesting. It doesn't make you immune to harm."

Damn the man. "I realize that. I just got here today and wanted some pictures as the sun was setting. I didn't get a chance to take any shots before that idiot jumped out at me."

Ronan shook his head. Another miniscule movement of his lips, a tiny twitch of amusement. "You were lucky he wasn't the serial killer. You should leave town and not come back."

She bristled. "I know my way around here, and a person can't live their life running from fear all the time."

He shifted closer and she caught a whiff of leather, bergamot, and another spice she couldn't identify. He smelled so delicious. Arousal heated her face with a blush.

"Sure, and you may think common self-defense is enough, but it isn't. Not against this killer. You cannot fight him."

How do I know it isn't you?

"How do you know it's not me?" he asked.

An eerie shiver ran through her as he echoed her thoughts. As powerful as this man appeared, she wouldn't have much chance of escape. Clarissa wondered if she'd made the worst mistake of her life.

Reality and rising dread slapped her in the face. Her heart fluttered with a peculiar combination of fear and renewed admiration. "You saved me from the pirate just to hurt me?"

Ronan crossed his arms. "You heard me say this is my territory."

Think fast, Clarissa. "I'm expected for dinner at six. If I don't show up they're going to come looking for me."

He nodded. "Undoubtedly. But if you're already dead, what good would it do if they found you?"

"Are you threatening me?"

"I might be."

Ire made her lash out. "Then get on with it. This witty repartee is starting to piss me off."

A laugh burst from his throat, deep, rumbling and tantalizing. She didn't want to feel anything for this irritating man, but the resonance in his laugh made desire center low in her stomach once again.

It was insane to feel yearning and trepidation at the same time. Absolutely, irrevocably nuts.

When had she encountered a man this contrary, this frightening and amazing at one time? Never. The fact she couldn't control it confused Clarissa down to the marrow.

"Are you willing to risk all you have for a feckin' photograph?" he asked. "And for what? A place of the dead? That's bollocks."

Irritated, she whirled and headed toward the front gate, intent on putting as many miles between her and the Irishman as she could. This situation was too weird.

Lightheadedness assaulted Clarissa and her eyelids fluttered. She swayed and reached out. Her hands landed on stone as she touched the side of a crypt and leaned against it. Panic trembled in her chest.

Powerful arms reached around her waist and pulled her back against hard-as-rock muscles. She gasped and tried to writhe out of his grip. He clasped her wrists, effectively pinning her arms against her waist. God, he was so big. He could snap her like a twig.

Something primitive, old, and perceptive motivated this man. She knew it down deep with certainty. She'd experienced these uncanny sensations before about people. Individuals who held secrets didn't realize she could sometimes see those mysteries when she touched them.

Just like she saw Ronan Kieran's.

Danger crackled and burned around him like untamable wild fire. Visions came alive as she excavated them from his mind.

The first vision slammed into her.

Ronan sat on a huge black warhorse, swinging a massive broadsword over his head in a gesture of defiance and strength. All around him mayhem raged. Other men rode horses toward a line of combatants holding axes, spears and swords. Archers drew back and fired longbows and the volley of arrows pierced the air.

The visualization shifted like smoke on the breeze.

Weak, she sagged in his arms. Blurred images scurried into her mind. *She saw him crouched over a petite young blonde woman dressed in gray garments. The blonde lay on an overgrown path, her throat punctured and dried blood on her dress. He pulled the blonde into his arms, and when he looked up from her ravaged body, his eyes held an untamable anguish. He closed his eyes, threw his head back and cried out, the sound of a man in inconceivable torment.*

She jerked out of the revelation and struggled against his grip.

Ronan tucked her tight against his body. "*Shhh.* Easy. I'll not harm you."

"You killed her," she rasped, her throat so tight it hurt.

He stiffened. "Who?"

"The little blonde."

"Damn it woman, who are you talking about?"

Woman? Oh, now she was pissed. "On a path. Her throat was bitten—"

"How did you know about her?" His voice went hard and rough. "How did you know?"

"I saw it. A vision." Her voice weakened as fear rushed her.

If she expected to hear disbelief in his voice, she didn't.

"Don't speak of her again. I didn't kill her." Fresh pain entered his words, the rawness and authenticity so cruel it spilled into her system like acid.

Then clean sensations replaced her fear and ire. Pressed along his long, muscled body, everything focused to a fine point, an awareness of him as a man reaching deep into her sensibilities. Each breath she took sounded magnified, every brush of his body against hers created prickles across her skin.

"There are forces at work here you don't understand, Clarissa. Forces that would destroy you."

His words were potent, as effective as a sleeping draught for her senses. As his heat sheltered her against the cold night, she savored his strength as energy injected straight into her bloodstream. With one hand he tilted her head to the side. Warm breath puffed on her neck as he touched the side of her skull. A cross between a moan and a growl issued from his lips. Power seemed to radiate from him like the sun, a coiled strength she knew could protect or annihilate.

"Your head hurts a little?" he asked, the words tender.

Compelled to answer, she licked her dry lips. "Yes."

His fingers brushed over her jaw, so light she almost didn't feel them, right over the spot where the pirate had smacked her. "There's no damage. If he had hurt you severely he would be dead now."

In the primitive part of her mind, she liked his possessiveness and the assurance that he would kill to keep her safe.

A gentle kiss touched the side of her head, a mere brush of hot lips over skin.

"Please," she said softly, not understanding what she wanted.

A seductive groan drifted from his lips, like a man in the throws of the deepest erotic need. "I would like to please you."

Please me? Oh God.

When had a man ever said this to her before?

As his lips touched her cheek, he whispered words. "I could give you pleasure beyond your wildest dreams. Here. Now."

She shivered, not from fear but from new, dangerous feelings. "I don't understand what's happening to me."

Feel your true needs. Feel the way we could be together. His husky voice poured into her, lulling her into an indolence she didn't resist. Couldn't resist. He didn't speak, yet she heard him again in her mind. *You would know ecstasy.*

Primitive needs intruded. Clarissa's prickled with hypersensitivity and with every hot breath on her skin, wild vibrations shivered over her. Alarm couldn't penetrate.

Nor the will to escape.

The dark stranger's left palm flattened over her belly and heat and heaviness breached deep inside her. A burning craving built in her loins with staggering quickness. She gasped.

With a flick of his wrist he opened all the buttons on her coat. Her sweater buffeted the cold, but when he pressed against her ribs in exploration, she felt his touch straight through. For one sane second she struggled against unbidden sensation. A tiny moan escaped. His lips brushed her cheek, and her nipples peaked against the thin confines of her bra.

She couldn't move, didn't want to move.

Her mind whirled, two parts separated from the whole. So what if this dangerous, handsome man took her right here? Brought her down to the snow-covered ground, ravished her among headstones and made her body feel things she'd never imagined. Forbidden needs roared up from some place primal. Instincts long restrained broke free.

She wanted him.

His hands drifted up her ribcage until he cupped her breasts. Light, not hurtful, his touch made her squirm. Her nipples tightened at the hot, heavy feeling of his palms. He didn't squeeze, he didn't caress, but kept her captive by mere touch.

Then erotic visions filled her head.

Lying naked on a soft bed draped in a canopy of pink and white tulle, she watched as Ronan stood near in his black clothes, his long leather jacket still on him. He looked down on her, a gentle smile touching his mouth. As he admired her, Clarissa's skin felt hot. She knew he intended to torture her with nibbles and licks, and the exquisite suckling of his mouth.

The image disappeared from her mind.

A whimper broke from her. "What's happening to me?"

She should have been terrified, but Clarissa couldn't form a coherent panic. Swallowing hard, she brought her hands up and clasped the big hands holding her breasts.

"Breathe deeply." His voice dropped, softer and reassuring. "Take me within you."

She couldn't resist, and at his command she inhaled. Spicy, musk-filled, and heady with sensual promise, his scent wiped away the cold and their location. All she wanted or needed would be provided. Every rapture could become hers. How she knew this she couldn't say.

He allowed his touch to drift and her hands followed his movement. He cupped under her breast, the other hand drifted low until it rested above her pubic mound. An ache migrated from her belly to between her legs. Moist heat dampened her, and her nipples tightened into even harder points.

His words rumbled in her ear. "Do you see now? Do you understand how defenseless you are? I can do what I want with you, where I want. You have no defense against me."

"You wouldn't hurt me."

"No, sweet lady, I would not. But there are creatures you don't understand wandering this place. They would not hesitate to harm you. Now, promise me. Leave this place and don't return."

Anger managed to leak through. She groaned and fought against the hold Ronan had on her mind. "Let me go."

"All you need to do is ask."

Instantly he released her and she snapped into sharp focus. All fog left her mind and she whirled around to face him. She stepped back until she bumped into a headstone. Her camera case lay in the snow several feet away. When had she dropped it again?

Using the hard surface as a prop, she stared at him with renewed apprehension holding her captive. His dark eyes again burned with that unholy fire. His nostrils flared, his breathing quick as his broad chest rose and fell. She gazed at the front of his jeans and only one thought penetrated. One exhilarating realization she savored despite the bizarre circumstances.

The impossibly gorgeous man in front of her possessed a serious hard-on. Her mouth popped open in surprise. No doubt about it, he had the look of a man filled with desire. A man badly in need of her as his cock pressed against his jeans, full and long.

What came out of her mouth denied the inconceivable sexual interlude. "What the hell just happened? *What* are you?"

For this man wasn't ordinary. The strange mental pictures told her that.

But had she seen his previous incarnations? Did he know about them?

He put his hands on his hips, and she remembered the sensation of his touch on her body. Ronan's hands had been warm despite the winter in the air.

When he didn't answer her query, she managed to command her muscles in to action. Mixed feelings challenged her to discover more about him. At the same time, she knew he wouldn't tell her anything.

The man had secrets miles deep, and he wouldn't give up answers without a fight.

How she knew this she couldn't say, but the certainty frightened her. But no more than wondering if everything she'd experienced really occurred. Had she lost her mind? Or did Pine Forest's usual brand of supernatural insanity cause this hallucination?

Without another word she retrieved her camera bag. She wrestled her car keys from a side pocket on the bag and walked toward her old red Acura, moving as fast as icy snow would allow. She didn't look back, though she could feel his heavy stare boring into her with every step she made.

* * * * *

After Clarissa left his arms and the graveyard, Ronan tried to control the raging, wild temptations surging through his system. He gritted his teeth as deep shivers ran up and down his tortured body. He turned and leaned against a crypt, palms flat against the stone. As he drew in ragged breaths, his undead heart pounded out his need. He closed his eyes as pain darted through his groin.

You almost had her, old man. Sure, and her blood would have tasted beyond sweet. Like the darkest honey, she would have flowed down your throat with sizzling fire and sexual ecstasy.

Shit. Shit. Shit.

But no. He'd given up tasting human blood that way a long time ago. His body wanted hers, wanted her spread out under him as he inserted his cock deep into her wet, welcoming body.

His fingers clutched at the hard stone under his fingers. When he'd seen the pirate wannabe assaulting Clarissa, red-hot rage had made his gut burn. He could have killed the cretin with one well-placed twist of his fingers. But then he would have been no better than the creep who tried to mug her.

He straightened, taking more deep breaths to control his bloodlust and heady craving.

Anger and desire.

A deadly combination.

Bloody. Feckin'. Hell.

Snow landed on his nose and he wiped it away with an irritable movement. Wind ruffled his hair as the moon peeked out from behind a cloud. Although the night grew bitterly cold, a fire continued in his belly.

He'd come to the church to think and discovered a woman with incredible copper penny red hair tumbling in ringlets down her back to her waist. She was a tall beauty about five-seven with curves that fit against his body with agonizing perfection. Her full hips, rounded and soft under those jeans had felt so good. And sweet Mother Mary. *Her breasts.*

Better not think about the ripe fullness he'd cupped. The weight of her breasts had driven him to within an inch of seducing her. He'd wanted to pluck those nipples, feel them under his fingers. He'd wanted to rip the shirt off her and suck her, lick the round orbs until she writhed and begged to be taken.

His groin throbbed with unsatisfied passion he hadn't suffered for decades.

"Damn it."

Who was he kidding?

A few moments of coaxing and she would have been his. Here in this forsaken graveyard he could have taken her right up against this crypt.

So why had he stopped?

He'd stopped because Clarissa Gaines didn't deserve what he'd done to her any more than she'd deserved the pirate's filthy attention. He'd vowed to keep his hands off mortal women a long time ago, and he'd refused to use his seductive powers to possess one.

If a mortal woman came to him it would be because she wanted him, not because he'd convinced her by some vile means that she wanted him when she didn't. Even seven hundred years ago, after he'd been turned into a vampire, he'd never taken a woman against her will. Rape sickened him and he abhorred all who used their power this way.

Yet with one glance at two beautiful blue eyes, he'd lost complete control and tried to seduce her.

Feck. He couldn't afford distraction with the ancient one still haunting this town.

When he turned and looked at the churchyard, he remembered what he'd told his friends only a day ago. What he'd vowed to Sorley, Lachlan, Erin, Gilda, Tom, Micky, and even Jared. He'd promised to find *the* woman.

This so-called woman would be everyone's salvation from the ancient one and the parade of darkness, according to the Irish seer and to Yusuf.

A warm feeling entered his weary vampire soul, one with far-reaching consequences. Clarissa Gaines had heated to his influence, and a woman who didn't find him attractive in the first place would have struggled more against his embrace.

Ronan smiled. Besides that, he'd heard some of her thoughts. Reluctantly she'd admitted to herself she thought he was handsome.

Ruggedly handsome. In a mortal, very ridiculous way her attraction gratified him. Something else kept his interest high; his weakness for wanting to solve mysteries. When he'd held her in his arms she'd murmured about things from his past, things he wanted to forget. A dart of mental pain lacerated him. Somehow Clarissa had known about sweet Fionnghuala or Fenella as her anglicized name would be known. Clarissa had seen the horrible memory of Fenella's death as if the memory were her own and not extracted from the deepest, most agonizing part of his mind. How?

His gaze fell on the abandoned fanny pack on the ground nearby. He smiled again. Maybe he had found *the* woman after all.

Chapter Two

As Clarissa walked into the town community center, memories flooded her. The old saying about not being able to come home again was true, yet the building smelled, looked, and felt the same as it had twelve years ago.

Long and wide, the log cabin structure seemed a little gloomy this evening. Although the cutesy Halloween decorations should have looked fun and inviting, they managed to appear clownish in the more sinister sense of the word.

She'd noticed as a child that the buildings in Pine Forest owned a special dimness. They lacked the verve and essential glow of happy areas. When she mentioned this oddity to her parents they'd indulged her with a "yes, dear" and then said no more. She'd chalked up her impressions as her imagination, since she seemed to have a tremendous quantity of it.

Shadows lingered here as they did everywhere else in this odd town. Determined to map this community by word and photograph, she knew she'd get her book written and designed despite the bizarre circumstances plaguing Pine Forest. Photographing haunted places during this Halloween time when the veils between the worlds were thinnest might be advantageous. Who knew what she'd pick up on film?

She stepped through the main foyer and saw the large meeting room to her left bustled with activity. People milled around the room greeting each other and settling into metal folding chairs. Tonight the topic of discussion would be whether to hold the annual Halloween party or to cancel. After all, a serial killer prowled the streets and no one appeared safe. The entire month of October had been rife with murders; Clarissa had lost count of how many had occurred.

How could they celebrate Halloween as if nothing drastic had happened? Halloween was in less than a week. Much could happen in that time, including the capture of the serial killer.

Or, as she knew only too well from the information she had, everyone in this community center could be dead by Halloween night.

She found a chair near the back. No one seemed to notice her, which seemed funny considering she recognized many faces in the room. Then again, she'd been gone for so long and had changed enough they wouldn't know her. Instead individuals appeared tense, alert but not quite with it. Maybe the entire town had been strung out on anxiety.

Although she still trembled from the experience she'd encountered with Ronan Kieran and the pistol-packing pirate, she didn't ignore the thoughts entering her mind now.

She liked this place. As a kid she'd been here many times. Brownies, Girl Scouts, even a high school dance. The place smelled the same with a hint of rose and lavender mixed with old wood. She recalled old Mrs. Bassett and her cologne had a rose and lavender scent, and since the lady worked in the community center for almost fifty years there was a good chance her ghost lingered here. At least that would be Clarissa's theory.

She doubted anyone in this room would be interested in hearing her conjecture. Yes, people believed Pine Forest had ghosts up the ying-yang. But twelve years ago she'd left this town with people's disbelief in *her* ringing in her ears. They hadn't believed her story, no matter how often she told it.

For twelve years she'd resented their treatment and hadn't been back.

Until now.

When the murders started she knew she had to return. Not just to photograph Pine Forest for her new book, but to exorcise the demons running around in her head and perhaps to find the killer in the process. To save this entire town from imminent ruin.

Her mind kept dragging her back to the graveyard. She couldn't stop thinking about what happened to her earlier in the evening, or the odd way Ronan Kieran made her feel. The visions she'd seen could have been past lives for him, and perhaps he didn't know about them. Reincarnation didn't explain the strange glow she'd seen in his eyes, or the bizarre and immediate attraction that held her in his thrall for several minutes.

She'd almost been mugged and then a strange man had saved her life and turned her on so much she could barely walk a straight line. Her entire center of being, the things she believed about herself were rattled in that graveyard. Her mind shrieked at the danger and wanted nothing to do with it; practicality said it would be hazardous to probe into the thick aura of mystery surrounding Ronan Kieran. The other side, the one searching graveyards for intriguing pictures and even more interesting ghosts, said she couldn't resist the challenge.

"Ladies and gentlemen, please take your seats!" A tall, thin man banged a gavel on the podium at the front of the room as he called above the din.

He brushed a hank of gray hair away from his forehead. With his longish hair and tweed suit he looked more like a studious middle-aged professor than Harry Bold, mayor of Pine Forest.

No one paid much attention to him, caught up in the typical summit mentality of no one in charge but everyone wanting to speak. The mayor was flanked by a tall, buxom young blonde and a short little man with thinning black hair and a Hitler mustache.

"People, please!" Harry rapped the podium and the talking and general noise decreased. "We have a lot of business to get through tonight." As soon as the coughing and shuffling died down, the mayor started. "We're discussing, in light of current events, the feasibility of the annual Halloween party."

Several voices went up, but the mayor used his gavel. His brows pinched into a severe frown. "We're doing this rationally. There will be no heavy debate, only sound decisions." When voices cried out again, he put one hand up. "Now, listen here. This is the plan. Despite the fear and chaos this murderer has caused, we are not giving into the fear. This town has been here over one hundred years, and Pine Forest isn't giving up."

"What about the killings?" One shrill female voice rose above the crowd. "It's the worst thing this town has ever seen. I say we cancel the party."

The mayor held up his placating hand once again. "I can understand your concern. But what I really want to know is if you plan on letting this murderer run us out of our homes, our town, our activities?"

"Yeah," another female voice said. "Maybe that's what this bastard wants."

Not surprised by the vitriol in the crowd, Clarissa took in the argument with interest.

A distinct female voice reached above the crowd. "We have to reconsider the party. It leaves too many people out after dark and vulnerable."

Clarissa turned to see a young woman with short black hair and a strikingly handsome man with long brown hair standing not too far away. She knew about the couple from her lifelong dreams and because she'd pumped waitress and long-time friend, Chestnut Buttercup Creed—Chessie for short—for information when she'd arrived in town today. The man was Lachlan Tavish and the woman was Erin Greenway, a local librarian.

Chessie had filled in Clarissa at lunch, explaining the amazing tale of Erin's ordeal with the serial killer and her miraculous escape from the so-called vampire-like creature. Although the town teemed with believers in the supernatural, few agreed a bloodsucker committed the serial murders over the last month.

Chessie also told Clarissa about strange goings on at the Gunn Inn, a secluded place on the outskirts of town. A series of murders occurred recently at the inn.

"That's hogwash," an older woman said, and Clarissa knew she'd lost part of the conversation. "There are no such things as ghosts in this town and there sure as heck ain't any vampires running around either."

"You've got to keep the curfew going to save lives," Lachlan Tavish said. "This isn't an ordinary killer we're talking about."

"He's right," said a handsome man with short-cropped brown hair. He stood next to an almost elfin-like woman with windswept short blonde hair.

Clarissa also knew their identity from what she'd learned in the last day and her dreams. The man was Denver police detective Jared Thornton, and the woman Micky Gunn, the owner of the Gunn Inn.

The crowd babbled and the mayor rapped on the podium. A headache started to blossom and Clarissa rubbed her temples. She'd missed dinner and that might be part of the problem.

"Come on, people, let's be calm-headed about this," another man said from the front row. "Whether you believe in the supernatural or not, the fact is someone is killing people in this town and the cops can't stop it. We're going to have to take care of this menace ourselves."

"Wait, now, we are not advocating vigilante groups," the mayor said.

"Neither am I," the man said. "What I'm saying is we need some sort of neighborhood watch. A group of people who wander the area in numbers each night as a part of a patrol."

Several voices went up in favor of the idea. The concept jumped from one incarnation to the next until the mayor nixed the idea. Some of the crowd grumbled and others cheered.

The mayor straightened his red power tie. "The question is whether to keep the center open for Halloween. It would certainly be safer for all of you to bring your children here rather than trick-or-treating."

After listening to another reason why the party shouldn't continue, Clarissa tried to imagine how disappointed the children would be with no festivities. Maybe their homes were decorated, but it wouldn't be the same as roving the streets in costume or enjoying the thrill of a good scare near a decrepit old house. She realized how lucky she'd been as a child to enjoy a more carefree town. Then she remembered that there was no such thing as the good old days. As a child she'd discovered, through nightmare and vision, that something possessed this town in a deep, evil way. To be frightened meant a temporary rush. Now…well, she couldn't say what it meant.

Then again, the purse-snatching pirate had scared the crap out of her, and so had Ronan. She'd experienced enough fear in this night to fill up her Halloween quota for the year.

Weary of the merry-go-round assembly, she looked for Lachlan and Erin and saw they'd moved to the back of the room. *Okay, time to regroup and maybe try again tomorrow.* She didn't have the energy tonight.

"What are we going to do, mayor?" a man nearby her asked. "Just let this fiend take over the entire town?"

That's what he wants to do, all right. If her dreams and visions came true, she knew deep in her heart the town would be devastated.

The mayor's face wrinkled with uncertainty. "The counsel will take everyone's concerns into consideration and vote in thirty minutes on the fate of the party."

A female voice chimed in. "But mayor, this is wrecking our quiet, safe little town. Why when I was a kid stuff like this never happened. We've always known this town is different, but nothing horrifying happened. We've got to do something to make this town like it once was. A totally safe place to be."

Another rush of voices went up, arguing, joking, and making mincemeat out of rational possibilities. She shook her head. Sometimes people drove her insane with their insistence on knowing what came around the corner the next few minutes. Didn't they understand security was an illusion? Obviously this woman had the mistaken impression that the good old days were golden.

Like a whisper, a strange sensation replaced Clarissa's aggravation with a far more potent feeling. All the hairs on her neck prickled and she knew the cause.

Someone watched her.

She glanced to the right. Ronan Kieran stood near the entrance to the foyer in all his arrogance, his gaze pinpointed on her as if he possessed all the time and resources in the world. Immediate impressions flew at her, rising from the depths of her well-honed intuition. Something dark and unusual commanded him, a man with nothing to lose, hardened by history and his decisions. Battle-scarred, his ego remained a powerful force. As her gaze stayed locked with his, she felt his interest in her rise and his heated attention. She felt an increase in suspense, as if she watched a spooky movie and now perched on the edge of her recliner biting her nails. An odd breathlessness made her heart pick up speed.

Ire rose along with a wave of female pleasure. In the full light, no longer obscured, his masculinity screamed out for all women to see. In fact, his blatant gaze, dark and potent as sin, seemed to have attracted significant female attention. Two women in their late twenties stared at him from the back of the room. While she couldn't see their expressions, she imagined the hunger she would see there. This man inspired instant arousal, immediate compliance to his sexual will. Her nipples grew tight and hard as she watched him.

He looked away and broke the trance.

Thank God.

She shivered, a delicious tickle warming between her legs. She would have to ask Chessie if she knew who Ronan Kieran really was. Yes, he was Irish, and yes, he looked better than any romance cover model or movie star she'd watched on the silver screen. That still didn't explain his identity or whether he could be trusted.

You can trust me.

His voice, husky and filled with his distinctive accent, filled her thoughts.

He can't be speaking to me like this. A deep shiver quivered through her and she glanced at him. He stood in the doorway watching the mayor.

Okay, so maybe his voice in my head was all imagination. Had to be.

Another voice spoke up, this real and familiar. A voice somewhat changed over the years by maturity, but the same masculine sound.

The voice came attached to a man with a notebook and micro recorder. His tone of voice, hurried and aggressive, made the guy sound like a reporter eager to find a story.

"Mayor Bold, do you have any comment on whom or what could be committing these murders? Several papers around the country say there's conjecture the killer may be El Chupacabra. You can't honestly say you believe in that sort of thing."

Mayor Bold rolled his gaze to the ceiling for a second, then pinpointed the man with a contemptuous stare. "We've answered these types of ridiculous questions over and over for the last few weeks. No, we do not believe El Chupacabra is responsible because there is no such thing as El Chupacabra. You could have gotten the information from the Pine Forest Sentinel. Talk with their office if you want to hear chicanery on the subject."

The man continued. "Mayor Bold, is it true several local individuals have approached you with an idea about how to trap the creature?"

Leave it up to him to keep slamming home the creature angle.

"Sir, I don't know how many times I have to say it. There is no creature. We are dealing with a very sick individual here," the mayor said, his face tight with anger.

Keep it up. The mayor will probably have his cronies throw you out on the street.

About six feet tall, with short-trimmed, wavy golden blond hair and a distinct resemblance to a young Robert Redford, this man couldn't be mistaken for anyone other than up-and-coming paranormal researcher Jim Leggett.

The man she would have married.

The man she'd left behind when she quit Pine Forest twelve years ago.

She blinked the memory away of Jim's face as she'd left him standing on a street corner, his bewildered expression stamped in her mind with indelible ink. Over the years Chessie had filled her in on Jim's adventures, but she tried not to think about him or what might have been. A little pain still resided in her heart.

"Mayor," Jim said, "what about the assertion by some that this killer is possessed by evil?"

The mayor's eyes narrowed, his lips drawing into a tight line. He smoothed his labels, his displeasure evident as he shifted on his feet and surveyed the room as if someone might rescue him. "Well, Dr. Leggett, I'm afraid there's nothing paranormal for you to investigate in this town."

A grumble went up from the crowd. Before Jim could launch into another line of questioning, the mayor took more suggestions and questions from the crowd. While the conversation went on all around her, Clarissa pushed back memories of what used to be in Pine Forest. Her life, her family, her love. Much of it came in a painful wave filled with remorse and bitterness.

Girl, you've got to rid yourself of this sourness before it eats a hole in your stomach lining.

The gavel came down on the podium, and she started out of her thoughts. Tiredness crept in around her enthusiasm and nervous energy. Part of her wanted to talk with Jim, the other with Lachlan, Erin and Jared and Micky. From what they'd said this evening their belief systems seemed similar to hers. They might know how to stop the menace that would engulf the town by Halloween. Maybe if she shared what she knew with them, she would feel better and have a chance of saving this town. It sounded like a project for tomorrow after she'd obtained some sleep.

"That's settled," the mayor said. "We're having the party."

Drained by loud voices and the constant hum of negativity around her, she stood. Others left their seats, some grumbling, others smiling. When she looked toward the foyer, she saw Ronan had left. Good. She didn't savor the idea of meeting up with him again.

A voice called out as she entered the foyer, and when she glanced over her shoulder, she saw Jim heading her way, a big smile parting his lips. Sparkling blue eyes cajoled her, pleading for instant friendship.

"Clarissa? Is that you?" Jim asked, his grin saying he did really know her.

She stopped and held out her hand. "Jim. Good to see you again."

"Man, it's been a long time." He cracked a wider smile, almost as if he were campaigned for office. "I couldn't believe when I saw you here."

His big hand held hers gently. His frame appeared thinner than when she'd known him in high school, but it was a deceptive leanness. His strong, callused hand proved that.

She tried a grin but it felt plastic. "I'm a little surprised you recognized me. I've changed a lot since I left here."

"The long, spirally curls gave you away. I don't know anyone who has red hair that curly, thick, and long."

A reluctant chuckle came from her throat. "I never could talk myself into cutting it. Trims now and again, yes, but nothing more than an inch at a time." As she took in his appearance, she realized his face had taken on a flattering maturity, growing better with age. "You look good."

He lowered his voice. With an admiring glance starting at her face and working downwards, he said, "So do you."

She waited for pleasure to creep in from his compliment. Nope. Not a twinkle of satisfaction from his admiration. *Good. One less link to the past that needs to be broken.*

"Thanks, Jim. Are you sure you don't have ambitions to become a reporter? Those questions you asked were pretty hard-hitting."

He shrugged. "You remember I was on the school paper in high school? Guess it never quite left me. I'm a paranormal investigator in the psychology department at DU."

"Actually, I heard that a couple of years back."

"Who told you?"

She yanked down her stocking cap until it almost covered her ears. "I honestly don't remember. It might have been Chessie Creed. She keeps tabs on everyone."

"Say, have you had dinner yet?"

She hadn't, but she didn't quite feel like replaying old times with Jim. She pulled her leather gloves from her pocket and slipped into them. "I got into town this afternoon and had a late lunch." She put her hand to her stomach. "I'm still stuffed."

He frowned. "Why did you come to Pine Forest? It isn't safe."

"You're the second person to tell me that tonight. I'm here to write a story about this place and capture ghosts on film."

"Maybe we can explore together. I plan on going into the graveyards around here and some of the houses to see if I get electromagnetic readings or EVP."

She'd heard of EVP. "Electronic Voice Phenomena?"

"Right."

"I thought you didn't believe in the supernatural? At least you didn't when we were kids." She couldn't help injecting that last bit.

He winced as if she'd kicked him. "I still don't believe in it."

In the wake of his continued skepticism, disappointment waged war with expectancy inside her. "So you're here to debunk."

"Exactly."

Jim stood in the most haunted town on earth and yet he doubted. He reminded her of a tourist trying to see nine countries in seven days. He would skim the surface but never see deeper than the crust.

Before she could speak, he asked, "How about we set a time to meet up tomorrow at the graveyard just outside town? We could do some exploring."

He hitched his camera bag over his shoulder, and she matched the gesture with hers. For the first time she realized she didn't have her fanny pack.

She groaned and slapped her forehead. "I'm a dolt. I can't believe I'm just now noticing I don't have my fanny pack." She reached in her camera bag and pulled out her car keys. "I must have left it at St. Bartholomew's. About the graveyard, I don't think you and I could work together on the project."

His brow wrinkled. "Why?"

"For obvious reasons, don't you think? You're a debunker and I'm not."

"You accept everything you read and see as authentic?"

A legitimate question, even if she didn't like it. "Of course not. But I prefer to work alone. I've got to go. See you later."

She left, heading out to the parking lot and her car.

He caught her elbow in a gentle grip. "Wait. I know that you always believed in the phenomena in this town and I didn't. But it doesn't mean we can't look out for each other. There's a serial killer in

Pine Forest." He gave her a tentative smile. "We might not see eye to eye, but I'd worry about you if you were out there alone."

Deep in his eyes she saw the old Jim, the good-looking boy who always seemed to have her best interests at heart on the outside, but not where it counted. "I appreciate your concern, Jim—"

"Please. You've got more common sense than anyone I know. It's not like you to go out by yourself."

She gently pulled away from him. "It wasn't like me twelve years ago. I'm a different person now."

"So am I. I'm a lot more considerate, I hope."

She smiled tentatively, unwilling to feed his ego by reassuring him. "Of course."

"At least let me go with you tonight and I'll help you find the fanny pack, all right?"

He sounded more than determined, and she knew after the experience with the pirate that she should be more careful. "All right. I'll meet you at St. Bartholomew's."

"I'll be just a few minutes. Don't get out of the car and start looking until I get there, okay?"

"Okay."

Clarissa turned away and walked down a row of cars near the community center entrance. She passed the side of the building when a figure appeared off to her left and not ten yards away. She gasped and put hand to her mouth. Ready to run, she took a step backwards.

When she saw who it was she didn't know whether to be relieved or scared.

Ronan Kieran stood near a secluded spot between the community center and a storage shed. His black coat hung open and flapped a bit in the gentle breeze. Clarissa tried to recall the last time she'd seen anyone so lethal. She wouldn't have needed the incident in the graveyard to understand this man took no shit off anyone. Ever.

His gaze held her like a magnet and a strong rush of feelings pinned her to the spot. Anger. Fear. Desire.

She'd never experienced all three emotions at once.

Since childhood she'd used her radar, as she thought of it, to detect people she couldn't trust. With him she couldn't be certain of anything. This man displayed a restlessness tempered by steel resolve and determination to see through any mission. But what mission? In the graveyard he'd driven away the mugger and protected her. Yet part of her continued to be scared spitless of him.

He lifted his hand and her fanny pack dangled from his hand. "Your pack."

"Oh, thank you." Her voice sounded wimpy and she hated the breathless quality. She cleared her throat. "I was going back there to pick it up."

He shook his head, exasperation clear on his handsome face. "Are you mad? You would ignore my warnings?"

Anger rose inside her at his patronizing tone. "It's none of your business what I do, so I'd appreciate you keeping your opinion to yourself. Look, I'm not ungrateful for what you did for me." Her cheeks flushed as she remembered he'd done more than *one* thing for her, all right. "But I don't appreciate you talking to me like I'm—"

"A silly cow who doesn't know when to quit?"

She gasped and took a step closer to him, indignation rising like hot lava in her gullet. "How dare you?"

Ronan grinned, and the stunning transformation dazzled her down to her foundations and short-circuited her fury. Wide and unrepentant, his mouth curved in the most attractive, seductive male smile she'd ever seen. In the shadows she almost couldn't see his eyes, but what she could view warmed her. Like melting dark chocolate, his gaze took her in, seducing her. His demeanor appeared receptive, and for a second she saw gentle caring and curiosity slip through the enveloping heat in his stare. It made him even more infuriatingly attractive. The man looked delicious.

And she was certifiably insane for thinking so.

I just want to strangle him.

Yep, that would do it. She would walk right up and wrap her fingers around his insolent throat and wring some common courtesy into his gorgeous person.

Teasing sparked in his eyes. "Damn, woman, but you are a stubborn one. I think I like that."

Unexpectedly, she wanted to hear him laugh. She wanted to know what this exasperating yet intriguing man thought, felt, and wanted.

I am losing my mind.

His grin returned, as if he'd heard a joke.

Clarissa frowned in counterpoint. "Just give me my pack, please."

If she wanted to retrieve the pack she'd have to come closer to him, and that unsettled her in a whole new way. She forced one foot in front of the other until she could reach out and take the pack. Their fingers brushed, but thank goodness she couldn't feel his skin through her gloved hand. She retreated, walking backwards.

It was his turn to frown. "You're frightened of me. Why?"

When he shifted closer her heart did a double flip. "I'm not afraid. I didn't expect you to be here."

"You saw me in the community center."

"Yes, but I thought you'd left already," she said, her voice tight with apprehension. "When I looked you were gone."

One of his eyebrows twitched up. "You were looking for me?"

She bit her lip and almost groaned. "No, I wasn't. I just saw you in the doorway. What are you doing lurking around here like a phantom?"

"I'm waiting for my friends." His voice sounded almost bored.

"Friends?"

"You saw them inside. Thornton, Tavish, and their women."

She lifted one eyebrow. "Their women. That almost sounds like a phrase from another time."

"I am from another time."

His strange phrase lodged in her mind, but she ignored it. "You know them well?"

"Yes."

She swallowed hard. Time to be cheeky. "Can you introduce me? I need their advice."

His eyes narrowed. "What kind of advice?"

She shook her head. "It's private."

Ronan's skeptical expression came through in the critical shine in his eyes. "I'll mention you to them. Where are you staying?"

Reasonable caution made her say, "I'll give you the phone number and they can call me."

He nodded. "Very well."

After strapping the fanny pack over her coat, she retrieved a pen and piece of paper from the pack and wrote down the number for the

Clary Ridge Hotel. As he took it from her hand she made sure his touch didn't linger. He stuffed the paper in his coat pocket.

"You are more cautious now then when we met earlier this evening, Clarissa."

Remembering the way he'd touched her in the cemetery sent a wave of startling arousal over her skin and mixed with instant shame.

Her throat tightened, but she pushed the words passed her lips. "Look, I'd appreciate it if you didn't tell anyone what happened."

"You're making a police report? You should have gone—"

"I know, I know. I should have made a police report right away, but I didn't want to miss this meeting."

"Why?"

"None of your business."

"Ah, so we're back to that, are we?"

"Yes, back to that."

He edged closer, his pace slow and certain. As he walked her heart started to pound, her skin flushing. He stopped when he stood within a few inches of her. Unwilling to be intimidated, she held her ground.

"All right, I'll accept that for now." His strong voice held a seductive purr even when he spoke of inconsequential things, and it sent a deep stirring straight into her loins. "I saw you with that man a few moments ago. He's a friend?"

The contempt in his voice gave her pause. It sounded like Ronan was jealous.

No, that's ridiculous. Ronan barely knows me. "From back in high school when I lived here. Why?"

"Even old friends can be deadly sometimes. How *well* did you know him?"

She made a disgruntled noise. "He was my high school sweetheart, not that it's any of your concern."

His hands clenched into fists, and she wondered how he kept his hands warm in this brittle weather. She thought she detected regret in his penetrating eyes. Then the hesitation retreated, overlaid by an anger she didn't understand.

"Everyone is suspect in this town. Even some women, perhaps," he said.

"Well, given that criteria, I could be the serial killer."

"But you're not. You could never hurt someone unless it was to save your life or someone you love."

"Thanks for the vote of confidence," she said dryly.

The hard edge in his eyes melted to a passionate, golden glow. The blazing fire froze her to the spot with a primitive, aching sensation that stirred from fear to desire in a heartbeat.

Caught up in the intensity, she couldn't look away. "Goodnight, Mr. Kieran. There's a nice, warm bed waiting for me."

His face etched with something that almost appeared like pain, and he closed his eyes. Free from his mesmerizing attention, she turned and walked the last few feet to her car. After unlocking the vehicle and sliding inside quickly, she relocked the doors. When she looked, he was gone.

Clarissa stopped by the cemetery at St. Bartholomew's and waited for Jim to show up. Sighing wearily, she remembered that Jim had a habit of being late to everything. It didn't look like he'd changed much. Surprise, surprise.

The back of her neck felt tight, and she rubbed it in order to ease the strain. Damn, but she would be tired as hell before this night finished. To while away the time, she thought back to the cemetery and the set of stupid moves that brought her to this point in the first place.

She thought back to Ronan's warnings, his incredible strength and sexual energy flowing from him into her as he'd touched her in ways no man touched her before.

How can that be?

His incredible gentleness mixed with overwhelming strength, a powerful alpha presence she'd never encountered in another man. Thinking back on what happened, she realized a sort of daze had clouded her judgment. She could chalk it up to the pirate's attack. She'd been attacked and maybe felt a little grateful to Ronan for rescuing her.

Um, no. That wasn't it either. With a horrifying sense of reality hitting her over the head, she knew if Ronan had caressed her more intimately, that would have been it. She would have had sex with the man right there in the graveyard. Frightened by the idea, she cursed her insanity. Had she lost all sense? What the hell had she been thinking?

Her cheeks flushed as mortification and incredible shame made her feel weak.

Frustrated by her thoughts and Jim's tardiness, she finally gave up and left the graveyard.

Chapter Three

The next morning Erin Greenway heard a screech, something between a banshee and an irritated bird, coming from her living room. Her skin prickled.

She turned to Lachlan, who stood in front of the bathroom mirror. "What on earth was that?"

"Sounds like the one and only Sorley Dubhe." A smile tilted the corners of his finely carved handsome mouth. "He's up early."

She glanced at the digital clock on the bedside table. "For a vampire, I'd say so. It's seven thirty in the morning."

Bright sun hit the snow outside the bedroom window, a blinding tribute to the morning. They'd have to keep the shades pulled so the vampires wouldn't be irritated by too much sunlight.

Her heartbeat returned to normal. She came up behind Lachlan and circled the big Scot's waist with her arms. She peeked over his shoulder and ogled him in the mirror. God, he was...a god. She grinned. The man didn't understand how drop-dead, one hundred percent absolutely handsome he was. More than that, he'd stood by her every step of the way in the fight against the ancient one. He'd brought her love, security, and endless strength. With him by her side, she could face anything, no matter how horrible.

"For a minute there I thought a brand-new creature from hell invaded my house," she said.

Lachlan chuckled, and the rich, husky sound sent her heart into overdrive. "The creature from hell part is still accurate."

"I don't know whether to be surprised or disturbed by the fact you actually recognized his scream. Does he do that often?"

He turned in her arms and gathered her close, then pressed a kiss to her forehead. "Aye. When he's pissed he has a whole repertoire of sounds."

She sighed and tunneled her hands through his luxuriously thick, long, dark hair. "Uh-huh. I guess I should have known that, considering how long he's been in our house."

Two vampires occupying her house took a toll on her as a mortal. Sorley, a thin, weasel-faced vampire and Ronan, a devilishly gorgeous vampire with a killer smile.

"Shouldn't he be sleeping?" she asked.

"He's got insomnia, probably."

"I know he's your friend, Lachlan, but I can't wait until Jekyl's reopens. That way he can have his own place to scream."

Lachlan's wide grin made her heart flutter, and she wondered if this besotted feeling would leave her.

He kissed her lips softly. "I know what you mean. With Ronan, I don't mind. Sorley…well…he's just Sorley."

"Then again, maybe they shouldn't go back to Jekyl's. You know how Danny Fortesque is out for blood."

He released her, a worried frown marring his features. "They should keep a low profile until this is all over."

This was something that didn't seem to have an end in sight, and Erin wondered how much longer they could battle the ancient one and survive. "They should stay here until this is all over. Of course, Ronan is hardly ever here anyway."

Lachlan nodded. "Something is on his mind, but I'll be damned if he'll tell me what it is."

"I'm worried, Lachlan. I can't believe they're still having the Halloween party. It's suicide if the ancient one regains enough power by that night."

Lachlan's thoughtful expression showed true concern. "I know." He released her and headed for the closed bedroom door. "Let's see what Sorley is up to."

Sorley sat in an easy chair in the living room and rubbed his stocking-clad foot. "Feckin' hell!" He gestured to a chest near the fireplace. "What's this chest made out of anyway, feckin' stone?"

Lachlan chuckled. "Try pine."

Sorley's thin face creased into an unexpected smile filled with mischief. "Sure, then I guess it doesn't hurt that badly."

Erin laughed as she started toward the kitchen. "Have you seen Ronan around, Sorley?"

Sorley trailed behind and almost bumped into her when she stopped at the kitchen counter. "Didn't see him all day yesterday."

"Well, we saw him at the community center meeting, then he just disappeared," Erin said.

"Vampires have a way of doin' that, you know." Sorley grinned.

"No shit," Lachlan said.

As the coffee perked, Lachlan made breakfast with Erin's help.

"Maybe he's found the woman he's lookin' for. The one he doesn't mind havin' sex with to help save the world," Sorley said.

The irreverent tone in his voice made Erin smile. A few days ago, she couldn't imagine finding anything about this situation entertaining. Now the black humor eased her tension.

"What makes you think that?" Lachlan asked.

Sorley put his hands on his skinny hips. "Wishful thinkin' actually." Sorley bumped into Erin and Lachlan as he searched for a glass in the cupboard. He snorted a laugh. "Though I have a hard time imaginin' Ronan giddy over a woman."

"Giddy?" a deep, almost scornful voice said behind the thin vampire. "I don't *do* giddy."

Ronan's chest felt tight as he materialized in Erin's kitchen. He'd felt out of it since the ancient one terrorized them all in the tunnels under Micky Gunn's establishment.

Erin scowled while Sorley gave a laugh. Although she trusted him now, Ronan remembered a time not so long ago where the sight of him frightened Erin. He couldn't really blame her considering all she'd been through with the ancient one.

Ronan slid the cape off his head and shoulders and tossed the garment on a dinette chair. He glared at Sorley. "Now what were you saying about giddiness?"

"Uh..." Sorley swallowed hard. "Well, not quite giddy. Maybe mildly interested?"

Lachlan smiled. "You could knock, you know."

Ronan felt surly, his temper up after his two encounters last night with Clarissa Gaines. He shrugged. "Since you invited me over your threshold a long time ago, why should I bother?"

Erin's frown said he'd pissed her off. "Hasn't anyone ever taught you manners?"

"Just long enough ago for me to forget them."

Lachlan turned to Ronan with curiosity written on his face. "What's going on with you? Since the last fight with the ancient one you've been moping."

Sorley laughed, his high-pitched noise grating on Ronan's ears. "He's goin' for a particular attitude, don't you know? All dark and pensive and vampirish."

Lachlan peered at Sorley. "Vampirish? Is that even a word?"

"That's not it." Ronan scrubbed a hand through his hair. "I'm hacked because we haven't finished the job. We know we didn't kill the ancient one. He will walk the streets again before Halloween. And if he absorbs the amount of power I think he'll absorb on Halloween, then we're all buggered."

"Sounds like we need another caucus to decide what we're going to do," Erin said.

Deciding he should let the group know about Clarissa, Ronan said, "I met the woman last night."

"See, see, I told you," Sorley said with a huge grin.

"Discussing my love life again, I see," Ronan said.

Sorley shrugged. "Nothing else better to do around here."

"Who is she?" Erin asked, anticipation in her voice and on her face.

Ronan groaned inside, unsure how much he wanted to reveal. He explained how he'd met her in the graveyard, but conveniently left out the part about them becoming cozy.

Erin crossed her arms, then looked into the distance with concentration. "She sounds perfect."

Sorley snorted. "Even if she does decide Ronan's an all right chap and she doesn't mind doing the nasty with him, we still don't know how havin' sex with him is going to solve our problems with the ancient one."

"The seer wasn't specific," Ronan said. "She simply said the power would manifest once the woman and I have sex."

Ronan saw the displeasure on Erin's face, but decided it wouldn't do any good to gloss over the facts.

Lachlan's expression held concern. "At the community center you disappeared before any of us could talk to you. Where did you go?"

"Out for fresh air. So many mortals in one area suffocates me."

Erin strolled toward him as she wiped her hands on a towel. "When do we get to meet Clarissa?"

"Today. Tonight if you wish."

Lachlan's eyebrows lifted. "Wow, that was fast work."

Ronan's frown deepened. "It wasn't my idea. She was at the community center meeting last night and wants to meet you."

"Why?" Lachlan asked.

"She told me it was none of my business." It irritated him, her defiance. "Wench."

Sorley laughed. "Sure, and she must be mighty comely if she can get that reaction out of him."

Ronan glared at him. "Shut up."

The much smaller vampire did as told.

Erin leaned on the kitchen counter. "Do you think she's trying to get a story out of us? Maybe she's a reporter in disguise."

Ronan prowled back to the other side of the room, his impatience grinding inside him. "No."

"Have some of this." Erin took a mug of coffee to Ronan.

Ronan took a sip of the brew, then put it down on the kitchen counter. "Clarissa asked me to give you her number so you can call. But I could bring her here."

Erin smiled. "Now wait a minute. Do you think a woman who doesn't know you would go with you? Especially with everything happening lately?"

Damned if he hadn't thought of that. "Of course not."

Lachlan rubbed his chin. "Ronan, why don't you feel out this woman's intentions?"

Ronan felt a rare laugh emerge from him. "Feel her out, eh? That shouldn't be much of a hardship. Although I'll have some work to do to get her to trust me. Besides, that, I may have competition. She talked with a pansy-assed mortal from out of town while she was still at the community center," Ronan said with distaste.

"Sounds like a lick of jealousy to me," Sorley said matter-of-factly.

Ronan admitted in his heart it *felt* like jealousy, but he refused to allow the sensation to build. He prowled the room like a restless animal. "I listened in on their conversation. The man she was talking to is a paranormal investigator from a university in Denver. Apparently the blighter was her boyfriend in high school. I get feelings about people. He's dangerous, perhaps to Clarissa." His gut burned at the thought of her being hurt. An odd, almost forgotten ability to feel tenderness made him pause. A strange yearning entered his undead heart. "I don't want her near him."

"You want to protect her?" Erin asked, a smile teasing the corners of her mouth.

Ronan slipped into his cloak again, tossing the hood over his head so that his hair and a good portion of his face stayed covered. "I must. That is, if she doesn't try to stake me first."

Erin's eyes widened. "You think she'd do that? But—"

"No." Ronan waved a hand in dismissal. "She doesn't know about vampires. But she's stubborn and will get into serious trouble at this rate."

Erin tilted one eyebrow. "Ronan, you were nice to her, weren't you?"

Nice. Feckin' yes. And it had felt damned good. "Very nice. But it frightens her. I frighten her."

Lachlan appeared grim. "*It* frightens her?"

"When I touched her I felt her emotions. She loved and hated the heat moving between us." His groin stirred at the thought of what she'd felt like in his arms. "She felt out of control."

Sorley's face screwed up. "Ewww. I don't know about the rest of you, but this is too much like listenin' to your parents havin' sex. Please don't share."

Lachlan and Erin smirked at Sorley, but Ronan ignored the pesky immortal. "Clarissa is very, very strong. Whether she understood she was doing it or not, she resisted my powers of persuasion. It takes a very strong woman to hold off a vampire in any way."

Lachlan's expression lightened. "And you didn't like that, did you?"

"Hell, no. Being with her was challenging. She's stubborn and tough."

Erin crossed her arms. "Sounds like someone I'd like to meet."

Sorley's irreverent expression said what he thought about the statement. "Pfft. You can convince any woman to spread her legs and—"

"Shut up," Lachlan said.

Not appearing the least chastised, Sorley snatched a piece of bread as it popped from the toaster.

"What time do you want me to bring her by?" Ronan asked.

"I've got to go into work today," Erin said. "What about inviting her to dinner?"

Ronan's bowed slightly at the waist. "It shall be done."

Without so much as a pause, Ronan snapped into invisibility. He heard and saw the last of the kitchen conversation.

"He's feckin' leavin' me behind again," Sorley said around a bite of toast.

Lachlan sighed. "Of course he is. You don't think he wants your hairy hide around if he's romancing a woman, do you?"

Erin threw Lachlan an appreciative grin as he slipped an arm around her waist and tugged her against his body.

"I know I wouldn't want Sorley around anywhere if you were romancing me," she said.

Ronan heard the small vampire ask, "Is that all anyone thinks about lately? Love and hearts and sticky things?"

Lachlan's mouth hovered over Erin's parted lips. "Go away, Sorley."

Still grumbling, the wiry vampire disappeared with an audible snapping noise. His disembodied voice echoed around them. "Bloody hell."

Ronan laughed and heard his mirth ringing in the air before he, too, disappeared into the ether.

* * * * *

Clarissa wandered down a murky tunnel, the night enshrouding her with pinpricks of fixed dread. She smelled damp earth, felt soil moving beneath her booted feet. Her breath came quickly, her heart pounding a frantic beat. She wouldn't escape now that she'd entered.

Something would come for her soon.

She couldn't breathe and her hand went to her throat.

She jolted awake with a semi-shriek. As her eyes popped open she saw sunlight streaming under the curtains. She'd fallen asleep on the bed last night fully clothed. She remembered stumbling into her room after talking with the police, then feeling so exhausted she decided to lie down one minute. Obviously she's slept more than a minute.

A knock on her hotel room door startled her. She took a deep breath to regulate her heart, then went to the door. As she ran her fingers through her tangled hair, she figured she probably looked like something the cat had dragged in for a meal. She checked the peephole and opened the door to Jim Leggett.

"This is a surprise." She smiled, trying not to feel angry with him and failing. "I thought we were meeting at the cemetery at St. Bartholomew's last night?"

Jim smiled ruefully. "I'm sorry. I got a call from Denver and by the time I got off the phone and headed toward the cemetery I realized you'd probably already left."

"How did you find me this morning?"

"I saw Chessie and she told me where you were staying." He took a big breath and let it out slowly. "I had to see if you were all right."

Frowning, she backed away from the door and gestured for him to enter. "Worried? Why?"

He stuffed his hands in his pockets as she closed the door. A flush spilled over his cheekbones. "I saw you with that man in the alleyway near the community center."

"Ronan Kieran?" She put her hands on her hips. "I don't know if I like you spying on me."

The flush increased, easy to see with his pale skin. "I wasn't spying. When I drove away I saw you there with him. I noticed him at the meeting, and when I asked a couple of people about him, they didn't know who he was. So when I saw you with him it worried me."

She crossed her arms. This was getting better and better. "Yet you left the parking lot. You didn't stop and check on me."

Guilt crossed his features. He licked his lips. "I figured you'd pull one of your independence routines and yell at me."

Not impressed, she twisted her mouth into a semblance of a smile. "You're probably right." She sighed. "Ronan is visiting friends in town. He's harmless."

"You knew him before you came back to town?"

"It's a long story, Jim."

His eyes took on a harder mien, as if he didn't quite like what he heard. "I also saw him give you the fanny pack you lost at the graveyard."

She rubbed a hand over her face and decided to tell the truth. She reported a quick run down of the mugging in the graveyard and the fact Ronan came to her rescue.

Jim didn't say anything for a second, then he leaned back against the dresser and shook his head. "Why didn't you tell me last night at the community center what happened?"

She decided being candid again would be the answer. "Because I was tired. I didn't think it was important."

His frown reminded her of the night they'd broken up not long before she left Pine Forest. She saw the same stubborn expression. Twelve years ago they'd fought about her beliefs and what she saw in the future for Pine Forest. She knew for certain things couldn't be different between them.

When he didn't speak, she said, "Jim, this isn't going to work if you're intrusive into my personal life."

As he nodded, he rubbed his hand over the back of his neck. "I know our breakup went pretty badly. But we can start fresh."

She made a small sound of disbelief. "A professional relationship only. And I'm not even sure if we can have that."

His eyes narrowed. "We're not the same people we were then."

She glanced at the digital bedside clock and it read eight-thirty in the morning. God, she hadn't slept this late in a very long time. "Can't we talk about this later? I've got to take a shower and get dressed. Can I call you?"

"Sure." He didn't sound too pleased. He gave her his cell phone number and she scribbled it on a hotel message pad on the small desk.

She opened the door for him, and he turned as he stepped out. He took her hand in his and grasped her wrist for a moment as if he couldn't stand to let her go. When his fingers tightened in one of those sharp, man-doesn't-know-his-own-strength ways, she winced and pulled her hand from his grasp.

Without another word, he went down the hallway. She flipped the lock when she closed the door, then leaned back against the cool surface and closed her eyes.

Just wonderful. Barely a day in town and two men seemed intent on driving her batty. She ran her hands over her face and yawned. She needed to get moving but she still felt exhausted. Falling face downward on the bed, she groaned. This expedition to Pine Forest had started with a bang. Maybe, if she was really lucky, nothing more exciting would happen.

If she could only believe that.

She rolled over on her back and sighed. Tiredness won out and she fell asleep again. She didn't know how much longer it was before she realized someone was in the room with her. On the bed.

Her eyes popped open in panic.

Ronan Kieran's face appeared in her line of vision, and she flailed at him instinctively. With one hand he pinned her wrists above her head, then put his other hand over her mouth. He used his leverage to hold her down.

"Quiet," he said with a low, soft voice. "Someone will think you're being harmed."

Oh, my God! How did he get into my room?

As if sensing her compliance, he took his hand away from her mouth and released her wrists. Even with his immobilizing grip he hadn't hurt her.

When she dared look at him, his eyes burned with a fiery gold more breathtaking than anything she'd seen. She moaned as a strange sensation slithered through her midsection, then bolted straight between her legs. In an instant her senses went on high alert. Her breathing quickened, her skin heated. His musk, a combination of his leather coat and something uniquely male, made her heartbeat stutter. Every long, hard muscle in his body seemed to touch her. She could feel his chest moving, his body poised on the verge of action.

Danger, she'd heard, could heighten the sexual appetite, and this man spelled perilous in capital letters. He must be throwing hormones off in spades, because all she wanted to do in that one, startling moment was to spread her legs for him.

Sharp and breathtaking, the instantaneous sexual feelings upset her more than his appearance in her room. When she'd encountered him twice yesterday and experienced the same insane excitement, she thought maybe her imagination played tricks on her.

Yet he appeared in her bedroom, almost lying on top of her and she liked it. No, she *craved* his warmth and hardness and unbelievable musculature pressed along her body.

He shivered against her and whispered, "Mother Mary, that's incredible. So hot and new."

"What? What are you talking about?"

"Your sexual needs. I can feel them in my body." He closed his eyes, and his sinfully thick, dark lashes fanned downward. "You haven't had a man in a very long time."

Astonished at his straightforward, outrageous statements, she gaped at him. "I beg your pardon?"

He opened his eyes. Without smiling he said, "You sound like an outraged virgin."

A gasp escaped her before she could think how it sounded. "Ridiculous. I may be outraged, but I'm not a virgin." Her face blazed with embarrassment. *Damn him all to hell.*

A laugh, half-mocking, half-enjoyment, slipped from his mouth. "Some would say I'm already in hell."

Shock silenced Clarissa better then a slap in the face. *He read my mind.*

Heat flickered in his eyes and restarted that stunning fire deep in her groin. Whether she liked it or not, whether she wanted it or not, it seemed this man attracted her on a deep, primitive level.

He frowned. With a feather-light touch, he brushed his fingers over her jaw line. "There's a tiny bruise here. Does it hurt?"

"No."

Feral intent erupted in his eyes, vengeance clear in the tilt of his mouth. "I might reconsider harming the pirate that did this to you."

Fear jumped past the arousal, and she twisted on the bed and tried to knee him in the groin. Growling low in his throat, he settled his long, powerful leg over both of hers, drawing her thighs together in a tight grip.

"Stop struggling," he said near her right ear. "I'm not here to hurt you."

She trembled as genuine fear struck inside her body like lightning. She swallowed hard. He twitched one eyebrow and she knew he'd thought of it already.

"If you're not here to hurt me, why didn't you just knock on the door?" she asked with venom.

"Funny how that theme has run through today." He smiled wryly. "I was asked to use the door earlier by a group of friends. I guess I need more finesse."

"I'll say. Now get off me."

"I apologized, now you need to calm down. Next time I won't pop into your room like this. But I needed to see you, to talk to you."

"How did you...how did you get in this room if you didn't use the door?" She heard her voice trembling and hated the fear plain in her tone.

"Trade secret. I'll tell you later."

"Oh, and that's supposed to placate me?"

"I doubt much would appease you, beautiful one."

His compliment spoken in that husky, sexy voice made her toes curl with forbidden delight. This guy screamed sex and secrets.

I'm pleased you think I'm sexy. His exotic voice trickled into her mind.

Fascinated and discomfited all over again, she stared up at him in awe. "You're a mind reader of some sort?"

With a dry tone he said, "Of a sort. But then so are you."

She sighed. Nothing like being obtuse, the bastard.

His hot breath tickled her ear and he pressed a tender kiss to her cheek. His expression went harder, cooler. "I saw that redheaded man come to your door earlier."

He almost sounded jealous. She frowned in disbelief. "You've been spying on me?"

"Watching out for you. I don't trust that biped."

"Biped?"

"He's not to be trusted. Stay clear of him."

She wanted to kick him in the nuts for his presumptuous manner. "Why you—this is ridiculous. I know Jim and he wouldn't hurt me. I don't know you from Adam."

His eyes danced with returning amusement. "Of course you know me. And you're going to get to know me a lot better." Before she could make another indignant comment, he said, "I entered your room to make sure you were all right."

"What were you doing?" She almost barked the question. "Listening at my door?"

"I have very good hearing."

She could see from the gleam in his eyes that he wouldn't give a better explanation. "It was just a bad dream."

"I saw it. You dreamed of a dark tunnel."

"What?" Shock made her pause. "How could you?"

"A secret for now. I'll tell you later."

His partial revelation compounded her belief that Ronan Kieran wasn't your average, run-of-the-mill man. Frustration made her cheeky. "Tell me now, or I *will* scream."

"No, you won't." His lips caressed the side of her jaw. "Or I shall do more than just this and give you a reason to scream?"

"You said you wouldn't hurt me."

"I wouldn't. But there are other screams."

Another flush filled her face, and she tried to remember the last time she'd felt this out of control and excited. "Such as?"

His smoldering gaze coasted over her body in caressing assessment. "I could make love to you until you quaked in ecstasy."

Wild thrills darted into her belly and moisture trickled between her thighs. "Oh God."

"You feel it, don't you? It is relentless between us."

She shook her head, and his lips stopped torturing her jaw. "You said you wouldn't hurt me and here you're restraining me and kissing me against my will."

"I would never take a woman against her will. But I could make your will mine." His eyes went lambent. "I know you want me. I can feel it in the way you move, the way your pupils dilate, your skin heats, the scent of your arousal."

Shaken by his blatant description, she couldn't say a word. She shuddered against his big body, the heat and power tantalizing beyond reason. Apprehension and disbelief threatened to overwhelm her senses. She closed her eyes to avoid his intense gaze.

With this man, though, it didn't seem to matter.

"Your feelings are open to me now with us so close together," he said. "Sure, and I can understand your worry. You think I can read your mind all the time, don't you?"

She kept her eyes closed. "What's to stop you?"

A long pause almost made her open her eyes again, but she resisted. Maybe if she didn't look into his strange, exciting gaze he couldn't read her thoughts.

"I can read your mind when I wish, closed eyes or no." His accent purred across her senses, seducing. "Most of the time I choose not to. Sometimes your mind is shouting it and I can't help it."

Indignant, she opened her eyes. "Oh, so now it's my fault?"

"It is sometimes."

Perturbed, she tried looking tough. Her actions drew another one of those scarcely there grins to his lips that disappeared like fog in a wind seconds later.

Ronan's gaze left her face and moved with hungry attention down to her breasts and lower to her hips. When his attention found the area between her legs, a tingle built and grew. An ache pulsed, pulled and tugged at her loins. Her vagina throbbed and widened as if to prepare for a deep thrust.

"No," she said to her traitorous imagination. *I've lost my mind. I can't feel this way.*

When she gazed into the shimmering, continual fire in his eyes, Clarissa knew an intoxicating awakening that grew more intimate by the minute. Fighting against it didn't seem to make a difference. Desperate, she pushed against his shoulders. He didn't budge, his solidity like rock.

"Do you think desire and sex are impure?" he asked out of the blue.

"Of course not. But I don't jump in bed with men I've just met."

"Except, perhaps, me."

Righteous anger threatened to override lust. She stuttered. "You — I can't believe you."

"Believe me. I'm real."

She almost screamed. Almost. Until she saw the expression in his eyes.

His gaze devoured her breasts. Her chest heaved up and down with her quick breathing, and when he palmed her stomach she stiffened.

"What are you doing?" she asked.

Fire curled in her loins as his big hand moved with the slightest caress over her bellybutton. Soothing, the motion also aroused. Her nipples tightened in response. An ache started in her core, her body longing to grip and hold a man's cock. Her fingers gripped his shoulders tighter.

His touch slipped down, dipping under her waistband. For one frightening, yet thrilling second, she thought he might unbutton and unzip her jeans. And to her horror, she wanted his touch between her thighs, over her breasts. Anywhere she could imagine he would claim and give.

An image expanded in her mind, and she groaned as she arched her back and her eyes closed with delight. This wild, reckless man slid between her thighs, naked and willing. His cock probed at her wet folds, tantalizing her as she arched her hips. *Oh, yes. Oh.* Her lips parted as her breathing increased and her chest rose and fell.

Oh God, yes. She wanted desperately to feel his cock inside her, to know the mystery he provoked.

Clarissa's eyes snapped open, her body trembling.

Blazing with seductive light, his eyes drew her into a world containing only them. He licked his lips. "I see what you see, Clarissa. Is this what you want? Do you ache as I ache? I want to know what your wetness feels like tightening around my cock. I want to know what it feels like to slide in and out of you slowly, then fast until you scream in ecstasy."

Although some of the glowing yellow temperature subsided from his striking eyes, his gaze held a lambent, sensual haze that made her want to writhe in pleasure rather than fear, but she couldn't relinquish power to this stranger. Had she gone insane? What if he *was* the serial killer?

When she squirmed with panic, his lips touched her brow with tender deference. "Hush. Easy. Easy. I'm not a serial killer."

"How do I know that?" Her voice trembled. "Only a crazy man invades a woman's room and forces himself on her like this."

"Well, in truth I've been called a crazy man before." When she continued to struggle, he said softly, "Calm down. What do you feel in your heart?"

In her heart she sensed heady sexual turbulence, a raging need almost out of control, but never with the intent to injure or humiliate.

"That's it." His voice dipped even lower, a balm on her tender nerves. "Stop and listen to me. You honestly believe I would've saved you last night if I wanted to rape and murder you?"

It didn't make much sense, but neither did his actions now. "What do you expect me to believe? You turn up at my bedside, you kiss my…my jaw. You lay on top of me. You start fondling me. I don't even *know* you."

An arrogant, sultry smile covered his lips. "You will know me. Very well. In your dreams, in your fantasies we are intimate. As I read your mind earlier, I saw your vision of me between your legs, ready to thrust inside you."

His words burned her, heating her to overwhelming need. Clarissa's breathing quickened as his words turned her on.

"Is it of things to come, sweet Clarissa? Do you see the future? For it is surely not the past." The mysterious man removed his touch from her stomach, sliding his fingers under her sweater to rest between her breasts. "Your heart is pounding but not from fear."

Damn his black Irish heart.

She rarely used crass language in anger, but the words erupted in desperation. She pushed against his shoulders again. "Fuck you."

He laughed, throwing back his head. Rich and deep, his mirth served to excite her so much she couldn't help the restless little squirm she made with her hips.

"Oh yes," he said. "Make no mistake. I do want to fuck you."

She blushed like a schoolgirl and hated it. "How dare you?" Enraged by his overblown ego, her anger overran previous trepidation. "You bastard."

To her surprise, regret and maybe even shame touched his gorgeous face for one moment. Then it disappeared like a light bulb extinguishing. He moved off her and stood near the side of the bed. As she levered into sitting position, she tugged her sweater over her belly.

"I've frightened you."

"I'll say." She sat on the edge of the bed and jammed her feet into her boots. She laced them in a hurry. She wouldn't get caught barefooted if she had to make a quick escape. As she glanced at the digital bedside clock, she groaned. "It's almost nine o'clock in the morning."

"To be sure my timing is off, but this can't wait." He reached in his pants pocket and withdrew a piece of paper and handed it to her. "Erin Greenway's number. You can call there anytime today."

Silence hovered like a shroud, dark and somehow filled with apprehension.

"And?" she asked.

He cocked one dark eyebrow. "They want to see you. Would you have dinner with me—with them—tonight? We'll meet at Erin Greenway's home."

The ire simmering in her blood cooled. "All right. I'm busy today until about six."

"What are you doing?"

Ronan's nosiness astonished her, but it shouldn't have considering his earlier behavior. "Again, that's not your business."

His eyes brightened, the fiery yellow tempered by warm brown. For the first time she realized his long leather jacket lay on a chair by the desk. A blood red sweater enhanced the burnished red highlights running through his chocolate hair. Black wool gabardine pants fit him as if specially tailored. All his clothes looked Italian designer, expensive and right for his powerful body. In the graveyard he'd looked dangerous and incredible, but casual. Now his attire screamed confidence. He didn't wear any jewelry, and for some reason she liked that. Maybe because the last man she'd dated had been obsession with gold necklaces and earnings she didn't appreciate.

She tried to remember, despite her annoyance with him, if she'd ever seen a more striking male specimen in her life.

No.

As she perused Ronan his gaze stirred hotter and appreciative. While she'd been looking him over, he'd done the same with her. He licked his lower lip and the sensual gesture jolted like electricity in her belly. Desire sparkled, refusing to react to her displeasure and concentrating in her loins.

Oh, man. If he could read her thoughts right now—

He took a step forward, and the movement startled her. She stood up, ready to run.

Instead Clarissa found she couldn't move. Ronan's potent gaze pinned her to the spot.

What's happening?

He whispered in her mind. *We are happening.*

She shivered. "No. You aren't in my mind. I must be losing it."

As a comforting glow surrounded her body like a blanket, he said out loud, "Please don't be afraid."

"What are you? *Who* are you really?"

"You've asked me that before."

"And you didn't answer."

In the blink of an eye he seemed to move several feet. He stood right in front of her with almost no inches to spare.

He reached out and she flinched. Instead of retreating he brushed his fingers over her cheek. "You feel it, I feel it. There is something between us."

Clarissa swallowed hard. "Huh. If that isn't the biggest line I've ever heard."

"Line?"

"You know what I'm talking about. A come on."

He grinned and the overwhelming sensuality in his face made her heartbeat pick up the pace. "It is, isn't it? I'll give you full disclosure down to the last desire. Emotional and physical reactions, thoughts, needs, desires. Would that ease your fears?"

All suitable retorts flew out the window. She didn't have much experience with men revealing their inner thoughts to her, especially not on short acquaintance, but maybe if she knew more about this mysterious Irishman she could decipher his game.

"Right now? I have somewhere to be," she said.

He gave a slight bow at the waist, an old-world gesture she found charming. "My apologies, Clarissa. I'm not always at my best during the day. I'm a night owl."

"Somehow that doesn't surprise me."

He laughed, the sound brushing over her erogenous zones like a lover's caress. For an unfathomable few seconds she sank into the odd but pleasant sensation. She shivered with a finely drawn ecstasy she could only describe as a peak experience. In one moment she felt cherished, protected, and loved.

How ridiculous. I don't even know him and I'm weaving these elaborate feelings and fantasies. Insanity.

A secretive smile touched his lips, then disappeared so fast she couldn't be certain she even saw it. "Whatever happens between us will be natural. Nothing malignant."

"The only thing that's going to happen between us is you explaining what this is all about. This mind reading thing, how you got into my room and so forth. You'll cough up answers or I'm kicking you out right now." She rustled up courage. "I *will* call the police."

Ronan took a step closer. Despite her independence and ability to take care of herself, something about him made her feel feminine and delicate. Standing so near, his presence drew her closer and closer. She inhaled deeply as her heart pounded. As she breathed in his tantalizing scent, a strange dizziness overtook her, and she let out a little gasp. A vision clouded her sight, and as her knees weakened she felt his arms go around her waist in support.

"Clarissa." His voice went husky with worry. "Clarissa what is it?"

His voice faded as she slipped into a dream world where she could see Ronan dressed in colonial garb like that worn by men during the American Revolution. As they marched into battle against the Redcoats, another man walked alongside him, a skinny fellow with a narrow face and small frame. She could smell sweat and urine, the vile stench of human fear as men walked towards certain death. Shivering, she suffered a deep, sorrowful ache for those who wouldn't survive. Seconds later Clarissa realized she resided in Ronan's body and saw what he saw, felt what he felt. His heart didn't pound with fear, nor did he flinch at danger. He knew what he would do and how he would do it. He understood the thin man beside him would back him up.

She hardly registered Ronan's rough Irish accent coaxing her from the vision. "Clarissa. Wake up. Wake now, darlin'."

Her eyes snapped open. He sat on the bed with her cradled her in his arms. Her head rested on his shoulder. The whole episode shook her to the core. Struggling out of his grip, she immediately stood and looked down at him. Her breath sluiced in and out of her lungs and her heart continued to pound. Everything, including her attraction to Ronan, moved way too fast for comfort.

He frowned. "Are you all right?"

"Of course. I just...you may think it's insane, but I have visions sometimes about people or places. It's nothing to worry about."

His eyes narrowed. "What did you see?"

"The American Revolution. You were there, and I could see through your eyes part of the time. There was a skinny man next to you."

When he remained sitting on the bed, looking at her like she might have grown a second head, she burned with embarrassment. On the other hand, if he believed her to be a couple chess pieces short of a set, maybe he'd leave her alone.

He stood and it brought him too near again. "Sorley. He's a friend in this life."

"So you believe in reincarnation."

"I do." He shifted, his gaze penetrating and asking her things she didn't think she wished to answer. "We'll have to take more time to talk about reincarnation." Again his attention caressed her, his eyes warm and filled with definite male interest. "After we've taken the edge off what is happening between us."

She jerked from the sensual haze threatening to overwhelm her common sense. "Nothing is happening and nothing will happen between us. Like I said, I can call the police if you don't leave."

He shrugged one shoulder insolently. "If you called the police it wouldn't matter. I'd disappear and they wouldn't find me no matter how hard they'd try."

A new worry formed inside her. "You make a habit of running from the police?"

"No."

"Are you a criminal?"

His irreverent grin made her angrier. "If I was, would I tell you?"

She sniffed. "Considering your impudence, yes, I think you'd admit it."

"All right, here's the truth. I'm not a criminal nor at any time in my life have I been a criminal."

"How do I know you're not lying?"

"You can ask Lachlan Tavish and Erin Greenway. Call them before we have dinner tonight."

Her fears eased, though the danger she sensed circling him didn't relieve her trepidation one hundred percent. "You're assuming I'm having dinner with them."

"Of course."

Flabbergasted by his arrogance, yet more and more curious, she sighed. "Right. If I was some mysterious woman who entered your room at night without knocking first, would you trust me?"

"Depends on her proposal. It's been awhile since a mysterious woman has been in my bedroom. Once you've talked with Erin and Lachlan, you'll trust me. Now is not the time for elaborate explanation, Clarissa. Tonight I'll explain some of it." His fingers slipped over her cheek again, the touch so light and caressing. "Then you'll understand."

Before she could resurrect a protest, his fingers slipped into the back of her hair and he leaned in close. She put her hands out in defense and her palms landed on the hardness of his wide, muscled chest. His strength revived primitive female responses that screamed for fulfillment.

"What are you doing?" she asked.

His mouth almost brushed hers. "Showing you we are meant to taste passion."

Another brush of hot lips made her quiver with delight. Her eyelids fluttered half closed as his lips hovered over hers. "But I think—"

"Don't think," he whispered against her lips, his breath hot and minty. "Feel what we have together."

And his mouth covered hers.

Chapter Four

Clarissa made a muffled protest in the back of her throat as Ronan's mouth molded hers. At first she couldn't think. Her nipples tightened immediately as arousal smoothed warm and seductive and drifted downward. As his lips shaped hers, desire rose with new flames, taunting her into responding.

She couldn't believe this. How could she respond to this stranger, a man she didn't even like? Rational thought left, removed by the wild sensations streaking into her body with furious intensity.

She savored his touch and wondered at his ability to make her feel treasured, worshipped. Her world went into riot, a million sensations taking root in her body as he deepened the kiss. Her fingers clutched at his sweater, needing him as an anchor. She palmed his muscles and enjoyed the male authority beneath her fingers. He was hard and rough, his muscles bunching and releasing as he moved against her with the subtle gyrations of rugged male animal. Relentless, his lips searched hers, asking for passion she wished to show but knew she shouldn't.

She melted against him. She'd never swayed into a man's embrace or his arms with whole abandon. Stunned by everything she felt, she allowed Ronan's essence, what made him unique, to touch her heart and soul. His kisses set her on fire, a combination of spine-melting tenderness and soul-searing sex.

When she eased closer, he moaned low in his throat and slipped his arms around her waist. Her breasts crushed against his chest, his cock pressed into her stomach. New, burning hot desire heated her body, dancing over her skin like lightning strikes.

When his muscled thigh pushed up between her legs and pressed against hot, intimate folds, she moaned softly. With rhythmic, insistent motion his thigh slid against tender areas that pulsed and dampened. His palm slid over her ass, testing and caressing. He shaped her with that hand, branding her his own. She shivered against the intimate invasion, focusing on the way his touch cupped and shaped her butt and the way his thigh rubbed against her intimately. His tongue slipped into her mouth, plunging and exploring.

Searing new sensations took hold, driving her toward an unknown passion. A tight, uncontrollable ache pulsed between her thighs and she undulated against him, dying for some relief from restless desire. She needed more. *More.*

Deep in her mind she felt something, a tickle in her brain as if someone searched inside her psyche. Each brush against her thoughts startled, yet aroused. Heat moistened the folds between her legs and she gasped against his mouth in tortured need. Again the tentative probe of her thoughts warmed her from the inside out, demanding an answer.

So she gave it. *Yes. Yes.*

Deep and undeniably Irish, Ronan's voice entered her head. *My beautiful, beautiful colleen.*

As his palms warmed her back, searching and caressing, his lips plied and coaxed. Incredible desire built as she arched in his hold, pressing into his muscled frame. Craving rose at the core, and she unleashed desires without a second thought. Responding to his ravenous kiss, she stroked his tongue with her own.

Delicious.

Seductive.

Beyond compare.

Desire had never been this strong.

She shivered and pulled back. His arms banded her tight against his chest as she stared up at the Irishman in blatant surprise. "What was that? What did you do?"

Blazing with an intensity that seized her breath, his fiery dark gaze enveloped her before he dove in for another kiss. With any other man she might have kneed him in the groin to escape. Instead, uncontrollable desire kept her in his arms.

He twisted his mouth over hers, effectively parting her lips as his tongue sought hers. Clarissa felt like a virgin tasting a man for the first time. With warm, deep strokes, he pumped his tongue into her mouth. Her loins clenched and ached as another hot pulse immediately took up residence between her thighs as he continued to press his thigh against her swollen labia and clit.

Yes. Oh, yes.

Releasing her lips, he whispered fervently, "God's blood, you are sweet. Hot and warm and beyond bearing."

He took her mouth again, a hungry, carnal assault that started wild feelings deep down in the most secret recesses of her soul.

A vision speared into her head, taking her by surprise. Ronan smiling and laughing with the little blonde woman, her eyes sparkling with joy at being near him. His eyes held a youth and innocence, a glow of a man who believed she would be his for all time. Love surged back and forth between Ronan and the young woman, and a strange heartache lanced through Clarissa.

Ronan broke the kiss and drew back several steps, his chest heaving, his eyes filled with ever present flame. To her surprise, shock also covered his face, as if she'd said or done something amazing.

Before she could ask him about the blonde, he turned away and headed for the door. He paused to put on his coat and the strange cloak lying on a chair. Without looking at her he unlocked the door and left.

Stunned, she didn't move for a full two minutes. She approached the door and relocked it, then turned and leaned her back against it while her breathing synchronized and her heart stopped pounding.

Amazed at the spectacular arousal that had jumped back and forth between her and Ronan, Clarissa couldn't think. Couldn't move.

She touched her lips. "What's happening to me?"

And why on earth should I be jealous of some blonde woman in one of Ronan's previous lives?

Or had it been simple empathy for the doomed couple? She couldn't be sure. She closed her eyes and tried resurrecting what she'd seen in her mind's eye. Ronan's clothing and the woman's came from a time in the distant past. She concentrated and brought the image she'd seen clear in her mind. They'd been sitting on wooden benches behind the tall, imposing castle. She thought back to what she knew about castles. This one, what little she'd seen of it, appeared to exist sometime in the twelve hundreds or perhaps later. The symbol of feudal power went beyond a simple motte and bailey erection of wood and clay. Sun had glinted off its massive stone walls in afternoon sunlight.

She opened her eyes with a start and found she sat on the floor with her back to the hotel room door. She glanced at her watch. Damn, she'd done it again. More than twenty minutes passed while she'd cruised around in the past. Shrugging off self-admonition, Clarissa stood and went into the bathroom to wash up. She had a lot of work to do.

Once she had a shower, she decided she needed to make that call to Erin Greenway. Clarissa hesitated before she lifted the phone. Intuition said to call Erin, but another part said the spooky buildings here in Pine Forest called to her camera and she should get out to the cemeteries while she had daylight to burn. She wanted to parade through Pine Forest and search out the memories of growing up here.

She tapped one peach-painted nail against the plastic receiver. Could she trust Ronan, a man with otherworldly eyes, amazing strength, and an odd ability to turn up in her hotel room without using the door?

Other than the fact he'd suffered through some past lives, the man had other talents, and a strangeness that defied logic.

"Okay," she said to the empty hotel room. "Should I be afraid of you, Ronan Kieran?"

Shaking her head, she decided to call Erin, then locate Jim Leggett to see if he could accompany her to the graveyards. She didn't relish going anywhere with Jim, but who else would be interested in helping her with the photographs but a ghost hunter?

She tried Erin's number at the library and reached her there. "Erin, this is Clarissa Gaines."

"Hi, Clarissa." Erin's soft, enthusiastic voice made Clarissa feel at ease. "Ronan mentioned you and said you wanted to get together with Lachlan and I. There are some other friends you should meet, too."

"You must mean Jared Thornton and Micky Gunn."

Her hesitation came clear over the line. "How did you know about them?"

Clarissa sighed. "I've known about the four of you for some time. I would have approached you at the meeting last night, but the crowd was a little much for me."

"Since you were there, you know we tried to stop the community center Halloween celebration."

Clarissa closed her eyes, a strange lassitude enveloping her. "I'm sorry it didn't do much good."

"I think people believe if they cancel the party they've given in to the fear. And really, they're right. But they don't know how dangerous things will be on Halloween."

Clarissa sighed. "Of course they don't. It's easier to deny the worst than to come to grips with something being wrong. I remember…"

"Yes?"

"When I was growing up here the townspeople denied the supernatural to each other's faces. In secret they may have believed, but in public they lied about what they thought. Maybe they thought saying it out loud would make it worse."

Clarissa heard papers rustling, then Erin spoke. "People told me that the town admitted that the place is haunted."

Clarissa stared at the dingy off-white ceiling. "I remember it a little differently. My parents were part of the denial crowd."

"What about you? Did you believe in ghosts as a child?"

"You could say that." She didn't plan to tell Erin everything this minute. When she had them all together it would be different. "I'll let you go now. I don't want to keep you."

"Don't worry." Erin's voice held humor. "Library attendance dropped dramatically since the murders started. After those young people were found murdered under the Gunn Inn...well, that slowed turnout significantly."

Clarissa glanced at the bedside clock, concerned she hadn't done much yet. "I read about the last murders."

"Then it sounds like we really do need to talk soon. You can come to dinner at my house, I hope."

"Of course." She wrote down directions on the pad next to the phone. "Seven o'clock it is." Clarissa's curiosity pushed her to ask more questions. "Before you go, I have a couple of questions about Ronan. Do you know what he was doing in the cemetery last night?"

"Ronan has been patrolling since the murders, trying to keep people safe."

Confused, Clarissa wrinkled her nose. "Patrolling? Is he employed by the police department?"

Erin's chuckle sounded breathy. "Not at all. He told us about you being in the graveyard last night and that he warned you away from going out alone. Please listen to what he has to say. He knows what he's talking about."

"The police sanction him playing neighborhood watch?"

"They don't know." Erin sighed. "I suppose I shouldn't have told you that. Please, for all our sakes, don't tell the cops what he's doing."

What if he was participating in something highly illegal? But if he was, could Erin, Lachlan, Jared and Micky be in on the activities? From the little she knew of them, it didn't seem likely. Ronan, though…

"Ronan's from Ireland, right?" Clarissa asked.

"He couldn't get more Irish."

"His language pattern sounds like he might be from an earlier time."

Erin laughed. "He's *definitely* old-fashioned and has old world sympathies." Erin's voice lowered. "When you come to dinner there are a few more things you'll learn about him, too."

Clarissa didn't know if old-fashioned could be considered good or bad. She guessed it depending on which part of old-fashioned Erin meant. "How long have you known him?"

"Less than a month, but he's a good friend already. Lachlan knows him from way back and can vouch for him in case you're concerned."

Feeling a little steadier about the mysterious Irishman, Clarissa finished the conversation and they hung up. Urgency made her think about the graveyard and how she needed to get out there and take pictures. She was finished doubting. Time to get moving.

* * * * *

Clarissa sat in the car at the graveyard outside of town and wondered if she tempted fate. She half expected to see Ronan here, demanding she leave the area. She figured she'd start here taking some photographs, then work her way back over to St. Bartholomew's where she'd encountered the mugger last night.

Outside the cozy warmth of her car, the temperature dropped, and although she wanted to take photos now, she felt torn between three things. Getting her work accomplished, not encountering a serial killer, and meeting up with Jim, the man who'd broken her heart all those years ago.

She watched trees sway in the wind near the black iron fence line. Like many old cemeteries, this one featured the proverbial scraggly looking, winter-barren trees, their gnarled, snow-covered branches reaching like bony fingers into the sky. Time-worn gravestones sat like old, neglected people, their ravaged gray faces worried and uncertain. Even the white cap of snow on top of each stone gave them a special creepiness.

She smiled.

Perfect.

The cemetery possessed the ideal atmosphere for the shots she needed. Gravestones competed for attention with crypts, the graveyard not exactly huge, but not small either. Hilly in places, the area seemed more welcoming in some ways than Pine Forest itself.

Something came to her with a jolt of surprise. She'd been here as a child and a teen but somehow the place didn't frighten her the way it did then.

Thank goodness.

Maybe whatever evil she'd felt long ago no longer walked among these resting places. One less monster to fret over, perhaps.

She almost left the car to start work, independence demanding action. Instead she recalled Ronan's warnings. She heard a car engine approaching and seconds later a sedan approached with Jim in the driver's seat.

With a wave he gave her a cheerful smile. Half concerned she'd made a big mistake meeting up with Jim, she climbed out of the Acura with her camera bag in hand.

"Hi." Jim walked around the car, the bag slung over his shoulder laden with electronic doodads she knew he used for his ghost hunting. "You're right, this place has atmosphere. Think we'll meet up with a Freddy Kruger?"

"I hope not. One time was enough for me, thank you very much."

As they made their way through the open gate, a breeze rustled through the trees and snow floated from the treetops. They wandered through the graveyard, scrutinizing various gravestones and marveling how some older stones appeared better preserved, while newer ones sometimes didn't weather the elements as well. As she always did when she took photographs in places of the dead, she wondered if any ghosts stood and watched.

As she snapped a photograph of a Celtic cross, Jim held his electromagnetic counter in front of him. "Do you ever get any ghosts in your photographs?"

She took the shot before she answered him. "Yes, actually."

She didn't look at him, well aware he'd offer her a skeptical grin laced with his usual know-it-all bravado. "You'll have to show them to me sometime."

Although ready to take another picture, she lowered her camera. "I don't have time to show my etchings these days."

His eyebrows tilted up. "I heard over the grapevine you've been traveling a lot for your books."

She started wandering again. "That's right."

He followed, holding the meter out in front of him, his gaze pinned to the reading. "So this book about Pine Forest would be the third one, right?"

Surprised, she looked at him as they walked. "You've kept track?"

"You'd be surprised how much I know about you."

"That sounds ominous."

"Don't worry. I'm not a stalker."

A little amazed he'd paid attention to her career, she kept her gaze on him.

"Look out!" Jim reached for her, dropping his meter in the process.

She tripped headlong over a flat gravestone and started to fall. A squeak of surprise left her throat at the same time she kept a tight grip on her camera with one hand. Jim grabbed her, tugging Clarissa against his chest.

Her breath whooshed out as she landed against him and her camera jabbed into her breasts. "Ow!"

He released her immediately. "You okay?"

Chagrinned, she straightened her stocking hat. "Yes. Sorry, I'm not usually this clumsy."

Jim bent over to pick up his meter, staring at it with a frown. She waited for the expected explosion. "Damn, I think I broke it."

"I'm sorry, it's my fault."

He shook his head. "Accidents happen."

A little surprised, she peered at him. "The old Jim would have exploded."

He shook his head. "The old Jim was an asshole." Her eyebrows went up and he laughed. "I realized that was one of the reasons why I lost you. After you left Pine Forest I started to change." He looked deep into her eyes. "When I saw you last night at the meeting, I knew I had to see you again, and not just to make sure you were safe. I wanted you to know the new Jim Leggett."

Taken off guard by the sudden confession, discomfort made her take a step back. "Okay, that's fair. It's been a long time since we've seen each other."

He smiled. "You expected me to get mad and unreasonable. To prove that people with red hair have a temper."

Her eyebrows rose. "Some do. I'm not the most conservative person with my anger."

"Oh, I don't know. You sure knew how to handle me. You kept calm when I was going off the deep end about you leaving Pine Forest."

Memories flowed strong inside Clarissa, a fountain of images and regrets she'd long forgotten until this moment. A mingling of disappointment for what never was and could never be swamped her. Old regret bit like teeth into her recollections.

She took a deep breath. "We both didn't know what we were doing then."

"That's for sure." His voice held a little sarcasm. "I know I'll never make mistakes like *that* again."

Damn him. Why did he have to remind her of her stupidity? "Maybe we should finish up and get out of here." She stuffed her hands in her pockets. "So, we need to get you another meter?"

He looked down at the instrument. "Look at that. It's working again. Weird."

"Ha. Nothing unusual is actually weird in this town. Remember that."

They continued, and this time she kept her attention on the ground. "So if you're a skeptic about supernatural phenomena, why did you turn to psychic research? You could have gone on to be another type of scientist."

"I *am* another type of scientist, remember? Psychology?"

"How easily I forget." She took a photo of a contorted tree, menacing clouds rearing behind it in the afternoon sky. "How long have you been into the psychic research side of things?"

"About three years."

"And before that?"

"I was a private practice therapist."

"That didn't satisfy you any more, I take it?"

He shrugged, his movement nonchalant. "I wanted to research the phenomena that made people believe in things that weren't there. I wanted to prove to people that psychic phenomena are a figment of the imagination."

Smiling, she turned her camera on him and clicked off one picture. "I think you're going to fail miserably. You're going to spend your entire life chasing something and never have the answer."

She saw his deep frown through the camera lens as she snapped one more photo of him. "Thanks for the vote of confidence." She walked on and he caught up to her seconds later. "You've got an edge I don't remember you having when you left Pine Forest. I'm not sure I like it."

Without looking at him or slackening her pace, she said, "Yes, I've changed. I'm not the same hopeful, grateful girl you knew. My edge, as you call it, is maturity. I know what I want, and I don't need anyone to tell me it's okay to want it."

His silence weighed heavy in the air. She knew she'd taken him off guard with her honesty. Okay, her bluntness. Her edge had sharpened over the years, and she didn't regret it.

"So you put down others to make yourself feel good."

Shocked, she stopped. He came to halt beside her, reading his meter apparently forgotten. She gaped at him a minute, then found an indulgent smile somewhere.

How can I grin without feeling like tearing his arrogant head off?

"I'm sorry if you felt I was putting you down when I said you wouldn't be able to debunk psychic phenomena. It wasn't my intention to downgrade you. I was giving you what I believe about the supernatural. Yes, there's much we don't know about the world. I don't think anyone knows all the answers until we're dead. Before that it is speculation and small truths revealed here and there." She took a deep breath, on a roll. "This is one of the reasons why I said you and I shouldn't work together. My opinions have nothing to do with my confidence in you as a psychologist. It has to do with the phenomena itself. The mysteries curious people chase after aren't ultimately definable. I learned that a long time ago."

"Then why are you here taking photographs? Aren't you investigating psychic phenomena in your books?"

She pulled her stocking cap down over her hair a little more as a crisp wind picked up. "Not really. I'm cataloging it."

"How?"

"I can see you haven't read one of my books."

He shifted, a flicker of discomfort in his eyes. "No."

"I take photos of the mysterious. By giving people a glimpse of what I see in the supernatural world. It's an art form to make ordinary things look scary, or to take pictures of scary things and make them seem even more frightening."

He smiled. "You always did love Halloween."

"Still my favorite holiday, I'll admit. Except for Easter. I still like hunting for eggs."

That made him laugh.

They walked on in silence for a few more minutes, and Clarissa drank in the graveyard like a woman in desperate need for water. She loved this place and the atmosphere.

"This place has such personality. Like it's a living, breathing person," she said. "It's almost like evil stopped here for a break, then left."

"Now that sounds like something to put in a book." He snorted a soft laugh. "Wait a minute. You don't still have those strange…visions, do you?"

Exasperation reared inside her, but she kept ire in check. Better to give him a calm, smooth façade even though she wanted to belt him. "I've never stopped having them."

A tolerant expression replaced his teasing. Before he could make another comment, she moved off. She snapped photograph after photograph, conscious of her discomfort at being around Jim and his disbelieving personality. She meandered as he concentrated on making notes on a little pad he produced from his jeans pocket. Putting distance between them seemed like the best way for her to come to grips. Jim Leggett had changed a little, but not as much as he claimed. Had she come out here hoping he might be different and they might rekindle something?

Then again, would any man support her in her endeavors? Believe her when she told him that Pine Forest would be destroyed on Halloween?

She headed toward a crypt on a low hill. Sitting alone with a few trees to shelter it, the crypt looked like a small Greek temple perched lonely and forlorn. She stopped at the bottom of the hill and took photos, then moved onward. As she walked up the slope she noted the hillside had been spared most of the snow, the rocky surface easier to navigate.

Clarissa imagined the person who'd been buried here had been wealthy or revered in some way. Her muscles drew tight the closer she came to the crypt. A strange throbbing started in her temples and she took a deep breath. When she reached the top of the hill a wave of apprehension floated over her, her heart pounding with a bizarre fear she hadn't tasted even when she'd been mugged. Her mouth went dry and she swallowed hard. The crypt door was smashed in, and at the angle she couldn't see much inside. Good thing she'd brought the right lens for taking shots in the dim interior. Still...

Something was here.

She felt it in each joint and sinew as she stopped and breathed deeply. She had to keep control or let the panic swell and burst. Running and screaming was an alternative, but not dignified. Since she didn't plan on letting Mr. Skeptic see her freak out.

Jim stood at the bottom of the hill. "This is weird. The meter is going nuts. I'm getting extreme readings right here."

Why doesn't that surprise me?

She gestured at him. "Come on up and see what you can find."

Ignoring her nervousness, she stepped inside the crypt and stood at the top step. She would need three more steps down to reach in the interior.

She whispered to herself, "Come on, girl, don't wuss out on me now."

One step. Two. She wished she'd brought a flashlight, and then wondered if Jim brought one. She started to turn back when the floor broke away under her.

A gasping scream left her throat as she fell straight down.

Chapter Five

The drip, drip of water landed on Clarissa's forehead like Chinese water torture. A jumble of impressions bombarded her. She only knew she must flee the darkness and the horrible choking sensation that clawed at her throat and stole her air.

Succubus? Incubus? A demon of unfathomable hate?

Jumbled words floated through her mind.

Must get out of the darkness. Must.

How much time passed she couldn't be sure. A dull pain in her head persisted. Impressions returned with distressing slowness as she realized she lay flat on her back. She reached up for her camera and discovered when she'd tumbled into the abyss she'd lost it somewhere.

Her mouth tasted like it had been stuffed with cotton and she licked her dry lips. She trembled as cold seeped through her parka. As she opened her eyes she couldn't see much in the gloom.

Light shimmered down from the hole she'd fallen through. Instead of full sun the light was watery. She wondered if Jim had gone for help; if she'd been unconscious for long assistance might be on the way.

"Jim!" She waited, hoping for an answer. Nothing. "Jim, I'm down here!"

Again, nothing.

As full consciousness returned so did pain. She felt battered and bruised. She groaned and touched her temples with her fingers. Her skull might fall off and then she'd be a ghost like Anne Boleyn, wandering this subterranean hell moaning and looking for her head.

Now I know I'm okay. I have my sense of humor.

She groped in the semi-darkness for her fanny pack and rummaged for her cell phone. She turned it on but when she tried dialing 9-1-1, static buzzed in her ear. She tried two more times, but the phone wouldn't cooperate. The display lit up, so maybe the signal didn't reach down here. If the walls acted like a cave, she doubted anyone could hear her unless she kept shouting. Glancing into the blackness around her, she realized light disappeared, swallowed up not far in either direction.

"Drat."

After stuffing the phone back in the pack, Clarissa shifted her fanny pack from around her stomach to around her back.

"Stay calm and everything will be all right." She tried once more. "Jim, can you hear me? Jim!"

Nothing.

Sighing, she decided she couldn't sit there and wait for rescue. There had to be something she could do. She stood and leaned against the rocky wall. Refusing to panic would keep her alive and kickin' one way or the other.

"See if I ever go into another crypt without a flashlight."

Seconds later she heard a strange noise, something like an exhale, but not quite. She waited, her hearing zeroing in on the sound lingering in the air. An echo? She took a shuddering breath. *Keep calm. The way to make it out of here is to stay tough. Anything less is foolish.* Drawing a cleansing breath, she tried to think about what she could do to get the hell out of there. Damp, dark, and smelling like earth, the chamber was cold. Glad for her long parka, gloves and stocking hat, she decided standing would be preferable to lying or sitting on the hard packed earth.

Rather than leaning against the wall, she stood within the circle of pale light streaming down from the hole above. Clarissa paused, searching her intuition for answers. While no one in their right mind would like this place, she felt vulnerable here. As if something or someone watched her from a spot too dark for human eyes to detect. This place seemed odd, out of sync.

Come on. It's just a hole.

A dungeon.

No. A strange crawling sensation heralded rushing emotions that didn't belong to her. A few whispers touched her ears.

Then she felt it. People had been down here before, searching for someone else, though she couldn't say how long ago. With reluctance she allowed her senses to accept and catalog, to discover *what* resided here in the blackness. For no one would ever stay here, if they valued sanity. She didn't dare close her eyes while experiencing the heavy emotions caressing the edge of her senses. Like a lead weight negative feelings touched her, starting first with panic, despair and disbelief.

It made sense in the grand scheme of things. Anyone who'd been trapped here for long might know all these thoughts. She didn't have to worry about approaching any of these emotions. Jim wouldn't leave her down here to die. Seconds later came a wave of repulsion. This time she couldn't say if the feeling came from her or from another soul that had once trod this dark corridor.

No matter what happened, she wouldn't allow insecurity to take over. Drawing another breath deep into her lungs, she plotted how to escape this nasty place and pushed away the disturbing feelings.

After she shivered she realized her hands felt cold. She located her gloves in her coat pockets and slipped into them.

She heard a strange popping noise not that far away from her, and she jerked in surprise and alarm. The same sound she'd heard in the graveyard last night when—

Ronan stepped out of the blackness, his eyes ablaze with yellow fire.

Her mouth opened, but she couldn't say a word, her surprise more than profound. She didn't have to respond, he moved forward with purpose, his gaze filled with fury. His unhappy expression made her shrink back against the rock. Her fanny pack jabbed into her back.

For an unguarded moment she thought he meant to harm her.

"Are you hurt?" When he spoke his voice sounded rough with worry, strained by emotion, taking her by surprise.

Trust took a backseat to fear, though, and when he took another step toward her she inhaled quickly.

"You." Her voice warbled and trembling suddenly racked her body.

His brows creased together. Faster than a blink he stood directly in front of her. Shocked by the lightning-quick move, she let out a small cry.

Radiating warmth and tenderness, his eyes held her captive. He clasped her head gently between his palms. "You're hurt."

"I'm...no, I'm fine."

"Never mind the headache?"

"How did you know—?"

"Your brow is furrowed. You're in pain or frightened." When she looked up into his eyes and didn't speak, he continued. "You didn't panic, Clarissa." His voice held a soothing quality laced into liquid seduction. "Sure, and with all that's down here, that's surprising."

"What's down here?"

His voice whispered in her head. *Darkness.*

His lips hadn't moved, and her fear renewed. "What are you doing here?"

"Looking for you."

Although she knew her brain should be operating at full throttle, she couldn't quite focus. Instead she sank into those fire-filled eyes and felt alarm return. "But how...how did you know I was here?"

His warm breath touched her forehead as he leaned in close. "Instinct."

God, his touch felt so good, his presence engendering security and wild fear. Her throat felt dry and hoarse. "What are you doing?"

His fingers gentled, warm and reassuring. He slipped his fingers over her cheek, then fingertips to jaw.

Close your eyes.

His lips hadn't moved again, and she wondered at her grip on reality. She placed her hands over his as his thumbs caressed her skin. "No."

Close your eyes. His voice echoed in her mind again.

Eyelids growing heavy, she fought to keep them open and couldn't. As her eyes shut, she struggled against his relentless influence.

He possessed her.

Took control.

Banished her will.

Ronan eased her against his body, gathering her tenderly against him.

He pressed her head against his shoulder as he whispered in that sensuous, stirring voice. "You are safe. I won't allow you to be harmed. Trust me."

As his soft plea reached her ears, she relaxed. She'd never felt this safe in a man's embrace before. How he'd known she was down here didn't seem to matter. Only staying in his arms had any significance.

Slowly the ache in her head retreated, inch by inch. Seconds later he moved her back a bit so he could look into her eyes.

"Feel better now?" he asked.

"Yes, I'm better." She looked up at the hole in the crypt above. "How do we get out of here?"

The Irishman did something she didn't expected. He winked. "We fly."

His grin held megawatts of pure charm. His eyes sparkled and the effect set her heart racing.

You're insane. You're trapped in a subterranean hellhole with a dangerous man and you're getting all goo-goo eyed over him?

Grateful beyond belief that he stood nearby, she closed the small distance between them. She placed one gloved hand on his chest. "Thank you."

An undeniable glow of orange fire punctuated his gaze. That uncanny glimmer that once frightened but now intrigued. "Thank you for what?"

"For calming me."

His fingers drifted over her forehead with a strange caress. His attentive gaze touched her lips. "If you don't stop looking at me like that…"

She felt free, dangerous, and willing to do almost anything to keep this strange exhilaration going in her blood. "What?"

He edged nearer until she brushed against him. Even through her coat and sweater she enjoyed the touch of his body against her breasts. She made a soft, sharp inhalation at the exquisite feeling.

"I know what you want." His voice filled with unrestrained passion. Darkly seductive, his tone promised endless delight. "Now is not the time to fulfill your needs, but later I will give you everything you want."

Puzzled, she frowned. "What are you talking about?"

"You've thought about our kiss. What it did to you." He brushed his hand over her cheek, cupping her face in warmth. "You want me inside of you more than you want to breathe."

She shivered against his warm touch as lightning arousal mixed with embarrassment. Mortified that she'd given away her innermost thoughts and yet astonished he could read her, she muttered, "You're insane."

She backed away and the movement made her dizzy. She swayed and he took her arm again.

Yanking from his grip she said, "Don't touch me. I don't—"

Ronan's mouth captured hers, a low, almost purring growl coming from his throat. She shivered as the kiss went supernova. Without preliminaries he tugged her closer, his arms unbridled steel around her waist and back, his mouth twisting over hers relentlessly. His tongue took immediate charge, plunging deep and devouring. As his tongue rasped over hers again and again she moaned into his mouth and responded. Entering the dance, she forgot where she was and how she came to be there.

She was in the bowels of a crypt, but the man holding her would protect her against evil. Clarissa knew he would guard her with his soul, his heart and mind. A restlessness grew inside her to put out this conflagration that heightened by the second. Ronan Kieran wanted her in all ways a man could want a woman, and she felt the hard press of his erection against her stomach.

He pulled back and stared into her eyes and she thought about moving away. Instead his voice whispered in her head. *Stay with me.*

With a deft movement he reached between their bodies and unzipped her coat. He slipped his arms under the coat and brought her into his warm embrace. Against his hard, hot body, safety and comfort enveloped her. Since his long coat lay open, she felt the hardness of his chest and the solidness of his thighs. Everything about this puzzling man spelled unbelievable strength and willingness to use power. His force, his essence was infused by a living inferno she didn't understand.

As he kissed her again, she succumbed to the overwhelming desire to remain close to him, to caress and cherish and thank him for finding her. She slipped her hands into his chocolate dark hair and caressed the thick strands, then touched his face.

His voice whispered deep in her mind. *Touch me. Feel me. Know me.*

He cupped her ass with a gentle but exploratory grip. She moaned in delight as he kneaded her flesh, testing and shaping. As his fingers brushed and cupped, she cherished the erotic need building deep in her belly, urging her to let go. Let go and discover what sensual delights this dangerous man offered.

He released her mouth, and his lips traveled over her ear. Clarissa kept her eyes closed, wanting to remain in this desire-filled world. Without restraint she caressed his hard arms and broad shoulders, needing to experience more than what she could through his leather jacket.

His breathing, heavy and rasping with a desperate desire, fueled her senses the way nothing else could have. "Sweet colleen, you have no idea what you do to me. You're the fire in my body I cannot erase. If this was the right time and place, I would show you how much I want you." He groaned softly against her neck, his frame racked by a fine shivering. "I'd take you to my lair." His hands traveled from her back to her butt again and he cupped her ass cheeks, kneading softly. "We'd drink champagne and taste each other."

"Taste each other?" she said, her voice shaky.

"Mmm." He licked her ear. "Caress." Warm and hot, his tongue darted into her ear, then out. "Taste." Ronan palmed her ass with long, soothing caresses. His mouth traveled to her forehead where he planted a warm kiss. "We'd connect. I'd do anything and everything you wanted to bring you to ecstasy. I'd feast on your luscious body until lust overwhelmed us. Then I'd take you."

A delicious shudder rippled over her. Deep between her thighs the ache built, hot and moist and desiring what he could give her. "Take me? As in make love?"

He chuckled a low, soft rumble against her ear. "It would be more than making love. It would be...mating."

"Mating," she whispered.

"Sweet, tender mating." His tongue lingered on her earlobe. "Or hard, hot, fast mating."

Wild shivers overtook her. "Yes to both."

Clarissa forgot the darkness around them, the strange fear she'd experienced and the trauma of falling down the hole. Instead she snuggled into Ronan's incredible, intoxicating embrace and accepted his wanton words, his mental lovemaking.

He brushed the curling fringe away from her forehead and his lips toured her skin. "Do you want to know how I'd feel inside you?"

It sounded so forbidden. "Please tell me."

He murmured against her temple, "You'll be so hot, so warm and dripping with sexual need that I'll slip inside easily."

To her immediate surprise and delight, she could feel a hard cock pressing between her legs. She knew it wasn't happening now, but the images, the feelings inside her head were there nonetheless. As the imaginary cock eased inside, spreading her walls, she groaned with the desire, the heavenly sensation.

"That's it," he said softly. "Take me inside." Mentally pushing, he progressed, parting her sex with steady pressure. "More, Clarissa. Open to me."

She shuddered and writhed as the sweet feeling continued as she opened wide to his intrusion. He pressed as high as he could go.

"When I'm deep, your warm pussy will grip me."

"Oh, yes. I can feel it now."

"You'll feel my heart beat in my cock, you'll shiver against my hardness. I'll feel every ripple of your hot walls."

More feelings darted into her system, as forceful as a blizzard, as incredible as anything she'd thought in her wildest dreams. She could feel him pressing deeper between her thighs, his hungry cock inserted fully into her hot passage.

Her head feel back, offering him her throat. "What will you do then?"

"I'll fuck you. Moving inside you with deep pumps of my cock."

His graphic description fired her libido higher than she could have imagined, and the sensation of his hardness sliding into her and then drawing slowly out made her quiver in his arms. "Oh. Oh, my God."

As she made the breathy sounds, his lips touched the hollow of her throat. "You'll feel me parting your sex time and again. Deep and slow."

When she issued another soft, "Oh, my God," he continued his assault on her crumbling defenses.

"Your heart is beating faster as your channel drips with your need. With each thrust you draw me tight against you as your pleasure grows."

At his words she felt the heat climbing from her groin all the way up her chest into her face, everything inside her responding to his words of seduction. Somewhere, in the part of her brain that could still reason, she wondered if his words were designed to lure, to make her weak. She wanted to struggle against him, but found she couldn't.

"No," she managed to push through the fog in her thought processes.

Immediately the sensations of him fucking her stopped.

It was if she'd never felt him inside her.

A warm laugh came from Ronan's chest as he nuzzled her cheek. "You try my control, but I would never force myself upon you."

She didn't know what to say, and with effort she opened her eyes. He stared down at her; the fire remained high in his remarkable gaze. Then the fire winked out, as if he forced it to disappear. "What did...? How did...?"

At her confused rambling he brushed his fingers over her forehead. "We came together mentally."

Sarcastic humor rose to forefront. "In other words, we just had a real mind fuck."

He chuckled, and the sound almost made her forget she stood in a dark hole with a man bent on seducing her. "Sure, and you could say we had quickie, but we didn't finish."

Finish. Now that would have been interesting. She shook her head, amazed beyond belief. "I must be insane standing here with you."

"Why? Because you allowed desire to overrule your fear of this place and of me?"

"Yes. I should be afraid of this place, just as you said. I've felt strange things here."

"You have the sixth sense to see beyond what many others do."

She nodded, at least assured he wouldn't ridicule her for the talent. "Sometimes. I saw you on more than one occasion in what might be another life."

He drew in a deep breath. "You see me as I am. Nothing more, nothing less."

"But you're not like most people. You can do things. Your power, your amazing agility—it defies sanity. You haven't explained the strange light in your eyes. This is all crazy."

His grip on her loosened. "There's nothing sane in Pine Forest anymore. Not I, not you. For you're crawling around in graveyards looking for ghosts. There are many worse things here to be found. Much worse."

His tone, almost harsh, made her ease from his arms. His hands clutched into fists at his side, but she didn't see anger in his eyes, only passion. This man wanted her, no doubt about it, but she felt him retreating from her, too.

When he took a deep breath, his trembling appeared to stop. "You're putting yourself at risk being in Pine Forest."

"No kidding. I walked right into this crypt and straight down a hole I had no way of knowing was there." She looked around. "I'm stuck here with a man who drives me nuts and who speaks in riddles. And apparently he has telepathy as well. Do you?"

"That's not what I meant."

Okay, so she'd intentionally misinterpreted his meaning. With the serial killer loose any woman could be in danger. Yet she knew the first danger came from Ronan.

I won't lie to you, Clarissa. Yes, I have telepathy. Very strong telepathy.

"All right. So we've established that you can read my mind and send thoughts to me."

He narrowed his eyes. "You take that knowledge calmly."

She shrugged and the sore muscles in her body protested. "Because I believe in the supernatural. Why do you think I take photographs of haunted places?"

His gaze calmed, the fire retreating to a slow, intermittent burn. Fascinated, she couldn't seem to resist looking into his eyes. And that frightened her in the most elemental way possible, deep down where lust and desire couldn't cloud her senses.

She backed away a bit, and he held his hand out. "Don't. Don't go far."

To her surprise his voice sounded a little scared. "What are you afraid of?"

His desperate look disappeared under a hard veneer, the heat retreating from his eyes like a banked fire. "I fear nothing."

Somehow she couldn't believe that, but she decided not to challenge him. "Were you following me, Ronan? Is that how you knew where to find me?"

"No. An odd question considering I told you I found you by instinct."

Confusion warred with indignation. "*You're* the oddest man I know. You appear at the most interesting times, especially when I need you the most. You've kissed the hell out of me, and you have the strangest eyes I've ever seen. You can read minds and I can hear your voice in my head—as if that doesn't creep me out enough."

"There's a lot you don't know about me. A lot you don't want to know."

"Oh, I see. You're one of those men who gets off on being dark and dangerous. I hope you enjoyed sleeping with me in your mind."

His perplexed frown almost made her think he didn't understand until he said, "That sounds like an insult."

If she hadn't been tired, aching, and still longing for his touch, she wouldn't have pushed the issue. "It is. What are you, some kind of cop?"

He stepped forward until once again their personal space amounted to almost nothing. Eyes glittering with insolence, he said, "No."

"Then what do you do?"

"Prowl graveyards trying to keep foolish women safe."

"Foolish—why you—"

When she cut herself off, he said, "Whenever you need me, if ever you need me, all you have to do is tell me with your mind. I'll come for you."

This gorgeous, intriguing man at her beck and call with one little thought. It sounded like a fantasy come true.

Although she'd seen clear demonstration of his ability to read her mind, part of her couldn't quite accept the idea. "Why would I need you?"

"For protection."

"Why would I need protection?"

He grunted. "You do. And you still want me."

His blatant statement increased her discomfort and her ire. She held up an index finger for emphasis. "I've run into enough self-assured-to-the-point-of-sickening men in my life. You're assuming a lot if you think I'll hop into bed with you because you saved my life once, possibly twice. And to top that all off, how *did* you get down here?"

One of his dark brows winged upward, a sardonic expression covering his face. He looked up at the hole she'd fallen through. "I flew."

Before she could respond to his preposterous answer, a harsh, rushing wind blew cold into their faces. Unease made her shift closer to him, and he put his arm around her waist. She didn't know what lurked in the strange darkness surrounding them, and she didn't think she wanted to understand.

The darkness is closer. We must leave.

She glanced up at him. "You're doing it again."

He smiled this time, and sensual nuance in his grin and his eyes turned her heart over. "Touching you?"

"You know what I mean. Talking to me in my mind."

"You don't like it?"

"You're invading my privacy."

"Mmm. There's more I'd like to invade, sweet colleen, but we've got to leave here now. We've lingered far too long." He put his fingers against her temple.

Reassuring and flowing, his voice filtered into her mind again. *We're flying, Clarissa. Flying.*

Before she could protest or comprehend what would happen, a strange languor overcame her. Unable to keep her eyes open, she sagged in his grip. Seconds later, the remaining light in the cavern disappeared and with it her consciousness.

* * * * *

Again Clarissa awakened enveloped in a man's arms. At first she smiled, happy Ronan still held her close. She felt as if she lay on a solid surface, cold and unforgiving.

"Clarissa? Can you hear me?"

The male didn't belong to Ronan's husky Irish inflection. Disappointment and apprehension made her struggle against the arms holding her. Her eyes popped open as the man kept her in his grip.

The arms released her as she struggled upright. "Whoa. It's just me. Jim."

Leaning back on her palms, she blinked at Jim in mystification.

He held his hands out in a gesture of nonaggression as he sat on the crypt floor with her. "I heard you scream and when I rushed in here and saw you down below in the hole, I tried to use my cell phone to call for help. I couldn't get a signal worth a damn, but when I rushed back with some rope to try and get down to you, I saw you lying on the floor next to the hole. How did you climb out?"

"Good question," she said, feeling dazed. "I don't remember."

"We've got to get you some medical assistance."

"No, I'm fine."

When she tried to stand, Jim sprang up and clasped her shoulders for support. "None of this makes sense. It didn't take me that long to go from the crypt to the car and back and in that time you found a way up here?"

She shook her head. Her senses had cleared and the ache in her head from the earlier fall hadn't returned. "Maybe this was all a dream." She reached out and touched Jim's chest. "Maybe I'm dreaming you."

A puzzled, worried frown touched his lips. "Damn it, Clarissa, you need to see a doctor. This isn't a dream, and I think you hit your head, because you're not making sense."

Maybe she did need to be looked at, because she couldn't be one hundred percent certain about what happened in the hole. If Ronan had rescued her, found a way out of the hole, why hadn't he stayed?

"Maybe I just dreamed the part where Ronan appeared."

"Who?"

His puzzled expression made her realize she'd made a hash of her explanation. "The man who saved me from the mugger. That Ronan."

"Ah." He nodded. "Right. He was down in the hole with you? Then where the hell is he?"

She shook her head. "Beats me. Come on, let's just get out of here. I can't believe I'm saying this, but this place actually gives me the creeps." Then she remembered one precious item. "Wait. Where's my camera?

"It must still be down there."

"Damn it."

"We'll come back for it later. It's not important now. You are."

She allowed him to lead her out of the crypt and back to the car. On the way back into town she pondered whether she'd lost her mind, or if she'd really encountered Ronan Kieran in the graveyard. How much she should tell Jim.

She chose, without being sure why, the avenue of not revealing anything about her encounter with Ronan.

* * * * *

Ronan rammed his toe against the refrigerator door as he wandered into the dimly lit kitchen in Erin's home. "Feckin' A."

Vampire vision or not, he'd managed to be more clumsy than usual popping into her home. He inhaled the delicious scent emanating from the big crock-pot on the kitchen counter. Definitely the smell of meat. His mouth watered. He hadn't taken mortal food in at least a week, and he was in the mood for it.

Frustrated from his encounter with Clarissa, and sensing that the woman had captured part of him beyond his control, he'd popped into Erin's home to get a supply of long-needed blood. The entire house sounded quiet. He also didn't detect Sorley around anywhere.

Just as well. He didn't want to explain to anyone where he'd been. He almost groaned as he adjusted his jeans, his body still wanting something it couldn't have. Fire ran through his body, his undead needs roaring and tossing like a tornado. It took everything he had to shove Clarissa's sweet, beautiful warmth to the back of his mind.

I'll be feckin' lucky if I ever get rid of this hard-on.

He wanted and needed relief, and he could take things into his own hands, but he didn't think masturbating would do the trick. It would take the edge off, but not the longing he'd felt since he first saw Clarissa Gaines in that bloody graveyard the first time.

A little disgusted with himself for trying to seduce her in that horror movie tunnel, he leaned against the refrigerator. She'd tasted so damned delicious, ready to be taken, to feel his teeth along her beautiful skin. His breathing, deep and not yet controlled, rasped from his throat. Denying more than their deep kisses and the sexual feelings he'd given her had been agony. Mentally she didn't need his help. Yet he sensed she wanted him. Her desire had drowned his senses in a corporeal inferno and demanded he take her away where no one could find them. Only supreme control had kept him from transporting her to a hidden spot where he could have taken her. Supreme control had prevented him from coming in his pants when he delved into her mind and felt what she felt.

The slick, gliding motion of his thick cock as he slipped it into her warm pussy. The steady, rhythm of his hips as he thrust inside her again and again.

Even now the fever that danced and burned inside bothered like an eternal itch. He wanted her more than anything.

Worse, he wanted her trust.

Shit. He desired her for more than a quick fuck to appease sexual appetite. He felt a yearning to protect her from anything and anyone.

Double shit.

He closed his eyes to true darkness, enjoying the oblivion as he did when he slept most days. He tried imagining something boring, like an overlong conversation with Sorley about any one subject. Sorley could turn any conversation dull, given time.

No, he couldn't banish the desire, no matter how much he tried. Possessiveness welled inside him, almost knocking him on his ass with the force. He took a steadying breath. He couldn't recall the last time he'd felt this way about a woman.

Aye, but you can remember.

Yes, he could recall if he tried hard enough. The last time he'd felt this hungry, this demanding about claiming a woman body and soul...the last time had ended when Fenella lay in his arms almost seven hundred years ago, dead.

He shivered with the painful memory. Mother Mary, would the pain never leave his heart?

Ruthlessly he tore the agony out, denying the feeling and using his lust for Clarissa to destroy unwanted emotions. What he felt for Clarissa amounted to staggering lust, nothing more. No one could ever replace Fenella, not in this century, not in any century. If he must take Clarissa to save Pine Forest, to save his mortal friends, he would do it. He'd made the decision and he would follow through.

He opened the fridge and he saw Erin had the refrigerator stuffed with delicious items. His vampire stomach growled. He closed the cold section and reached into the freezer to extract a packet of blood.

"What are you doing?" Lachlan asked as he strode into the kitchen without bothering to turn on the light.

Lachlan's vampire-like abilities allowed him to see as well as Ronan with no problems. The man's eyes sparkled with yellow fire. Lachlan wore only jeans, his chest and feet naked.

"Did I wake you?" Ronan asked.

"No. We're getting ready for the dinner with Clarissa Gaines tonight. Did you forget?"

Ronan shut the freezer door and walked to the microwave. "I just spoke with her. She is very difficult to forget."

One of Lachlan's eyebrows tilted up in query. "Just spoke with her? You've had a lot of contact with her in the last two days."

He knew what Lachlan implied and couldn't deny it. "Of course I have. You know why."

Lachlan smiled. "Yeah, I know why."

"She was in trouble and I helped her." Ronan gave the short version of events in the tunnel, leaving out the passion.

"Damn," Lachlan said, "she could have been killed. I thought the city council said they were going to seal up that passageway after we told them about it."

Ronan snorted. "Takes them awhile. They probably want to leave it open because it goes under the graveyard and right to the Gunn Inn."

Lachlan went silence, his eyes widening a little. "You're kidding me."

"I wish I was."

"So you've been exploring rather than just patrolling at night. Any sign of the ancient one?"

"No."

"Good. Maybe we have more time before the bastard recharges."

Ronan shook his head. "Sure, and he might just stay away long enough for me to fuck Clarissa."

Ronan didn't expect his friend to look shocked, but Lachlan's face hardened with disapproval. "I thought you said you couldn't sleep with her unless her feelings were genuine?"

Part of Ronan wanted to deny the truth. He wanted to say that Clarissa Gaines would come to him whether he put images of mind-boggling sex into her head or not. But he didn't know that. "I sense strength in her. I can't read her mind all of the time. That's unusual, since with most women I can read any of their thoughts at any time."

"So what you're saying is you probably can't read her mind any better than I could read Erin's?"

"Partially. But I think it's more to do with her strength. I can see she has psychic ability, though I'm not certain how much."

Lachlan sighed. "All right. So where do you go from here? Halloween's coming up fast. How can you possibly make her fall in love with you before then?"

Ronan chuckled softly. "This coming from a man who fell in love with Erin not long ago."

"All right, all right. I suppose it's possible. But what if she finds out you're a vampire?"

Shrugging, Ronan said, "She already knows something is different about me with the mind reading, the ability to teleport, and my eyes. She'd have to be totally out of it not to notice." They sank into silence for a moment before Ronan said, "Did I ever thank you for letting me and Sorley stay here?"

"Yes, you did."

Ronan managed a sardonic smile. "You know I'd pick a nice crypt somewhere if I could find an empty one not tainted by the ancient one's stench."

Lachlan grinned and crossed his arms. "No problem, but it's Erin who deserves the thanks."

Ronan nodded and put the blood into the microwave. He pushed a button and set it to defrost. "Any clue where Sorley might be?"

"Nope. Haven't seen him."

They waited in silence until the microwave pinged and Ronan took the blood out. After he retrieved a plastic tumbler from a kitchen cabinet, he poured the liquid into the tumbler and took a sip. Warmed enough to go down smooth, like the finest whiskey he could imagine.

Lachlan flipped on the light switch. He leaned against the kitchen counter as Ronan drank the blood. Lachlan's expression said it all; he didn't like seeing his friend consume the sanguine liquid.

Ronan put the cup down on the counter. "I suppose I should find some nice snow bank to store my blood supply."

"Why do you say that?"

"Because if the police ever decide to search this house for some hare-brained reason, do you think they'll understand packets of blood in your freezer?"

"No. They won't understand. But we can take that chance."

Ronan finished the blood, rinsed the tumbler, then put it in the dishwasher. "I'll move it as soon as I can find another place to sleep." He sounded mournful, almost lonely. He stopped, astonished at the emotions. "Damn, I sound like a feckin' geek."

Lachlan laughed softly. He cocked his head a little to the side, questions written all over his expression. "Hurry up and get with it, vampire. Clarissa will be here soon."

* * * * *

The ancient one put on his cloak just before nightfall, the garment shielding his body against the draining effects of the remaining sunlight. With one last look at his temporary home, he considered if it would be worth coming back to the crypt before dawn. Perhaps. Unless he found somewhere equally safe and intriguing. He didn't consider the tunnels under the Gunn Inn an area to sleep in any longer. He could visit with the darkness there, but not to stay.

Dusk edged through the woods as he emerged from the crypt. Winter air rushed over his face, but he barely noticed. His cloak swirled in the breeze, the flapping sound loud to his sensitive ears. Snow, freezing again after a day of melting, crunched under his feet. He breathed in earth saturated by centuries of evil and relished the power. He would need more time to regain everything taken from him by Ronan Kieran and his meddling mortal friends. He moved away from the crypt, the long-forgotten sepulcher of some pitiful soul. Time had ravaged the tomb, but time would not destroy him. Invincibility guaranteed, he strode toward his goal with confidence. If anyone saw him they'd think him dressed in costume for a party.

Of course, if anyone came within visual distance, he would kill them.

He prowled, with advancing strength, along the woods toward the tunnels under the Gunn Inn. He wondered if Micky Gunn and Jared Thornton still resided in the cavernous old building and if the stupid mortals continued to believe they could reclaim the property. Hadn't they seen enough of his glory? Enough of what he could do?

He sensed Pine Forest's unease.

The townspeople feared Halloween.

He smiled, pleased. He fed off the thought, allowed it to grow the way mortals allowed their fears to run them.

Before Halloween, Pine Forest would feel his ultimate wrath, and this time they couldn't stop him. Damnation grew in the tunnels beneath the graveyard and the inn. It spread like the locust, the fly after death, the maggots over a dead body left out in the elements too long.

So much percolated beneath the townspeople's feet, and little did they know. Soon the volcanic eruption of fear and hate would cause them to destroy themselves from within. Their petty prejudices, their ridiculous beliefs would bring them false certainty. Like all mortals their foibles would lead them toward disaster rather than strength, to pestilence rather than joy.

He smiled as he walked, then put his hands up to the sky as clouds obscured the last of the sun. He flipped back the cape hood and allowed the night to bathe him.

"Ahhhhh." Every fiber in his body seemed to expand, to cherish and absorb the darkness within and without.

At the same time anger and determination surged inside him. Two times the mortals had foiled him, had taken what belonged to him. And Sweet Dasoria, his reincarnated lover, refused to recognize him. Where once his undead soul ached that Erin refused to acknowledge her past life as his lover, now he felt his feelings turning toward hate and death. Malevolence wended through his thoughts and memories until he could no longer recall how much he'd once loved Dasoria. He would treat her as he treated all other mortals. Erin would find her death in Pine Forest before Halloween came.

No more fighting to see her, to bring her over to the undead once again. No more desire to share his love with her. Next time she would feel his lacerating teeth against her throat for one reason only.

There would be no mercy.

Chapter Six

As she drove toward Erin Greenway's home, Clarissa's headache returned. This time she knew the pain originated from tight muscles in her back and neck.

Jim had insisted she see a doctor, so she'd driven to the emergency room with him following behind. The doctor who examined her declared her sound of body. When Jim asked her if she'd like to have dinner with her that evening, she explained she had other plans and left it at that. He'd looked disappointed, but she had no intention of jilting Erin and Lachlan for a dinner with Jim. While a little surprised at the extent of Jim's concern for her, she didn't quite trust his motivations. Their past together kept her feelings distant.

She rubbed the back of her neck, then turned down a street leading to Erin's home. She checked her watch. In less then five minutes she'd be there, and the tension seemed to build second by second.

As she found Erin's address and turned into the driveway of the Victorian home, she noticed two other cars parked along the street. She imagined Micky and Jared would be here. Maybe even their mysterious Irish friend, Ronan. If he was, she planned on cornering him at some point to find out how he'd gotten her out of that hole under the crypt without her remembering a thing, and why he'd disappeared without a word.

Nervous butterflies fluttered in her stomach. From everything she'd heard about the events occurring in Pine Forest this month, Erin and Lachlan would have no reason to doubt her story. Instead nagging worry plagued her.

After she turned off the lights and switched off the car, she unlocked and opened the driver's door.

A figure loomed up next to her. She gasped as her heart leapt.

Ronan stood there, his gaze watchful.

"Do you make a habit of popping up unexpectedly?" she asked.

"Yes. Dinner will be ready soon. Come."

His old-fashioned courtesy, mixed with his brusqueness took her off guard again.

"You're about the most intriguing man I've ever run into, you know that?" she asked without thinking about how it would sound. "And sometimes the most challenging."

"Thank you."

She closed and locked the car. "Were you skulking in the bushes when I drove up? I didn't see you."

Ronan slipped his arm around her shoulders. "In a matter of speaking, yes. I should have escorted you from your hotel this evening."

"It wasn't necessary. I'm a big girl and can take care of myself."

His gaze held teasing and exasperation. "Sure, and here I am talking to the woman who got mugged last night, then falls into a hole the next day."

She searched those deep, enticing eyes, so sexy and exciting even when they held an uncanny light. A deep ache centered in her gut that had nothing to do with irritation and everything to do with arousal.

She almost moved out from under his arm. "Thanks for your vote of confidence."

He drew her nearer until the heat of his body touched all along her side and he turned her slightly toward him. "You're a wee, bonnie thing, as Lachlan would say. A beautiful woman and a strong one. I'm not saying you can't take care of yourself. But remember what I've told you already about how dangerous it is in this town." His insistent words sounded rough with sincerity and the husky liquid of his accent. "I don't want anything to happen to you."

When she saw the truth in his eyes, heard the deep conviction in his voice, she felt like melting into his arms. She'd never wanted a man's protection before she met Ronan. Even the odd things about him she didn't understand didn't stop her heart from racing or her body from responding.

"Thank you," she said softly.

"My pleasure, my lady." Warm and low, his voice simmered with promises too exciting to ignore.

She smiled slightly. "I should be wary of you."

He tilted her chin up with his fingers. "Most definitely."

As his mouth closed over hers, she expected a sweet little peck of affection. Instead she got more. As she kissed him back, a soft moan left his throat. He slanted his mouth over hers and tasted, his kiss somewhere between cautious and lusty. Dazed by the tenderness, she ached to sample more of the mint freshness of his breath. With startling rapidity her nipples peaked, aching to be touched. Warmth filled her stomach and between her thighs. No man had turned her on as quickly or fully in a matter of seconds.

Ronan broke the kiss, his breathing coming harder. Looking into his eyes, she saw the same staggering need she'd witnessed when he'd kissed her in the catacombs beneath the crypt. Not only did his eyes simmer with a sun-filled yellow, his expression was ravenous.

"You try my patience," he said huskily.

She smiled, warmed through and through by his adoration and the affection that mixed with his hunger. "I think we've gone over this territory before."

One corner of his mouth twitched, as if he wanted to smile but didn't dare. "You're difficult to resist."

He tore his gaze away and started walking with her to the front door.

When he rubbed his hand over her shoulder in a soothing fashion, her stomach tumbled in excitement. Attempting to kick-start her brain after his embrace took all her effort.

"Did you drive here?" she asked.

"I'm staying here for the time being as Erin and Lachlan's guest. So is my friend Sorley."

"Sorley?"

"Aye. You'll meet him as soon as he arrives tonight, which could be any time he sees fit." A wry smile curved his mouth. "Jared Thornton and Micky Gunn are also here."

They'd taken a few more steps toward the front door when he asked, "Are you all right?"

"Of course. Why shouldn't I be?"

He made a doubtful sound. "You fell through a crypt floor today."

Deciding she could be as enigmatic as he was, she responded. "I know. Nasty experience I don't plan on repeating."

Ronan knocked on the door and it swung open to reveal Erin and Lachlan.

While Lachlan couldn't be more than six feet tall, Erin was petite enough to look small standing next to him. Her black hair was cut short below her ears, a pixie that seemed to barely tame her windblown style. His blue-black, wavy strands fell just over his collar. Lachlan's voice held a husky, Scottish accent, distinct from Ronan's Irish tones but equally intriguing.

Clarissa couldn't help comparing Lachlan's staggering good looks to Ronan's more mysterious handsomeness. Ronan's glittering dark eyes and short beard concealed so many things, yet that air of secrecy seemed to suit him. She couldn't remember another time she'd been in the same proximity of two more gorgeous men at one time.

Amusement at her train of thought almost made her smile. *All this delectable male flesh is enough to distract a woman big time.*

Ronan glanced at her quickly, one of his eyebrows hitching up as if he'd heard her thoughts again.

Damn, she'd have to be careful from now on.

Immediately the couple's kind smiles and warm expressions made her feel welcome. Tension eased in her neck and she could relax. A flurry of introductions started and after taking their coats, Lachlan and Erin drew them into the living room.

Jared Thornton sat near to Micky Gunn on a couch. Both of them smiled when Clarissa and Ronan came into the room, and their genuine words of welcome soothed Clarissa's apprehensions. After more introductions, Erin and Lachlan retreated to the kitchen to uncork wine and check on the dinner.

"I'd be happy to help," Clarissa said as she followed Ronan into the kitchen.

Erin waved a dismissive hand and smiled. "The chicken has been cooking all day. The veggies are keeping warm in the microwave, and Lachlan's already uncorked the wine." Erin shooed Lachlan and Ronan out of the kitchen just as Micky walked in. "Unless you big lugs are going to help, there are too many people in the kitchen."

"Hear that?" Jared asked from the living room, his voice teasing and good-natured. "Why don't you guys come out here and have brandy and cigars with me."

Ronan and Lachlan looked at each other, then laughed.

"No cigars in this house," Lachlan said.

"But we do have brandy, right?" Ronan asked with a hopeful tone. "For later, that is?"

"You got it." Lachlan sauntered out of the kitchen, his attempt at countrified accent deplorable. "I guess the womenfolk ain't got no need for us, boys."

Clarissa groaned while Erin smiled.

Ronan winked at Clarissa. Then almost as an afterthought, he slipped his fingers into the hair at the back of her neck and leaned forward to press a tender kiss to her forehead. She blushed right to the roots of her hair as he left the room.

The knowing looks Erin and Micky gave her almost made her squirm. At the same time, a guilty pleasure pulsed through her at this show of affection.

"What can we do to help you get dinner ready?" Micky asked.

Erin gave them an appreciative smile. "If you ladies would like to set the table, feel free."

While anxious to start discussing what she knew with the whole group, she knew jumping into the middle of her fears wouldn't be the best thing. Better to ease her way into the topic. "Thank you for inviting me here, Erin."

"Any friend of Ronan's is a friend of ours."

Friend. An interesting word to describe her relationship with the mysterious man. Could she be called his friend? Some of the feelings he generated inside her had more to do with lust than friendship, but what else could you call their relationship?

Small talk ensued while Micky and Clarissa set the table. The dining room was beautifully furnished in a true late Victorian style without being overwrought. The burgundy tablecloth over the long dark wood table looked beautiful against the crystal wine glasses, the crystal vase centerpiece, and the pretty blue and white English ironstone.

Micky moved the large crystal vase centerpiece and put it on the sideboard. "You've had a traumatic couple of days in Pine Forest, Clarissa. It seems to happen to all of us when we get here. Welcome to Creepsville."

"Oh, you can say that again," Clarissa said.

"Good thing Ronan was there to save the day."

Clarissa looked at Micky to see if hidden sarcasm resided there, but she didn't detect anything but a genuine smile on the other woman's face. "I owe him, believe me. There are things I don't understand about what's happened to me since I got here. I'm hoping everyone can help me clear things up."

Micky paused as she put plates on the table. "In just the short time I've been in Pine Forest, I've had a rude awakening."

"How's that?"

"By discovering there is so much in Pine Forest that's strange and evil. So much bizarreness it's hard to define. Some of it is like a nightmare."

Clarissa smiled. "I've picked that up already."

"Are you prepared to listen to things that might not make sense? Things that don't seem real?"

"Believe me, I'm used to that."

For several moments they exchanged information on their connections to Pine Forest.

"I read about what happened at your inn, Micky. So are you living there now?"

"We thought at first we would, but everyone encouraged us to stay out at least until we can decipher what's going to happen here in Pine Forest."

Clarissa knew what would happen in Pine Forest if they didn't stop the darkness from overtaking the town, but she wanted to wait until they'd gathered around the table before she explained what she knew. She returned to the kitchen with Micky and they'd been there less then a minute when Ronan walked in the room and came up behind her.

He placed his hands on her shoulders and squeezed gently. "Hurry up. The men are getting ravenous."

She elbowed him gently, and his deep, rumbling laugh made her entire body tingle with sweet, gentle arousal. Being with him in a nonsexual environment still guaranteed she'd be driven batty in more ways than one. As his hands massaged her shoulders, she placed her right hand over his. When she realized what she was doing, she took her hand away.

Micky and Erin moved into the other room a moment, chattering away. *No, no. Don't leave me alone with him.*

If you don't want me to touch you, sweet colleen, just tell me.

The telepathy shocked her each time it happened, even when it shouldn't. After the evening ended she'd ask him about his extraordinary ability once and for all.

He leaned down and whispered against her ear. "Feeling more relaxed?"

"No."

His hands moved with gentle persistence, his voice low-pitched so no one else could hear. "Because my touch makes you aware of things you haven't felt before?"

She turned toward him, and his hands dropped from her shoulders. His gaze appeared more serious than passionate, more worried than seductive.

Before she could answer, Micky and Erin came back into the kitchen.

Erin clapped once. "Okay, everyone, I think this show is on the road. Let's eat. Sorley is late again, but we aren't waiting on him."

After placing serving dishes on the table, Micky, Erin, and Clarissa settled into their chairs. Lachlan and Jared sat down while Ronan filled everyone's glasses with wine. They settled into a companionable pace, passing around dishes and making the inevitable chitchat.

As they started eating, Clarissa experienced a strange tension entering the room she didn't understand. Everyone seemed tired, and she understood the feeling. It had already been two long days for her. Maybe they waited for her to speak up, to tell them why she needed to see them. If she didn't get this off her chest she would scream. She might as well jump into the fire.

"Tell us why you needed to see everyone tonight," Ronan said.

Clarissa paused as she sipped the delicious fruity white wine. Had he read her mind again? His calm façade told her nothing.

"I don't know where to start."

"Maybe she'd like to eat first," Erin said, glaring at Ronan. "Give her a little time."

Ronan winked at Clarissa, then smiled at Erin. "Sorry. I'm just eager to hear her story."

Clarissa took another healthy swallow of her drink before she answered. "It's all right. If I don't tell you now, I might lose my nerve."

She cut into the succulent chicken and began. "I mentioned to Erin on the phone earlier today that I grew up in Pine Forest, so I'm aware of its strange history." She smiled. "It was a weird place to be a child."

"Was it frightening?" Jared asked as he speared a cauliflower floret.

Clarissa took a deep breath. "I imagine it was for many children, but it was especially bizarre for me. I was able to see and hear many things other children couldn't."

Before she could continue, a strange popping sound came from the living room. Everyone seemed to go on full alert. Ronan sat up straighter, and so did Jared and Lachlan.

"It's just me," a distinctly Irish male voice said from the living room.

A skinny man walked into the room, his smile wide. His narrow, slightly pockmarked face would never be called handsome. Yet the charm in his grin almost made up for his lack of looks. Short, untamed black hair tousled over the small man's head. He was dressed in a blue flannel shirt, jeans, and boots.

As he walked toward Clarissa, he said, "This must be the lovely Clarissa."

Ronan introduced them. "Sorley, this is Clarissa Gaines. Clarissa, Sorley Dubhe."

"Or as they said in Ireland many moons ago, Somhairle Dubhe," Sorley said.

"Your Gaelic name." Clarissa shook his hand and smiled.

"That it is. Has the big guy here—" he slapped Ronan on the back, "—told you his Irish name?"

"Not yet," Ronan said. "We're barely acquainted."

Ronan sat to Clarissa's left, and she felt the weight of his stare. The implication lay in his eyes, saying for her what she couldn't admit for herself. Despite their ravenous physical reaction to each other, they didn't know each other well.

"It's Ronan Ciaran," Sorley said. "Which really means little seal black. Very strange name if you were to ask me."

"No one's asking," Ronan said with a polite, but definite edge.

Suitably chastised, Sorley made a courtly bow.

Unable to resist his quirkiness, Clarissa returned his grin. "Very pleased to meet you, Sorley."

"Sure, and a supreme pleasure it is to meet a friend of Ronan's," Sorley said.

While everyone else looked amused, Ronan's raised eyebrow and cynical expression made her hesitate to joke with Sorley.

Sorley sat in the vacant chair between Ronan and Erin. "Sorry I was late. The feckin'—" he glanced at Clarissa, "I mean the weather is gettin' weird again. A front is comin' in. Might snow again before it clears for a good strip tomorrow."

"Lovely," Micky said with a sigh. "I think we've had enough snow for awhile."

"On a different subject, I thought Gilda and Tom were comin', too?" Sorley asked.

"Mark has the flu," Lachlan said, then turned his gaze on Clarissa. "Gilda works with Erin at the library and Tom is her husband. Mark is their son."

Erin poured more wine for herself, then offered the bottle around the table. "Before you came in, Sorley, Clarissa was telling us about why she needed to meet with us tonight and what brings her to Pine Forest."

Clarissa reached for her water glass and took a fortifying sip. "It's a long story."

"We've got all evening," Jared said.

Unfortunately her nerves jumped and pinged with worry. She stared at the tablecloth. "When I was a little girl, I used to have precognitive dreams. Sometimes I still do."

She waited, glancing around the table to see the reactions she obtained. Everyone gazed at her with genuine interest. Maybe they wouldn't think she'd lost her mind after all.

"And?" Micky asked softly.

"I was a toddler when I started having night terrors. I never remembered what they were about until I was about five. I dreamt the same thing over and over, sometimes as much as three times a week."

"That must have been horrible," Erin said, her expression sincere and worried.

Clarissa nodded. "I didn't know what to do or how to make it go away. My parents took me to a local doctor, a psychiatrist. He claimed I was trying to get attention from my parents, even if it was negatively. When he questioned me about the dreams, I always felt like he was patronizing and telling me to stop making things up." She toyed with her food, pushing her chicken around the plate. "My parents stopped taking me to him after about a month of appointments. They thought I was cured because I didn't mention the dreams anymore. At least not for a while. I figured if I was going to get punished every time I told them about the dream, there was no point in telling them."

Ronan frowned. "Your parents punished you for telling them about a dream?"

His incredulous, angry expression made her feel gratified in a strange way. Every time this man defended her, regardless of how small the gesture, something deep and profound moved inside her. Satisfaction. A sense of belonging and a deepening of feeling inside where she'd never been touched before.

She didn't want to feel anything extraordinary for this odd, yet compelling man. The more she tried to resist the reaction, the more it tortured her.

She continued. "The punishment was metaphorical. If a child discovers there are negative consequences like going to a psychiatrist who tells you that you're making it all up, the child sometimes stop what they're doing. In my case I pretended I wasn't having the dreams any more."

"That must have been so hard on you." Micky's voice held sympathy. "What happened then?"

"The dreams continued into my teens, though by then I had the nightmares maybe once a month."

"What were the dreams about?" Ronan asked, his eyes a liquid warm brown that encouraged her.

Clarissa put down her fork. Despite the resolve she'd felt returning to her childhood stomping ground and coming here to confess what she knew, a wave of uncertainty washed over her. She stared at them, frozen.

"It's all right, sweet colleen, you can tell us." Ronan's endearment, spoken in that husky, unmistakably Irish tone, reassured her. "We aren't going to condemn you."

"Sure, and we've seen enough buggered strange things in our lives to tell forty more tales," Sorley said.

"Believe me, whatever it is, you can trust us," Micky said. "And if it helps us to save this town, we need all the information we can get."

Clarissa couldn't seem to speak of it, her throat tight. Tears filled her eyes. Embarrassment followed close behind. "No...I...maybe this was all a mistake." Flustered beyond anything she expected, she pushed back her chair and stood up. "I'm sorry, I shouldn't have come here and—"

She didn't know how to explain her behavior. She didn't know what to think. As she headed into the living room, awash in mortification and unbelievable sadness, she heard Ronan mutter a curse.

She hadn't gone far before he clasped her shoulders from behind and halted her. "Wait. It's all right."

Clarissa shivered, her mind filled with confusion at how she'd come this far and now couldn't seem to push the words passed her throat. "I...no. I can't."

Ronan turned her to face him. Instead of anger she saw worry and determination. "Come with me."

"Where are we going?"

"To talk."

His big palm and fingers enclosed her much smaller hand as he led her down the hall and into a room a couple of doors down on the right. Ronan clicked on the light and turned the dimmer switch to a lower, less glaring illumination. He released her hand and closed the door with a solid click.

He returned to Clarissa and cupped her shoulders, his grip more reassuring than anything. "Let's cut to the chase. Everyone in this house understands the paranormal and believes in it. Do you honestly think we'd chastise you for telling us about the dreams?"

Clarissa wanted to believe him the way she wanted to breathe. "I'm sorry. I thought I was all prepared. Then, in spite of the weird things I've experienced the last two days, I couldn't tell you about my dreams."

"Do you know why?"

She pulled out of his grip, unwilling to give away all her secrets in a rush. If she allowed him to touch her, she'd lose her perspective. Maybe touch made it easier for him to read her mind.

She glanced around the room, noticing details for the first time. Decorated like the rest of the house in an understated Victorian motif, the large bedroom featured blue and green tones in the wallpaper and in the fluffy comforter that covered the dark wood four-poster double bed.

Before she could turn back to Ronan, he clasped her upper shoulders by her neck and restarted that maddening yet comforting massage. "You came to this town to write a book and take photographs of haunted places, right?"

"Yes."

"And you want to capture other haunted places here, eh?" His fingers pressed into her muscles, kneading away the tension with slow rhythm.

"Of course."

"Let me be your escort while you're here."

She did turn around then, surprised at his offer. The caring in his dark eyes made her stomach flutter with attraction, that steadily melting combustion that hovered whenever he came near. This close she felt his heat, his force of personality.

"Why would you want to?" she asked.

"You have to ask?"

"Yes."

With slow deliberation, he leaned in and placed a tender kiss on her lips, then drew back slightly. "This is why." Her lips tingled, her breath coming faster, her heartbeat calling to the male in him. "And this is why." His lips tasted her again, then he pulled back. Again he dipped in for a soft kiss. "And this is why."

She put her hand up, covering his mouth with index and middle finger. "Everyone is going to wonder what is taking us so long."

"Who cares?" he murmured, diving in for a kiss that went a little longer. She responded, tasting him as he tasted her. Once again he backed off. "Are you worried they might guess we're kissing?"

"Yes."

"Would that be so bad?"

She thought about it, then sank into the burning attention in his gaze. The smoldering fire in his eyes warmed her at the same time it challenged, and when that slow burn turned to a full bonfire she'd better watch out. Deep in her body, her pores, her very soul she acknowledged the essence of Ronan Kieran that defined him. It called to Clarissa in a mysterious way she couldn't quite understand. The way he looked at her now said the next kiss, and the one after wouldn't be so tentative.

Ronan's arms slipped around her, drawing her against his hard chest as his fingers plunged into her hair. His mouth took hers, his kiss a hungry exploration that demanded to find answers. As his mouth twisted over hers, he didn't hold back. Her lips parted as she followed his lead. His tongue moved inside, stroking and teasing her mouth with a sexual prowess that made her body shiver with cravings. She arched against him, her arms going around his neck as she dove into the embrace with her heart. Moments lengthened as the kiss lingered. His hand caressed her back, then he cupped her ass and pressed his hips into her.

Oh, my God.

The Irishman owned a hard-on that felt as strong as a spike. An ache started between her legs, a demand for fulfillment she knew she couldn't have right now, and most likely not with this man. Everything within her responded as his tongue took her mouth repeatedly, his hands pressed and kneaded her flesh deliciously, and her nipples tingled with the need to be touched. She felt something simmering inside him, something that wanted to break free. She couldn't concentrate on it, not with her needs shifting and changing, her physical wants screaming for total completion.

She knew restlessness built inside him. He didn't want one kiss or two, he wanted all she could offer. Wrapped in his heat and strength, she moved against him with need and desire. Her mind melded, blended, sought Ronan's with a demand for fulfillment.

She tested his shoulder muscles, loving the way the material of his sweater felt over the hardest muscles she'd every touched. As his tongue and lips teased beyond endurance, she wished they had a room, any hotel room but here. She slipped her fingers into his hair, savoring the sweet silkiness against her skin. Inhaling deeply, she savored his clean and totally masculine allure.

That's it, sweet colleen. Open to me. Feel me inside your soul.

She tore her mouth away with effort. "Ronan. You're reading my mind again."

"Mmm." He brushed his lips over hers. "You're in my...blood. I want to be inside your mind...in your body..."

My body. The idea made her shiver with delicious needs, and a desire to relinquish control.

"This is dangerous," she said.

He buried his face in her hair. "Sure, and there are more dangerous things in this town then you and I kissing. Much more dangerous things. You've nothing to fear if I'm with you."

"What if I fear you?"

He pulled back far enough to look down at her. "I'd never harm you. I'll keep you safe."

His tender words, so unlike the fierceness she'd seen in him when he defended her against the mugger, contradicted the violence she sensed inside him. With a sigh he released her from the intimate embrace.

Ronan clenched his hands into fists, and she saw the glow depart from his gaze like a fire extinguished. "My offer of protection stands. Now tell me what you couldn't tell my friends. What were your dreams about?"

If she stayed in this intimate setting with him any longer, she knew she wouldn't think any clearer than if she went outside now and told everyone. "I'm ready to tell everyone now."

His eyes narrowed. "You're sure?"

"Yes."

With a grin, he said, "So the next time I need information out of you, all I need to do is kiss you?"

Succumbing to the almost boyish charm in his smile, she crossed her arms and smiled back. "Well, that's a possibility. It's not a guarantee, though."

Trust him? How can I?

Because you know I wouldn't hurt you.

Once again he'd proved he could read her mind. "That's supposed to make me trust you?" A smidgen of exasperation sparked inside her. "How can I feel safe and comfortable around a man who has glowing eyes and reads minds?"

Ronan's grin was a bit wolfish. "The glowing eyes thing didn't send you running. Neither did my ability to read your mind. Most women would believe I'm a monster and wouldn't have anything to do with me."

"Right, like I believe that for a minute, Ronan Kieran. Tell me another one. *Are* you some kind of monster?"

Suddenly tired, she sank down on the bed a moment. He followed, sitting much too close. Again he put his arm around her shoulder. "A monster friendly to many, but not to all."

"Why would you be affable to me in particular?"

His trademark melting eyes kept her attention. "A beautiful woman should always be admired."

Humor ignited the cold place inside her. "You've kissed the Blarney Stone, haven't you?"

"More than once. It's an Irish thing."

"Humph."

Like a man determined not to be ignored, he leaned in until he nuzzled aside her hair and whispered in her ear. His breath wafted hot and stimulating over her neck.

No, she didn't feel comfortable, not at all. Frustrated, she sighed. "I can't feel relaxed with you. You're too unnerving. Too mysterious. Too...too..."

"Yes?"

Sexy. She couldn't say it. She couldn't have complete confidence in a man who drove her insane with his high-octane, fuel-injected sexual allure. If she didn't get away from his closeness right now, she'd do or say something monumentally stupid. Like how much she'd started to want him, how much she needed his touch and kiss to give her reassurance.

"What can I do to convince you?" His lips touched her ear for a whisper. "Relax in my arms, allow my touch, allow me to love you as you've never been loved before."

His enticing words made her heart thunder into a treacherous ride. Her emotions fluctuated, her soul afire with a sudden need to surrender.

"I don't indulge in one-night stands," she said in defense.

"I'm not talking about a one-night stand."

Oh, shit. Well...she couldn't...didn't want to answer him now. "Can we talk about this later?"

He gave her breathing space. "Of course. When I take you home."

"When you take me home? But I've got a car here."

"I know. I'll still accompany you to your hotel. We can talk there"

She laughed. "You are sure of yourself, aren't you?"

He cupped her face in both his hands, his palms warm and gentle. "No matter what you may think of me, I'm not protecting you just to get in your knickers. I would never do that. My protection is not conditional. You may have it whether or not you and I make love."

Oh, man. Was this guy for real? She'd tried to imagine, all her adult life—all thirty-two years of it—a man like this one. Dark. Dangerous. Willing to shelter a woman from harm and love her with equal strength. But he didn't guarantee or speak of love, nor did he claim to want happily-ever-after. No, he wanted her body and nothing more.

Without giving him an answer, she stood and opened the bedroom door. She headed out first. When Clarissa and Ronan reentered the dining room, everyone was eating apple pie. When they all looked up at her and Ronan, they smiled. Nothing but welcome and acceptance showed in their expressions.

"There she is," Sorley said. "Praise be. We thought maybe Ronan had kidnapped you for the night."

"Shut up, Sorley," Ronan said matter-of-factly, his voice as pleasant as if he'd been talking about the weather.

Clarissa slid back into her seat and Ronan returned to his. A piece of pie sat on a plate in front of her. "I'm sorry I walked out like that. I let my fears overwhelm me."

Erin's eyes held clear acceptance. "If this is too difficult to talk about, we don't have to do this now."

Clarissa shook her head. "Halloween is coming up fast, and if we don't find a way to band together to stop this horrible force, it will gain strength." Silence reigned supreme for a moment. "And then there might not be a November first for Pine Forest."

Chapter Seven

Ronan watched and listened to Clarissa, his mind if not his undead soul open to her story. If he cared too much the ache would return, the one he'd vowed never to allow again when Fenella died seven hundred years ago.

Watching this fascinating woman, the one he wanted in his bed, turned his sanity upside down and inside out. He couldn't decide if he wanted to leave her to her own devices or insist she listen to him. But this was the twenty-first century, and despite the fact he'd lived seven hundred years, he never found lording it over or commanding women to do things a savory prospect. Independent, strong women gave him a serious hard-on, and he sensed stubbornness inside Clarissa that matched any woman he'd known over the centuries.

Tonight he'd lost supreme control, his body and mind unwilling to listen to logic or protest. He wanted her with a burning need he hoped would ease. Anything else would consume him as he resisted following the awakening of his most primal instincts.

And if she saw him in his most primitive form she would run. She would leave Pine Forest and perhaps the doom she predicted for this town would come true.

No. He would do whatever he must to have her in his arms and his bed. Lives depending on them consummating their attraction in the most ancient way possible, and he couldn't allow his friends or this town to die because of moral ambiguities.

He returned his attention to what Clarissa was saying.

"My dreams always started out the same. I'm an adult in the dreams, which is strange considering I had this dream as a child. It always comes in stages, like viewing scenes in a movie. At first I see strange things happening in Pine Forest." When she paused Ronan could hear every other sound in the room. The wall clock in the living room bonged out the hour. Outside a tree branch scraped against the kitchen window. "People start calling each other names in heated arguments; they disagree vehemently about things of no consequence.

People are unhappy about old squabbles they thought they'd buried years ago. Fires are set and the fire department has difficulty keeping up with the mess...and there's the big fire on Halloween night."

"When does the first stage happen where people are building resentments?" Jared asked.

"In the first segments of the dream I think its a few days before Halloween."

"Right now, in other words," Micky said, shoving her empty pie plate to the side and picking up her wine glass. She took a healthy swallow. "So we're well into it."

Clarissa turned her citrine ring around and around in a nervous gesture. "At the very beginning, I think. At least it seems so to me."

"Let me guess," Ronan said, "the next thing that happens is they get violent and crime starts to skyrocket in the town and makes it almost impossible for the police to keep up."

"Yes. How did you know?" Clarissa chewed another piece of pie.

Ronan exhaled a deep breath. "Because I've seen it happen before. Back in—"

When he cut himself off Clarissa asked, "Back when?"

When Ronan looked at her, a flicker of embarrassment made him wince, almost as if he'd slipped a top-secret government project to lothe enemy unintentionally. Clarissa's gaze darted from person to person, as if she detected everyone's discomfort. Bugger all, he wished he'd kept his mouth shut.

"Explain," Clarissa said, her peach-hued skin radiant under the lights, her tumble of red hair falling over her shoulders like a cape.

God, how he wanted to touch her again.

Pulling in his desires, he sent reassuring thoughts to her. *Easy, girl. That's not a new sentiment. Just like what you're talking about. I'll tell you all my secrets later.*

Clarissa's cornflower blue eyes widened. A tiny smile flicked over her mouth, then disappeared. He felt her anger disappear, and he sighed in relief. Even though she looked bloody beautiful pissed off at him, he liked it better when she melted against him in passion. While she'd worked hard to conceal her sexuality, he felt it moving molten and heavy between them whenever they touched—hell, whenever they came within sight of each other.

Yeah, he would take her...soon.

Then, perhaps, all their troubles would be over.

Sorley had started talking, and Ronan barely heard what he had to say.

"Several years ago in Morocco, they had a strange problem, something like this," Sorley said. "They blamed it on evil spirits."

"We know it is evil this time, too." Clarissa chewed and swallowed the last piece of her pie slowly, as if contemplating what she should say next. "Anyway, I'm getting off track. First comes the arguing about new resentments, then old. Then the crime spree, and fires."

"So why did you see this in your dreams?" Lachlan said. "Why you?"

Clarissa shook her head. "I wish I knew."

Ronan understood all too well. "From the moment I met Clarissa, I detected her abilities with the supernatural. She is a sensitive with great empathic abilities. She's capable of even more, though she may not know it." He decided to go for it, to concede something he could keep hidden but saw no reason to do so. "When we first encountered each other in the graveyard, she saw a piece of my past."

Clarissa's gaze snapped to his, and Ronan absorbed her surprised expression. Her soft lips parted, as if she might refute his claim, then she subsided. He heard her thought and chose not to respond.

Ronan Kieran, just you wait until I get you alone.

He smiled, not caring if the rest of the room wondered why. How could he not be pleased that she wanted to get him alone? He didn't care if she wanted to kick his ass or kiss him into oblivion. A warm, satisfied tingle raced through his undead body, and for a moment he almost felt mortal again. While he might be immortal and vampire and didn't begrudge his lifestyle or his powers, he sometimes longed for a normal life. Being inside this woman's body would remind him of the mortal life he once possessed.

"So in the dream you're at the community center on Halloween night and the center is burning?" Micky asked.

Clarissa was solemn. "I never see how the fire starts, unfortunately. If I had that information I'd tell you. I hear screaming. Men, women and children. It's beyond awful. I'm in the building with the flames, too, and I can't get out."

Silence covered the room, and Ronan felt a lump rising high in his throat, a mortal reaction to the idea of carnage. He hadn't experienced that emotion in some time.

"How did you know we've been involved with what's happening in this town?" Erin asked. "How did you recognize us at the community center the other day and know to contact us?"

Ronan saw Clarissa swallow hard, as if she couldn't force words past her throat. "Because in my dream I know you are all in the community center with me before it starts to burn. And you don't come out."

Another heavy silence, this one filled with yawning horror, blanketed the room like a dark storm cloud. Ronan felt the onrushing worry in his gut as he tasted the last of his wine.

Then the quiet broke like rushing floodwaters.

"That's horrible," Erin said, her voice sounding dry and cracked. Lachlan took her hand and held it in both of his.

Few things rattled Ronan's wiry, feisty friend Sorley, but this seemed to do the trick. The little Irishman's eyes widened. "Jesus, Mary, and Joseph."

Jared looked at Micky. "Then we just won't go into the community center Halloween night for any reason."

"But her dream is prophetic," Sorley said, the slightest panic in his voice.

Ronan pinpointed his worried friend with a stern look. "Even prophetic dreams can be changed. Now that we know what may happen on Halloween night, we have a defense against it."

"So you don't see anything else in the dream after the fire?" Erin asked.

A sheen of tears made Clarissa's eyes look glassy. "Not a thing. The sound of the screams sends me running, then I pop out of the dream. I'm ashamed because I'm running and my heart fills with excruciating pain."

Ronan reached under the table and covered her small hand with his much larger one, pressing gently. She glanced over at him, tears threatening. He wanted to draw her into his arms and assure this woman he could keep her safe.

"I knew you all lived here or at least were visiting," Clarissa said. "I went to the restaurant at Jekyl's and talked with Chessie. I also knew

I could trust her, because I've known her all my life. When I described you she told me your names. By going to the community center the other night I'd hoped some of you would be there. When I saw you there, protesting against the Halloween party, I realized the dream was genuine once and for all." Clarissa shook her head. "I'm sorry I brought this bad news to you."

Lachlan stood, then held up the empty wine bottle. "I think we might need another one of these."

As Lachlan went into the kitchen, the table seemed too silent to Ronan. Too sedate and willing to let things lie. He waited to speak until Lachlan returned with the wine. Lachlan refilled his glass, Micky and Erin's glasses, then poured some for Ronan. The others decided they wouldn't indulge.

Ronan picked up his wine goblet and studied the intoxicating liquid. Intoxicating for everyone but vampires. He took a long sip.

"There's more for you to know, Clarissa," Erin said.

Lachlan slid his arm around Erin's shoulder, and suddenly Ronan almost wished he possessed the same comfortable relationship that his friends had found. The sweeping need startled him, and he pushed it away with a vengeance. No time for strange, mortal wishes. He was damned satisfied with his immortal life.

"Who wants to tell her what's happened this whole damned month?" Jared asked with a clear, weary tone.

"There's a lot of information to assimilate," Micky said, "but she should know now. It's not like we have days and days to explain."

"What about the vampire part?" Sorley asked.

Another hush filled the room, until Ronan decided he would cut to the chase. "She has to know or none of this will make sense. She must know about the ancient one and the fact that Lachlan, Micky, and Jared have certain...extraordinary talents."

"Vampires?" Clarissa said, her eyes widening again.

The others in the room pinpointed Ronan with stark expressions, as if they expected him to tell Clarissa everything.

"Did I just hear you right?" Clarissa asked, this time her expression edging into an incredulous smile.

"It's all true," Jared said. "Everything we're about to tell you about is deadly business."

"Can we clear the table and settle in the living room before we start talking about this?" Erin asked.

It didn't take long for the group to load the dishwasher and clean up the dining table. Once they settled into the living room with the wine bottle on the coffee table, Ronan figured it would be smooth sailing explaining this last month's events. He could hope, anyway.

Sorley started the gas fireplace, then settled down cross-legged in front of it. Erin snuggled in a chair with Lachlan, the two of them managing to scrunch into the big chair. Micky and Jared shared one side of the couch while Ronan took the other side.

Clarissa didn't sit next to him as he hoped she might; she settled into the loveseat next to Ronan's side of the couch. Deep inside him a craving built, the need to touch Clarissa driving him to an internal desperation.

Tonight he would show her the power of his seduction and she wouldn't resist it.

Taking a deep breath, he calmed his agitation. They needed to inform her on the particulars. Without the details she'd be unsafe, wandering in the morass of peculiarities that promised to swamp the town in unimaginable misery.

Slowly the others gave Clarissa the low-down. Lachlan and Erin explained how they met, including the part about Lachlan and Erin being able to read each other's minds. Ronan didn't expect Clarissa to question that information, considering she already knew he could read her mind. Erin eased into the vampire discussion.

Clarissa waited until the couple paused in explanations before she spoke. "So Lachlan was bitten by a vampire and as a result he has some of their powers."

"You got it," Lachlan said. "I can move fast like a vampire, although not with quite the speed they can."

Erin laughed. "Quick enough." She went on to explain the first time she'd seen Lachlan demonstrate the ability when he saved a glass from crashing to floor. "I wasn't sure I'd even seen him move, but there was the glass, safe and sound."

"What else can people bitten by vampires do?" Clarissa leaned forward in her chair and propped her elbows on her knees, clear interest etched into her face.

"Micky and I can answer that one," Jared said, "because we were bitten by the ancient one."

"Ancient one?" Clarissa asked.

As explanations continued, the twisting and turning felt like molasses to Ronan. He didn't add information, knowing his friends would do a better job. He noticed, though, that they left out the fact he and Sorley were vampires.

One bottle of wine and three hours later, Clarissa had the entire story from the first day to the present, from the ancient one to the dark force that had taken Micky and how Gilda had found her way into the other dimension to help save Micky.

Clarissa looked shell-shocked but still intrigued. Relief made Ronan happy, an emotion he couldn't count on feeling often over the years as he hunted the ancient one.

"There is a very important part they ingeniously left out, Clarissa," Ronan said as he cast a wary look at his friends.

Clarissa lifted one auburn-hued eyebrow as she sagged back into the pillows piled on the loveseat. "There's more?"

She sounded exhausted.

"One very big more," Sorley said his gaze fell on Ronan. "One gigantic piece I wouldn't feel right tellin' you."

"Well?" Clarissa asked. "Don't stop now."

Ronan shifted to the edge of the couch. "You've had enough for tonight. Tomorrow we need to caucus here again and make plans."

"So," Clarissa said, her eyes sad, "what do we do now? I'm willing to help whatever way I can."

Sorley smiled. "There's a way you can help, that's for certain."

Ronan gave the Irishman a stern glare. "I'll tell her later."

"Why later?" Clarissa asked, frown lines appearing between her eyebrows.

Ronan couldn't tell her, tactlessly and carelessly in front of everyone, that she had to have sex with him to save the day.

No. That would be just too feckin' rude.

He said instead, "We've known for some time that there's another solution—or possible solution—to the horror that's haunting this town."

"Oh?" Clarissa asked.

He breathed in her subtle perfume, a soft musk that drove him crazy every time he caught the scent. "Like I said, I'll tell you in private."

Clarissa's smooth brow creased and she sat forward one more time, her hands gesturing, long figures elegant and poised. "I need to know now. We need to plan what to do, now."

Right. She'd decided to be stubborn. "I'll take you back to the hotel and we'll talk there."

Good, Kieran. Now she'll just think you're using this as an excuse to get her into bed.

He decided to project a thought into her mind. *It's very private and you could be embarrassed if I talk about it here in front of the others.*

When he purposely captured her gaze, he thought he saw understanding there. Then a thought whispered from her mind. *All right you stubborn bastard.*

He grinned, satisfied and amused. Knowing looks passed around the room, and for the first time in a long time, Ronan felt his cheeks heat. Shit, he hadn't experienced a blush...a real honest to God, mortified blush in decades. *Feck, no. Try centuries.*

This pretty colleen would drive him to his end, one way or the other.

Ronan retrieved their coats from the hall closet and her fanny pack. As he helped her on with the coat, Micky and Jared prepared to leave as well.

"Do you see anything else in the dreams?" Lachlan asked Clarissa. "What do you think starts this whole disaster sequence Halloween night?"

Sadness twisted Clarissa's features. "I wish I knew."

"Even if we know all this disaster is coming, how can we stop it?" Micky asked as she slipped on her coat.

"I was hoping you all could tell me." Clarissa's sad voice, a little resigned, gave Ronan pause. He didn't like that this strong, tough woman sounded like she might give up. "Because I haven't got a clue."

* * * * *

As Ronan and Clarissa piled into her car, Ronan offered to drive her back to her hotel. A little less feisty then when she'd arrived, she acquiesced. She found she liked throwing him off balance. Maybe this big, conceited man thought he could keep her under his constant watch, and that he could pull something on her with his intellect and persuasive personality.

Little did he know.

As they pulled out of the driveway and headed down the icy road, Ronan drove cautiously, much to her surprise and satisfaction. She'd never liked guys who drove like maniacs, especially in bad weather. Clouds obscured the stars tonight. Light traffic traversed the streets, and a hush seemed to settle over the town as it cowered under the threat of a serial killer.

With a shiver of cold and fear, Clarissa adjusted her hat. Ronan flicked a glance her way.

"You're awfully quiet," she said.

"There isn't much to say after everything we told you."

She drew in a cleansing breath to resurrect her equilibrium and courage. "Except for one thing. What was so important and so embarrassing you couldn't tell me until we were alone together? Go ahead, spit it out."

His voice, when it came, held a husky, sexual nuance that made her heart beat faster and anticipation tingle in her stomach. "I suppose if I say I'd like to wait until we get to your hotel room you'll be angry and suspicious."

As if he'd switched a light bulb on she felt both emotions. She tugged her hat down on her head and wiggled her fingers in her gloves. "Exactly."

Ronan's grunt sounded assured, one of those noises a woman could expect a testosterone-laden male to make when he thought he knew the lay of the land.

"Then it sounds like I'm better off if I wait until you're in the hotel room."

She glared at him. "Why don't you just spit it out? What are you afraid of?"

"Nothing frightens me."

"Huh. Right."

Another glance, this one tinged with that golden fire, came her way. "Do you believe everything we told you tonight?"

His subject switch surprised her. "Yes, of course. Why?"

"I'm glad. It means what I'll tell you later won't be so difficult to swallow."

He turned down Main Street and headed for her hotel.

"Were you bitten by a vampire?" she asked suddenly, hoping her question would get a quick answer from him.

"Yes."

His ready answer took her aback. She'd expected more quibbling. She took a deep breath to gather her thoughts around this startling information.

"Okay. So you're like Lachlan, Jared, and Micky then."

Without a word he turned into the hotel parking lot and located a space close to the front door. He turned off the ignition and handed her the keys.

"It's more complicated than their situation. But yes, I'm like them in many ways."

"Then why the big secret? They told me what they are. Did you think I wouldn't believe you?"

His gaze didn't turn golden as she expected, an unearthly calm settling around him. He gazed through the front windshield into the night. "Your acceptance of what we told you is amazing. Micky and Erin had to have more proof. But I'm thankful you believed us."

"Micky saw shadow people all her life and yet she needed more proof?"

"She didn't tell anyone for years for fear of ridicule. And Jared needed more proof even after she told him about the shadow people."

Before she said another word he opened his door. She'd barely taken a breath when the passenger door opened and her heart slammed up into her throat. Ronan stood there patiently, as if he hadn't been in the driver's seat a second ago.

"Ronan." She put her hand to her chest. "You scared the hell out of me."

He held his hand out and gave a devilish smile. "I can move far more quickly than Jared or Lachlan. I can move faster than the human eye can see."

Feeling a tad breathless, she placed her hand in his and allowed him to draw her from the car. "What do we have here? A little competition?"

He winked and drew her closer, the mischievous look in his eyes making her wary. "I don't need or want to compete with them."

As he closed the passenger door with a solid click, she said, "Because your ego is large enough?"

"Because as powerful as Jared, Lachlan, and Micky can be physically and mentally, I'll always have more strength."

Curiosity made her say something she wouldn't have a few days earlier. "Come inside for a few minutes. You've got some explaining to do."

With one hand he touched her cheek. Warm and gentle, his gesture felt like precious gold and diamonds, a gift bestowed only to a woman he cared for a great deal.

"Oh, I can come inside for more than a few minutes if that's what you want."

Liquid heat poured into her loins at his double entendre.

I mean it. His voice whispered in her mind. *If you want me, you only have to ask, Clarissa.*

Surprise at his bluntness threw her off balance for a moment. Her mouth felt dry, her throat tight with expectation and nervousness. Excitement also welled inside and demanded fulfillment. Without a word, uncertain how to express her chaotic feelings, she slipped her hand from his grip and started for the front door of the hotel.

Two female clerks and a security guard stood behind the front desk in the small hotel. The ladies, middle-aged strawberry-blonde twins, smiled and nodded to Clarissa and Ronan. The short, rotund guard gave Ronan a suspicious glare. When Ronan gave the man a bored expression, the guard turned away.

Stifling a smile, Clarissa continued to the elevators. She pushed the button to go up. Keeping her voice low, she said, "You have an interesting effect on people."

One of his thick, roan-dark eyebrows lifted. "Sure, and it's only your imagination."

She cleared her throat delicately. "Bull. I'll bet women faint at your feet and men cower."

"You haven't fainted."

She snapped her fingers. "Darn, that's right. But maybe it's because I'm immune to your charms."

Oops. Wrong thing to say.

He didn't use his preternatural speed, but within seconds his arm slipped around her waist and he drew her against his side. Warmth enveloped her body in comfort and a dreaminess she'd felt many times whenever she came near him. She shivered with pure delight, captured up in one of those eternal moments.

Nuzzling aside her hair, he whispered into her ear. "If you think you're immune, I can prove otherwise."

The elevator pinged and the door opened. He led her inside and when the doors closed he didn't release her. She could hardly reach the button to push for her floor.

"In fact," he said, "I'll prove right now that you can't resist our attraction."

His gaze flashed yellow, their light brilliant enough to make his pupil and iris disappear. She gasped. "Ronan."

Metal groaned loudly. The elevator jerked and she started to lose her footing. Ronan tightened his hold, chest to chest, thigh to thigh.

With a mechanical sigh, the elevator stopped.

Blinking, she looked into his yellow eyes and watched as the glow disappeared. His glorious dark eyes returned to normal.

Disbelief made her mouth pop open, but for a second she couldn't believe. "You didn't."

He grinned.

"Holy shit," she said. "You did."

Chapter Eight

Ronan's unrepentant grin would have irritated Clarissa if she hadn't been so fascinated by what had just happened.

Her mouth opened, but he cut her off. "There's more I can do."

With a smile both cagey and sweet, he snuggled her closer until they couldn't have fit a piece of paper between them. Clarissa's heart did double time as she marveled at his cheekiness.

"Okay, so I've seen your parlor trick. Someone is going to realize this elevator is out of commission."

He brushed his lips, warm and tantalizing, over her forehead. "Not unless we push the emergency button or they realize we're stuck in here."

"Are you saying you've somehow hijacked this elevator and you can't start it again?"

"Nope. Didn't say that."

She pushed against his chest in token protest. "You're worse than a boy with a toy."

He chuckled softly. "I can be." Filled with heated desire, his voice lowered yet another notch into pure sex. "When I see something I want I go after it."

"Consequences be damned?"

"Sometimes."

She shivered, a drop of fear lingering.

Ronan's voice eased into her mind, liquid, soft, and sensual. *I would never harm you. I will always protect you.*

Her heart sped up. Once and for all she knew it in her soul. He might be the scariest, strongest man she'd known, but he wouldn't hurt her. Not physically, at least. All along her body she savored his masculinity. Although he held her in an unbreakable grip, she never felt more cherished or alive.

"Why did you stop the elevator?" she asked. "Other than to prove you could, of course."

To her surprise and disappointment he released her. He started walking around her slowly. As he ambled, Ronan caught her gaze, his concentration as intense as a touch. "I like the thrill of a little danger. Don't you?"

She made a little huff. "With everything that's going on in this town you think we need another challenge?"

His pace eased as he circled, then came to a stop behind her. "This danger is different. Beyond anything you've experienced."

"I've been trapped in an elevator before. Ten years ago."

"Were you frightened?"

"Actually I was bored. I was stuck in there for an hour with my aunt. And believe me, you don't want to get caught in a department store elevator with Aunt Liz."

His hands gripped her shoulders and started to massage. His fingers kneaded relaxation into her muscles.

His breath brushed her ear. "Are you bored now?"

Her heart thudded, her breathing quickening. "No."

Ronan's fingers soothed her, asked her to relinquish control. "Afraid?"

"No."

Everyone is afraid at one time or another. His thoughts came into her head. *What do you fear the most other than hot, wild sex with me?*

She inhaled, drawing in a calming breath. It was unbelievable the way he twisted and turned everything back to sex.

He drew her back against him, and she remembered the first time she'd met him and they stood in the cemetery like this.

"You think all I want is sex?" he asked.

"Isn't it?"

His lips brushed her earlobe. "No."

"Then what else do you want from me?"

"Your trust. We don't have much time to understand how to destroy the ancient one. But I do need you to believe in me without question if we're going to accomplish that."

"How can I trust you? I barely know you. It doesn't matter that your friends have faith in you...you're not having sex with them." A wild, ridiculous impulse urged her to say, "Or are you?"

She felt him stiffen, his rhythmic massage coming to a halt. Instead his fingers trailed down her arms, then back to the collar of her coat. Without hesitation he unbuttoned the garment. Not with the quick flash he'd performed before, but with the methodical motion of a normal man without extraordinary abilities.

"I think it's getting hot in here." His voice rasped in her left ear this time as he drew her coat off her shoulders and down her arms. He tossed it in a corner. "Do you have fantasies about ménage à trois?"

As his fingers slid down to her waist and lifted her thick, marled-wool sweater, shock slithered into her. His warm hands cupped her waist.

"I'm totally heterosexual," she said. "And I'm not interested in sex with another woman."

"More than one man?"

Amazed at the direction of their conversation, her senses a whirl and her composure cracked, she sputtered the next answer. "I haven't...no I haven't done that."

"Haven't done it or haven't fantasized about it?"

"Neither."

"But you do fantasize."

"I've been too busy and too tired to fantasize lately."

"Too bad. We'll have to do something about that."

He gathered her thick, long hair with one hand and then kissed the back of her neck.

Yearning centered deep in her stomach and moist heat gathered between her legs. Her body didn't seem to care that she didn't trust him. He turned her around and gathered her into his arms again, his hands sliding down to cup her ass. Once again those fascinating eyes radiated potent energy, a shimmering fire that commanded at the same time it compelled.

Still cautious, she said, "How long can you keep this elevator stopped?"

"As long as I need to."

"Uh-huh."

He sighed. "I hear the mistrust in your voice. You want to know everything about me? We've got all night to talk and plan and discover."

She turned toward him, momentarily breaking his hold. "Who says I'm going to be with you all night?"

His cocky mouth turned up a little, a sardonic grin that ran across his lips, then vanished. "If you're truthful with yourself, you know we don't have time to waste. This isn't about long-term negotiations. It's about now. About what we feel and what we have to do to save this town." He pulled back and looked down on her. "You can spend a lifetime denying your feelings for someone."

"Sexual feelings aren't necessarily emotional," she said in last defense.

"They can be."

She hadn't expected him to say that. Not this man with enough testosterone to make most males look like all-time wimps. With curiosity and trepidation she took a step in a direction she never thought she would. "Are you saying you want to have sex with me because you have feelings for me? Because if all you want is some woman to screw, I'm not the one."

New emotion gathered in his eyes, one akin to frustration. It almost overthrew the continual saturation of need in his gaze. "My coupling with a woman is never just screwing."

"So you're saying you've got to be emotionally involved to make love to her?" She knew she sounded skeptical, but she couldn't deny his statement seemed flawed. "Why don't I believe you?"

"You don't believe me because most of the men you've known can fuck a woman without caring for her. It's difficult for me to make love to a woman I don't have feelings for. It's always been that way."

She laughed softly. "Right. You've never made love to a woman without having feelings for her?"

"I didn't say that. I said it's very difficult for me."

A long pause settled between them, and she could tell he wouldn't be the first to speak. "Is there another motivation driving you, Ronan?"

Surprise and admiration skittered across his face. "You could say that. Let's say for now that the ancient one took something from me long ago. Something precious and irreplaceable. I want revenge."

Unreasonable jealousy did a cartwheel through Clarissa, stunning her into silence. Disconcerted, she couldn't believe the feeling was real. Circumstances and confusion must be a part of her envy. Being this man's center of attention did funny things to a woman. She couldn't be thinking straight.

"Was this something precious a woman?" she asked.

"Again, very perceptive."

Remembering the blonde she'd seen him cradling in her visions, she spoke without thinking. "Are you the type of man who would kill for love?"

Ronan's face hardened, all trace of desire disappearing. "If you're thinking what I think—"

"Did you kill the blonde woman because the ancient one wanted her?"

The fire in his eyes turned an interesting shade of crimson, adding to the darkness of his iris.

"The ancient one murdered her." His voice went rusty, and for one glimmer she saw moisture in his eyes along with overwhelming hurt. "He murdered the woman I loved with all my heart."

An ache centered in her soul, one filled with regret and sorrow for his loss. She slid her hands upward over his powerful shoulders. She cupped his face and felt the prickly, all male texture of his beard. "Oh, Ronan. I'm so sorry. I didn't mean to bring back bad memories."

His gaze stayed centered on her for a long time, as if he assessed her credibility, her genuine concern. "You believed I murdered her when you first had the vision, didn't you?"

She shook her head. "I didn't know what to believe."

She released his face, but his hands caught hers and he gathered them in his palms. Big and strong, his hands warmed hers. "Understandable. I was a stranger and you had no reason to trust me."

Glad he'd accepted her apology, she sighed and smiled. "Okay, now we have that settled, don't you think you should get this elevator started?"

Mental pain left his face, replaced by unquestionable male interest. "Not quite yet."

"But—"

"You haven't finished telling me your fantasies."

"Like I said, I'm too busy to think about sex right now."

He smiled. "Oh, I think right now is a perfect time."

"Ronan…"

"What about elevators? Have you ever wanted to fuck in an elevator?"

Heat warmed her face. With any other man his suggestion would have offended. Instead, the temperature simmering in her loins increased, turning into a scarcely banked inferno.

"Have you ever done it up against a wall?" he asked.

"No."

"In a car?"

"No."

"Tell me what you need. What you've always wanted," he whispered huskily. "And I'll make it come true."

Skeptical, she slipped her hands from his and started to pace the elevator. "No man can do that no matter how handsome he is."

A brash grin parted his lips. "You think I'm handsome?"

Okay, she could be honest. "I think you're the most gorgeous man I've ever seen. There. Does that gratify you?"

He leaned back against one wall and crossed his arms. Wonder touched his eyes. "A woman's never told me that before."

"You're kidding me?" She walked toward him, amazement overtaking her caution as she came closer to him. "Are all the women in Ireland blind?"

"I usually scare women. At least initially."

She could understand that. He'd certainly frightened her the first time she'd met him. "Even when you're rescuing them from harm?"

"Even then."

"Then they must be insane."

She meant it from the bottom of her heart. She couldn't be afraid of this man any more with the powerful need roaring inside her.

More than pure sexual necessity welled within her whenever she saw him. Dawning awareness made her pause, made her pay attention to emotions coursing through her. Treacherous or not, mysterious or not, he'd kept her from harm on two occasions and he'd opened a gate inside she'd denied too long. She could spend the next fifty years pretending she felt no attraction to him, and that her heart didn't melt at the sight of the big Irishman.

But God help her, she *did* have a strong reaction to him. The way he looked at her, touched her, talked to her made Clarissa a jumble of roiling passion. She felt agelessness within him, a wisdom coiled in among the bubbling attraction. His enigmatic nature made her want to know more. Ronan Kieran tasted like chocolate truffles, a sinful dessert impossible to resist and keeping her in danger of wanting more.

He uncrossed his arms and left his position against the wall. She couldn't help it; she moved as well. As they walked toward each other, everything paused in time for her but the continual flow and surge of yearning she felt.

"Clarissa," he said softly as he stood close, his gaze holding hers.

Without hesitation or leading up to a slow pass, he plunged in and took the kiss building between them since they'd arrived at the hotel. With gentle persistence his lips demanded a response, and she gave it. Easing into his arms, she allowed his embrace. He plunged both hands into her hair. Kiss after kiss, he bestowed everything she needed, just as he'd promised moments ago. As Ronan's powerful arms cradled her in intoxicating heat, she felt a prevailing desire to assent to any demand he made upon her body.

She craved.

She wanted.

Feel it, Clarissa.

His voice tantalized her mind as he kissed her, as his tongue caressed hers. *Give in to the desire. Imagine again how it'll feel when I'm sliding deep inside your tight, hot channel. Imagine me staying there, feeling your wetness and tightness holding me.*

As he slipped the erotic thoughts into her mind, she knew what they had together would be extraordinary. Heat leapt, desire flaming as she twined her arms around his neck. Her will dissolved as her heart thundered, and her breathing quickened. She absorbed the sensation of his wide, hard chest through his open coat. Cold leather could do nothing to hide his powerful muscles. She knew the tantalizing erotic fantasy he'd planted in her mind in the tunnel under the crypt would pale in comparison to what they experienced next.

She didn't care where the hell they were or if someone opened those elevator doors right now and found them kissing.

Because that's what she wanted to do.

Immediately.

God, yes. His words, groaned softly into her mind, fired her libido into gear.

When they broke the kiss he wrestled his coat off in three quick moves she could barely see. He let the coat drop.

She blinked. "Wow. Can you...um...?"

He cupped her face gently. "What?"

"Make love that fast? I mean when you're..." Her face flamed. She couldn't say it.

Instead of answering verbally, he kissed her again. Then his mind whispered to hers. *When I'm inside a woman I can fuck her as long as she wants it. As hard or as deep or as shallow as she needs. I can keep her hot and moist and make her want me so high up inside her she'll never stop coming.*

She shivered and moaned softly at his arrogant and erotic words. She ached, mad with rising passion as her nipples tightened. Her breath rasped in her throat as she took the kiss away from him and thrust her tongue in his mouth. He tasted mint-fresh and delicious. She wanted to lick him up, search every corner of his mouth, his body until no mystery remained. With yearning she plunged her fingers into his hair and enjoyed the soft texture. Silk spun and thick, his gorgeous hair seemed to curl around her fingers with a mind of its own, capturing her as sure as his seductive persuasion enticed her to leave common sense behind.

With a quick move he turned them and pressed her up against an elevator wall. His cock pressed against her stomach and she arched against it. His fingers inched up her sweater to caress her as his kiss went on and on. She gasped into his mouth as he flicked open her front clasp bra and cupped her left breast.

As he shoved up the sweater and took in her breasts, his big hand encompassed and held. "Ambrosia. You're all the nectar I need."

Reverently his gaze caressed her breast, and under that hot attention her nipple hardened even more. She waited, anticipating his tongue and lips and fingers showing her the way to paradise. Instead he kissed her.

A few moments later he'd unzipped her jeans and yanked them and her panties down past her thighs.

Startled, she jerked in his embrace. The man had done it again, taking her off guard with his lightning movements whenever he saw fit to share them. His lips touched the side of her neck. He licked the erogenous zone between her shoulder and neck, his tongue a fiery spark against her equally hot skin. The sweet, insistent pressure of his hand under her breast made her nipples ache for attention. He brushed his thumb over her nipple. She gasped in startled pleasure. Capturing the aroused nipple between thumb and forefinger, he tugged.

As he tormented her breast, he slid his hand down her belly and through her pubic hair. She felt vulnerable and raw. Exposed to the last degree.

Open to me.

She did as told, and he tested gently. He circled her wet, aching labia and the exquisite feeling made her tremble. Probing, he plied her wet folds with tender attention. Tightness coiled in her belly, a fervent hunger. She leaned her head back against the wall and sighed with ecstasy as he fingered her swollen clit. She moaned softly. As he circled and rubbed, her wetness made the friction oh so right. It felt so good she couldn't keep still, and she moved her hips.

His lips skirted her mouth, brushing across her flesh to her chin, then to her neck where his voice came dark and deep as his breathing deepened, control close to breaking. "That's it, Clarissa. Now."

She clutched at his shoulders and held on for dear life. She whimpered with an irresistible desire to have him inside her when she climaxed. "Ronan."

One more brush over her sensitive clit and she fired into orgasm. Ecstatic fire invaded her loins as he pushed two fingers deep into her cunt. He rubbed and stroked inside her, working his fingers back and forth as she clenched around him, drawing the climax out for an eternity of pleasure.

As she came down from the hard orgasm, she shivered and buried her face against his chest. The scent of sex was all around them. She whimpered as he removed his fingers.

Feeling lightheaded and yet aroused, she wanted to give him everything he'd given her with such rapid success. While she'd never been bold in sexual relationships before, she wanted to satisfy Ronan. A flush spread over his cheekbones. He smiled, self-assured looking and pleased. She'd lost her composure so swiftly and she wanted to make him lose control.

She reached between them and touched his cock through his blue jeans. His eyes closed and his head tilted back as he sucked in a breath.

"Clarissa," he whispered.

Pleased at his reaction, she allowed her touch to glide over a large, very hard erection. How would it feel inside her? Would he even fit? Shyness came out of nowhere and ambushed her. She jerked her hand back.

He grinned and opened his eyes. A feral grin touched his mouth. "Oh, I'll fit all right." Before she could react to his statement, he reached between them and unfastened his pants. "Touch me."

Heat blazed across her face, but she wanted to explore him so much. She palmed his cock through his black briefs and then slipped inside to draw it out. She'd had two lovers before, but they'd been average men. Ronan's sizable erection was big and beautiful. She'd always thought some erections looked intimidating and ugly, but Ronan's gorgeous cock made her want him inside with a fierce ache. Long, thick, and tightly engorged, his flesh felt smooth and hot under her touch. She drew her hand up from the base to tip, base to tip, base to tip. Her rhythm stayed slow and sure, using pre-cum to slick the surface. With each stroke he moaned softly, the sound growing with each upward movement. And with each glide of skin over skin she felt her response heighten.

Then something devastating popped into her mind. She removed her touch.

"What's wrong?" he asked, his eyes glazed with passion and a yellow glow.

Feeling dazed and wanting, she said, "We don't have birth control, and I don't really know you —"

"It's all right." He kissed her forehead. "I can't have children and I can't have disease. Trust me. I'll take care of you."

There was that word again. Trust.

But as she looked into those flame-filled eyes, the out-of-this-world unreality hit her again and she didn't care about anything but having him buried in her. The ache inside demanded immediate fulfillment.

He smiled. *Yes. Now.*

The emergency phone rang and Clarissa almost jumped out of her skin.

"Feck," he said through gritted teeth.

Breathless, she laughed. "I thought you could hold this elevator indefinitely."

"I can." He grabbed the phone and answered gruffly. "Hello?" Seconds later he said in a less rough voice. "No, we're fine. Yes."

He closed his eyes and tipped his head back. He took a deep breath and a long shiver ran through him. When he opened his eyes, the elevator creaked and started to ascend.

"It seems to be working now," he said into the phone. "Thank you."

He frowned and hung up.

Surprised, she asked, "Why did you start the elevator?"

"As much as I want you, I didn't think holding up the elevator any longer was fair."

This man was worried about fair? She never would have guessed when it came to full on, raging sexual hormones, that Ronan would yield to anyone or anything. She didn't know whether to feel angry at the interruption or relieved, but his expression guaranteed the animal inside him couldn't be appeased by anything but sex.

"I haven't shown you anything yet, Clarissa. If you think I'm an animal, just wait until we get into your room. Then you'll know the meaning of the word."

He frowned and proceeded to stuff his huge erection back into his pants. Within less than a blink of time he'd put himself back together, including his long coat. She realized with a jolt that her shoes and coat lay in the corner. Frantically she pulled her pants back up and refastened them, then grabbed her boots and put them on.

Therein, as Shakespeare once espoused, lays the rub. She'd known him barely two days and she had almost performed full sex with him in the elevator. A forbidden shiver of excitement mixed with her shame. When she drove into this town the other day she never would have expected she'd be lusting after a man and ready to do the two-backed beast with him without hesitation. But here she was, contemplating making love and trying to decide whether she should change the game plan and run instead.

She'd just picked her coat up from the floor when the elevator doors opened and they stepped into an empty hall. Thankful they were alone she headed down the hall toward her room, Ronan in tow.

When she unlocked her door and stepped through, she felt a whoosh of wind. She turned on the light and almost cried out when she saw Ronan standing in front of her. He glanced past her and she heard the door behind her lock by itself.

A little irritated, she asked, "Are you doing these parlor tricks for a reason?"

"Yes. Because now you know some of the things I can do, I don't have to hide it from you."

She paused, aware of a dawning understanding. She decided to feel a little ashamed. What must it be like to hide your abilities for fear of what others would say or do? When she glanced at him again, though, she couldn't think of how different he might be. Instead she felt his strong personality, his high intelligence, and the attraction she couldn't shake. A jolt of sexual electricity rammed her, as if he'd touched a live wire to her body and kept the hum going in a steady stream. Trying to distract herself from the jumpy feeling, she put her hat, gloves, and coat on a modest chair by the desk.

Ronan's gaze surveyed the room and took in the small space with its cozy-looking queen bed. When his gaze slipped back to hers, he drew his coat off slowly and tossed it on hers. His erection pressed against his jeans with a vengeance. He wanted her without a doubt. Unfortunately, his fierceness both frightened and aroused her. He might be intrigued with the idea of sleeping with her, but could he be patient?

Renewed apprehension made her say, "I'm...I'm not sure this is a good idea."

He stalked toward her until she backed up against the door. He brushed his hand over her hair, twisting long strands around his fingers. "What are you terrified of Clarissa?"

She breathed in his all male scent, the intoxicating blend calling to her senses. The heat in his eyes lowered to a slow simmer. She tried not to respond to his overwhelming presence, to the maleness inside him that demanded a female response.

"I need more time to think about what we're doing," she said. "What we did in that elevator was...was...crazy."

He brushed a finger across her jaw line, then whispered low, his voice a temping growl of brisk and gentle. "And that scares you?"

"Frankly, yes."

"You've never been into wild sexual experimentation."

"No. And if you're talking about sex with two men and one woman or two women and one man, I told you I'm not into that. And if you are—"

"In the past, many, many years ago, I indulged once with two women at the same time."

She sniffed, feeling slightly disappointed in him. "Well, it isn't for me."

"So you want me to think you prefer white bread sex?"

Embarrassment sent heat into her face and she glared at him. "There's nothing wrong with white bread sex."

"No, there isn't. But what if I told you there was something more incredible than you ever dreamed?"

"I thought what we did in the elevator was pretty unbelievable as it is."

He chuckled, the sound deep, slow and sexy. "But there's more. Much more."

With reverence he kissed her forehead, then her nose, then her mouth. She leaned into his tender touch. She needed more than a wild fling with a man that was half-vampire.

With determination she pulled away from him. "Ronan, we've got to talk this through. I'm not into one-night stands."

A gentle smile curved his mouth. "I'll want you for more than one night, believe me."

The overconfidence, the old-fashioned possession in his attitude should have affronted, but instead it fascinated her. "Give me a compelling reason why I should finish what we started in the elevator, Ronan. And don't leave anything out."

He released a soft growl. "Woman, I don't think I'm going to be able to take much more of this."

"This?"

He cupped her cheek, caressing the skin with his thumb. "Looking at you, being near you, touching you without being buried inside you is driving me insane."

His words rasped over her and warmth filled her lower belly once again. She grinned. "You're a big boy. You can handle it."

A teasing smile came back to his lips. "You think I'm a big boy, eh?"

Without a hint of remorse he leaned into her so she could feel his erection pressing against her stomach again.

She trembled. "Wow, that doesn't want to go away, does it?"

He laughed, the sound caught between strangling and hilarity. "All right. I'll tell you what you need to know. And as soon as I tell you, you'll do one of three things. You'll either run like hell, never speak to me again, or you'll be terrified."

Apprehensive, she wished his disturbing presence didn't keep her libido and her sense of obligation to him so prominent in her mind. She glanced down and tried for humor again. "Oh, I see. You're not going to tell me you've got two of those bad boys, are you?"

Again he chuckled, and she loved the rich, whisky and velvet sound of his voice. Dark. Smooth. Sinful. "Now that might be interesting to have two cocks. Think of what I could do with them."

She tried not to smile and didn't succeed.

"But no," he said, "I've only got one cock, and it wants you damned badly. Sure, and if you don't put me out of my misery, I'll have to take the problem into my own hand."

Arousal boiled and built inside her like a hurricane. She'd never fantasized about seeing a man jacking off, but she had a feeling tonight in bed she'd close her eyes and dream about Ronan Kieran wrapping a big hand around his cock and stroking until he exploded.

"Shit," he said. "I felt that, Clarissa. What are you thinking? It must be sex."

Trying to be brave, she decided to confess. "You're right. It was. But I think it's over now."

He groaned softly. "Damnation, woman—"

"Do you know you speak like someone from another century sometimes? It's really interesting. Layer it on with that Irish accent and I'll bet women follow you all over."

"Trying to avoid the subject, eh, Clarissa?"

She sighed. "Please be patient with me. I might understand the paranormal, but everything that's happened in the last couple of days has me rattled."

Clarissa knew she would have been in big trouble if she'd let him take her in the elevator.

I would have let him take me if the phone hadn't interrupted.

He knew it and she knew it. So how could she put him off now? Staring into his luminous eyes sent trails of fire dancing along her every nerve ending. She may have delayed sleeping with this man, but not for long.

"It's getting late." She kept her tone mild and polite. "It's been a long day. Tomorrow I need to go to the crypt and try and find my camera. I can't believe I didn't even think of it until now. I really must be losing it. It's probably damaged beyond repair."

Alarm darted over his features. "You will *not* go out there without me."

One of her brows twitched upwards as she responded to his imperious tone. "What makes you think I want you with me?"

He sighed and closed his eyes. "Damn it, Clarissa, don't do this to me." He rubbed a hand over his jaw. "Mother of Mary, the seer never told me—hell—Yusuf never told me it would be this difficult."

She frowned. "Who?"

He shook his head. "You're right, it's late." He looked at the bedside clock. "Stay here and I'll get your camera tonight."

She smiled. "You can see in the dark, I take it?"

"Exactly."

"Okay, it's a deal. Just bring it to me in the morning."

With a groan he reached for her, his mouth coming down on hers with a heated passion that made her warm all over again. He tasted her deeply, his tongue intruding as he caressed her mouth.

She didn't even get a chance to respond before he stepped back abruptly. He slipped into his coat. "Don't leave this room tonight and don't open the door to anyone but me. In the morning don't leave until I'm here to escort you."

With a blink and that strange popping sound, he was gone.

She gasped. Startled beyond belief, she stared at the spot where he'd stood. Okay, now she'd seen everything.

"That would explain how he appeared in the crypt and how Sorley appeared tonight," she murmured to the empty room. "What have I gotten myself into?"

Apparently, something really, really bizarre.

Puzzled and caught between lingering arousal and irresistible curiosity, she sank down on the bed.

Chapter Nine

The ancient one explored the tunnels, though in his trip through the insidious maze he'd yet to discover the resting place of the evil. He thought once he'd entered the tunnels under the Gunn Inn he'd feel the power of the black hell immediately. Instead he experienced only the drip of water as it made its inexorable way through the caverns.

"Where are you?" he asked the dark.

Nothing answered him back, no feelings intruded to prove iniquity other than himself existed in this tunnel. A twinge of worry raced into him, making him wonder if he'd imagined the evil shadows that had helped him as much as the good shadows helped Micky Gunn not long ago.

Where had the wickedness gone?

Malevolence this potent didn't dissipate with ease, no matter what some thought. Few mortals or immortals could perform a ritual to rid their world of the purest form of evil, which he'd felt in these tunnels before Ronan and his band of mortals had fought him.

He wanted the sinister energy with a blazing necessity that demanded fulfillment this minute, and the longer he wandered to find the evil, the angrier he became. Darkness parted for him as he walked.

It didn't take much longer.

As he stepped into a tunnel he hadn't traversed before, the power hit him like a punch to the stomach. He gasped for breath, then dropped to his knees as emotions burst through him like an explosion.

Fear. Hate. Loathing. Desperation. Panic.

He laughed and threw back his head. "Yes! Yes! Come into me! Make me one with you! For I will be the greatest evil!"

Power surged inside him like a draught of fresh air for a drowning victim. He inhaled deeply.

"Yes! Yes!" He threw his hands up over his head and laughed again. "Come within me!"

Night flowed like new rain over his drought, a renewal of gloomy spirit, a pouring of unimaginable hate deep into his psyche.

He achieved his wish to be replenished by the hate, his body jerking as a kaleidoscope burst inside his head. Yellow, red, blue, green, the spectrum of the universe invaded his dim spirit, his despicable vampire soul.

When the feeling eased, he opened his eyes and rose to his feet. He licked his lips and smiled. He required sustenance and the empowerment he'd received assured success. A deep chuckle issued from his throat.

Time to feed.

With his newfound energy bursting forth, he left the tunnels and rushed toward Pine Forest.

Cloaked, he waited outside Jekyl's Hotel until the restaurant section closed for the night. He saw a young waitress leave from the back entrance and make her way to her car, start it up and defrost the windows. He smiled. Little did the poor soul know stepping out of the hotel restaurant would be the stupidest thing she'd every done. After she left and proceeded down the main street, she drove until she reached her home on the outskirts of town.

Stupid humans. Despite fear and the cops suggesting they stay home at night, the woman didn't care. Perhaps her employer demanded she work late. She would wish she'd defied her employers.

He pondered, as the waitress stepped out of her car, if she thought she was immune to horror and death. So many humans thought they couldn't be harmed, their relentless sense of immortality their eventual downfall.

As the woman whistled, the vampire hovered nearby, ready to uncloak and show her what he could do for her. If she'd never experienced ecstasy in her small life, she would this last time.

A crackling in the nearby bushes made the woman jump back, a gasp coming from her throat as she showed fear. He laughed as a cat jumped from the hedgerow. The waitress looked around, her eyes full of fear. She'd heard his laughter, no doubt.

Before she could react, he popped into visibility in front of her. Her mouth opened on a silent scream, and before she could squeak he grabbed her and yanked the woman into the bushes by the side of the house.

Settling her under him, he held her arms over her head and looked deep into her eyes. He used his considerable charms to seduce her, to bring her into a state of languor that meant she would no longer struggle. As he probed the woman's long repressed fantasies and made her warm for his explorations, he bit into her neck. Blood spurted in all directions. Gore would be all over everything, a greeting for the police when they came to the scene.

As the sweetness of her life force drained down his throat, he gulped and enjoyed the musky scent of her arousal. He loved it, thrived on it, and inhaled it with a glorious and profound need. She tasted delicious. Until now she'd never known such excitement. He wouldn't leave her to her miserable life. Instead, he would take all she had to give and leave her to be found in the morning, cold and alone but having satisfied his needs. Several moments later he reared out of the bushes with a roar of strength. He didn't care if the neighborhood could hear him. Instead he screamed again with his newfound invincibility. With the addition of the woman's blood, he felt equal to anything Ronan and his crew might throw at him.

No one could defeat him this time.

With a final smacking of his lips, he dissolved into the night.

* * * * *

Ronan took his time walking through town, keeping to the backstreets. Cold wind brushed across his cheeks, a light snow flurry coating his hair with white. Snow crunched under his feet.

He could have popped into the cemetery outside town and searched for Clarissa's camera and located it within seconds. Then he could have been back in her room and handing her the camera. Maybe he could have convinced her to sleep with him, without getting into the complicated particulars of his immortal status.

Right. At this point, he didn't see that happening. He'd missed the power curve and now she'd want a full explanation, just as he'd vowed.

"Damn it, why did I promise her?"

Maybe because he'd never intentionally hurt a woman in any way, and when he promised a woman something, he followed through.

Instead of rushing back to her, he chose to wander and take time to think. God, how he needed to think.

He wanted to take Clarissa more than anything he could remember wanting in a long time. If the phone hadn't interrupted them in the elevator he would have had her. Experiencing the glorious sensation of her hot, wet cunt squeezing his cock and rippling around him in orgasm would have been fantastic. He gritted his teeth in exasperation.

Who was he kidding? It was a lot more feckin' complicated.

His emotions jumped from staggering desire to total frustration. From the first time he'd seen her in the cemetery, a punch of attraction had hammered his gut, but he'd never guessed the other emotions that would come from knowing her. It scared the hell out of him.

As he thought about her alone and vulnerable in her hotel room he almost went back, almost popped into her room. He *had* to keep her safe. He didn't like this atypical alarm crawling inside him like maggots, eating away at his defenses. He stopped and allowed the wind to flow over him. Wait a minute. What was he afraid of? She'd asked him that earlier and he hadn't answered. He feared for her safety, yes, but something else worried him. The suspense and danger rippled around this town like a live wire unleashed. Something felt off in the breeze, more odd and misshapen than the ancient one's ugly head.

Damn it all to hell. He couldn't afford this wimpy attitude. He stuffed apprehension back where it belonged. Moments later he realized what created his original concern.

In order to keep Clarissa safe he must seduce her. Even if it meant using some unscrupulous vampire tactics.

He stopped in his tracks.

Saints preserve me. He couldn't do this to her. She already understood he didn't live like a normal man. When he saw her again he would explain about his seven hundred year existence, and he would tell her the facts. Besides, he knew too well they didn't have forever to come together as man and woman. He must bed her and do it soon.

Once he reached St. Bartholomew's and entered the cemetery, he wandered into the crypt she'd fallen through. The tunnel under the crypt, dark and freezing, didn't bother him. He'd stopped at Erin's house long enough to grab his weapon loaded with silver bullets. His superb senses of hearing and sight detected little life nearby; most animals had taken shelter against the cold and increasing snow. He found Clarissa's camera where they'd forgotten it and snatched it up.

Before he could move he felt the pressure start. Like a hot, nasty poker the feeling intruded into his stomach. He looped the camera around his neck and checked the immediate darkness. At first Ronan couldn't be certain what he felt was real. The creeping sensation walking up and down his spine appeared on rare occasions.

Then it hit him. What if the ancient one managed to revive earlier than expected? Although he hadn't anticipated fighting the ancient one by himself, he always knew it could happen. A chill, unexpected and unprecedented in his immortal state, rose inside his body and threatened to resurrect fear. Taking a deep, fortifying breath, he clenched his fists together and braced his feet wide apart to take whatever might come next.

The darkness came alive, rippling around him like bat wings.

What the hell – ?

Red eyes burst from the tunnel toward him and he saw the gargoyle head upon the tall, cloaked body as the ancient one came to a stop directly in front of him. Ronan drew back several steps for leverage. Preparing for attack, he felt his immortal blood flow as it warmed and glowed within his body.

The ancient one's cloak flapped around his body in nonexistent breeze, revealing a tall body encased a black leather coat much like his own and leather pants. The ancient one hadn't stopped growing for some time after he first became a vampire a thousand years ago, and he towered over Ronan's six-foot four-inch frame. Nothing like encountering an almost seven-foot vampire in a dark tunnel to make Ronan feel ready for a fight.

Blood speckled near the corner of the creature's mouth, and Ronan realized with a sinking feeling the ancient one obviously had enough stamina regenerated to feed. The stench of blood made Ronan's stomach clench. Where blood might have aroused him at one time to feed, evidence the ancient one had killed made Ronan ill.

Damn the stinking hell rat.

The bastard stayed in his gargoyle head form, too spineless to transform into his true shape and reveal the face no one alive had seen. "Hello, Ronan." The ancient one's voice enveloped the tunnel, gravel-filled and layered with hatred deeper than Ronan remembered from their last encounter. "Fancy seeing you here."

Spiced with a bit of Scotland, the thousand-year-old vampire's voice would chill mortal hearts to the bone. Not Ronan. He'd talked with this beast on too many occasions to dread the effect the vampire's voice could inflict.

"Ancient one. You've called off your sleep too early."

A chuckle reverberated in the tunnel. "Too early for you, perhaps. Aye, you and Lachlan and your other weakling friends will regret my early return. You thought you would have more time to work on defeating me. Well, you were sadly mistaken."

Evidently. If he didn't think of something right here and now, all hell would break loose. He took one step back from the evil so he could tilt his gaze upward and obtain a better look at his enemy. Shit. This wasn't good. He couldn't remember the last time his confidence felt so in the toilet.

"You should give up." The ancient one held out a thin, scaly hand as grey as death. "I've too much power for you to defeat me. Now it's assured once and for all."

"No. I've tracked you down, and now I'll have my revenge."

The laugher echoing down the tunnels almost hurt Ronan's ears. "That is all you want, isn't it? Not to help the stupid mortals. Why don't you turn away from this fruitless chase, and I'll allow you to leave unharmed. As one vampire to another, a gift."

Unbelievable. This stinking piece of flesh wanted him to quit? "I don't think so."

"Then prepare to die."

Ronan had heard lamer lines in B-grade movies, but coming from the guttural voice of this vampire, it sounded too serious for celluloid.

Before Ronan could do more than brace for impact, the ancient one launched across the small space between them.

"Feckin' A," Ronan said under his breath.

Ronan twisted to the side and avoided the head-on force of the ancient one's heavier body.

Twirling in the air like a top, the ancient one stopped before he impacted with the wall ahead. "Come here, little vampire. I can make this hard or easy. It's your choice."

"Since when, asshole? I don't remember you making your bloodsucking easy on anyone."

The ancient one walked toward him. "Since I've discovered new strength."

Renewed anger made Ronan cocky and he braced again. "Bring it on, tit meat."

The ancient one laughed, his harsh laughter once again making Ronan wince. "My, my, but you've become a trash mouth. Spending too much time with little dick Sorley."

"I wouldn't be so confident if I was you."

The ancient one charged.

Ronan yanked the weapon out of his holster at his waist and aimed. He pulled the trigger and hoped the silver bullet would find its mark. As the pistol barked out a report, the ancient one moved with laser speed.

Ronan tried to dodge, but the old vampire's impact threw him backwards at a tremendous rate. Ronan hit a wall and his breath whooshed out. Pain careened into his whole body, and he knew a mere mortal would have been crushed like a bug. He lost his grip on the weapon.

The ancient one rushed again, this time coming in with a two-handed grip around Ronan's neck. Ronan's throat hurt like a son-of-a-bitch, but at least he couldn't be strangled. The ancient one drew Ronan off his feet and swung him by the neck in a wide arch. As Ronan was tossed away like a weed, he used his catlike agility to twist his body and attempt to land on his feet. Instead he skidded on the rocky soil. He tripped and landed face down. He stood immediately and swung around. The ancient one paused a short distance away, his smile filled with satisfaction. His razor-sharp teeth, as pointy and revolting as anything owned by a demon, made his grin particularly disgusting.

"The evil in the tunnels beneath the Gunn Inn has given me all I need to defeat you and everyone else in this pitiful town, Ronan Kieran."

Ronan gritted his teeth in regret. Okay, how the hell would he get out of this one in one piece? If he'd fucked Clarissa tonight he might have more strength. Might survive this attack. He'd waited too long.

"Are you hoping to outwit me?" The ancient one asked. "I don't think so. You can't save your friends anymore than you could save sweet, innocent little Fionnghuala."

Taunted beyond endurance, Ronan's hot anger sent him rushing toward the older vampire. "Fenella loved me, you piece of shit and you took her away from me. Go to hell!"

Ronan attacked, kicking the bigger vampire's legs out from under him. The old vampire went down with a roar. Ronan's energy surged and he leapt into the air just low enough not to hit the ceiling but to come down on the ancient one's stomach area with both feet. As he growled and pushed his feet deep, the other vampire yelled and grabbed Ronan's ankles. With a shove of tremendous force, he flipped Ronan backwards end over end. Ronan managed to get his hands under him and executed the flip onto his feet as if he intended to do it all along. He retrieved his weapon and took dead aim at the older vampire's heart. He fired.

The bullet hit. The ancient one reeled backward, arms flailing. With a screech like an enraged bat, the ancient one staggered for a moment.

Feckin'-A yes! Ronan prepared to take another shot. Maybe he could —

The old vampire wavered but didn't fall. Then he put one hand to his heart area and the bullet popped out in his hand and to the floor.

Mother Mary. The bastard couldn't be hurt by silver bullets anymore.

Shocked, Ronan didn't move.

The ancient one repositioned on the far side of the tunnel. The gargoyle-headed creep might be the most powerful vampire on earth, but he seemed bigger, hardier and far more pissed than Ronan had ever seen him.

Something had changed in the ancient one, and not for the better.

Then, before Ronan could blink, he felt the vampire behind him. A powerful punch landed in Ronan's back and red-hot pain lanced his entire body. Groaning in extreme pain, Ronan started to fall. The ancient one grabbed Ronan by the waist and picked him up. With a mighty roar he tossed Ronan like a ball toward the opposite end of the tunnel.

Beyond the pain rocketing through his body, Ronan tried to slow his rate of speed as he came toward the T-junction wall between two tunnels.

I'm going too fast.

Oh, shit.

The wall came up and he hit full force. Everything went black.

* * * * *

Clarissa's nightmares came alive as she tossed and turned in the hotel bed.

Chills rippled over her skin as she walked in the tunnels beneath the crypt. Freezing cold, without a jacket, she walked fast toward an unknown area. She must locate Ronan right away, though she couldn't understand why.

Her heartbeat thundered in her ears, her limbs tight with exhaustion as she trembled in the biting cold. In her gut she knew something had gone dreadfully wrong.

She dared to speak. "Ronan! Ronan where are you?"

No answer. Fear leaked into her bloodstream as sweat formed on her forehead. Anxiety and worry formed out of nowhere and took her prisoner. She couldn't remember feeling this devastated, as if someone she loved beyond all things had been taken from her.

"Ronan, damn it, where are you?"

Then she saw a form against the wall at the far side of the tunnel and her heart wanted to stop. "Ronan?"

She ran toward the figure and when she reached it, she saw him lying unconscious in a crumpled heap on his back, his face bloodied, a gash in his side and blood soaking his sweater. "Ronan!"

She started to reach out for him and his eyes snapped open.

She inhaled sharply. "Thank God."

His right hand went out to her but she couldn't move. Tears of worry and fear stung her eyes. She tried to form words, but no sounds came from her throat.

His eyes widened, his lips parting as he struggled to convey something to her. She heard him strain to say, "Clarissa."

A horrible sense of dread crept over her and she swung around.

A gargoyle head, red eyes flashing with hatred, glared at Ronan and then laughed. She shivered with repulsion. Spikes of cold, unholy fear invaded her.

"No!"

Clarissa snapped out of her dream with a jolt as she sat upright in bed. Quivering, she reached for the bedside lamp and turned it on. Frantic, she slipped out of bed and grabbed her robe. She put it on and fastened the ties around her waist with shaky fingers. She grabbed her slippers by the bed and jammed them on her feet. Then she stopped.

"What am I doing?" Sinking down on the edge of the bed, she crossed her arms and waited for some of the shaking to subside.

As in her dream, she obeyed reflex action. Rubbing her temples, she closed her eyes and took deep breaths. She must calm down and think.

"It was just a dream."

Wasn't it?

Ronan said he'd retrieve her camera, but why would she dream about him being injured unless...unless this ancient one had harmed him? Determined to forget her reaction to the weird dream, she took off her robe and slippers. When she saw Ronan tomorrow she'd tell him about the weird dream and he'd laugh.

Terror lingered and with it the contrasting memories of Ronan's extraordinary lovemaking. How did a woman stand being around Ronan Kieran without liquefying into a writhing mass of sexuality on a regular basis?

She glanced at the bedside clock and it read four o'clock in the morning. Today would be a long day. No doubt Ronan would try to monopolize all her time. She supposed she couldn't avoid him; he'd managed to evade answering many of her questions and they hadn't discussed how to defeat the ancient one and how she fit into the picture, other than prophetic dreams.

With a sigh of exhaustion, she closed her eyes and hoped for sleep.

* * * * *

Clarissa waited in her room until nine in the morning but Ronan didn't show. With the residual disturbance of last night's dream continuing to haunt her, she paced the room, dressed in her warmest turtleneck and sweater and her flannel-lined jeans. The weather channel on the television said conditions would hover around the freezing mark for the rest of the week.

Damn Ronan. Didn't he understand she needed her camera to do her work? Then she sighed in self-recrimination. The man offered to get her camera to keep her safe and here she was complaining about it? Guilt stopped her mental carping.

A few moments later, Clarissa dialed Erin's home and Lachlan answered. She asked if they'd seen Ronan.

"No," Lachlan said. "We didn't see him after he left with you. "Why?"

"When he left me last night, he said he'd return this morning with my camera. I figured he'd be here by now."

"I wouldn't worry about him. He's one tough son-of-a-bitch. If he hasn't turned up this morning it's for a good reason."

"I wasn't worried about him. I was concerned about my camera."

Lachlan laughed. "Okay. If I see him I'll be sure to tell him. By the way, if you want company, Erin is working at the library this morning. We could swing by and pick you up. You'll be safe there."

"What I really need is an escort to take me around to get more photographs."

"Clarissa," Lachlan's voice sounded a little perturbed, "don't you think staying safe and figuring out how to finish off the ancient one is more important?"

For a moment she'd forgotten that everything wasn't normal. "Yes. But I can't help any of you figure out what needs to be done while I'm stuck in this hotel room."

"Good point."

They made plans to meet in the lobby in thirty minutes. She left a note on her bed stand and at the front desk for Ronan telling him where she'd gone.

As she stood in the lobby, she half wished Ronan would come striding into the hotel. Ronan's absence felt wrong, and she wished she understood why. By the time Erin walked into the lobby with Lachlan's arm around her, Clarissa's nerves felt a little frayed. She envied the easy love she felt flowing between the big Scot and the petite woman. Erin managed to look happy despite the events surrounding them. Lachlan's initial expression, stern and watchful, changed to relaxed.

Erin and Lachlan greeted her with smiles and hugs, but Clarissa saw the worried expressions on their faces. They walked out to Erin's Subaru Forester, piled inside, and Lachlan headed toward the library.

Erin turned to look at Clarissa in the backseat. Her brows were pinched together a little. "Now tell me why you're frowning so hard."

Shrugging, Clarissa tried pushing away her fears. "I wish I could tell you. It's just a niggling feeling I've had since I woke up this morning. A dream."

"A prophetic dream?" Lachlan asked.

"I'm not sure." Clarissa thought about it a little more. "Not all of my dreams are prophetic. This one was frightening and weird."

"Tell us," Erin said.

"I was walking through the tunnel area beneath the crypt. The one I fell into. I could see in the dark, which is weird. I saw a body at a fork in the tunnel. I realize when I get there its Ronan. He looks bloodied, like he's been in a fight. At first I think he's dead, but then he opens his eyes and reaches out for me. He says my name, but then I realize there's someone behind me. I turn around and there's this gargoyle-faced figure."

"Oh, no," Erin whispered. "You've seen the ancient one in your dreams."

A shiver ran over Clarissa. "So this could be a prophetic dream. Something that might happen to Ronan in the future." Worry added to the cold feeling inside her. "I'll tell him as soon as I see him."

Erin glanced at Lachlan, then back to Clarissa. She cleared her throat. "There's something else we should discuss. I mean, I feel a little awkward asking you—"

"Then maybe we shouldn't ask," Lachlan said.

Glancing at her fiancé, Erin allowed a crooked grin to part her lips.

Curious, Clarissa spoke up. "Ask me what?"

Erin hesitated, a flush spreading up her face. "Did Ronan tell you what must happen before the ancient one can be defeated?"

"No. He started to. I thought for certain he'd explain considering how important it is we figure out how to stop the ancient one right away."

Lachlan made a sound between a groan and a growl. "Damn, Ronan. He should have told you by now."

Rather than defend him, Clarissa said, "Since he's not here, maybe you should tell me."

"It's a little difficult to talk about, but...well..." Discomfort etched Erin's face. "It's very personal. Ronan will probably be mad as hell if I tell you."

A little guilt crept into Clarissa as well as embarrassment. She couldn't say Ronan had been too distracted by sex to give her any important information. "He probably would have told me, but I mentioned my camera and he volunteered to get it."

"But he said he was going to come back last night?" Lachlan asked as Clarissa saw him glance in the rearview mirror.

"He was supposed to stop by this morning," Clarissa said. So, did these two think that she'd slept with Ronan? That could explain the awkwardness. She considered them new friends, but her sexual relationships weren't their business. "He'll probably stop by the hotel first and when he sees my note he'll come by the library right away."

Erin nodded. "We'll leave explanations to him."

"Erin," Clarissa said with a warning in her voice. "Come on, 'fess up. What's going on? What should he have told me?"

Erin managed a weak smile. "It has to do with saving Pine Forest, as you know. But there's much more." Erin's gaze darted to the snowy landscape outside. "An Irish seer that Ronan consulted and Yusuf, a long time vampire hunter in Morocco, told Ronan the only way to defeat the ancient one is if Ronan makes love to a woman."

Clarissa blinked. "What?"

Erin flushed again. "Ronan must have sex and from that mating the town will somehow be saved."

Clarissa sank back against the seat, amazement and disbelief warring inside her.

"I see we've left you speechless," Lachlan said a short time later.

Resentment eroded Clarissa's control. "Oh no, I'm not speechless. I'm mad as hell."

Chapter Ten

Clarissa thought Erin looked a little startled, but then who could blame her. Just as no one could censure Clarissa if she kicked Ronan's handsome ass the next time she saw him.

"I'm going to kill him," Clarissa mumbled, staring at the floorboard.

Erin put up a placating hand. "It's not an easy thing to tell someone." She cleared her throat. "I mean, he should have told you before things became...intimate..."

Aha. So Erin thinks I already slept with him.

"So you all knew this last night?" Clarissa asked.

Erin's gentle eyes held remorse. "We've known for a long time what Ronan would have to do."

Clarissa chanced a glance in the rearview mirror and the seriousness in Lachlan's eyes.

"We'd never dream of getting into a couple's personal business like this if it wasn't important to the survival of this town," Lachlan said.

Clarissa nodded and released a breath. "I'm not angry with either of you. I'm pissed at Ronan."

"Maybe he was *afraid* to tell you?" Erin asked.

Clarissa considered the possibility for two seconds. "That doesn't seem likely. Have you ever known him to be scared of anything?"

Lachlan sniffed. "No way. He's a fearless bastard."

Bastard is right.

They arrived at the library a few moments later, and when they went inside Clarissa hardly noticed the quiet and the few people milling around the area. Instead her thoughts centered around how many ways she could kill Ronan.

Then it struck her and she stopped. Erin almost bumped into her.

"What is it?" Erin asked as she stripped off her coat.

"Why does it have to be Ronan? Why would Ronan in particular be the one who would receive the power to destroy the ancient one?" Clarissa asked.

Lachlan looked around, then kept his voice low. "He didn't tell you that either, I can see."

Frustration made Clarissa's voice go tight. "There's more?"

Erin hesitated, and for a moment Clarissa thought she might not answer. Then she sighed and opened up. "Ronan is a vampire, Clarissa. He doesn't just have a few extraordinary vampire abilities like Lachlan, Jared and Micky. He's a full-fledged, seven hundred year-old vampire."

As Clarissa's mouth dropped open she thought the world would open up and swallow her. She didn't care if she sounded like a Mynah bird repeating her own phrases. "I'm going to kill him. I'm just going to kill him."

"We need to get this resolved between you," Lachlan said, his expression stern. "There's no time to lose."

New anger made Clarissa bristle. "Oh, I see how it is. It's perfectly all right for a vampire to use me as a means to the end. We just need to get it on and everything will be all right with the world?"

Erin scowled at Lachlan. "That was insensitive, Lachlan."

"And it doesn't explain why Ronan has to be the one," Clarissa said.

Exasperation touched his expression, and as he spoke his accent became more pronounced. "For God's sake, we haven't got that much time to quibble. Ronan is the one because he's the only vampire right now other than Sorley who is hunting the ancient one. The others are either too afraid of the ancient one, know they aren't capable of fighting him, or are evil themselves. Ronan has been hunting this bastard since the beginning. He knows more about him than anyone other than the seer and Yusuf. Think about that when yer both bein' indignant." He held up one finger when Erin looked like she might object, then he stared at Clarissa. "It's up to you now, Clarissa. Think about what you're goin' to do and how that decision will affect Pine Forest and everyone in it."

Clarissa glared at him then stalked toward the bathroom, her thoughts awhirl and her heart aching. When she slipped into the room she found a small lounge area with a chair and plunked down. Her breathing felt choppy, so she inhaled deeply and tried to relax. She must wrap her mind around everything she'd learned this morning.

Okay, she could handle this. Ronan Kieran was a vampire like the creature that wished to kill, maim, and destroy everyone in Pine Forest. Yet Lachlan and Erin, Jared and Micky seemed to have a high opinion of the Irishman. Ronan's dedication to removing the ancient one from the earth remained strong. He'd probably do anything to destroy the old vampire.

Even if it meant sleeping with a mortal woman for the greater good.

She hated it.

Sure, in a twisted way she liked that he'd chosen her, but at the same time, it sucked. No pun intended. It hurt her pride to discover the sexual interest he'd displayed had as much to do with necessity as it did lust or…

No, she refused to go there. She'd known Ronan for such a short time the feelings she experienced for him couldn't be more than sexual attraction.

So what should she do? Have sex with him to save Pine Forest as Lachlan had implied moments ago?

Everything inside Clarissa rebelled now she understood Ronan's real reason for wanting her. Hurt mixed with genuine desire to strip a piece of hide off the vampire when she next saw him.

Vampire.

That explained a hell of a lot of other things about the man, too. Abilities like appearing and disappearing and his knack for moving at the speed of light. Curiosity made her wonder what else he could do. Her face heated. Had he used some weird sort of mind manipulation to make her feel sexual interest in him? A gamut of emotions ran over her as she processed the information. She'd been kissed, caressed and almost screwed by a vampire, for heaven's sake. Now if that wasn't a shocker she didn't know what was. Granted, he was one of the good guys, but that didn't negate the shiver running up and down her spine or the doubts about her sanity. Despite her brushes with the supernatural when she'd lived here as a child, she'd never imagined she'd discover vampires stalked the earth or that she would kiss one. She remembered Jim Leggett and her one other lover and then added Ronan to the list. Romantic failures, each one.

But no man had ever made her feel the way Ronan did.

"Hell and back," she said to the empty room. "I can't believe this is happening."

Allowing herself a few moments of self-pity, she speculated if the humiliation would go away, or would she be reminded every time she saw him? In any case, the next time he got within screaming distance she would give the big, handsome, infuriating vampire a piece of her mind.

Tears stung her eyes and she fought them back. She possessed a bigger problem than hurt feelings. What if this Yusuf and the seer and everyone else turned out to be right about Ronan's need to mate with a mortal woman? Her imagination kicked in and she thought about Ronan making love to any other woman to get the strength required to kick ancient vampire ass.

No, she didn't like that one bit.

She put her head in her hands and allowed tears to trickle down her face. What could she do? She wouldn't become emotionally attached to a creature that sucked human blood. Another quiver ran over her skin and despite all her efforts, more tears escaped as her heart ached with desolation.

* * * * *

Clarissa wandered the enormous stacks in the library, determined to find two books she'd read as a child. Until she'd stepped into the library she'd forgotten about the books. Excitement pushed her to find the volumes fast. At the same time she noticed the strange vibrations in the library. The place echoed with the stain of bad events, of the past and things that might yet happen. Stony quiet didn't help things; few people visited the library these days. She shrugged and tried to ignore the atmosphere. What else could she expect in Pine Forest?

Eventually she located the books on local legend and took them to a workstation in a secluded area. She went through the first volume, a brown leather-bound work. Old and yellowing, the book had a million fascinating stories in it that she'd forgotten.

Skimming a first chapter for information, she came across an entry that made her pause. It reminded her of what Sorley and Ronan had said about the town in Morocco being plagued by a similar evil. This entry proved what she suspected.

Pine Forest, according to old-timers who'd related the story, had seen a mini apocalypse not too long after its founding. The town had suffered the appearance of ghosts and goblins right from the beginning of its founding. So often people believed hauntings transpired in old buildings. Not necessarily. Perhaps the elementals lingering in the tunnels under the Gunn Inn and the crypt were the same thing as the shadow people who plagued Micky. From what she'd learned the other night, the shadow people assisting Micky were good, unlike the ones in the tunnels.

One story in the volume mentioned a disturbance at a home on the outskirts of town where a young woman complained of being visited by an incubus night after night. The young woman turned up dead two days later outside the house that would in due course become the Gunn Inn many years afterwards. The woman had been drained of blood. A few days after that the same thing had happened to an older woman who was found drained of blood in her home one evening.

Two more murders of a similar nature happened. Ridiculous fights broke out among long-time friends and accusations ran rampant. Arrests took place and people threatened with lynching before the mayor put a stop to the madness. Now history threatened to repeat itself with maybe worse results.

In a weird, twisted way, what happened to Pine Forest in the past resembled an abridged version of the Salem Witch Trials. Could the same hysteria envelope the town again?

Could her dreams about the end of Pine Forest on Halloween night have anything to do with reading this as a child? Had she internalized all this and her mind played tricks on her all her life? How could she have forgotten so many things about Pine Forest?

"No," she said.

Bad things occurred in Pine Forest now that mirrored the events of over one hundred years ago. Facts were facts. As she read it all started to come back to her that she had read it before...had known the information previously. Perhaps her mind protected her by keeping some of the more horrific information locked away.

Did that mean the ancient one had visited this town one hundred years ago? If so, what had kept him from destroying the town at that time? She glanced at her watch and saw that time frittered away while she researched the town she thought she'd known well. She closed the book and put her head on her folded arms. Closing her eyes, she thought about how the information could work to their advantage. Her tired mind slipped into a dream world.

She stood over Ronan as he lay on the floor of the cold tunnel, his face paler then the last time she saw him in the dream. Her fingers trembled as she leaned down and touched his wide chest. She recognized the long leather jacket, sweater and jeans as what he'd worn when he left her last night. She searched his chest and found no breathing, no sign of life. Though he might be immortal he didn't possess a single sign of animation. Panic rose in her throat as she tried to cry out, to see if anyone could help her. He looked so cold.

"No," she said in her dream. "Oh, no."

Tears threatened again. She'd give anything, anything at all for this not to be true. Ronan couldn't be lifeless. Not a powerful vampire with charm, wit and a brooding sensuality that made her feel things she never believed she'd ever feel.

Someone touched her shoulder and she vaulted out of the dream with a startled cry.

"Clarissa?" Erin stood by the cubicle workstation, her hand on Clarissa's shoulder. "Are you okay?"

A fine trembling ran through Clarissa's body and she rubbed her arms. "I was dreaming." Raised voices came from the far side of the room, and Clarissa glanced that way. "What's going on?"

Erin shook her head. "One of the patrons flipped out on us thirty minutes ago upstairs in the children's section. I'm surprised you didn't hear the commotion. Lachlan had to restrain him until the police could get here. They're taking him out now."

For a moment Clarissa felt shell-shocked. She stared at Erin in dawning comprehension and her heart felt like it might stop.

"Don't you see...it's the beginning of the fighting? People are starting to turn on each other." Clarissa stood and grabbed her books. "And Ronan's in trouble. We've got to help him."

Erin trotted to keep up with Clarissa's longer stride. "What? How do you know Ronan's in trouble?"

"I had the dream again but this time it was different. Ronan was cold, pale. Lifeless."

"Well, he *is* a vampire. The undead."

"But he's not normally cold. No, he's very, very warm. I noticed whenever he touched me that the outside weather doesn't seem to affect him and his skin is always toasty." Her voice trembled. "What if he's been lying in that tunnel under the crypt since last night after he left me? Has anyone heard from him?"

Erin shook her head. "Sorley just popped in a moment ago and he's talking with Lachlan now about where Ronan could be." Her gaze turned troubled. "Let's get our coats and let Lachlan know about your dream."

They met up with Lachlan and Sorley a few moments later at the front desk. She left the books on the counter.

One librarian stood nearby and continued talking to the police in a worried tone.

Erin nodded toward the librarian. "That's Fred Tyne, the head librarian. He's been acting unusually hard-nosed lately, but then I noticed the last few days several people have been on edge. I chalked it all up to nerves over these killings, but after you talked with us last night about the dreams and how people begin to act strangely, I realized it's started already."

Lachlan slipped on his coat as they moved away from the front counter. "Great. Just what we need."

"What was the altercation upstairs about?" Sorley asked.

Lachlan's expression went semi-amused. "One man was accusing another of having an affair with his wife. They were doing all this in the kid's section of the library."

Within moments they piled into the car again, this time with Sorley next to Clarissa in the backseat.

She glanced at him and he smiled. "Don't worry. Ronan is the toughest vampire I know." His face paled, if that was possible for a vampire. "Um...I...I hope he told you—"

"We told her," Lachlan said as he started the car. "She knows you're both vampires and she knows what the seer and Yusuf said must happen between her and Ronan to defeat the ancient one."

Sorley's eyebrows went up. "Good. I didn't want to let the cat out of the bag."

Ire still simmered in Clarissa's blood. "Lucky you."

The skinny vampire smiled again. "I take it Ronan's in mighty big trouble when you meet up with him again?"

The truth hit her square in the stomach. "No, not anymore. I just want to find him alive."

Sorley looked anxious for the first time, his elfish expression pinched. "And in the dream he looked dead?"

"Yes."

"He can't really die," Erin said.

Two parts relief ran through Clarissa, and two parts concern. Apprehension managed to cancel out the respite. "If vampires can't die, how do we expect to stop the ancient one?"

Sorley shook his head. "Vampires can't die unless they are shot in the heart with a silver bullet or stabbed with a silver stake and most of the time even that doesn't work well. The ancient one is so old and powerful all it does is slow him down but it won't kill him."

Exasperated, Clarissa asked, "So this whole sex thing cures the ancient one plague, eh? It sounds too pat. Too easy. There has to be more to it."

"There is," Sorley said. "We just don't know *what* it is."

"We have to stop by the house first," Lachlan said. "We need the first aid kit, rope to climb down into the crypt, and weapons with silver bullets."

"What about Micky and Jared?" Erin asked. "We could always use Jared's extra power to help find Ronan."

Lachlan agreed and Erin pulled out her cell phone to call their friends. When she finished the conversation she said, "They'll meet us at the house."

They proceeded to Erin's home and rushed in to pick up the provisions. Less then twenty minutes later Micky and Jared drove up to the Victorian house and parked at the curb. When they came in the house they seemed worried.

Micky hugged Clarissa. "The dream sounds awful. I don't blame you for being concerned about Ronan. But we'll help you find him."

Before long they'd taken off again, this time in two cars. Clarissa pondered the unreality of the whole situation. She sat there silent and grim, watching the pine trees rush by as Lachlan drove them to the cemetery and the crypt.

She glanced at the cloak Sorley wore.

"What is that cloak all about?" Clarissa asked. "It looks old-fashioned."

"You've seen Ronan wearing one, right?" Sorley asked.

She nodded.

"It's to protect us when the sun is up."

She smiled. "I should have guessed. When I first saw Ronan that night in the cemetery he wore one then. He had the hood up and when the sun went down completely he took off the cloak." A horrifying thought came to mind. "Wait a minute. Does the sun kill vampires?"

Sorley chuckled softly. "A lot of people wish that was true. It can kill us, but only after our force has been drained by repeated exposure. It isn't like the movies where we burn up before your eyes." He rolled his eyes and held his hands up. In a falsetto voice he said, "I'm meltin'. I'm meltin'!"

Clarissa chuckled. "Wizard of Oz, eh?"

"That was water, Sorley," Erin said. "And it was the Wicked Witch who was melted by water, not a vampire."

"Picky, picky," Sorley said.

Everyone in the car tittered with restrained laughter, as if they couldn't resist Sorley's sick sense of humor. As they subsided into quiet, concern inundated Clarissa again. She wished she'd ignored her dreams and skipped coming to Pine Forest. If she had maybe Ronan would be safe right now.

"I'll never forgive myself if Ronan's been hurt because I asked him to get my stupid camera," she said.

Erin turned to look at her, eyes filled with understanding and sympathy. "I'm sure he's all right. Like we said, Ronan isn't afraid of anything. Let's just hope your dream was born out of fear and not truth."

Clarissa's voice wobbled. "That sounds like something he would say."

The remainder of the trip passed in silence. When they reached the gates of the cemetery, Jared and Micky pulled up beside them. They all piled out of their cars, Lachlan took the gun with the silver bullets, then handed another lethal-looking gun to Sorley.

Sorley hoisted his weapon. "We picked up another one of these this week just for safety."

"Sorry we don't have one of these for you," Lachlan said to Jared.

Jared unzipped his big coat and pulled his service revolver out of his shoulder holster. "This should even the odds a little."

Lachlan put the circle of rope over his shoulder, and Erin took the small first aid kit.

Sorley gestured at the gates. "I could scout the area quickly for Ronan."

Lachlan shook his head. "No. We'll stay together. Besides, if anything happens to me, I'll need you to help me protect the women."

"Please don't say that," Erin said as she placed her hand on his shoulder. "You're scaring me."

Lachlan kissed her gently on the lips. "I'm sorry. If I could have left you at the house and you'd be safe, I would."

Clarissa thought about protesting Lachlan's statement; she didn't want to think her, Erin, or Micky were vulnerable. "Why isn't she safe at home?"

Lachlan cleared his throat. "Like we told you last night, the ancient one wants her and if she doesn't have my protection day and night, he's sure to try and hurt her again."

Lachlan handed flashlights to Clarissa and Erin.

Though she didn't ask for an explanation, Jared turned to Clarissa and said, "Lachlan, Sorley, Micky, and I can see in the dark."

Remembering the startling glow present in Ronan's gorgeous eyes, she wasn't surprised by Jared's confession. Sure enough, a subtle glow started in the men's eyes and in Micky's gaze almost immediately.

They left the car and went through the gates. The rescue party headed straight to where Clarissa had seen Ronan in her dreams.

While crusted snow broke under her booted feet, she was once again grateful for her hat and gloves. Her breath frosted as freezing air touched her. An uncanny sensation crawled its way up her spine, forcing Clarissa to take a deep breath to control her nerves. She could do this. For Ronan she would search this graveyard tooth and nail.

A crow cackled from a nearby tree and she started. A breeze ruffled through the trees, icy and almost as strange as the bird's call. The wind seemed to whisper to her.

Weareherewearehereweareherehere.

Micky stopped cold and Jared put his arm around her shoulders.

"What is it?" Jared asked.

Micky smiled. "I heard the shadows. The ones that protect me."

Amazed, Clarissa said without hesitation, "I heard them, too. They said they are here."

As she turned toward Clarissa, Micky's eyes widened. "You heard them?"

"There are a lot of strange things I can see and hear," Clarissa said as she stepped forward and they renewed the pace toward the crypt on the hill.

"This is happy news," Sorley said, "that the good shadows are here."

His sardonic tone made her glare at him, and when he turned those yellowish eyes on her, a shiver rolled up her spine. He might be on the side of good, but the fact he could drink people's blood gave her second thoughts about trusting him.

The crypt, outlined in the smallest light from the moon, loomed up before them. Standing stark and framed by the leafless trees, it looked as ominous as a monster movie set. She had to remember reality. Everyone hesitated at the bottom of the hill and stared at the monstrosity. Night seemed to speak with murmurs and guttural obscenities. She shivered as slithering dread radiated up and down her body like a mild earthquake.

"This place." Clarissa rubbed her arms, her coat no longer keeping her warm. "It's infected by that evil. The one that comes from the tunnel and tried to harm Micky. I feel it in my gut."

Sorley and Lachlan insisted on walking ahead, while Jared took up the rear behind the women. Sorley went inside the crypt first. After he gave an all clear, they stepped inside one by one. Clarissa allowed her flashlight beam to illuminate the structure and the hole in the middle gaped like the maw of some great, awful monster. Her throat felt tight with anticipation, with panic that they'd find the worst.

Sorley said, "I'm going scouting now we're here. I'll be back in a flash."

He popped out of their sight and a rush of wind accompanied his departure. Dust floated up from the floor.

"Damn him," Lachlan said. "I told him we should stick together."

As they waited in the crypt, Clarissa felt a strange sensation she hadn't experienced in some time. Her vision started to dim.

Oh, damn. Unlike her dreams, a vision could strike her at any moment and the physical consequences could be either mild or violent. When she'd seen what she believed to be Ronan's past lives, she'd had no physical reaction to the event.

This time, regrettably, that didn't seem to be the case. The flashlight started to slip from her fingers, so she tightened her grip. Her breathing quickened as a sickening wave of nausea punched her in the stomach.

She placed one hand over her midsection. "Oh, great."

She felt a hand gripping her arm and then Erin's voice near her right side. "What's wrong?"

Clarissa's eyes fluttered shut.

The vision hit full force.

She saw the gargoyle-headed creature. He walked Main Street, passing by several women who walked together for protection. He grinned at them and they all gawked at the tall man with the ugly mask and huge cape fluttering around him almost like bat wings.

"No," Clarissa said, her hands going out, the flashlight slipping from her hand and crashing to the floor. "Don't get near him."

"What's happening?" she heard Jared ask.

Then the ancient one kept walking, leaving the women alone. Weakness swept into Clarissa as she watched him traverse the street, passing by unsuspecting people who believed he wore a mask.

"The ancient one walks the streets of Pine Forest in full view of others," Clarissa said through her aching throat. "He has no fear any longer. He just passed a group of several women walking down Main Street and even though they saw him he didn't seem worried about it. The women sensed something wasn't right, but they don't understand he's evil. They just think he's dressed up for the holiday."

Before she could see where the ancient one planned to go next, the vision snapped to the group of women. They started bickering. They stopped in front of a bar and argued, their voices rising in a miasma of sudden hate and uncontrollable emotions.

"The women are fighting. Their emotions are out of control." The vision blinked out. Clarissa felt her knees tremble as she opened her eyes. "It's gone. The vision is gone."

"Damn it," Lachlan said harshly. "He's getting bold and it means he's fully recovered. The women are feeling the effects of evil. We've got to find Ronan."

"Why would you have the vision now?" Micky asked.

Clarissa explained. "It's not predictable how or when I'll get the visions or why I even have them. They just come or they don't. I have no control over them."

Not a minute went by before Sorley popped back into the crypt, his eyes wide and his words jumbling together. "Hurry! Ronan is lyin' there at the end of the tunnel, and he's white as mortal death. I swear to all that's holy, he actually looks dead!"

Fear slammed Clarissa. Tears spilled into her eyes as she put a hand to her chest. "Oh, God. Please no."

She couldn't even glance around to see everyone's reaction to the stunning news. She'd feared this from the moment she had the dream.

Ronan could be dead right now because of that stupid camera. Dead.

She felt Erin pressing her shoulder. "He'll be all right."

"Come on," Jared said. "Let's get down there."

Sorley popped out of sight again.

Slowly, one by one, they traversed the rope down through the hole and into the tunnel. As Clarissa shimmied down through the aperture, she felt out of breath with anxiety for Ronan, a staggering recognition that she cared about the vampire far more than she could have imagined on short acquaintance. While she once wanted to kick his ass into the stratosphere, now she couldn't wait to put her arms around him.

Please, oh please, let him be alive.

They headed down the tunnel. It didn't take long to see a pair of glowing eyes at the end of one tunnel. Lachlan came to a dead stop and Erin almost ran into the back of him.

"Is that Sorley?" Erin asked.

"Aye, I think it must be," Lachlan said.

Sorley's voice echoed down the long stretch. "Come on!"

They broke into a trot, and despite her uncertain footing and the uneven surface of the tunnel, Clarissa ran. Their flashlight beams bounced along, the light hardly enough to see by.

When Erin's flashlight beam illuminated Ronan lying on the floor, Clarissa gasped. Blood had dried on his forehead and a large bruise had formed near his temple. His skin looked hard, pale and cold.

"It's just like the dream only worse." Clarissa dropped to her knees beside him and touched his chest. "Please. Damn it, Ronan, please don't do this to me."

Tears rose in her eyes again and she let them fall. Trembling, she touched his face and felt the icy surface. Emotional agony far deeper than anything she could remember before arrowed straight into her heart. She didn't care what anyone thought as her insides seemed to quake with pain.

She'd sent Ronan to his death.

Chapter Eleven

Lachlan knelt near Ronan's head, his expression filled with stark fear. He looked up at Sorley, who stood at his fellow vampire's feet. "Sorley, what do you think? Could he be…?"

Sorley looked shaken, bravado washed right out of him in the bleak moment. "If he fought the ancient one his body might have injuries. It would take him a little to recover. But he should have come out of it by now."

Clarissa couldn't speak, couldn't believe the iced-over sensation encasing her heart. She leaned over and placed her lips against Ronan's. She rubbed her palm over that chest, still firm and powerful. A tremendous ache centered in her heart, so excruciating she wanted to cry out. Instead she touched his lips with all the tenderness inside her. She took a shaky breath.

As she did so she felt warmth growing in the vampire's lips. Before she could react, Ronan let out a soft groan and responded. His mouth stirred under hers and with one quick movement his hand speared into her hair. His lips opened and he kissed her deeply. His tongue plunged into her mouth and she met it with her own in dazed and growing happiness.

She wasn't imagining this. She wasn't going mad.

Ronan is alive.

Of course I am, darlin' colleen.

For a few seconds she knew nothing, felt nothing but the overwhelming knowledge that he lived and his body heated by the second with immortal life. She put her palm to his cheek and his skin flushed with warmth. Alive and strong he kissed her like no one else watched them, as if he would devour her with his hot embrace.

She pulled back in stunned excitement, a smile breaking over her mouth.

"Jesus, Mary and Joseph," Sorley's voice went hoarse. "Feck me!"

Ronan's eyes popped open and a weak smile touched his lips. "Sure, and I thought maybe for a moment I was dreamin'." His accent thickened as his eyes glowed with the welcome fire of a vampire alive and kicking. His gaze centered on Clarissa. "If you aren't the most beautiful woman I've ever seen."

Lachlan laughed and soon the rest of them joined in, their voices rising in the darkness and overpowering the night.

Relief made her feel weak. She put her hands over her face and took a heavy, shivering breath.

"Clarissa." Ronan's deep voice touched her like a warm caress. "Are you all right?"

She took her hands from her face and wiped at her tears. "Am I all right? We thought you were..." she gulped. "We thought you were dead. Of course I'm not all right."

A broad smile broke over his mouth. "I thought I *was* dead. After the ancient one..." He tried to sit up and failed, sinking back to the ground with a gasp as pain flickered across his features. "Shit! I almost feel mortal."

"What's wrong?" Lachlan asked.

"I think my ribs broke during the fight." He explained how he'd encountered the ancient one and quickly discovered the monster had regained his power and then some. "I couldn't believe how quick he was. Quicker and nastier than any of the times I've met him before. When I hit the wall all I felt was pain. Then I was out. I woke up a couple of more times and it was bizarre..."

His gaze centered on Clarissa, simmering with something that almost looked — dare she even imagine it? — love.

Love.

"I saw you," Ronan said as he reached up and cupped Clarissa's face with one hand. "I thought you were real at first, then your image shimmered, as if you were a ghost."

"It's my dream," Clarissa said in wonder.

"Like an out-of-body experience," Micky said softly.

Clarissa nodded. "That's what brought us here. It's the reason we knew where to locate you." She leaned into his palm and enjoyed his skin against hers.

"Okay you two lovebirds," Lachlan said with a grin. "Let's get you out of here. Can you stand?"

"Wait a minute, what if his ribs really are broken?" Clarissa asked, concern spiking through her.

Ronan shook his head. "Don't worry. They've mended. They're just a little tender." He felt the skin along his forehead. "I probably had a concussion, too. I'm okay, now, though." He winked at her. "It was your kiss that brought me out of the coma. I heard you calling my name and talking to me. Then when you kissed me—"

"Enough," Sorley said, his grin caught between cocky and disgusted. "This is way too much information for me. Let's get him out of here before I start to blubber."

They all laughed again, and this time Clarissa's heart felt lighter and happier than it had in a long time.

"What do we do if he can't walk?" Erin asked.

Ronan grunted as he forced his legs under him. "I *will* walk." Jared and Lachlan looped his arms over their shoulders so he could amble along with maximum support. "Nothing keeps me down for long."

Clarissa felt a slow burn of anger rise up as she followed behind him. "Right. You've been unconscious for most of the night on top of most of the day."

"But I'm a—" Ronan started.

"I know," she said and her voice rose. "A vampire. So I found out. But only because your friends told me."

"Ah, shit," Ronan said.

Clarissa smirked. "Exactly, vampire boy."

"I think he's in trouble," Sorley said. "What do the rest of you think?"

"Definitely," Erin said.

"Without a doubt," said Micky.

Lachlan let out a sigh. "I'd say he's about as low as shit on a boot heel right now."

"Well, *feckin'* hell," Ronan grumbled.

* * * * *

"You're staying with us," Erin said as they drove up to Clarissa's bed and breakfast. Sorley, Micky and Jared had gone back to Erin's home already and planned to wait for them there. "And no more arguments. We've got the extra room tucked away in the attic. It's a little dusty but I'm sure we can clean it out."

"You won't get any argument from me," Ronan said with a smile as Clarissa sat next to him in the backseat. "But I'm feeling better already."

"No patrolling for you tonight," Lachlan said.

Ronan glanced at Clarissa and winked. He reached for her hand and squeezed it quickly. "You've got that right."

Clarissa smiled, enjoying the resurgence in her energy. She knew his words meant something deeper. She knew he wanted to spend tonight with her. Alone.

She still rode high on Ronan's incredible resurrection. Whether her kiss had revived him, or he would have repaired his body soon without her help, she couldn't recall feeling this joyful in a long time. Deep inside her soul she'd realized one thing in that tunnel. She cared for Ronan Kieran more profoundly than any man she'd known. And it didn't matter in that moment, as she'd kissed his cold lips and wept for him, that he was a vampire.

No, not at all.

"I'll go with you," Ronan said as Clarissa opened the door.

She looked back at him. "Oh, no you don't. You're not well enough. Just stay there. Erin and Lachlan will help me get my things."

To her surprise he grinned and didn't argue. Amazing. Maybe the powerful vampire didn't mind having someone else take charge, at least for a smidgen.

It didn't take long for Clarissa to gather her things and check out. When they returned to the car Ronan sat with his head tilted back and his eyes closed. For one paralyzing second Clarissa's heart leapt with fear. What if he'd relapsed? His eyes opened immediately as they entered the car, and she sighed in relief.

They remained silent as they took the short drive back toward Erin's home. They hadn't gone too far when they saw a glow above the horizon.

"What's that?" Erin asked.

"Looks like...no it can't be," Lachlan said as he made the turn down her street.

"Fire," Clarissa said softly.

"Damn it." Ronan clenched one fist.

Clarissa reached out and placed her hand over his. Tension exuded from him. "We knew fires would probably happen."

They arrived at Erin's house and saw Jared and Micky standing on the front lawn watching the red glow above the horizon. When they piled out of the car, Jared and Micky walked up quickly.

Jared spoke first. "We just heard on the radio that a house out in the woods close to the Gunn Inn has gone up in flames."

"I was worried about it being my place," Micky said, "but then the report gave the address and I was relieved it wasn't."

Clarissa gripped Ronan's arm gently. "Let's hope no one was hurt or killed."

Ronan didn't allow anyone else to support him as he walked toward the house. He glanced at the reddish haze in the night sky above the tree line.

Once inside the house, Ronan swayed a little. Clarissa's worry didn't diminish, and she kept a firm grip on his muscular biceps. "You've got to lie down."

He shook his head. "We don't have time for me to be sick. We thought we had problems with the ancient one, but its worse. A lot worse."

Clarissa described the vision she'd experienced about the women on Main Street fighting after being in the presence of the ancient one. "It had to be his influence." Clarissa relayed once again the information she'd discovered in the two old books in the library. "It's possible that the ancient one was here a hundred years ago."

"What about the other evil I encountered in the tunnel in our last fight against the ancient one?" Micky asked.

Everyone went silent for a moment before Jared said, "It would make sense. We don't really understand much about the evil other than what Micky learned."

Although Clarissa had heard about the additional malevolence when they'd grouped together the night before for dinner, Micky mentioned again how she'd gone into another type of dimension, remaining in the tunnels but not visible to her friends. "The evil wanted me to join with it, but it specifically said it wasn't a part of the ancient one. It said the ancient one was a part of *it*."

Clarissa eased Ronan down on the couch. "Nice and cryptic."

"Brilliant," Sorley said. "So this evil has an ego even bigger than the ancient one."

"I sent an urgent message to the seer and to Yusuf about this mega-evil," Ronan said. "I'm surprised I haven't heard back from them yet."

"Urgent message as in called them?" Lachlan asked.

"Right. Yusuf doesn't have a phone, but I contacted his cousin Jasmina and she said she'd relay the message. I tried reaching the seer by telepathy but she hasn't responded. So I left a message on her home phone."

Clarissa smiled despite the gravity of the situation. "You're going to have to tell me more about this seer."

"Oh, she's quite beautiful," Sorley said, a mischievous grin spreading over his face. "And Irish, too."

"Hmmm." Clarissa made a noncommittal noise because if she didn't something snarky would come out.

She couldn't afford to be jealous of the relationship this seer may or may not have with Ronan. She'd already experienced the sting of jealousy when Ronan had talked about the blonde beauty the ancient one had killed all those years ago.

Moments later Erin offered everyone beverages, but all declined. Erin and Lachlan went up to the attic room to get it ready.

Ronan's gaze appeared bleary, as if he hadn't awakened one hundred percent from the coma. She sat beside him, eager to keep close watch. He closed his eyes and ran his hand over his chin, the movement fatigued and nothing like the powerful man she'd come to know. Then he winced and put his hand to his ribs.

Renewed trepidation spiked into her like a lightning bolt. "Are you okay?"

"I'm getting there. It shouldn't be much longer before I won't even know I had a fight with the ancient one."

"What happened between you and that fucking creep down in those tunnels?" Jared asked.

Ronan cleared his throat and opened his eyes. "He jumped me. Kicked my ass, in fact. And that hasn't happened in a very long time." He gave Clarissa a weak smile. "Over a hundred years, in fact. And then he cheated. This time he tossed me in the air like a twig. Bad for my ego, it was. I didn't think I'd meet up with him in the tunnels, but even if I did, I didn't expect him to be that potent. The things he could do were phenomenal. He's finding a source of energy from somewhere beyond the ordinary."

"What about your weapon?" Jared asked. "You couldn't get off a shot?"

"Oh, I got the shot off, all right. The bastard is now immune to silver bullets entirely. The bullet hit him straight in the heart and it didn't faze him much. Then he put his hand over the wound and the bullet fell out."

"Ah, hell," Sorley said as he sat on the floor cross-legged. "This is not good."

"What if he's absorbing the evil from the dark shadows?" Micky asked out of the blue.

Ronan enlivened a bit, as if he hadn't thought of the possibility until now. "That wouldn't surprise me."

Clarissa decided to inject some good news for a change. "Micky and I heard the good shadows whispering to us in the graveyard tonight. They said they were there, as if they wanted to reassure Micky."

Micky glanced at Jared. "I wasn't reassured. I was still scared. None of us know who or what these good shadows are."

They continued discussions about what happened to Ronan in the tunnels. He finally turned to Clarissa. "I'm sorry about your camera. I know it was expensive."

She smiled. "You're right. But the camera isn't important right now."

His return smile held sensual warmth she felt right down to her toes. *It's wonderful to see you.*

Hearing his voice in her head took her off guard, but then she tried speaking to him in her mind. *I'm so glad you're all right.*

Thank you, sweet colleen.

A flush filled her cheeks and her eyes tried to tear up. He held her gaze, the intensity and heat in that stare tempered to a slow burn. Despite the others in the room, she responded to the message in his eyes.

Moments later Erin and Lachlan came downstairs. Erin smiled as she entered the living area. "We've got the room all set up. It's not large, but it's cozy. Clean linen and the works."

"Thank you." Ronan glanced at Clarissa. "I need to speak with Clarissa privately. Then we need to talk about what we can do to stop the ancient one."

"We'd better get back to the hotel. We'll let you know if we hear anything more about the fire," Jared said. "Just give us a call if you come up with anything else we can do in the meantime."

Erin hugged them both, and before they could leave, she said, "Please be careful."

After Jared and Micky left, Ronan reached for Clarissa's hand and encompassed it in the callused, warm embrace of his touch. "I need to see you. Alone."

Lachlan's expression was just short of conspiratorial. "Don't mind us. We'll be down here or in our room."

"If you need anything just let us know," Erin said.

Clarissa knew they'd taken her bags up to the attic, too. Everyone anticipated she would stay in the same room as Ronan and it made her want to scream a little. Assuming always made her angry. Still, as she walked up the narrow steps at the end of the hall with Ronan behind her, she felt as if they'd found an oasis where they could talk and she could understand more about this mysterious vampire.

Ronan opened the door. Despite the fact it was still daytime, the fan window high on one wall didn't illuminate the room much. Ronan flicked on the light switch and a warm glow came from a small Tiffany lamp on the bedside table.

To her surprise the little room seemed far nicer and cozier than she would have expected. A tiny bathroom off to the west side of the room would be convenient. A queen-sized bed dominated the room, the headboard against the north wall and opposite the fan window across the room. Near the window two piles of boxes filled the corners. The room felt a little chilled, but it didn't bother her. Just the idea of being in this room alone with Ronan did enough to warm her clear through.

She closed the door and locked it. When Ronan heard metal *snick*, he turned and stared at her, a knowing look in his flame-tinged eyes.

What are you thinking, Ronan?

He either couldn't hear her thoughts, or he decided to ignore them. Instead he walked back toward her. As he sauntered closer, she noticed the bruise on his forehead had diminished down to a light discoloration and he walked as if his ribs no longer hurt him.

"You do heal quickly," she said, awe in her voice.

"Believe it now? That I'm a vampire?"

She took a deep breath. "Oh, I believe it all right."

When he stood in front of her, he smiled gently, a flicker of emotion slicing through his eyes. Was that discomfort she saw? Uncertainty? In wonder she gazed back at him. Tension simmered between them, and it felt equal parts tender, sexual and defiant. She resisted the wild desire tugging at her heart, demanding she surrender a part of her soul she'd never given another man. Fear surged inside, along with a last smidgen of concern for her sanity. Surely no woman with half a brain would consider falling in love with a vampire.

No. Falling in love didn't describe what she felt for him. It was far more complicated than that. Perhaps for as long as she knew this man their encounters would be filled with both the sinful and the simple.

He touched her face with a quick, gentle sweep of his index finger, trailing from her cheek to her chin. A fiery tingle built in her belly, edged by a trepidation born of the unknown.

One corner of his sinful mouth turned up. "And now you need to know everything that's brought me to this point, don't you? My life up until I became a vampire and my life as an immortal. I can see it in your eyes."

"Yes. But I need something before you tell me your story."

"Anything."

With only the slightest hesitation, she reached up and plunged her fingers into the hair at the back of his neck. Her chest brushed against his, her lower body teasing his. Again, pure flame ignited his eyes. She'd have to be careful or this vampire would consume her before she could gather her wits.

She brought his head down and touched her lips to his, keeping the kiss gentle as she sampled him. He trembled and she knew right away his restraint hung in a balance. His lips parted only slightly, but he kissed her back. Ronan's chaste response surprised her a little. When she pulled away, a gentle, almost boy-like wonder remained in his eyes.

You never cease to amaze me, Ronan Kieran.

He smiled as she stepped back. *Come sit on the bed with me. Better yet, lie with me. I promise I'll behave.*

Amazed, she nevertheless sat on the edge of the bed. She pulled her boots off in record time and scooted up the quilted blue paisley comforter. After stripping his long coat off, he removed his boots and joined her on the bed.

They lay side by side, staring at the ceiling.

She spoke to him in her mind. *Talk. You've got a lot of explaining to do.*

He laughed. "So I'm not out of the doghouse, even if you did kiss me. By the way, what was that kiss for?"

She inhaled deeply, then exhaled. "Because I'm glad you're alive. Because I should never have let you go after that camera."

He reached across the small space separating them and took her hand in his. "Damn it, Clarissa, don't start blaming yourself. If anything, I was the idiot. I shouldn't have left you. I should have convinced you how important it is that we don't hold back with each other. We've got to make a decision on what we do next."

She swallowed hard. Despite the fact this man had touched her in many intimate ways, the idea of him actually taking her continued to scare her in a primitive manner she didn't understand. She chastised herself. *For God's sake, you're not a virgin, Clarissa.*

"You didn't respond to me like a virgin," he said.

"Even when you were using your mind games on me?"

"When did I do that?" His voice rose a little, offense creeping into his tone.

She licked her lips, her mouth so dry she could hardly say it. "In the graveyard the first night, and the time you described what...what I would feel when you were inside me."

He shrugged and released her hand. "You're right, but nothing else we've done together was false emotion or bogus physical attraction. In the elevator I didn't use any vampire influence on you at all." His voice went deeper and huskier. "You were ready to fuck me."

Again that word. A remark so many disliked, but she found extremely erotic coming from his lips. The four-letter word held the ability of an incantation; she felt the power of it roaring straight down to her loins.

She turned on her left side and propped up on her elbow. Looking down at his face, she saw he'd recovered his color; the bruise had almost faded to nonexistence. "You're feeling better, right?"

"A big change in subject, don't you think?"

"No. I was worried about you."

He grinned and cupped her face again, running his fingers down through the length of her hair with a smooth and caressing motion. "You know what it does to me to realize that? I don't want you to worry about me ever, but at the same time it feels damned good to think you might have some feelings for me."

Yes. She wanted to scream at him. *I have feelings for you.*

He went silent. She sensed a change, subtle but certain. While confidence and masculine clout held him, she saw an unusual tenderness.

"What happens now?" she asked.

"Whatever you want to happen."

Serenity and maybe a trickle of exhaustion remained in his expression. Staring at his chocolate sinful eyes made a trembling renew in her belly as potent as anything she'd felt with him before. Though he appeared calm and collected, she knew he wanted her with a ferociousness that hummed right below the surface.

She couldn't move forward with this relationship if she didn't understand all she could about what she'd gotten into.

"There's so much we need to know about each other," she said in defense.

"Of course. I can already guess your favorite color."

She lifted one eyebrow. "Oh?"

"Citrine. You love the color both in your clothes and jewelry."

She glanced at the checkerboard-cut east-west oval citrine ring on her right hand, the small princess-cut diamonds along the shank on the ring adding to the sparkle. It was true she wore greens and copper-toned hues most often because they went well with her penny-red hair. She shifted and the tumble of curls that almost reached her waist shifted around her shoulders.

"The ring is a part of what you really are," he said. "Softness wrapped around sparkle and brilliance."

She couldn't admit to that without sounding arrogant. "What else do you know about me?"

His eyes lost a little of their warmth and faded to an icy assurance. "Who gave you the ring? A man?"

She laughed softly. "Is that jealousy I hear?"

"You're feckin' right it is."

Wow. She'd never imagined in all her days a man would be jealous over her and admit it to her face. Oh, yeah. He was annoyed.

"Tell me. Did a man give you this ring?"

While she could bask in the raging green monster a little longer, she didn't feel it was fair. "I bought it two years ago with my own money. I gave up long ago waiting for a man to buy me jewelry."

Tension eased from his handsome face, replaced seconds later by gentleness. "You sound lonely."

"No. Alone, but not lonely. There's a difference."

She lay back again, and he studied her with those fabulous eyes. She felt his gaze travel over her jeans and thick wool sweater. Every gaze from him smoldered with a continual arousing fire. Despite what had happened to them since she arrived in town, her attraction to Ronan refused to diminish.

"You left Pine Forest because of Jim Leggett?" This time his voice held a little anger, but not jealousy.

"Yes. I didn't mention it earlier to you and your friends, but I thought I really loved Jim. I told my parents about the strange things I'd seen and experienced here in Pine Forest, and they didn't believe me. Neither did Jim. I can't say I blamed them, but it devastated me. I left town because of that." She shrugged. "I was young. Maybe if I'd been older, things would have been different."

His frown increased. "You thought if a man truly loved you, he'd believe you."

She nodded. "Yes."

"Your heart can't trust a man because of Leggett."

A little astounded that a rough-and-tumble man like Ronan gave credence to heartbreak, she found his concern touching. "Perhaps. I know all men aren't alike, but I guess I haven't found any man I could have that deep of a connection with."

A pause between them lasted for several seconds before he turned to another subject.

"You love all things Celtic," he said. "And before you ask how I know, I noticed the Celtic knot earrings and necklace you wore yesterday. They're silver."

"Does being around silver bother you?"

He smiled. "Not at all. Being shot with it is a different story."

"But shooting the ancient one with silver should have killed him."

"Should have, but it didn't because he's too old and powerful. That's why you and I—" He cut himself off, as if she might balk if he spoke of what they must do. "Never mind that for the moment." He paused and allowed his ravenous gaze to tour over her body again. "You think your body is too lush, but it's rounded and gorgeous and every man with half a brain would appreciate it."

She flushed and the heat crawled down her neck. "Well, most men prefer a slim body."

He rolled his gaze to the ceiling and sighed in apparent exasperation. "Colleen, darlin', any thinner and you'd blow away in a strong breeze." He cupped her waist with his big hand, then his fingers trailed down her thigh. "Your legs are long and curved to perfection." He caressed back toward her waist, and his attention riveted to her breasts. "Your breasts are deliciously round and taste like a special kind of honey."

She shivered under his praise, a new heat invading her body like an army. "You are so full of it, Ronan Kieran."

He frowned. "I'm not lying to you."

Once more his touch ventured, smoothing over the side of her breast so that she quivered. Then he touched her neck, feeling the pulse at the base. He closed his eyes and took a slow, deep breath. When he opened his eyes, a conflagration invaded once again, a blazing red and yellow combination that reminded her of a fire burning out of control.

"There are things I can detect in a woman, sweet colleen. Things you can't hide from me even if you want."

"Such as?" she asked breathlessly.

"Your breath is coming fast and your pulse is, too. Your body aches with need for sexual fulfillment. Your pussy is hot. Wet."

"Ronan," she said with a gasp.

An ache centered high inside her, and she wanted his possession with a staggering desire she could no longer deny.

"You're feckin' beautiful and don't ever allow anyone to make you think otherwise."

Ronan's touch drifted down her hip and stayed there, an intimate reminder of what might occur. Staring into his luminous eyes brought trails of fire flickering over her nerve endings.

He's so patient with me.

"Why does it surprise you when I'm patient?" he asked.

She sighed, so used to him reading her mind at various intervals that she couldn't find it intrusive anymore. "Because ever since I met you I sensed incredible power. There's something violent in you. Something so fierce."

"You know I'd never hurt you."

She did understand that, but his energy influenced her, creating havoc in her otherwise calm personality. "You do something to me I can't explain. Whenever I'm with you it feels like everything is clearer. As if my life's purpose came when I walked back into Pine Forest. Yet my nerves are on fire when I'm with you."

"Are you saying being with me causes you pain?" The rasp in his voice spelled deep concern.

She touched his forearm and squeezed briefly. "No. No. I don't know if the attraction I feel for you is real or some weird chemical reaction caused by the fact you're a vampire."

"We talked about this before."

She smiled. "Forgive me for being a little skeptical."

"There's nothing to forgive."

"Good. Then you can answer some more questions."

"Then we'd better start at the beginning."

"The very beginning of time?" Clarissa asked.

Ronan propped up on one elbow and looked down on her. "Back so far the only evidence that the civilization ever existed lay buried beneath sand for eons. So you'll understand how vampires came to be."

Even with his eyes calm deep pools, she sensed his internal heat, his vampire core filled with energy and potential. Lightning fueled him and centuries of stored memories and actions.

He passed his index finger over her cheek in a gentle caress. "The vampire legend is clouded with mystery and who knows if all of it is true. Like any history things are distorted with the passage of time." His eyes darkened, as if recalling the details caused him to enter a state of meditation. "This story starts around three thousand years B. C., even before Egypt was a great civilization." His words sounded ancient, like they touched the dusty past and they'd both stepped into another world. "Close your eyes and you'll see the story unfold."

Chapter Twelve

Clarissa closed her eyes as he requested. Then, as time seemed to slide backward with feathery fingers, she realized his words became images. Night became day, and sun-baked terrain, hilly and unforgiving came to her vision as unmistakably as if she'd stepped into the past.

His voice went deeper. "The story concerns the Sumerians."

Visions unfolded in front of her and she wondered if he planted them in her mind. She saw a growing city made up of flat-topped huts with walls of reed matting stretched between wooden uprights and waterproofed with plaster made of thick mud. The huts had wooden doors and the hearths were holes in the beaten mud floor. Newer buildings arose on the outer reaches of the city, this time of mud-brick and several rooms each. As she gazed out at the spreading city, she noticed this place was a gleaming production of temples and a royal palace.

"Erech," Ronan said. "It was resurrected by Utuhegal after hordes of Gutians rushed down from the mountains and destroyed it. After a hundred years of oppression, they are free. Their new ruler is Ur-Nammu."

"You're seeing what I'm seeing," she said.

"Yes. But I wouldn't be able to visualize it if it wasn't for your ability to see and feel the past. You have a power more formidable than mine."

Cows, oxen, pigs and other animals populated the village. People ground barley in rough querns to make porridge. A man flint napped arrowheads from obsidian. She saw painted pots and vessels with incised decorations. Villagers moved in the narrow marshes in canoe-type boats.

Then Clarissa saw a beautiful, very young woman of perhaps sixteen who wore a homespun cloth dress. Bone studs pierced her ears, and a heavy necklace of beads made from carnelian, shell, and crystal hung around her neck.

"Her name is Shub-ad," Ronan said.

"What time frame is it?"

"Around two thousand one hundred years B.C., about one hundred years before the Elamites will destroy Ur. The histories have perished, but some information survives from excerpts in Babylonian chronicles." He went on, "The woman was the daughter of an influential merchant and he wished great things for her. She wanted to marry a wealthy man, a retainer of the king. But her father wanted her to be a bride of the deity at Ur-Nammu's temple, a wonderful ziggurat dedicated to the moon-god Nanna. So her father didn't allow her to marry her love."

Clarissa gazed into the distance, entranced by Ronan's words and pictured what the young woman could see. The ziggurat rose high in the distance, a massive structure with three terraced stages rising at least seventy feet above the city. The vision slowly dissolved and Clarissa opened her eyes.

"Attached to every temple there were women who formed the god's household," he said.

"Let me guess," Clarissa said. "She had to take a vow of chastity."

"No. In fact, the temple women were all prostitutes. As it happened she didn't become the entu, a first wife of the god. Instead she was a Sal-Me, a priestess of the second caste. During this time she fell in love with a man who visited the priestesses for services."

"She couldn't marry him?"

"She could but she wasn't allowed to have children by him. Because of that he was allowed to take a concubine and the concubine had six children. Shub-ad was jealous of the concubine and concocted a plot to murder the concubine and blame it on the bride of the deity, a far more powerful woman."

Rubbing her forehead as an ache centered in her temples, Clarissa said, "This is complicated."

"So it seems. When Shub-ad murdered the concubine, she discovered her husband had fallen out of love with her and in love with the concubine. The law required that Shub-ad be drowned. Shub-ad's husband couldn't bear her being put to death, even though she had murdered his beloved concubine. So to help Shub-ad he framed another one of the concubines. The attempt backfired and they were found out. Before Shub-ad and her husband were put to death, she cursed any descendents of the concubine's children. Many years later each of those children had one child of their own and those offspring were born with a deformity no one had witnessed before. Everyone knew it was because of the curse and because Shub-ad and the children's father were evil. The defect was in the blood. Each child could become invisible at will and teleport. They could move faster than any other human. They craved human blood and could feast on mortals daily."

"Vampires."

Ronan nodded.

"What happened then?" she asked, caught up in his story.

His concentration pinpointed an area above her head, as if he could see more of the story unfolding, but this time wouldn't share it with her in a vision. "Whenever their anger was aroused, the children would roam the streets and kill and maim those people no one would miss. But as they grew to adulthood, they fanned out over the region and spawned a wider veil of death and destruction."

"Did they create vampires with their bite?"

"They did. This made the plague, as the people called it, a far worse thing. Now there were hundreds of vampires where there'd once been only six."

"Did these villagers fight back?"

Ronan eased up and sat cross-legged. "A team of assassins was sent out to kill the original six vampires. One was set on fire. Another was strangled. Yet another was shot in the heart with an arrow. They resurrected and left Sumer. No one knows exactly where they went."

A question hit her. "Wait a minute. These were the first vampires?"

"Supposedly."

She pondered for a couple of minutes. "This story was probably concocted because it was an easy way to explain how vampires came into existence."

He leaned his arms on his knees. "That's my guess. But it also explains why so few vampires are actually made over time. Once a vampire bites you, it's very difficult for him stop taking your blood. Most of the time you'd be drained dry. As you saw with Lachlan, Micky, and Jared, it takes only one bite to make a half-vampire."

She tried thinking of her newfound friends as something *almost* vampire and couldn't.

"You acknowledge me as entirely vampire," he said.

She gave him a rueful grin. "Because I've seen you in action, that's why. I've seen you lift a punk off his feet using only one arm. I've seen your startling eyes."

He returned her smile. "Wait until you catch Lachlan, Micky, or Jared angry. That's a sight to behold."

She reached up and almost without forethought traced her fingers along his bearded jaw. As a teen she'd never imagined being attracted to a man with a beard. Ronan had changed all that. He trapped her hand in his and touched her fingers to his lips for a quick kiss.

"The story doesn't end there," he said. "It's said not all six of the children were evil. Some were good and they tried to help others where they could. They also vowed to hunt down the destructive vampires and rid the world of them."

Heavy silence covered the room as she absorbed what Ronan had told her. She waited for him to continue.

When he didn't speak, she allowed the question to form. "Do you believe evil created the first vampires?"

For a long time he stared at the wall, as if uncertain how to answer. "I know nature creates aberrations. It doesn't take a curse to cause oddities on earth."

"So there isn't anything, in theory, that will kill the ancient one. Except for this sexual union between you and a woman."

"Right again."

"Why you?"

"Yusuf didn't know, but the seer just said she foresaw it."

She didn't want to admit to herself that maybe Yusuf and the seer really didn't know what they were talking about.

Ronan took her arm and leaned in close to her. His warm scent swept her up. *Trust me, they have accumulated enough knowledge and experience over the years to know.*

That's an incredible story, Ronan.

Incredible, but does it ease your mind?

She considered his mental question and knew she had to understand more. Renewed apprehension made her speak again. "How did you get to be this...this way?"

"You mean charming, devilish, and—"

She gently smacked his arm. "No, you turkey. I mean a vampire. How did you become a vampire?"

His grin said he knew what she wanted all along but liked teasing her. "I was born in Limerick, Ireland around 1300 to a poor peasant mother and a father who left her shortly thereafter. I was a bastard."

Though being a bastard didn't have the same stigma today as it did in his birth time, she felt his pain like a hot poker in the gut.

"I grew up in the most rat-infested area of the city filled with crime and prostitution and hate."

She cupped his face for a second to give comfort. "That must have been horrible."

"It was all I knew. Sometimes I didn't realize how bad it was because I never left my part of the city until I was twelve." His accent thickened, like he'd gone back in time and brought history with him. "My mother was a whore."

Dishonor tinted his voice, and she felt a deep ache inside. "What your mother did wasn't your fault. That was her choice."

He snorted softly. "You think she had a choice?"

"Come on, Ronan. You've been around seven hundred years. You know she did."

His eyes hardened, a glint of the vampire she'd first met in the graveyard returning. "Her mother was a whore, and probably her mother before that. What else did she know? What opportunities do you think she had?"

She sighed. "I'm sorry, I shouldn't judge her. I'm sure she did what she thought had to do to survive."

For a long time he said nothing, and silence made the room somehow gloomier, as if the comfort turned to solemnity.

He continued his tale. "I don't know to this day if my siblings were actually full brothers and sisters. I doubt it. I was the eldest, then came Elspeth a year later. We were best friends and I loved her, but—"

When he cut himself off again, she dared look into his eyes and saw a sorrow so deep and agonizing she wanted to cry. "What happened to her?"

"A john stabbed her when she was only seventeen. He took what little money she had and left her dead in an alley."

Her mouth dropped open. "Your sister was a prostitute, too?"

He closed his eyes and she mourned the way animation left his face. Reminded of how lifeless he'd seemed not so long ago, she squeezed his arm in sympathy.

He opened his eyes. "Yes." After taking another sustaining breath he returned to his story. "My brother Balcor took it even harder than I did. He was four years younger than me. He lived to be eighty but had no children."

"And you never really knew your father?"

He shook his head. "Never."

Clarissa swallowed hard. "How did you transform into a vampire?"

"After my sister was murdered my mother went into a decline. She blamed herself for Elspeth's death, but I blamed myself even more."

Moisture touched his eyes and she wanted to cry with him. Touched by the agony she saw building behind his memories, she said, "It's all right. If you don't want to talk about it—"

"No, I have to. You have to know it all before you'll trust me."

He was right. She needed to know the man before her more than she needed to breathe.

"Balcor said he'd take care of our mother, and I couldn't take living in the stinking city any more. I also realized I couldn't do anything to help her. She was a vile and hateful woman with spite in her soul. I left Limerick with a little money I'd gathered from working in a blacksmith's shop. I headed into the country and traveled."

"Did you see your mother and brother again?"

His sarcastic smile said it all. "I did. But not until after I was made a vampire. They rejected me when I told them what I'd become." He shook his head as if to dislodge the thought. "But that happened later. I stayed in Ireland, and eventually found work as a blacksmith at Allegheny Castle near the Shannon River. I made swords and shod horses for knights in Lord Allegheny's employ."

She swallowed hard. "In one of my visions about you I saw a fortress."

"That was Allegheny. The head blacksmith, O'Hennessy, took me under his wing. He was an expert swordsman and taught me how to fight."

She closed her eyes and remembered her vision of him attired as a knight.

He smiled slightly. "You know a lot about history?"

"Enough to understand the time period."

"Then you know that going to war with your neighbors wasn't exactly an unheard of thing in that century."

"You went to war?"

He nodded. "More than once I helped make the swords, the horseshoes, and the armor that protected those that went to war. Finally one day I couldn't stand to be left on the outside anymore. I put together my own suit of armor and fought for the castle."

He sat up, and she didn't see a wince or hear a groan out of him. He looked as if he'd never been mortally wounded twenty-four hours ago. Instead he slid off the bed, stood, and stretched his arms high above his head. His muscles rippled, and she felt renewed desire spike inside her womb. Heaven help her, he was the most exciting, gorgeous, incredible male she'd ever seen, and she itched to taste him again. Instead of acting on her impulse to go to him, she waited for him to finish the story.

"O'Hennessy had a sister that lived nearby outside the castle. She had a daughter…"

Clarissa felt a surge of jealousy. "The young blonde I saw in my vision?"

"No. Darina was like my sister. She was pretty, a brunette only sixteen years old. Far too young for me." His sigh filled with hurt, a sound she never expected a tough vampire to make. "Shortly after her sixteenth birthday, one of the men in the village raped and murdered her."

"It happened to you again. You lost someone you loved."

He paced to the fan-shaped window and peered outside. "Two innocent little sisters. I started to wonder what I'd done to deserve this kind of pain in my life."

"What happened then?"

He turned back to her. "I left the castle in pursuit of whoever murdered her. I chased the bastard across Ireland into Wales but there he faded into the countryside. I was never able to find him."

"I'm so sorry, Ronan."

Silence covered the room while she pondered the horrendous agony he must have suffered over the years as he lost women important to him. Then something more intense came to mind. "What about the blonde woman I saw in my vision? She was lying on a path with her throat bleeding. You were...you looked as if you suffered her loss."

Agony spread fresh across his countenance, and for a moment she wished she hadn't mentioned it. He licked his lips, and a sardonic smile touched one corner of his mouth as if he wanted to say something sarcastic. Instead he apparently swallowed the impulse.

"That event was still to come," he said. "When I was twenty-eight I decided Ireland didn't have anything more for me. After learning to read and write under the help of a monk, I thirsted for knowledge and information. I traveled to several other countries including Wales, Scotland, Italy and Spain. I traveled back to Ireland when I was thirty."

More curiosity washed over her and she couldn't help asking, "And during all this time I suppose you lived like a monk?"

This time, when he smiled, the grin seemed genuine. "Over the years I'd courted a few women, made love to them. But I never *fell* in love. I returned to Allegheny's Castle and there I finally met someone who changed my idea of love."

"The blonde in my vision."

"Fenella. She was the daughter of a friend of mine. After courting her in secret for a few months, I offered for her hand in marriage. She said yes and her mother and father agreed to the match."

"That's wonderful."

She imagined how it might feel for this man to care for her with all his heart and knew his adoration would be a glorious, unspeakably beautiful love. How lucky Fenella had been.

His gaze blazed hot with grief, an intense hurt and longing. *Luck wasn't with us, colleen. Evil was. The village outside the castle was plagued by a vampire, and I wanted to marry Fenella as soon as I could and bring her into my protection. We were going to marry on a Monday. I remember the day like it was yesterday. But then...*

Yes?

One night the vampire came to her home and killed her mother and almost finished off her father. Her father urged her to run for the castle and safety. When I went looking for her the next day I found Fenella on a path near some bushes where the vampire had dragged her. She didn't even make it out of the village but she was in sight of the castle walls. Her throat was...she was dead. And so was my heart.

Clarissa's soul clenched as she experienced his regrets and sorrows like daggers to the stomach. Pain manacled her soul, and she allowed her tears to fall.

She became a vampire? she asked in her mind.

No. He'd drained all her blood. A vampire is only made when the sire doesn't take too much.

"Sire? The vampire who killed her?"

"Yes."

Then Clarissa saw something she never expected in a million years. First one tear, then another trickled down Ronan's face.

Her throat tightening, she managed to say, "Oh Ronan. I'm so sorry."

She stood and reached for him, twining her arms around his waist and burying her face in his chest. She wanted to sob for Fenella, for the woman who'd first loved this man and lost him. More than anything, she wanted to do whatever it took to erase the ache ablaze inside him.

His arms went around her shoulders and he buried his face in her hair. "She was beautiful, Clarissa. Beautiful inside and out and she didn't deserve what happened to her."

"Of course she didn't. I wish I could...I wish I could remove the hurt."

He rubbed his chin over the top of her head in a slow gesture of comfort. "You can."

"How?"

"Be simply being here. You're the only person I've told the whole story. Lachlan and Sorley know the half of it. They think my first encounter with the ancient one was during the American Revolution."

"You didn't tell them the real truth because it hurt too much." Her heart lurched at the implication. "You must trust me, then."

"I trust you with my life."

Warmth stole into her where moments before only pain resided. Moved by his sensitivity, by emotions she never suspected lived inside his hardened exterior, she reached up and palmed his chest. She felt the strength under her fingers and the beat of his immortal heart. His body trembled once.

"Was it the ancient one who killed her?" she asked.

"I didn't know it at the time, but yes, it was."

"What did you do after Fenella was killed?"

"I heard rumors about the vampire. That he lived in caves and the forest not far from the castle. I hunted him, but he always eluded me. I traveled throughout Ireland until I ran into a vampiress in Derry. At the time I thought all vampires were evil."

"What happened when you ran into her?"

"We fought in a room in the inn. It didn't take much for her to pin me down." A sardonic smile tilted his lips. "She tied me to the bed."

Her eyes widened, imagining him struggling with a woman more powerful than him. Then her mind made an erotic leap. "What did she do after she tied you to the bed?"

"She could have killed me," he said. "But she didn't. We talked and she explained that she, too, looked for the vampire I sought because he was evil. She called him the ancient one and said no one knew his real name but all other vampires knew he was the oldest vampire still alive. She'd heard rumors that he'd killed Fenella."

She lifted one brow. "And then she slept with you, I suppose."

His hands traveled to her hair, where he plunged his fingers into the long mass. "Believe it or not, she didn't want my blood, even thought she wanted my body. But when we made love, I begged her to make me a vampire. I told her that all my travels amounted to nothing if I couldn't hunt down the ancient one. And how would I do that if my life gave out?"

As jealousy did a spiral through her again, she pushed the useless emotion aside. To give herself some distance, she gently extracted from his arms. "She was your sire."

"Yes."

"How old were you?"

"Thirty-two."

"That's how old you are now." She spoke knowing the truth and not expecting him to confirm.

"Thirty-two I'll remain forever, unless someone or something takes my immortality from me."

As her body quavered with a combination of dread and sadness that he could be taken from her, she realized his story wasn't concluded.

"When I found my mother and my brother in Limerick again they rejected me. They were horrified."

"I can only imagine how that must have felt." Clarissa had to know more. "What was it like to become a vampire?"

"Darker and more horrible than anything I'd experienced. It's not something I'd wish on anyone."

"Tell me."

He shook his head, adamant. "Another time, if at all."

Seeing she would no longer press the issue, he pulled his gaze from hers and looked at the floor. "I've traveled around the world again, this time to many exotic corners of the world until I heard that he might be in the New World."

"America?"

"Yes. I traveled to the Colonies and met Sorley."

"How old is the brat anyway?"

He chuckled. "Three hundred years."

He paced the room, a restless marauder with an agonizing story to finish. "What happened during the Revolution?"

"I made friends with another woman, this one in her late fifties. She was a vampire hunter who'd been turned into the undead four hundred years before. Her name was Anna and she was originally from England. She explained that she needed someone to take up where she'd left off. She said the ancient one was coming for her and she didn't believe she possessed the strength to fight him any more."

Clarissa feared what he'd say next, yet she must know. "What happened?"

"I told her we could fight him together. Over the years I'd learned a lot about warfare with other vampires." He stuffed one hand through the thick fall of his hair, then stopped pacing. He turned back to her with gloom making new shadows in his eyes. "I was a fool."

She stood and walked toward him. When she stopped close, he gazed down at her with the eyes of the condemned. "You could never be a fool, Ronan Kieran."

"I could. And I was." The determined, hard line of his mouth said he wouldn't take any argument. "We traveled together for a short while until the war broke out. She settled in Maryland."

She frowned. "You couldn't fight as a soldier, right? You would have to be out in the sunlight."

"You've got that right. I had to keep my whereabouts incognito so there was no pressure for me to enlist. I ran into Sorley one night. He was being plagued by a soldier in an alley and Sorley's patience with mortals was very thin at the time. I kept Sorley from killing the man."

She put one hand to her mouth. "I thought Sorley was a good vampire, like you."

His smile touched sardonic, then slid to warm. "Sorley and I have done things we're not proud of…long ago when we were first turned immortal. From that point forward Sorley and I were friends. He decided that learning to save mortals was more gratifying than taking their blood."

She almost couldn't make herself ask. "How do you maintain your…your blood habit?"

"Right now it's through a special supplier who gets blood for me whenever I start to run low. It's kept in a freezer until I'm ready for it. Once a day is all I need." His gaze searched hers, as if uncertain she could envision him drinking blood and accept his presence. "Does that repulse you?"

She expected to feel revulsion but whatever it took to keep this man alive was all right with her.

With a flash of insight Clarissa knew that she could no longer deny what she felt down in her deepest heart. She might have known him a short time, but he'd managed to wend his way into her mind and soul so overwhelmingly she couldn't bear not to see him, touch him, and be with him. All the apprehension she'd suffered when first learning of his vampire state faded into nonexistence.

"Nothing about you could ever repulse me, Ronan."

He tugged her closer, his body rock hard against her softness, and his masculine scent building a craving inside her. His gaze told her one thing.

He wanted her now.

"There's only one way we can defeat him. There's only one way I can get revenge for Fenella and everyone else whose life has been destroyed by the beast. Make love with me, Clarissa."

Chapter Thirteen

Make love with me, Clarissa.

His words whispered again, this time in her mind.

Not fuck me or take me.

Make love with me.

She thought them the most beautiful words to part his lips.

Clarissa saw Ronan's need written across his haunted eyes, a desire to take her to new heights and make an imprint on her haunted soul. A big part of him had stolen into her and would never leave, and if she didn't love him now, she would regret it with everything inside her.

"What will happen if we…?" Her words faded, then she gathered courage again. "If we make love, did Yusuf or the seer say exactly what would happen to us?"

"No."

Plain. Stark. Ronan's gaze captured and held hers in that strange golden light.

She couldn't look away.

Wild desires lanced through her, warning Clarissa if she didn't have his touch now, she never would. His fingers trailed down her back and hovered on the rise of her butt cheeks. This man would drive her insane before she made it to her next birthday with his unrivaled strength and mysterious, beyond-gorgeous eyes.

He smiled. Dance with me.

She glanced around. There's no music.

Suddenly she heard a soft click and a small radio near the windowsill came on. Static poured from the speakers. He glanced behind him and the tuner adjusted, obeying his mental command as it turned until a smooth jazz tune slid into the air.

She laughed softly. "That's amazing. Can the others do that, too?"

"Lachlan can, although it's a strain on him if he does too much. I don't know about Jared yet or Micky."

Throbbing music instantly worked on her libido like he'd known precisely what music would enhance her sexual needs.

"Wow," she said.

A low, seductive chuckle left his throat and caused a new avalanche of desire to pulse low in her stomach. He drew her closer, pressing into her. His body felt like refuge and home. As his body nudged hers she felt his erection pressing hard, thick, and long against her stomach. Oh, yeah. He was ready to love her, all right.

No more boundaries or waiting.

No more fear or ambiguity.

Ronan thought he'd died again, this time with Clarissa's softness taunting him and begging him to seduce. Though he felt a heat blaze and build at her center, he knew she needed sensuality and a soft, gentle wooing now that feelings flowed more easily between them.

In the elevator he'd almost taken her with his ravenous sexual appetite. And while he saw fast, hard sex in their future, he knew drawing out the explosion would lead to the greatest lovemaking they'd experienced in their individual lives. Other encounters with women would be erased from his mind like they'd never been.

The knowledge staggered him, and he drew a deep breath to regain equilibrium. He'd never imagined in a thousand moons he'd meet a woman like her or would soon be buried deep inside her soul, and not just her body.

If it took sex to save Pine Forest from destruction, he would have their memory of it be pure. Nothing greedy would surround them, nothing hollow or unsure. Sex, whether mortals knew it or not, defined a human at the nucleus. Sex showed a mortal's heart, the authenticity of spirit and the naked truth of their desires both inside and out.

Ronan knew what they both needed to make life triumph over death.

Only pure, raw, primal sex.

Edges would feel sharp, softness would be feather gentle, kisses would be deep and long and imbibed with every passion imaginable. He would build, with all his vampire strength, from soft lovemaking into the most exquisite feast imaginable between two people. This act felt sacred, holy in every aspect.

He threw back his head and groaned quietly as hot wires of desire darted into his cock. He looked down on her again and saw her eyes widen as he pushed his hips against hers.

"Ronan," she whispered softly.

"Mmmm." He couldn't manage another syllable.

He closed his eyes and started to sway to the music, and her arms went around his neck. She laid her head on his shoulder and he pressed his cheek to the side of her head. Drawing her womanly soft rose and lavender scent into his body, he dined upon her wishes, dipping into her soul to see what she wanted.

Inside her mind he delved into the darkest of her wishes, the most archaic of her sexual requirements. When he saw her deepest need he smiled.

Oh yes, Clarissa. We'll do that, too.

God, Ronan. Her whispery, fluttery tone held the tiniest embarrassment mixed with delight that he'd discovered what she wanted and would give it to her.

He turned them into a slow dance as the music grew in power, the saxophone wailing, drums thudding and pumping. He brushed his hands up her back as he slipped his hands under her sweater. Her body quivered as he palmed up to her shoulders, then caressed downward. He cupped her rounded ass with one hand and drew her tighter against his hips so she could experience the solid, heavy column of his arousal. Her breath drew in sharply and he smiled.

Movement smoothed into movement as his legs brushed hers, solid column of thigh to thigh. Warmth melted and swirled until he felt she might be one with him in spirit before their bodies came together. He tried to remember the last time he felt this out of control, this glimmering with a sexual energy that seemed to erupt from his gut.

Despite his normal reticence about talking when having sex, he knew the ideal seduction. Tell her precisely what he felt. He'd never spoken of feelings while having sex.

Somehow he knew this must be different.

"I've never felt this with another woman."

Her lips parted, her eyes widening a little.

He continued, "I feel like drowning in your body, in your mind, in the promise of what will come between us tonight. Beyond this minute, this hour, I couldn't care less about what happens to me. Only your happiness, your welfare means anything. Whatever befalls me in the days leading up to Halloween, I can withstand it if you live."

Clarissa's lips parted, as if in wonder.

He smiled, filled with a roaring, overwhelming thirst to love her. As her body slid against his again, he savored the heat and shape of her breasts, her curved hips.

Music throbbed, the beat going silky and smooth as a lover's touch.

As he twirled her, she giggled, and the unexpected humor made him grin. She continued to smile and he kept his gaze on her as the fever rose. He felt it surging inside him, demanding a release. Clarissa's smile faded, replaced by her own glittering, possessive expression.

"Mother of God, by everything that is holy," he whispered, "I want you to feel me in your blood and bones. Nothing matters but your acceptance."

"Ronan." Her soft response choked with emotion.

Emboldened by her positive reaction, he continued expressing himself. "I can't get enough of looking at you." He brushed his fingers over her cheek. "Your rounded cheeks, your perfect, small nose, and the rosy glow in your skin that compliments the copper penny red hair." He kissed her nose. "Your blue eyes sparkle like crystal and are more pure than the waters of the Caribbean. You're so damned beautiful."

Moisture touched her eyes and for a second he thought he'd made a terrible mistake. Then she smiled. "Thank you. I don't know what to say, Ronan. I'm..."

He kissed her lips softly, brushing over them. "Then just listen."

Her lips touched his chin, then traveled to his throat. Shivering under the tentative brush of her lips, he slipped one hand into her hair and gently tugged her head back so she would look into his eyes. He luxuriated in the sensation of her hair cascading over his hand and the way her lips parted as if waiting for a kiss.

Clarissa saw the change in him and his eyes went supernova. Dazzling light sparkled like stars in his irises. She felt Ronan in her mind, aware he searched for an opening, a vulnerability that would make her all his.

God, yes, she wanted it. His sweet words had disarmed her.

She'd never expected this tough-as-rawhide man to speak so gently, so openly of his feelings. She wanted to surrender at the same time she conquered, wanted to give at the same time she received. No other man could do this to her, make her feel like diamonds and starlight and infinite space all wrapped into one. As she danced with him, she couldn't imagine another world but this one in the future.

She would be with him, or with no man at all.

Her stomach clenched as he brushed his cock against her, and she ached with the deepest longing to take him high and hard straight into her center. Her touch traveled over his shoulders, caressing the hard musculature that cradled her so tenderly. Such a big, powerful man, and he treated her like fragile glass.

Oh, yes. They would come together tonight, and when it happened the fireworks might incinerate all in its path.

As her breath quickened and her pulse sped up, control departed. She didn't know if she'd be able to handle this rampant sensuality, this tantalization much longer. Potent waves of desire swamped her.

Doubt did one last dance. She'd always done the practical thing since she'd left Pine Forest all those years ago. Always played things safe to keep pain away.

No. His mind spoke to hers as he stopped dancing. He cupped her face and captured her gaze. Heart rose in his dark eyes and flickered like flames in a hearth. Don't let the past come between us.

She placed her hands over his and drew upon the tenderness shining through the staggering desire she saw within his gaze. Before she could doubt again he covered her mouth with his.

Eager, she relaxed into his touch, ready for a final showdown between their bodies. His lips moved with slow exploration. His tongue dipped, tasting the tip of her tongue with slight licks that enticed and teased.

Taste me, his mind whispered. Feel me deep inside you.

Yes. Oh yes.

This time she didn't want him planting the suggestion of sexual play in her mind. She wanted his naked body buried inside her.

When she shivered with longing he broke the tender kiss and spoke softly against her lips. "Now."

Liquid rushed warm and slick and dampened her panties. He inhaled deeply and instinct told Clarissa he'd scented her arousal.

"Mmm." He closed his eyes and drew in another breath.

His lips traveled to her ear, his words whispered dark and seductively deep. "Open all to me. Let me see you. All of you."

Without hesitation she stepped back from him and reached for the hem of her sweater. She pulled it over her head and tossed the garment aside. She reached behind and unclasped her bra, eager beyond words to comply. Her nipples went hard and tight as his gaze touched them.

His stare assessed her with pleasure, his lips parting and eyes gleaming with feral hunger. Her breasts felt larger, higher, taut with a desire for his caress.

Finally he did. He cupped her in his large hands. Every stroke around her nipples, every gentle squeeze sent a sweet, stinging need deep between her legs. She hungered for his kiss.

He released her breasts. Take what you want.

At his urging she leaned in and twinned her arms about his neck. Their mouths met and the kiss turned fierce. Tasting, melding, blending. His lips moved over hers ravenously in response. His mustache tickled her, but with an intense brush that heightened her yearning. To feel more of his masculinity, she palmed his hair-rough jaw.

Without indecision she sought a deeper meeting and the continual sweep of his tongue over hers sent wildfire into her veins and joy into her soul. His kisses searched and coaxed all her fantasies to life, even those she hadn't known she possessed. He drew back and his expression went from sultry to lightning hot.

As if he could no longer contain himself, his hands worked at her waistband and with two quick movements her jeans came undone. Then, with a grip that surprised her, he jerked and her jeans ripped at the seams.

She gasped and her eyes widened. Excitement mixed with total shock. "Ronan Kieran."

He laughed, enjoyment at her surprise dancing in his gaze. Her jeans fell to the floor in a torn heap.

His nostrils flared and his lips parted. "I'll buy you a dozen others."

Then with another faster than light movement, he tore her white cotton hip-hugger panties right off her ass.

Waves of desire rippled through her as he cupped her naked ass and drew her against him. He stroked her already sensitized skin and she quivered.

His lips traveled down her throat, kissing and licking. Cupping one breast lightly, he tested her skin with feather light touches. Aroused beyond all belief, she writhed in his hold. Gently he gripped her nipple between thumb and finger and pinched. She moaned as he continued the torturous movement, a steady delight that made her squirm in his grip. Then to make the sensation more excruciatingly wonderful, he reached between them and trapped both nipples between his caressing fingers. As he whispered into her ear, he massaged the tight buds with persistent but sweet twisting and plucking.

You like that, sweet colleen?

Do I like it? God, yes.

With relentless strokes he continued to torture her nipples. Ripples of pleasure scorched her veins. She saw the brilliant flash of his smile as he leaned down and took her between his hot lips. She gasped and leaned back as he cupped her breast and his tongue danced over her hardened flesh. Uncompromising, he switched to the other breast and flicked over the tip until she moaned. Hot, wet, the sensation of his tongue making coarse sweeps across her aching nipples drove her into a mindless state. She plunged her fingers into the thick, cool strands of his hair and held on for the ride. Persistent, he stroked and suckled until she thought she'd go mad.

Seconds later he growled low in his throat and gazed at her. She'd never seen a man's expression as molten, as full of desire as Ronan's and she knew she never would see another man look at her quite this way.

As if she belonged to him.

At one time the thought might have rankled. Hell, two days it would have pissed her off. Now it made her wet with lust and a thirst deep in her cunt that begged to be quenched by his body alone.

He backed her slowly toward the bed and urged her to sit on the edge. Watch me.

The sound on the radio edged a little higher. He drew off his boots and tossed them away. Without hesitation he slowly pulled his sweater over his head and it landed alongside her garments.

As the fire leapt higher in his eyes, she allowed her attention to glide over the broadness of his shoulders down the finely-carved, hard musculature of his long arms. Sighing, she eagerly devoured the sight of his sinew-bound chest. Hair curled over his pectorals, then slimmed down until it broadened over his six-pack stomach. Her lips parted in silent pleasure, her body reacting to his nudity with a fresh rush of liquid between her legs. Oh, my heavens. Ronan Kieran was, without any argument, the most gorgeous man on heaven or earth, bar none.

His flattened his hands over his stomach and drew them down with a slow movement toward his waistband. Instead of unbuttoning the fly, he allowed his hands to cup over his cock.

"Ronan." Her voice sounded husky to her ears, and she shivered as he caressed his cock once, then twice.

His ability to touch himself, his lack of modesty, served to inflame her more. Apparently knowing how much she liked it, he did it again.

"Please," she said. "If you do that again I think…"

"What?" His voice came rusty and low with desire.

"Please just take them off."

As the seductive music throbbed and sluiced through the airwaves, she licked her lips in anticipation.

He slowly flicked open each button, then drew the jeans down and off his legs. He kicked them away.

Her libido went into riot. Then she said something out of character, but oh so true. "Oh shit, Ronan. Holy God."

One corner of his mouth tilted upward. "Yeah."

Yes. The man had a lot to be proud of. Literally.

His cock stood at full attention slightly away from his belly. She'd known his cock was big, but now she saw his length and thickness nestled in a thick bush of curling black hair, it made her ache to devour him. Engorged, his cock looked so hard she knew it would caress places inside her no man had reached before. She wanted him in her mouth, in her heat, in—

As the forbidden idea slid through her mind, she gasped.

We will do that, too, he said in her mind.

You're so large—

You can take me. Everywhere.

A furious blush made her feel a little vulnerable. As his gaze coasted over her nakedness in appreciation, she wondered again where her reserve disappeared.

Burned away by the inferno between us, his mind said to hers. There is nothing we need to hide from each other. Open to me and I will open to you. Lie back.

She did, closing her eyes and awaiting what he had in store for her next. As he knelt between her legs, he parted her thighs and proceeded to dine.

With a soft touch he tested her moistened labia with his fingers. His tongue followed, licking with a swift, tickling swipe over the wet folds. She shivered and groaned with bliss as he feasted. Her breathing quickened, her heart beating faster and faster as her excitement rose. She felt a flush start in her skin spreading spread outward over her body in rolling waves.

He licked each fold tenderly and so lightly she quaked against him in building pleasure. Again and again he sipped her, pressing a kiss to a fold after he licked it. He slid his tongue inside her cunt. She arched up and moaned. She'd never felt anything so hot, so fantastic as he pushed his tongue in and out, in and out. He trapped her clit between his fingers and tugged and rubbed gently as he tongue-fucked her.

Clarissa couldn't stand it.

She wouldn't make it.

As his tongue left her cunt, he immediately slipped two fingers deep inside. He sucked her clit and she arched against him in overwhelming pleasure.

"Oh, Ronan," she whispered in desperation. "Please."

She grasped the comforter, gripping it tightly, then releasing it as waves of continual enjoyment passed over her.

Another lick passed over her sensitive clit and he moved his fingers within her slickness. Her walls clenched over his fingers as he moved silkily inside the sensitive, tight grip of her cunt. His fingers moved back and forth as his tongue tapped, licked, and his lips suckled.

When his tongue flicked over her clit one more time, she reached the end of her endurance. Everything within her body melted with a sensual ease and then ignited like dry tinder under a lightning strike. Orgasm burst through her center and poured into her like a flood. She gasped and cried out, the small whimper a mere sound of total surprise and shocking heaven.

All the while his fingers worked inside her, prolonging the contractions. Then he pulled out of her, his feral expression telling her there could be a lot more where that came from. She couldn't stand it. She had to have him now before the stars fell from the sky.

She said the one thing she never imagined saying to a man before, was too shy to say in other physical relationships. "Fuck me, Ronan. Now."

He smiled, a look of wonder and male lust mixed.

He reached down and pulled her up, his arms coming around her as she stood. She giggled softly, her breath still coming fast. He marched her backwards until she came up against a wall.

Ronan gripped her waist. "Wrap your legs around me when I lift you."

Lift her? She weighed too much—

He powered her upwards, and with a gasp of surprise she lifted her legs and started to anchor them around his waist. She didn't have time to wonder anything else, to think anything else. Clarissa felt the big, swollen head of his cock at her slick, aroused entrance.

His eyes glowed full force and she knew he'd take her with a hunger both frightening and potent.

Clarissa?

Yes.

She drowned in the fierce fire she saw in his eyes.

Blunt and unyielding, his sex parted her folds, inch by inch.

As the thick intruder burrowed into her, she groaned in shivery delight. "Ronan, Ronan. Oh, my God."

She quivered in ecstasy as each hot probe brought unbelievable bliss. His hardness stretched her wide but she was so hot for him it didn't matter. She opened easily to his intrusion. With a half groan he thrust full and hard and she gasped and moaned as he pressed all the way to her womb, his black pubic hair mixed with her russet curls.

Her sigh of satisfaction escaped as he pressed her back against the wall, his face buried in her neck. He breathed hard, as if his control teetered on edge. Instead of thrusting he rested inside her. She clenched around him, her muscles shivering as she adjusted to his tremendous thickness.

As she tilted her head back, his lips found the underside of her chin. With excruciating slowness he drew his cock out, his width sliding against her vaginal walls with a caress that caused her breath to sluice out in astonished pleasure.

Then his mouth found hers and his tongue plunged deep at the same time he thrust hard. She gasped against his lips as lights seemed to go off in her head and she climaxed around the hard, hot cock buried deep up inside her.

She wanted to scream but was so breathless she drowned in his kiss instead.

Slow. Slow, colleen.

She didn't know if she could stand it; her arousal continued to burn like a steady flame. The last two orgasms only made her want him more. He thrust with a slow, languid back and forth movement, her weight held easily in his grip. Each long, fixed thrust turned into another, back and forth, back and forth, until the friction caught her up in another inconceivable pinnacle. She shuddered and gripped his wide shoulders, her fingers digging into his flesh. He didn't seem to notice, his cock burrowing steadily as he fucked her through another climax.

It must be the end. It had to be.

No, his mind assured her.

She didn't know whether to protest or beg for more.

Again he drew the tempo out, a steady push and pull that kept her wet, aching, demanding more. She didn't care if she'd be sore in the morning, all she could feel was the tingling burgeoning again, ready to bring her to another climax.

We can fuck all night, his voice rasped in her head. Until the sky comes down. We can do it any way you want.

He gripped her waist tighter and moved them to the bed. As he laid her down he slipped from her heat and she made sound of protest.

Ronan grinned. "Don't worry. There's more."

As he came down on top of her, his hard thighs parted hers and he slipped easily back into her warmth. She gasped at the beautiful sensation. Wriggling a little, she tried to force him impossibly deeper.

Again he drew back and plunged hard. Her gasp turned to repeated moans as he thrust, hammering between her legs. Sharp and full, climax threatened to rip her to shreds.

Ronan buried his face in her throat, his breathing ragged. She felt the sweat running down his body, yet as he fucked her, his strength seemed to grow. His hips churned against hers as his sharp thrusts pounded deep inside her.

Vampire heat ran in his blood, but although he shoved deep inside her like a madman, it didn't hurt her. Lust conquered as she sensed his total loss of control. She clenched around him again as a sweet climax burst. She was crying, the tears of unrelenting ecstasy tearing her up. Arching against him she accepted his unyielding possession. Throwing her head back, her lips parted and a whimpering cry left her throat as her entire body trembled.

"Feck," he said gutturally.

She opened her eyes and saw the savagery still here, still holding sway over him. His eyes gleamed like a predatory animal, his lips drawn back as he held his cock deep inside her. "You. You're feckin' beautiful. And we're not done yet."

He pulled out of her, and when she frowned in confusion, he slowly turned her over so that she came up on her hands and knees. Before she could speak he pushed deep between her thighs. He took her with a steady pace. He reached under and clasped one nipple and tugged. As she responded to the sweet pressure, he also flicked his fingertip repeatedly over her clit. Sensitive tissues begged for more. He fucked her tirelessly, hammering with the stamina of a bull. His thrusting built in speed and she knew this would be it. She couldn't possibly come again. As the power built, she thought she might faint, her breath rasping her throat.

Seconds later, she detonated as a cry ripped from her throat.

He continued to fuck her, prolonging the waves as they rocked her.

Ronan rammed between her thighs one last time and shook as an uninhibited roar left his throat. Hot liquid spewed inside her as he thrust two more times, his breathing ragged.

Excitement filled Clarissa. She'd never known what it felt like to have a man's naked cock caress her inside, much less his ejaculate spill inside her. But this wasn't just any man, this was a vampire. Her vampire.

The immortal she might be falling for.

As her mind whirled with ebbing excitement and a growing sense she would never be the same, an act flashed into her mind. A sexual act she knew he wanted, but she knew she wanted, too. She was ready for it. Primal awareness split open, reviving long withheld needs she'd never indulged.

Aftershocks made her cunt tighten over his cock and he moaned. Intermingled with the tender emotions rocking her, a languid sense of total satisfaction and unbelievable pleasure made her sigh.

Now she understood what it meant to be fucked out of her ever-livin' mind.

"Do you trust me?" he asked, his voice husky with sex.

So softly she could barely hear herself speak, she said, "Yes."

He kissed her shoulder. "I won't hurt you."

She believed it with all her heart. "I know."

Gently he slipped from her body, and as she shivered with the sensation, he kept her hips tilted up. He reached between her legs and smoothed their liquids between her buttocks. As his fingertips touched her where no man had touched before, she quivered with sinful excitement. The more she thought about the act, the more it made her crave, delight, want what would come. With measured strokes he wet her forbidden entrance. She didn't know if she could stand the tickling that wasn't quite a tickling, the small forays of his middle finger just inside the entrance. Each tiny probe made her wriggle, tormented and aroused.

"More," she whispered.

His hot breath touched her neck as he laughed. "With pleasure."

Seconds later he pushed his finger slowly, inch by exquisite inch into her anus. As she absorbed the unusual but exciting sensation, she heard his voice in her head. Oh, holy Mother. Forbidden, all right. Tight.

As he moved gently, the friction caught her by surprise. Tingles of reaction zipped into her stomach as he drew his finger out, then pushed in, then out. Working her body, he kept his finger buried in her ass and reached around to touch her clit.

She jumped, unprepared for the duel pleasures. "Oh, Ronan."

All right?

Yes. Oh yes. More.

He complied. Manipulating her clit with steady strokes, he barely moved his other finger, keeping himself embedded. She writhed in his hold, unaccustomed to the amazing feelings rocketing inside her like quicksilver. When his touch left her clit and he removed his finger from her, she groaned in dissatisfaction.

Ronan moved around behind her and nipped her shoulder softly. "Easy. There's much more. Lean down on your forearms and tilt high."

She did as asked, including spreading her legs wide. She could hear his breath sluicing in and out, a testament to his excitement with what they planned to do.

Seconds later she felt the blunt tip of his cock nudge her anus. Clarissa gasped.

"Clarissa?"

She knew what he asked. He needed her permission again, her reassurance. "Please. Do it."

His hands grasped her butt cheeks and pulled them apart a little farther. With a small surge he probed and entered a scant inch. A light pinch made her inhale, but no real pain. Excitement made her press back against him, eager for more. A whirling eddy of needs began to emerge inside her, as if that first entry signaled to her body that she was free. Anything she wanted, nothing she couldn't handle; it would all be hers under this man's touch.

Without moving, he reached under and trapped a nipple between his fingers. He pinched and rolled the aroused peak and she writhed back, and another inch of his cock slid into her.

"That's it, sweet colleen. Open up to me. Open."

As he rolled her nipple, he found her clit and brushed over it. She shook in sublime pleasure as his fingers manipulated her clit and massaged her nipples one after the other in a play of delights. She moved back, wanting another inch of him before he was apparently ready to give it.

She moaned softly as a shot of pleasure zigzagged into her lower belly as he probed yet another increment. When he pulled back the friction made her gasp. "Oh, yes. Yes."

He didn't stop this time, probing back into her with steady pressure until she felt him filling, stretching her. Then he pulled back, thrust. Pulled back. Pushed. Until he established a steady, measured, but very gentle back and forth motion. He wasn't going too deep, and Clarissa knew that Ronan understood any more would hurt her this first time.

As she closed her eyes he tucked his cock back inside, then withdrew. His touch became aggressive on her clit and nipple. Each twist of her nipple, each brush over her clit fired new life into her arousal until she shook and shivered and wanted him to finish her excitement more than she'd wanted anything else they'd ever done together.

A soft growl left his throat and the primitive sound made her shiver with a delight that matched the incredible sensation of him moving inside her. The friction and his words set her off and she started to shake. As her body built into the strongest climax yet, he quickened his tempo.

Her mind in a total chaos of ecstasy, she couldn't stop the whispered pleas coming from her throat. "Please, please, yes, yes."

With a growl he burst into climax, and the feeling of his orgasm pouring liquid into her set Clarissa off. As he held tight inside her, Clarissa's womb seemed to clench and ripple with an earthquake so strong she sobbed a breath. Dizziness assaulted her as the last trembling subsided.

When he pulled away from her seconds later, he turned her around and drew her down to the bed with him.

Ronan could barely move let alone think. He wanted her warmth snuggled tight against him for the rest of the night, protected in his arms. The smooth jazz still pulsed in the room.

Through a haze he tried to recall the last time he'd had sex quite like this and couldn't remember. He hadn't slept with a woman since Selima in Morocco and that experience paled in comparison to the mind-blowing passion he'd felt in Clarissa's arms. He'd thought he would never stop coming. His bones felt rattled, his muscles exhausted, his body enraptured by a strange peace. Everything inside him stilled, as if ready for a great revelation. It was, plainly, the best feckin' sex he'd ever had.

Power swelled in his immortal blood, his skin, his sinews. Ronan thought he felt his muscles changing in some odd way he couldn't define. The tightening and releasing in each fiber made his body quake for one second.

He kept his eyes closed, and he felt her hands searching his face, his shoulders and arms. "You're trembling."

When he opened his eyes, he contemplated her sea blue gaze and saw deep concern. "I'm fine." He kissed her softly. "I think we could both use some sleep, though."

Her breath ruffled against his beard as she nuzzled him, then rested her head on his chest. "Uh-huh."

Ronan retreated to the bathroom to clean up. When he returned to the bed he brought her close against him. As tiredness started to take over, he remembered to use his mind to turn off the radio.

He drifted in a half-awake state of mind even after he noticed she'd fallen asleep. A sense of possession ran through his blood, a stamp on his life. No matter what happened from this moment, there could be no pretending they hadn't joined in the most erotic, most everlasting act between a man and woman.

An old worry kept him from sleeping for a time. He wanted to know how this joining would help him defeat the ancient one. What signs should he look for?

As he lay peering into the night, no answers came.

Chapter Fourteen

I could have killed him.

The ancient one wondered, as he walked through snow along the road not far from Erin Greenway's home, why he hadn't finished off Ronan Kieran when he had the chance. He wouldn't admit that the fight had drained him as well. His feeding, which included an old homeless man holed up in a shack near on the outskirts of town, didn't quite sustain him. No, a fresh killing before the night extinguished would bring him the power he needed for the next night's bedlam.

Yet he couldn't be happy knowing Ronan Kieran probably walked at this moment. He would have staked him, but he hadn't acquired silver stakes when he came on this journey to Pine Forest. He hadn't expected opposition.

Something else plagued him. Why, if he had acquired the force of the deepest evil in those tunnels...couldn't he kill the Irish bastard with one sweep of his arm?

Niggling uncertainty entered his brain. It hit sharp and painful, giving him an uneasy sensation.

In the meantime, he would get on with the business creating hell on earth, of formulating nightmares for everyone in town. Of course, he wouldn't turn down a heady draught of human blood if given opportunity, but he must plan for the time to come.

The Time.

He would call it that from now on. He thought of horrible events in the world that scarred it for life, the days where a mere mention brought mortals into a sinister place.

9-11.

December 7, 1941.

Perhaps 1066. Doomsday, some had called it.

He knew people fixated on these days but they eventually faded into memory, until all who'd heard of the event recalled it with the merest hint of emotion.

One hundred years ago in this little town people had thought the world was coming to an end.

Now they would think so again.

Curious, he continued down the road toward the fire turning the sky to molten red and yellow. His smile broadened for a moment before turning into a frown. The evil he'd called upon in the tunnels permeated his undead soul, his seething hatred growing by leaps and bounds. Yet one wicked part of him loathed that malice more dreadful dictated from now on what would occur from this point forward.

He didn't like being controlled at all.

He might be joined with the darkness that resided under the ground and in the night, but his ego stung. Discomfort wriggled over his undead skin, almost like the goose bumps suffered by mortals.

A new emotion, or perhaps an old one, crept closer to him. What was it?

Fear?

He tried to remember when he'd last been afraid and he couldn't recall. Perhaps before his immortal life began. But that had been too long ago to remember much about it.

The strange sensation almost made him want to run and pretend he'd never felt it. Because if he did it might mean something odd, something horrible could happen to him.

How can it? I am the one they all fear. Every vampire on earth knows of me, respects my power. When Pine Forest is consumed in the fire of its own greed and hate, I will have another hellfire notch to add to my legend.

Again the discomfort niggled at the back of his mind.

Sharp pain shuddered through his midsection and he fell to his knees in the snow. It was as if...as if the fight he'd had with Ronan Kieran actually did damage. Another jolt of electrified misery tore through his head and he fell onto the snow bank by the road. As he lay in the snow, he closed his eyes and rode out an agony so acute he considered screaming.

No.

No.

This never happened.

Each stinging jolt defied all pains he'd experienced his entire mortal and immortal life. Bewildered, he allowed the sizzling pain to lurch through him. Whatever happened, he would endure.

Then the voice came to him.

You are not the utmost. You are not the power, the voice said. My iniquity supersedes all others. And you will obey.

"Who are you?" he asked through a tight throat.

A laugh edged through his mind like knife cutting into cheese. You sought me in the tunnels and brought me into your body. I am you but I am not.

The ancient one realized then, with astounding lucidity, how much he'd given up to absorb the greater evil.

Again the voice commanded, and the pain started to ebb. You will obey or be destroyed. You will comply or suffer.

He waited for more instruction but nothing came. That which possessed him went silent.

Shrugging off the aberration, the ancient one proceeded. Shaken but not broken, he refused to acknowledge what had happened.

He smiled as he came to the road where fire trucks and police cars congregated. An old structure, its skeleton smoldering and smoking, caught his attention. Not entirely satisfied with the mayhem he felt building around him, he decided more must be accomplished.

* * * * *

The light went on next to the bed and a warm touch gripped Ronan's right shoulder. "Ronan?"

The soft voice belonged to the gorgeous woman he'd fucked into oblivion less then a few hours ago. Clarissa's fingers smoothed over his back in a comforting caress. He shivered under her palm. Tenderness and fierce protectiveness welled inside him. He drew Clarissa down on the bed and hovered over her.

He buried his face in her throat and slid his lips down the long, white column. As she shivered he knew he'd given her a tiny taste of what he could do to her. She thought what they'd done earlier was extreme. She hadn't seen anything yet.

"You all right?" he asked.

"Yes. I'm sorry I woke you. I had a bad dream."

He brushed stray hair away from her face. "I'm sorry about the dream."

"I don't even remember what it was about now I'm awake."

He savored looking at her breasts with their rounded curves and rosy nipples. He could almost taste her on his tongue. "Have I ever told you how beautiful you are? Because I'm going to tell you again. You're the sweetest, toughest, sexiest woman I've ever known."

Her brows pinched together. "I wish I could believe that. You've known dozens of women across seven hundred years."

"Shhh." He pressed a half dozen kisses across her forehead, her nose, her cheeks and chin. "Don't doubt yourself. From the first moment I saw you I felt fierce attraction."

Her eyes widened and she smiled broadly. "Oh, was that what that was?"

"Okay. Attraction is a mild word for it. I wanted to fuck you right there in the graveyard."

"That's kinky."

"It could be."

"Some would say sleeping with a vampire is insane."

He expected her to laugh, but instead her eyes shimmered with unshed tears. Her lower lip trembled just a little. That satiny curve tempted him to sin.

She cupped his face with one hand and slid her palm over his beard. "I can't believe this is happening. It doesn't seem entirely real. You're a vampire and I just made love with you. It's amazing and incredible and totally unbelievable."

"Think of me as just a man."

She rolled her gaze to the ceiling, then tested the muscles in his shoulders. "Right. You just made love to me for longer than any man ever has." A flush spread over her cheekbones. "I mean...you're supernatural, Ronan. No man I've been with has ever been able to manage that many thrusts for that—"

She gulped as her face turned more crimson.

He laughed, glad the tears had left. "Remember what I told you about vampires while we were stuck in the elevator? That we can fuck as long as long as it takes to get a woman off?"

Her nose was cherry red now. "Yes."

"That we can draw a woman's orgasms out and give her dozens at one session?"

"Yes."

"Then you know what we did earlier was just a start."

She shook her head, looking amazed. "I don't believe it."

"Well, believe it." When silence settled over them, he looked deep into her eyes.

"I have a strange question." One of her eyebrows quirked up. "Well, maybe it isn't a strange question. I thought vampires drank blood during sexual arousal."

He couldn't blame her for asking. "Sometimes they do. Disciplined ones who aren't interested in hurting mortals don't bite them on the neck."

"Oh." The quiet syllable sounded amazed.

"You wondered why I didn't bite you during sex."

She nodded. "Yes."

"Because I've had centuries of practice at not biting."

"Would you ever bite again?"

He brushed his fingers over her cheekbone then down to her chin. "I don't know. Sure, and it's very dangerous for a vampire to try and stop once he's taken blood from a mortal."

"Yet the ancient one did when he bit Lachlan, Micky, and Jared."

"More by accident than design. They were lucky. Their blood must have been rich and thick enough to satisfy him. It surprised me when they survived the attacks. You know how many people have died in this town since this mayhem started at the beginning of the month."

He remembered too well the fright in her face mixed with defiance on the first night he'd met her. She would be a worthy opponent for any vampire, but he didn't want her within ten feet of the ancient one.

She yawned and wriggled against him slightly. Her skin slid over his with sensuous results. A jolt of lust heated his body like a firestorm. His cock spiked into one of the most intense hard-ons he could remember having.

Shit. She would drive him insane.

The serene, trusting softness in her exquisite face drove him mad with need. He could barely keep from parting her thighs now and plunging deep inside. He knew she had to feel his cock against her, almost begging—hell, almost whining for entrance.

A tiny smile hit her lips. "Come inside."

"What?"

With gentle urging, she brought him over her. He melted with pure pleasure as he realized what she wanted, and he couldn't help but smile. Without hesitation he touched his cock to her soft creamy slickness, then pushed. When he rested fully inside her, he wanted to shout with joy. She felt amazingly hot and wet wrapped around him. With a staggering jolt he acknowledged heaven was anywhere he could be with her, inside her. Her eyes widened as he looked down on Clarissa, their blue structure drawing him down, down into a sea storm. Sensations lifted him up and away from thought and into the corporeal.

Instead of moving inside her, he licked across one nipple with slow, sweet consideration. One lap, two—he tasted her like she was the most exclusive delicacy. With one slow taste, he drew her nipple deep into his mouth, then feathered it with his tongue. She arched against him, moving her hips, but he refused to thrust. Instead he kept his cock buried high inside her and continued the torture of his slow, slow licking. He pulled a nipple deep between his lips, then suckled. On and on he licked, going from one nipple to the other with agonizing attention. He gently cupped one breast, then twisted the aroused nub. Moments later he settled in to suck hard and long while he tweaked the other nipple between thumb and finger.

Moans caught low in her throat and broke free as he devoured her breasts. When he felt her wet tightness start to clench around him, to shiver with approaching climax, his hips moved into a measured thrust. Push deep, pull away, push until his balls were tucked up against her buttocks, drawing out until just the tip of his cock remained inside her. He moved his hips in a stirring rhythm and she moaned each time he pulled back, then sank deep.

She came with a harsh inward breath as her silken walls tightened over his cock. Her eyes fluttered shut and her lips parted as her body gripped his. Her entire body quaked as a low gasp left her.

Music seemed to sing in his head, the gentle voice of an angel calling him to dance with her in the most ancient ritual of man and woman merging as one. Divinity resided in this motion, in the way he discovered light within her. Ronan continued his need for her, unwilling to let her body take his seed just yet. Although he could never have children with Clarissa, he ached for what couldn't be. He wanted to make a child with her with fierce need.

What would it be like for her genes to mix with his? To share in the generation of something new that only the two of them could create?

Tasting her lips, he kissed her thoroughly, willing to prove she belonged to him. With deep, stabbing thrusts he made another claim on her, one that any other vampire could detect. Unrelenting and without mercy his body danced inside her, worshiped her body as a holy place.

He felt the snarl rising in his throat as he jammed high inside her one last time and all restraint within him broke apart. He roared and spilled inside her. With a ragged sigh of satisfaction, he rolled to the side and brought her into his arms.

She glanced at the bedside table. "Nine o'clock."

"I have to get up. I can't believe I even slept at night. That doesn't happen often for me."

"Just after you've had sex?"

"Not just any sex. Mind-altering, out-of-this-world sex."

Her mouth, as tempting as any sin he could imagine, turned up at the corners. "Ronan we have to start thinking about what we're going to do. We don't have very long. Things are happening as we lie here. Bad things."

"Have you had any more visions?"

"No. Just feelings. I'm jittery and restless. I feel like something big might happen at any time."

He touched her chest with his index finger and drew a slow path around her right nipple. When she wriggled, he threw a leg over her thigh so she remained still.

"I feel it, too, Clarissa. There's edginess in the air."

A frown turned down the corners of the mouth he'd thoroughly ravished. Then one tear escaped and rolled down her cheek. The sight threatened to tear a hole through his heart.

He smiled and kissed her nose. "We'll get through this." He kissed her nose again and her mouth. "Please don't cry. I can't stand it when a woman cries."

As a few more tears escaped, she gave him a quavering smile. "Oh? What do you do when women cry?"

"It depends on the woman." Tenderness stirred in his heart. "In your case it makes me ache to hold and protect you."

Instead of allowing her to speak, he covered her mouth with a devouring kiss.

A new wave of heady, erotic stimulation raced over Clarissa's skin. She didn't want to think about insecurities, or the few doubts she harbored about bone-melting sex with Ronan. Instead she allowed his assurances and the way he touched her to drive away tears of fear and misgiving. She became a being of sensation and pure sexual energy. She'd started to lose track of the number of times they'd made love.

Raw need overwhelmed her as his kiss deepened. His tongue touched hers with light flicks, as if coaxing a virgin into compliance. She answered with silky strokes and sampled him as he'd tasted her. Plunging her tongue deep into his mouth, she demonstrated she knew something about driving a man wild. As he groaned he rolled over and pulled her on top of him. Their legs tangled together and she savored the feeling of one hairy, hard thigh as it pushed against her moist, sensitive tissues. His big hands slid hotly and possessively over her back and landed on her ass. He cupped, caressed and teased.

As she sat up, she nestled his hard cock against her clit and pressed downward. She found the perfect spot and lined it up. As she moved her hips, she rubbed her clit against his shaft. Sharp arousal spiked in her stomach.

"God, yes," he said, his eyes going from melting chocolate to sunlight bright.

He cupped her breasts and twisted her nipples lightly, his big hands gentle. She closed her eyes and took in every physical feeling as he heightened her need. Hot arousal spilled from her, dampening her core and making it ache. As the motion continued, she rocked her hips and he stroked her nipples without mercy.

When she opened her eyes, craving starkly lined his features. From the flush on his cheekbones, to parted lips, to the way his hips rotated against tender, wet folds and the way his muscles bunched and flexed, he defined male animal. It would be so easy to surrender everything to Ronan. Give over her mind, her body, her soul.

For this minute, give me your body. His mind whispered to hers. *Now.*

Desperate to feel that steel-hard thickness inside her, she lifted her hips and took his cock in hand. When she pressed him against her heated opening, he moaned.

"Please," he said with an ache in his voice. "Do it now."

Complying, she inserted him into her opening and pressed down.

Unexpectedly, she tightened up and only an inch of him entered. "Oh."

His forehead creased in a frown. "What's wrong?"

"I don't know," she said with a catch in her voice.

A soft, reassuring smile crossed the vampire's lips. "You're too excited. Relax."

"I can't. I want you too much."

With a deep, shaky breath, he lifted her off of him. When he touched her labia she gasped. It was just a quick sweep, a test. "You're not wet enough."

"Not wet enough?" She felt hot beyond belief.

"Not for what I have in mind. This calls for desperate measures."

He urged her over onto her stomach and she lay with her arms above her head. When he touched the back of her thighs she jumped a little and giggled because it tickled. With deliberation he pressed soft kisses to her ass cheeks, each one feather light.

Seconds later he brushed her long hair away from her neck. "Maybe you need a little something extra to make you relax."

With gentle persistent strokes he massaged her shoulders, working the tension out. Soon, his fingers found and eliminated every tense knot down her back and into her legs. But he didn't just massage her, he pressed slow, hot kisses to already highly sensitized skin. She linked up to him in her mind, amazed at the effortlessness of their mental communication.

I think the sex has made the communication easier, he said in her mind.

He nipped her neck and a tight little frisson of heat moved over her. *Oh, Ronan. That feels good.*

A deep, sexy chuckle left his throat. A wicked thrill, one born of the unknown, made her squirm under his touch.

He smacked her ass playfully. She yelped.

"Stop it," he said.

"Or what?"

His voice purred, engorged with sex and ultimate sin. "You'll have my cock up your darlin' little pussy. Then I'll fuck you and I'll keep on fucking you until you've come ten times."

"Ten times?" she gasped the question.

"I can make it happen."

She smiled as she teased him. "That's pretty arrogant." His touch drifted over the sides of her breasts and she sighed. "I don't know if it's even possible for a woman to come ten times in one bed session."

"It is." His voice went husky and his accent deepened in his passion. "I'll prove it to you, sweet colleen. I'll move inside you hard and fast, then slow and soft. I'll stay inside until I wring those climaxes out of you."

She loved his forceful oaths, but not because she wanted to be dominated. No, because she knew Ronan Kieran would fulfill every promise he made. That included all the suggestive comments filling her ears.

On and on he kissed her body, tempting her with little licks, long touches. His fingers drifted down when he brushed her ass she jumped a little. She felt so sensitive now she would probably come if he barely touched her between the legs.

He reached for a pillow and wedged it under her hips so they tilted up. Open your legs. His voice in her head demanded, and she complied.

As he palmed her ass cheeks, his heated exploration made her thighs tremble in anticipation.

"Mother Mary, you're wet now," he said in a breathless groan.

His fingers brushed lightly along her labia, smoothing her wetness. She jumped a little, then settled down as he continued to slide his fingers across her wetness with long, hot strokes. Her entire body quivered as she enjoyed his erotic touch. Clarissa didn't realize she could become any wetter, but to her amazement another gush of arousal dampened her.

He stopped and she almost commanded that he continue the extensive, exciting caresses. His hands coasted up her calves, his gentleness making her lower regions ache with the need to be touched. He parted her thighs wider and then she felt his tongue swiping over her folds.

She muffled a loud moan against the pillows. "Oh yes. Oh yes." She couldn't stop the words from tumbling out. "Please. Right there. Oh God, yes. Right there."

She'd never been wordy during sex, but Ronan seemed to have let something loose inside her. Arching into his touch, she let out a soft moan when he slid two fingers deep into her channel. He worked her body, pumping his big fingers in and out with a steady movement.

"Damn it, Ronan. More."

He chuckled softly. "Sure, and she's a demanding wench."

Wench? She ought to smack him. All she could do was enjoy the way his fingers plied her body. As the pressure built, all she thought about lie between her thighs. In and out. In and out. He removed his fingers and she felt his tongue plunge deep. She bit her bottom lip to prevent a squeal from leaving her throat.

"Mmm. Delicious," he said, his hot breath gusting over her tissues. "So wet. I can't wait to get into that tight slit. And when I get in there, I'm going to be there a long time."

Just his description of what he'd do made her crazy. She couldn't take much more of this.

He leaned in and dined.

That's the only way she would have been able to describe it if asked. Oh, yes, Miss Gaines. How did he do it? Why, he just stuck his tongue in there and fucked me with it. He thrust in and out with that amazing tongue until I thought I'd go nuts.

Plying her folds, he licked over one, then the other with feather soft ministrations. Then he would stuff his tongue inside and the wet, warm abrasiveness caressed her inner walls, licking up her juices and savoring the taste. He made sounds of approval, as if consuming a gratifying meal.

She screamed out in her mind, Lick my clit. Lick it.

She wasn't surprised when he didn't do as she asked.

Damn it, Ronan. Please, please, please.

He cupped and fondled her ass cheeks. By now she thought she could feel the wetness dripping out of her. She'd never been more aroused and ready to make love than she did at that moment. Her hips moved, her body needing a finish to the torture.

Then he removed his hands and his tongue and she almost whipped around to ask him—to beg him—not to stop. Then something hard and hot probed her and she groaned in breathless relief. With a quick, deep movement he speared her right to the core. A gasp left her throat, then a sigh of satisfaction.

Then she didn't need words and he didn't give them.

He shuddered against her, his entire body quivering as he made a sound of gratification. His hips started a grinding, gyrating thrusting that didn't allow for a slow slide into orgasm.

Nothing prepared her for the intensity, both physically and emotionally as they plunged into sex so heated she knew it would be imprinted on her memories forever. Ronan slipped an arm around her waist and lifted her onto all fours. His hands seemed to be everywhere on her body, every caressing touch driving her to new pinnacles of screaming arousal. He crushed her hair in one hand as he grasped the back of her neck. His other hand clasped her hip as he rammed between her legs.

Her mind went blank and she became a mass of corporeal sensation. A low moan shivered through her as she came, the sudden, tight little orgasm trembling through her.

"More," he growled.

Again his touch became relentless, moving across her hips, her ass, then flicking her clit. She twitched, possessed by a glory surpassing their previous encounter. Her body would have what it wanted, and if it meant animalistic fulfillment, she would take it. She pushed back against him, forcing her hips into a pace that matched his. Another orgasm caught her up, then rolled into another and another.

That was it. She was going to die right here.

Her head buzzing, she sagged to the bed and Ronan slipped from her. She turned over with a weak groan. When she looked up at him, the inferno in his vampire eyes looked highly explosive. Everything about him made her sex long for him. Pulse and clench and beg for him again.

His big shoulders, broad and muscled, looked like they could take on the world. His tightly roped, incredible arms said he could carry her through any storm. His pillar hard cock glistened with her juices and looked so tightly engorged she thought he couldn't be far from bursting. No, he most definitely hadn't completed his mission yet.

Good.

He reached for her, but she used her remaining strength to slip off the bed. When he made another muffled growl and tried to snatch her into his arms, she danced away.

Try and catch me, vampire.

His smug grin said he could do it.

In less then the blink of an eye, he'd trapped her up against one wall.

Oops. She'd forgotten he could move with the speed of lightning.

He cupped her ass, lifted her and plunged. Startled and so turned on she couldn't stand it, she jumped into another orgasm. Her mouth opened and before she could scream her fulfillment, he kissed her. He started thrusting heavily. He didn't stop kissing her as he took her with merciless fervor. Relentless, his cock moved in and out like a piston gone mad.

She knew this wasn't silk and sweetness and satin lovemaking.

It was animal. Primal down to the last cell.

He tore his mouth from hers, his breathing fast and hard. Pleasure became so acute she could barely breathe. Reaching for last reserves of strength, her body wanted yet another climax.

And she got it.

Dazzling lights went off behind her closed eyes and colors blended one into the other as her entire body felt like it might melt. The orgasm went on and on, firing deep in her with heavy spasms. Each hard thrust prolonged the contractions until the rise and fall of sensation threatened to send her unconscious with ecstasy.

With one last hard thrust, Ronan moaned deep in his throat and came in great, hot jets.

He gathered her up in his arms and walked with her to the bed. Even though she was beyond exhausted, the man had more than enough strength.

He put her down on the bed and smiled. Sweet colleen, you're incredible.

She couldn't help but smile up at him as he stood over her. I think that was more than ten orgasms.

He laughed. "You were counting?"

"No. But I think it was just one long..." She trailed off and blushed.

Mischief twinkled in his eyes. "There's more where that came from."

She yawned. "Mmm."

He pulled the covers over her. Tenderness came into his eyes, the fire now banked behind release. "Sleep now. I'm going downstairs."

Feeling a little insecure without his arms around her, she asked, "You're not leaving the house?"

"I might take a quick look around town to see if I can tell what's going on. Don't worry. Sorley is probably up. I'll take him with me."

Fear jumped into her like a sharp pain. She grabbed his arm as he started to move away. "Ronan, please don't."

He sat on the edge of the bed, more gorgeous than any man had a right to be and just as stubborn. "We won't go into the tunnels. Don't worry."

She hated feeling this vulnerable, but she knew her emotions ran high from what they'd experienced together. "It's dangerous out there."

Leaning down, he kissed her forehead. Then he brushed his fingers through the long tangle of curls that tumbled over breasts. Melting and loving, his gaze held hers for a long moment.

"And you're dangerous to me." His voice sounded shaken. After swallowing hard, he got up and went in search of his clothes.

She gloried in the way he'd looked at her and the unsteady cadence in his voice. She'd managed to affect the man on some level other then sexual. Smiling, she settled more deeply under the covers and closed her eyes.

Chapter Fifteen

As Ronan and Sorley walked through the early morning darkness, their invisibility guaranteed no one would see them. Not even the ancient one could see them when they chose to go invisible. Becoming unseen and teleporting used more energy than necessary at this point, so they'd chosen to walk from Erin's home to wherever bad vibrations took them. They also used telepathy, well aware inanimate voices could be heard by animals and other people. Soon light would come, and their cloaks would provide them with protection.

Why are we doin' this now? Sorley's voice asked in Ronan's head.

To get the lay of the land.

Speakin' of lay, Sorley said, *how was it?*

Ronan would have glared at his friend if he could see him. He could well imagine Sorley's smirk, though. *I'm going to pretend you didn't ask me that.*

The smaller vampire allowed an audible laugh to fill the air as they walked the long road and closed in on Main Street. *You weren't exactly quiet, mate. She wasn't either.*

For the first time in a century Ronan felt heat crawl into his face. With previous encounters with women he would have felt smug male satisfaction.

Feck off, Sorley.

Ronan could almost hear Sorley shrug. *Well, the mortals might not have heard you.*

Who was Sorley kidding? Ronan understood he could shut up Sorley by ignoring the topic.

His skinny friend, though, seemed obsessed. *So, if anything miraculous happened because you had sex, you'd be screamin' it from the rooftops, eh?*

Confession came whether Ronan wanted it or not. *Nothing miraculous happened. At least, not that I could tell.*

Didn't sound like it to me.

Bloody hell, that's not what I meant.

They passed the last row of Victorian-era houses close to the business district.

Then mean what you say. Or is that say what you mean? Sorley was clearly amused.

Ronan's patience with his irascible friend grew thin. *If you don't want a silver stake through your flea-bitten heart —*

Aye, I hear you.

They continued in silence, even their footsteps too quiet for any but dogs and cats to detect.

What about the fire near Erin's home? Why didn't we investigate that? Sorley asked.

Because we aren't doing this to investigate, only to help if we can. We can't help the people who've already been burned out.

So we're almost like superheroes. You know, Superman, Spiderman, you name it.

Ronan couldn't help smiling. *Those blighters have nothing on us.*

Oh, don't let the mortals hear you say that. You'll be dead meat, Danny Boy.

To Ronan's chagrin, his friend started singing *Danny Boy* in his head. He cringed as Sorley sang an off-key note.

A woman's scream burst out of the darkness, high-pitched and desperate. Ronan sensed Sorley's startled jump.

Where's that comin' from? Sorley asked.

Honing in, Ronan realized it came from the house they'd just passed. He turned around. Another terrified scream rent the night. *Here!*

What are you goin' to do?

I'm popping into the house.

What? Sorley sounded shocked.

I won't allow a woman to be hurt if I can do anything about it.

The painted lady Victorian, a combination of blues and grays, looked dismal and a perfect setting for a haunted house movie. Lights blazed from a second floor window. Without waiting for Sorley to speak again, Ronan gathered his energy and directed his body toward the second floor.

Ronan materialized in the bedroom where he sensed mortals, but kept his form invisible. He knew the popping noise would be audible to mortals no matter what, but by the sounds of the struggle going on, they wouldn't notice.

A tall man stood over a woman lying on the floor, his brutish features marred by three long, thin bloody slashes over his right cheek. The man wore a plain white T-shirt and red plaid pajama bottoms, his barrel chest heaving with angry breaths. Waves of malice rolled off the man as he looked at the crumpled form on the floor. The crude-looking bastard's powerful arms and body had assured the woman didn't stand much chance against him. Raking his hands through his short blond hair, the man licked his lips and looked down on his handiwork.

A fast glance at the woman, her bloodied head lying near a bedside table, told Ronan she was in serious shape, if not dead. Vampire rage built in Ronan and he knew justice would be served far quicker by him than by the police.

He returned to corporeal form right in front of the man.

The man's cold blue eyes about burst from his head. Taking two steps back, the asshole cringed. Ronan drew back his fist and hammered the man across the face. The creep went down and out.

Sorley popped into the room a second later, his expression verging on fear. "Sure, and what's goin' on in here?"

Ronan's battle rage rolled off him in waves, and he could feel it filling the room and adding to the already thick atmosphere. He pointed to the man on the floor. "This asshole was beating the woman."

Stepping around the man, Ronan crouched down beside the female and checked her vitals. When he found a fairly strong pulse and heartbeat, he sighed in relief. "Call the cops and find some rope."

After Sorley put in an anonymous 9-1-1 call and they'd tied up the man and gagged him, they considered taking him to the crypt where Clarissa had fallen through to the tunnels.

"Sure, and the bastard would think twice about hurtin' a woman," Sorley said.

Ronan nodded. "He'd be dead. The ancient one would find him and kill him. We can't."

Sorley looked disappointed for a moment. "Ah, bugger. You're right."

Ronan put his hand over the woman's wound, testing for how much damage had been done to her skull. "She's going to be all right, I think. It's not a fracture."

At that moment the man woke up and stared at his assailants. His eyes widened and he thrashed in his bonds as he lay on the floor. Ronan smiled down at the man with satisfaction as the bastard tried to speak. Sorley waved at the guy and as they disappeared, the man screamed against his gag. Sirens wailed in the distance.

"Good riddance, you dip weed," Sorley said.

* * * * *

Clarissa's restlessness drove her out of bed when the sun still slumbered. But day would soon be here. She couldn't sleep worrying about Ronan and Sorley. She dug some new jeans out of her suitcase, as well as a pair of panties. Smiling, she couldn't help but admit the animal way he'd ripped her clothes off had made her sex throb and her heart pound.

She headed into the bathroom and took a shower. As water slipped over her body she half expected the flesh between her thighs to be thoroughly sore. To her surprise she didn't feel overused. Pleasantly used, yes, but not as sore as she should be considering how long and hard Ronan had made love to her. His lovemaking had been everything she expected and beyond.

God, but the man could make love.

She'd barely rinsed the soap off her body when a strange sensation echoed in her stomach. A fluttering. She put her hand to her stomach in surprise. The feeling built until nausea rose over her once in a sickening wave. She shut off the water and stood in the shower a moment until the feeling subsided. Sweat broke out on her forehead for a second, then went away. Stunned and concerned, she toweled off quickly and dressed. As she stood in front of the mirror and looked at her long, wet hair, another wave of crazy feeling slipped over her, but this time it came as a hot flash. She shivered in distress, not liking the sick wave of discomfort one bit. Dark circles also rimmed her eyes.

"Damn it, you'd better not be coming down with something," she muttered.

She considered lying down again. To her surprise, though, the sickness left her and she felt wonderful. Energized, as a matter of fact.

"How bizarre," she said.

A cup of tea might settle her stomach and wake her up. As she went downstairs she became aware of the entire house, the subtle noise here and there that spoke of old times and old timber. Her senses felt heightened. Taking a deep breath, she allowed her body to relax for the first time since Ronan had left her in bed. Images of him hovering over her, ready to thrust his big cock inside her, made Clarissa shiver in remembered excitement. She reached the bottom of the stairs and closed her eyes as another heat wave, this one more to do with arousal, swept her from head to toe.

"Good grief," she said and walked slowly to the kitchen.

Digging around in the kitchen cabinets, she found a mug and made tea in the microwave. She settled down in the kitchen nook and sipped the drink. Relief settled over her as the tea warmed her and no more odd physical symptoms assaulted her. As she contemplated everything that happened between her and Ronan, she started to wonder when and if there would be any evidence that sleeping with him somehow helped their cause against the ancient one. Or had this whole thing been one big cosmic joke? Perhaps this seer and the man named Yusuf had lied.

Before she could think about it too much, she heard soft footsteps coming her way. Erin entered the kitchen and smiled as she slipped into a chair across from Clarissa.

"Good morning." Erin nodded. "Couldn't sleep?"

Clarissa took another sip of her tea. "No. I hope I didn't wake you up?"

"No, I was awake anyway. I've had trouble sleeping on some nights since I came to Pine Forest."

"I can't thank you enough for taking me in."

"No problem. It's like a big family here now." Erin shrugged.

Silence passed between them for a few moments, and Clarissa took another slow sip of her beverage. "You're handling all this strangeness very well. I'm impressed."

Erin appeared to go into deep thought a moment. "I guess you could say that with Lachlan beside me, I believe this is going to work out."

Clarissa put down her mug and leaned on the table. "So the visions I had don't frighten you?"

"Of course. But if we give up hope, what else is there but defeat?"

Clarissa gathered her still wet hair and pulled it away from her neck, then let the strands fall to her shoulders. "You're right. I shouldn't be thinking of this in terms of the glass being half empty. I'm glad you're all here together."

"And you're glad Ronan is with you."

"Oh, yes. He's... I don't know. Extraordinary. There's some sort of power that comes unleashed inside him. It's so powerful. So..."

"Arousing? I know. I get the same thing with Lachlan. But Ronan's powers are more extreme. Even I can sense that."

Clarissa considered her statement. "Dangerous looking, dangerous acting. Just plain perilous all the way around."

The sparkling amusement in Erin's eyes turned into a laugh. "That's for certain. I've seen him in action fighting the ancient one. He's incredible. Like a fierce warrior in battle. I've never seen or imagined anything like it. Don't get me wrong. I love Lachlan. But any woman who didn't respond to Ronan's virility would have to be dead."

Clarissa wrapped her fingers around the mug to keep her hands warm. She thought back to the life Ronan had described before he became a vampire. "He went from a blacksmith to a warrior in a heartbeat."

Erin frowned. "He hasn't told us everything about what happened to him. I take it he told you?"

"Yes. All of it."

Erin leaned back in her chair looking well-satisfied. "Good. That's very good. It means he's opened up to you."

"We...uh...talked. More than once."

As if sensing the nuance behind Clarissa's allusion, Erin laughed softly. "I know. We could hear you."

Clarissa's mouth dropped open and she felt the blush reheat her face. "I'm so embarrassed."

Erin laughed again, this time sounding a little like a schoolgirl giggling. She clapped her hand over her mouth for a second. "No, don't be sorry. It—" She cleared her throat. "It gave Lachlan and I some ideas."

Understanding hit Clarissa between the eyes and suddenly she saw the kinky, hysterical side of it. She started to titter and Erin joined in.

"What's so funny?" Lachlan's Scots accent broke through their laughing as he stepped into the kitchen.

"Nothing, nothing," Erin said.

This time Erin blushed and Lachlan's gaze latched on her with an intensity that went straight to the heart. Clarissa could see the love in his eyes for the petite woman and it made Clarissa wonder if Ronan could ever feel that way about her.

Oh, damn. It's true. I want Ronan to fall in love with me. I do.

Before Clarissa could form another thought, a different wave of heat passed over her. She put her head in her hands and closed her eyes. "Oh God."

"What's wrong?" Erin said quickly.

Clarissa pulled her hands away from her face and managed to speak through a second onslaught of nausea. "I feel like hell. When I was in the shower this morning I felt hot and cold and then nauseated."

Lachlan immediately went to Clarissa. He put his hand on her forehead and frowned. "You don't have a fever."

Clarissa willed the sick feeling into abatement. "Maybe it's just something I ate. I had tea thinking it would do me some good. Now I'm not so sure." Then a horrifying thought came to Clarissa, one that didn't bear thinking about. "Wait a minute. You don't think that this sickness is the result of…"

She couldn't say it.

Lachlan, apparently, had no qualms. "Sex with Ronan?"

Clarissa couldn't even nod her agreement.

Erin's eyes went wide and they all just stared at each other.

* * * * *

Ronan and Sorley rushed through town toward the next possible trouble scene.

As they crossed Main Street toward the restaurant where Micky had first met Jared, Ronan noted the police cruiser sitting in front of the all-night diner.

Sorley's voice slid into Ronan's mind. *Where are you goin'? That's a cop car.*

What of it?

I don't know about you, but I'm not to happy about gettin' close to the police. Didn't you say we need to keep away from them because that Fortesque creep is suspicious of us?

If someone needs help I'm not withholding it because they're a cop. Besides, what can they do to us?

No sooner then Ronan had spoken when a shot rang out from inside the building.

Sorley let out a grunt of surprise. *Holy shit.*

Ronan didn't wait for Sorley's astonishment to fade. The scene looked surreal, almost like a police drama come to life on television. A trembling waitress stood behind the diner counter. An emaciated man with long stringy blond hair and torn jeans held a gun on Fortesque. Sorley popped into existence behind the skinny man a second later. Fortesque looked stunned as he gaped at the vampires. The waitress fainted with a sigh.

In that second Ronan felt everything in the room. Dark emotions jumped from the feral man to Ronan, the sensation of the evil inside the man almost staggering. Ronan took a deep breath and closed his eyes for one second. He visualized mirrors surrounding his body so the malice pouring off the skinny creep would come right back at the guy. With a gulp loud enough to hear, feral man swallowed and stepped back against a stool. Testosterone was alive and well, pulsing from the skinny man, Fortesque and himself. Ronan could smell, feel it, taste it. He detected the fear in the cop, and the ready to jump into action that might cost the police officer his life.

For an instant uncertainty showed on the sweaty, drawn face of the long-haired man. "Fuck me. Who the hell are you?"

Ronan forced a smile and made sure to keep his voice light. "Your worst nightmare."

Long-hair's gaze darted from the cop to Ronan and back again. Finally his gaze settled on Ronan.

Good, Ronan. Draw his attention away from the cop.

Ronan took in Sorley's encouragement, aware the skinny guy hadn't seen Sorley quite yet.

Ronan put up his hands. "Sure and it's a fine mornin'. No need to get all excited."

"Bullshit. This cop here was going to arrest me. That ain't gonna happen, man."

"Then what are you going to do?" Ronan asked.

"I'm going to shoot him and you. Then I'm going to leave," the man said as his gun-toting hand started to shake.

Fortesque, looking beyond his realm, kept his hands up and didn't move an inch. At least Ronan could give the officer points for sense.

"Well, you see," Ronan said, keeping his voice calm, "I can't let that happen."

When the strung-out man pointed the gun at Ronan's head, Ronan knew the time had come. Take the guy down or get shot.

Taking him down sounded a lot less painful.

With vampire speed he moved toward the criminal. Skinny dude didn't have a chance as Ronan ripped the gun from his hand and delivered a punishing chop to the side of his neck. The man's eyes rolled up and he slumped to the floor.

"Jesus, Mary and Joseph," Sorley said. "If that wasn't a clean take out."

"Damn," Fortesque said, his voice strangled as he leaned over the man and handcuffed him. He checked the guy's pulse and looked satisfied.

A woman and a man came out of the kitchen area. Apprehension and terror marred their faces.

"Is it over?" the woman cook asked.

"Yeah." Fortesque looked at Ronan with disbelief. "I think so, anyway. What are you two doing here?"

Oh, good, Sorley's voice spilled into Ronan's mind. *You take the junkie down and Fortesque wants you to take it up the ass.*

"I'd like to be able to tell you that but—" Ronan started.

"But then he'd have to kill you," Sorley said.

Ronan glared at his friend, then looked back at the cop. Fortesque's frown faded into bewilderment.

Ronan cleared his throat. "Sorry Fortesque. It's just that Sorley expects to be arrested every time a cop sees him."

This statement seemed to make the police officer relax. For a moment Ronan wondered if Fortesque planned to arrest him anyway. Instead the cop called for backup at the location and relayed details to the dispatcher.

"We have to go," Ronan said and started to move away.

Fortesque put up one hand. "Wait."

Ronan turned back around, his apprehension in full force.

Keeping his hand on his holster, the cop surveyed Ronan and Sorley with skepticism. "Are you staying with Erin Greenway and that boyfriend of hers?"

Before Sorley could speak, Ronan said, "We have accommodations of our own."

When Fortesque scowled, Ronan asked, "What? Do I have something stuck between my teeth?"

Ronan smiled, aware his canines might be the tiniest bit longer. Though time and practice assured Ronan's canines wouldn't grow too long during battle or lovemaking, he knew sometimes he couldn't stop it.

Fortesque stared at him, then blinked. "Uh, no." He put his hand out to Ronan. "I don't know what the hell just happened, but I think you saved my life. Thank you."

While he'd never expected the police officer to react this way, he shook hands.

Sorley sauntered up to them. "I'll bet that killed you to say that."

Fortesque's lips twitched and he raised one eyebrow. "Almost. Look, with all the weird crap going on around here right now, I'm not going to ask if what I just saw really happened. And if what I saw *did* happen, that would explain a lot." Deep inside the cop's eyes, trepidation lingered, as if he half expected Ronan and Sorley to create mayhem on their own. "I knew there was something not quite right about you two."

Sorley grinned and slapped the cop on the back. "Oh, we're quite *right*, most of the time."

They started to leave again.

"Wait." Fortesque surveyed their cloaks. "Are you guys going to a Halloween party?"

"Of course," Sorley said. "Wouldn't miss it."

Fortesque's puzzled air made Ronan grin. Instead of going invisible and popping from the room, Ronan walked out. Sorley threw a comment back as he followed. "Have a good day."

Sorley smiled at Ronan as they walked along the street in the emerging morning light. "Hey."

"What?"

"That was fun."

Ronan chuckled. "Yeah."

They hadn't gone far before Ronan felt an odd, unusual foreboding. Deciding where to go next wouldn't be a problem. "There's significant tension on the south side of town."

As they continued their patrol, they headed into the more residential area in the south section beyond Main Street.

Do you think the cops have noticed somethin' wrong yet? Sorley asked.

If they haven't, they'd better do it soon. Not that it'll do them much good. They can't fight this.

Why are we trying to? We've failed twice already in the last month.

I can't believe you're asking me this.

Sorley subsided into quiet.

A block later Ronan saw a man being held at gunpoint at an ATM machine connected to a bank. "Let's move."

Remaining invisible, they descended on the mugger. Faster than the mugger could blink, Ronan plucked the gun from his hand and threw it against the wall. The weapon shattered into little pieces. He pulled the man into the alley. The young man who stood beside the ATM took off at a run.

Sorley lifted his fist and let out a yell. "Go ahead, run. Forget thankin' us for your stinkin' money and maybe your life."

Ronan knocked the man out and they left the alley without materializing. When the man woke up he would probably wonder if the whole thing had been a dream.

They hadn't gone far when they heard a loud explosion, this one coming from Main Street.

What was that? Sorley asked. *Sounded like a bleedin' nuke went off.*

Let's find out.

They materialized on Main Street. A small flower shop had burst into flames. People milled around the street, shouting, pointing and others running from the scene. A black sedan with dark windows roared away, almost knocking down a man rushing across the street. A cop car followed, sirens screaming.

Ronan gestured to the car. "Those bastards threw a Molotov cocktail."

Bloodlust turned Sorley's eyes carnelian red. "Let's get 'em!"

A flash of unease made Ronan grab his arm. "You see if there's anyone trapped in the building. I'll take care of the bastards who threw the cocktail."

Some of the red left Sorley's eyes and for a second he looked like he might argue. Instead he nodded and dematerialized.

Ronan didn't know how many people rode in the black sedan, so he didn't try to teleport and materialize into the car. As he flew in the air alongside the car, he could see three burly men occupied it. This called for heavy-duty ordinance; he couldn't rely on the cops doing all the work. He didn't have time to place an object in front of them unless...

He appeared in the road in front of the onrushing car and planted his hands on his hips and his feet wide apart.

Ronan watched the driver's eyes widen in horror. Seconds later the screech of tires on pavement pierced the night. The driver swerved and veered off the road toward a copse of small pines. Ronan closed his eyes and concentrated on slowing the car's momentum to a more survivable speed. As the car rammed into the trees, it ran over the smaller ones. With a crunch the right side of the front bumper hit a much larger tree. Steam poured from under the hood. Taking a quick look into the car, Ronan saw all three men sprawled in the car, unconscious.

Good. At least he wouldn't have to put them out for the authorities. He went invisible again. The police cruiser pulled up behind the car and out jumped three cops. He remained invisible and stuck around for a few minutes to make sure the police could handle the criminals.

A few moments later he headed east on Main Street, a strange new energy in his physical body and his soul. Sunlight crept toward the horizon, ready to bring on a new day. He almost felt as if he could fight the sun and its debilitating effect on him. Knowing the idea made no sense, he maintained his invisibility and flipped the cloak hood up to block intruding light. Again he popped onto Main Street closer to the fire. Firefighters worked the blaze.

Sorley, where are you?

Cold wind whooshed by him like a fast train.

Then he heard a deep chuckle he would know anywhere. *Sorley isn't here, but I am.*

Ronan stood on the sidewalk near a store and didn't move. *Gloating over your handiwork, ancient one? You're causing this mayhem, aren't you?*

I start nothing. Mortals have all the ability to create hate and crime and the iniquity of the ages.

You lie.

I speak the truth, but you choose not to listen. You would rather believe I am the root of all evil on this planet. That I do whatever I can to bring you personal pain. Have you ever thought you seek pain? That you want to punish yourself for Fenella's death?

Ronan couldn't stop the upwelling of hatred as it surged upwards in waves. Nothing irked him more, enraged him more, than people who couldn't take responsibility for their actions. This warmed-over shit pile hadn't taken accountability for anything in a thousand years.

You killed her, you asshole.

Her stupidity led her from home and into unguarded territory, just as it does any human who doesn't listen to the dark warnings in their heart. Humans deny that they must be on watch, and they don't understand that bad things lurk in the shadows and the light barely keeps it at bay. Their souls are haunted and yet they deny the dark side of their lives in favor of the light. When the dark comes, they do not identify it until it is too late and they're consumed. That's what killed your Fenella. There is something you didn't know about her.

Ronan's breathing came harder, his turmoil breaking loose. *You're lying.*

Just because I am the most powerful vampire on earth does not mean I lie full-time. You delude yourself as much or more than I would mislead you.

He couldn't trust what the ancient one said, but he could certainly probe the monster for answers. *You're saying Fenella had a dark side?*

She explored her dark side yet kept it hidden from everyone, including you.

No. He wouldn't believe it.

Believe it, Ronan Kieran. From the time she was young she played tricks on others and used her charm and wits to deceive. Just as all women do.

Ronan drew a deep breath. So that explained it. Respite eased his mind. The ancient one's taunts weren't really about Fenella, but about the old vampire's twisted categorizations and beliefs about females.

Deciding now he should try a new tactic, Ronan thought, *What is your real name, ancient one? The one your unfortunate parents gave you at birth.*

The laugh, rusted with hate, rolled over Ronan's skin and made it prickle. *My name is long lost, even to me.*

Ronan knew the ancient one lied and why he kept his name a secret. If anyone knew, the name might be used against the ancient one in a ceremony performed by a seer if that seer practiced magick.

I'm here now, Sorley said.

Relief filled Ronan. At least with Sorley and him combining energy, they may survive an attack from the ancient vampire.

Sorley's shaky voice filled Ronan's head. *The ancient one is here, too.*

I know.

Penetrate his mind for his name. Now!

Although Ronan knew what he planned was dangerous, he didn't see how he could ignore what he must do. He closed his eyes and threw the full power of his concentration outward. He would penetrate the psyche of the ancient one if only for a few seconds.

He pushed and pushed.

There.

A hitch as he intruded on the old vampire's brain slowed him down, like swimming through thick mud. Then he was in. *Give me your name, ancient one.*

Ronan sensed the ancient one's quiver, as if the awareness of Ronan piercing his mind felt highly unpleasant. *What have you done?*

The growl in Ronan's mind sounded like a lion, angered by the insistent teasing of a fly.

Taken a piece of your mind, Septimus Ademus.

Ronan could have cursed the old creature, called him a knave, a clump of shit on the bottom of his shoe, but didn't want to take the chance of bringing on another fight in this time or place.

Jesus, Mary and Joseph, Sorley's voice said, a rasp of fear and awe.

Get out of here, Sorley. Go!

With a harsh, guttural laugh, the ancient one continued. *You think knowing my name will save you and this wimp? Your other useless mortal friends? Then I gave you too much credit for intelligence.*

Ronan's heart seemed to thud with thick beats and his breath stuttered. He knew he couldn't maintain the connection much longer. A strange and foreboding malaise worked its way inside him and demanded surrender.

He'd felt overpowering evil in the tunnels the last time he'd fought the old vampire. When they'd saved Micky from the monster, he'd experienced the seeping, disgusting wound of evil that embedded itself in the very tunnel walls. Now he touched the wickedness with his own mind and it frightened him.

For added protection, Ronan inhaled deeply and imagined white and gold light surrounding him. A real glow, like the sun touching glitter, spread around his body.

Do it, Ronan said to Sorley, *Protect yourself now.*

Another shimmering sheet surrounded a shorter, skinner outline nearby Ronan's right side. Worried about his chatty friend's silence, he built the strength of the white and gold light around his own body. Because of the shielding the connection between the ancient one and him should break.

He's tainted now. The old vampire's slithering voice scratched over Ronan's mind like sandpaper. *The darkest has him.*

The darkest?

That which is darker than my soul.

Ronan couldn't believe it. He'd heard of such a thing, and the evil they'd encountered in the tunnels certainly qualified as the most evil Ronan had ever experienced. *You can't have him.*

The darkest. The darkest has him. He's been touched.

A mild panic flared inside Ronan, but before he could do anything the old one's presence evaporated like steam.

He glanced to his left and saw the glow around Sorley's body. *Are you all right?*

Of course I am.

The why the hell didn't you answer?

The glow around Sorley's form vanished. *Because I couldn't. After we made connection with the ancient one's mind, I couldn't move. I couldn't get my bleedin' breath.*

Let's get of here then and talk about this. Now we have his name —

No. We need to track more of the people wreckin' this town. We could have had some fresh blood tonight.

Ronan didn't like the way this conversation was going. *After seven hundred years I don't like the taste of fresh human blood anymore. You know that. And you said you don't either.*

The pause made Ronan wary.

Sorley spoke a minute later. *They're criminals. I don't see the harm in it.*

Anger made Ronan lose his patience. *Think about what you just said, Sorley. Do you think, after living on thawed blood from packets that you'd be able to hold back with a mortal? Do you think you could stop short of killing them?*

Sorley's voice, when it came, sounded almost as sullen as a teenage boy. *You may not be able to do it. But I can.*

Ronan held back, despite the fury that bolted through him like lightning. He couldn't believe what he'd heard coming from his old friend.

Sorley, though, couldn't let it go. *We'd be gettin' rid of the scum of the earth. What difference does it make?*

As they rounded a corner and started back toward Main Street, Ronan's irritation snapped like a whip. *Because that would make you no better than the ancient one.*

Feeling the ire radiating from Sorley was easy enough; the vampire was never much good at keeping his feelings under wraps. *You think because you're the older vampire that you can lord it over? Do you think the rest of us are under your command or somethin'?*

No. But you're not thinking clearly. You need to remember that taking fresh human blood will make you want more. You'll crave it every day until the need burns in your stomach like an ulcer. Don't you remember that?

I remember. But I won't need to worry about that if I've got the frozen blood.

What if all Hades breaks loose and you and I have to go without the frozen blood for awhile? Are you going to hurt a mortal for your needs? Think, man.

I am thinkin'. It's you that isn't bein' reasonable.

Like a monster long suppressed, Ronan's frustration burst forth. *If you even think about hurting a mortal, I swear to God —*

You'll what?

Sorley's voice held a surliness Ronan hadn't heard nor expected to hear from Sorley ever. It didn't make sense, but his jolly friend turned argumentative in no time. Apprehension crawled up his spine. Was his friend's behavior a symptom of what this town faced?

All around them people scurried in a panic and some wouldn't come out of their homes at all. Few people moved down the street, still slick with ice. None of them guessed two vampires conversed telepathically only a few steps from them. The entire scenario since they'd wandered the streets today felt surreal, a carbon copy of a horror flick with no ending.

Emergency vehicles littered the street as firefighters continued to put out the blaze and prevent it from spreading to other buildings on the street.

To Ronan the real terror came in acknowledging something had gone very wrong with Sorley.

Sorley, this isn't you talking. The ancient one said you'd been touched by the darkest. He has to be talking about the other evil in the tunnels. The evil that is worse than him. Did you go to the tunnels while I was arguing with the ancient one?

No. And I don't think I've got any bleedin' problem. I'm all right. Why do you believe what he says anyway?

Sorley, listen. This isn't us. We don't argue like this.

We do now.

No. Think. This could be a symptom of the darkness in this town.

I don't think so, mate. This is you tryin' to tell me what to do every time you get a wild hair up your arse.

You're telling me you can't wait until we get to Erin's and defrost a bag of blood?

Why wait? These criminals are worthless. The jails are full of 'em. I say we eliminate some of the pressure and drain the lot of them.

If Ronan hadn't been ready to strangle Sorley, he might have considered the dark humor. *If I hear you've harmed a mortal —*

Never mind it. I'm goin' for a walk. I'll be back at the house later.

Ronan didn't know whether to be relieved or more concerned when his old friend took off. His thoughts reeled. Sorley's biting argument had thrown Ronan out of sorts. It couldn't be Sorley's real personality creeping through because Ronan had known him long enough to see into the Irishman's deepest thoughts. Sorley might be a reformed thief, a man who'd done some wild and dishonorable things as a mortal. As an immortal he didn't stray much, despite his wildest talk. Perhaps he should go after Sorley.

No. If he did that he had a feeling there would be a physical confrontation this time. When he confronted Sorley next he would need tools to fight the *darkest*, the total absence of light.

Ronan jammed one hand through his hair and held back a sigh. Apprehension grew inside him and he realized with sudden clarity that Clarissa needed him.

He didn't know why or how, but he had to get back to her now.

Chapter Sixteen

Clarissa stared at Lachlan and Erin for several seconds in pure disbelief. "You mean to tell me that—" She swallowed hard as her voice went high. "That having sex with Ronan is going to make me sick?"

Before they could say anything, Ronan popped into the kitchen.

Clarissa almost came out of her skin. "Jeez, can't you give us some *warning* before you do that?"

"No," he said matter-of-factly.

Before Clarissa reacted to his cheeky statement Erin asked, "Where's Sorley?"

Ronan's gaze took on a haunted air, as if a weary burden had been added to his already battered soul. "He's cooling off somewhere."

Lachlan's eyebrows went up. "Cooling off?"

Ronan explained their patrolling adventures. When he finished everyone looked a little stunned, even though what he said didn't surprise Clarissa much. Despite the loyalty Ronan displayed toward Sorley, she'd sensed restiveness, an on-the-edge quality in the other vampire.

Lachlan's displeasure came out as he went to the refrigerator and took out the coffee. "That little pissant."

"You don't think he'd really hurt a mortal, do you?" Erin's voice took on a vein of fear that echoed in Clarissa's heart. "I mean, he's a bit naughty sometimes, but hardly the type to turn rogue."

Lines formed between Ronan's eyebrows as he brooded. "Naughty? That's not a word I'd use for a vampire, if I was you."

Determined to put a little levity in the room, Clarissa said, "What about stubborn, strong, and most annoying?"

Ronan strode toward her chair, his gaze tangling with hers in a heated way that made her stomach clench from arousal and not nausea. "Why do I get the feeling you're not talking about Sorley?"

She waved a dismissive hand as he stood close to her. "Sorry, I couldn't help it."

Tiny flames jumped into his eyes and despite the fact their friends stood around them, another hot flare of desire stirred inside her. His glare held hunger and exasperation melded. He made one of those typical male grunts females had been hearing since humans walked out of caves.

As he peeled off his cloak and tossed it on a chair, Erin went around closing the blinds to keep out the encroaching morning sun.

Lachlan seemed eager to return to the patrolling adventures. As he started the coffeemaker he asked, "So you think Fortesque is off your butt permanently?"

Ronan shrugged. "Who knows? Maybe for a little while."

Erin sighed. "What Clarissa saw is coming true."

Uneasiness hung in the room like a pall, and the weight of it made Clarissa want to curl up in a ball and erect shields against visions and vibrations that might come to her. Yet she refused to wimp out. These people had become her friends and she needed to help them.

Ronan explained more about what happened, and when he got to the part where he'd encountered the ancient one, Clarissa felt her heart skip a beat. "He's tainted now by touching the ancient one's mind?"

"It's the only explanation I have for his sudden turn in behavior." Ronan marched to the freezer and unceremoniously pulled out a bag of frozen blood. He plopped it in the microwave on defrost.

When the microwave dinged Ronan retrieved his blood packet. He poured it into a large plastic blue tumbler. Clarissa was grateful the tumbler wasn't clear. The last thing she felt like doing was watching him drink a glass of blood. To her amazement he tipped the tumbler to his lips and started drinking. His throat worked and worked. He didn't sip his life force renewal like fine wine, but like the requisite it had become.

When he finished swallowing he licked his lips. A red stain held her attention as it lingered on his top lip. Fascinated, she watched as he licked again and caught all remaining evidence he'd just consumed an entire tumbler of human blood. He captured her gaze a second and the concern she saw there surprised her. It looked as though he felt ashamed of what he'd done, even though it remained necessary. He tore his gaze from hers and went to the sink. He rinsed out the cup, filled it with water, then took several sips of water. Once he'd finished that ritual he placed the tumbler in the dishwasher and leaned back against the kitchen counter. No more signs of bashfulness or worry lingered in his eyes. So she'd seen him consume blood for the first time. So what?

Lachlan went to the small radio sitting on the windowsill and snapped it on. He tuned it to a local rock station. "Maybe we can get more information about what's going on out there."

Sure enough, the news superseded music, the announcer's almost excited voice announcing the bizarre crime wave sweeping Pine Forest. So far there had been two armed robberies at convenience stores, five assaults, and one arson fire.

Then the announcer mentioned the incident at the diner. "This is the second such incident in this diner in the last two weeks. Also, a man was robbed at gunpoint at an ATM, but claims mysterious unseen rescuers subdued his attacker. Not long before this bizarre episode, a woman was almost beaten to death by her estranged husband. This man was found tied up in the woman's home. Police say the 9-1-1 call was anonymous, and the man who assaulted his wife claims he didn't call them and his attackers were invisible and then materialized."

The announcer switched to the blaring entrance of an old rock tune.

Clarissa's mind tumbled back to the conversation she'd been having when Ronan came back to the house. She didn't think she could restart the topic considering how odd it sounded. She didn't have to.

Pain ambushed her in the side and she gasped. She put her hand to her waist in reaction and tried to hold back a moan.

Ronan crouched down next to her chair and placed a hand on her thigh. As he looked up at her, she saw deep anxiety in his eyes. "Are you all right? What's wrong?"

"Something is wrong," Lachlan said, "but probably not what you'd think."

Ronan's glare cut right through his friend. "What?"

"Sex?" Clarissa asked, willing to just let it all hang out.

The handsome vampire's frown intensified. "Sex?"

Erin reached out for Clarissa's hand and patted it in sympathy. "She's been feeling ill all morning. Nauseated, some pain."

Ronan's touch felt comforting through Clarissa's jeans, but radiating hurt made her wince. Plus, she didn't like the theme or the speculation. Embarrassed, she started to stand. Dizziness filled her head.

"Whoa, easy." Ronan slipped his arm around her.

Another wave of pain made her bend a little at the waist as she put a hand to her stomach. She gasped.

Before she could protest, he lifted her into his arms. "Come on, you're going to lie down."

Clarissa tightened her arms around his neck, savoring the reassurance and safety easing into her as he held her cradled to his chest. Because she continued to feel dizzy, she laid her head on his shoulder. "This isn't necessary."

"It is. You need to lie down." His eyes held a firmness that said he wouldn't take an argument. "If this doesn't go away you're going to a doctor."

Once inside the attic he put her down on the bed. With a tenderness that calmed her fears, he took her shoes off and then pulled a fleece blanket up over her.

"So what would I tell a doctor, Ronan? That sex with you makes me sick?"

He flinched as he looked down on her. "Does it?" He sat on the bed and stared at her, the rhythmic motion of his hand brushing her hair away from her face making her feel cherished. "Clarissa, I'm so sorry. If I'd known—"

"That can't be it. I mean, unless there is something about vampires making love to a mortal woman that you haven't told me. Is sex with you *supposed* to make me ill?"

"No woman has ever been sick after we've slept together." She closed her eyes for a long moment and he leaned over and touched his lips to hers in a heartbreaking tender kiss. When his voice came again it held the rasp of deep regret. "Damn it, Clarissa, did I hurt you when we made love?"

Her eyes popped open. Worry etched across his face showed true remorse. "No."

"Are you sure? I wasn't exactly gentle. I felt like I couldn't get deep enough inside you. I wanted to stay there day and night. It felt so damn good I lost control. But if I harmed you physically in any way—"

"Shhh. Stop it. You were *wonderful*. You think I could have climaxed if you were hurting me?"

Some concern eased from his eyes. "No."

"Then I rest my case. Yes, we got a little wild."

"A little?"

She knew right then Ronan needed her to confess, and she couldn't hold these feelings inside any longer. "Okay, we were down right insane. But I wanted you so much, Ronan. You made me feel things I've *never* felt before and never imagined I could feel in a million years. Please don't blame yourself for what is happening. It's probably nothing."

Anxiety returned to his eyes. "I can't bear seeing you in pain. I don't mind telling you right now that it's worrying the hell out of me to see you this way."

All the masculine reassurance and brawn she was used to seeing in this vampire dissolved. The ache in her side eased until it disappeared. "You're sweet. In fact, if you keep looking at me like that, I just might have to kiss you."

Instead of rising to the bait, he asked, "Do you feel a little better?"

"Yes."

He put his hand to her forehead.

"Lachlan already did that. I don't have a fever."

"That isn't what I'm checking for." He frowned like a doctor who'd discovered something disturbing.

"What is it?"

He gathered her hand in his and brought it to his mouth. He kissed her fingers one by one. As he closed his eyes, she fixated on his long gorgeous male lashes. Her heart ached with yearning. She wanted to kiss him, but more than that, she wanted to remove his concern.

He pressed more tender kisses to her fingers. "Something's changed. Your system is out of balance."

"How can you tell?"

A gentle smile touched his lips. "Most vampires have the ability to tell if someone is sick and what the problem is. And some can heal."

Intrigued, she asked, "Can you heal?"

"I can keep someone from dying by touching them, though I can't heal them one hundred percent."

She considered this new information. "Could making love with you alter my chemistry?"

"I'll have to ask the seer. This whole situation is pissing me off." Anxiety turned to anger as his eyes glittered with that danger Erin had talked about not so long ago.

She reached up and gripped his biceps, feeling the muscle bunch and tense. "I'm going to be fine."

"Of course you are, because I'm not going to let anything happen to you."

She saw and heard it in his voice, a brutal protective streak that she couldn't deny. "It isn't that bad. I can take care of myself."

"You can't."

Feminine independence couldn't let that one go by. "Wait a minute. I'm a grown woman and I can take care of myself."

His scowl held daggers. "Sure, and you think if the ancient one came in here right now you'd be able to fight him? You're under my full-time protection until that bastard is gone forever."

Then she understood, in a small way, what motivated him. "I'm not Fenella, you know. I'm not going to leave like she did."

His fingers caressed hers, but his words came out hard. "She didn't leave me." Passion-laced Irish tones spilled from his voice. "She was taken from me. I won't let that happen to you."

Clarissa allowed quiet to settle between them, the emotions crackling in the air full of potent sentiment and even sex. It would do little good to argue with him. This amazing, gorgeous, attentive, *hot* man wanted to keep her safe.

She couldn't help but smile.

The ache in her side had disappeared and other than being a little tired she felt great. A stirring in her stomach, this one more from desire than anything else, took her by surprise. Sharp carnal need flared into her body like a rocket explosion and she gasped.

"What is it? More pain?"

"No. Something else." She reached up and brushed her fingers over his mouth and tried to erase his displeasure.

His gaze intensified, fixating to her mouth as his nostrils flared a little and his pupils dilated. "Don't look at me like that."

"Like what?"

"As if you'd like me to lie with you right now."

"I would."

With a tiny snarl he moved in, his mouth molding to hers. He kissed her deeply, his tongue plunging and moving against hers. Her arms slipped around his waist and she moaned low in her throat. He pulled back and her arms dropped to her side.

"Clarissa, we can't. You need more time before we do this again."

Feeling bewildered and dazed by the high-impact sexual craving, she shook her head. "Now."

A smile moved over his mouth, sexy, masculine and tender. "Ease down."

She didn't know if she could. "Do you think this has anything to do with what the seer and that Yusuf guy were talking about? Maybe this strange sickness is what happens before I'm able to help you with the ancient one."

"Maybe."

She yawned unexpectedly, and he said, "Get some sleep. I'll be downstairs if you need me."

"But we *should* be discussing what to do about the ancient one."

"I can do that with the others. Just get some rest and I'll check on you a little later."

"Stay." She glanced down at his jeans and noticed the hard length of his erection pressing against the fabric. "You really want to leave the room like that?"

He glanced down and then smiled. "I can't help it. It's what you do to me."

She knew what he needed and wanted to give it to him with everything inside her. "Come here."

He walked toward her, wariness in his eyes. "Demanding wench."

His teasing tone said he didn't mean to offend, and she laughed softly. "Don't argue with me, vampire. Just get over here."

When he stood in front of her, she reached for his hips and tugged him closer. His growing erection strained against his jeans, and she ran her hand down over it.

He sucked in a breath and his hands landed on her shoulders. "Clarissa."

"Understand what I'm doing now?"

"I think I'm getting a clue."

He might have protested, if she hadn't unfastened his jeans in record time. Instead his eyes widened as she tugged his jeans down. She palmed his ass cheeks through his snug briefs as spirals of arousal obliterated all illness she'd experienced earlier.

"God, Clarissa." Ronan's eyes blazed down into hers as he slipped his fingers into her hair and caressed her scalp.

She grabbed the waistband on his briefs and pulled them down his hips. As he hissed in a breath, she stared without embarrassment or hesitation at the hard thickness that pulsed with need. Without waiting for a buildup, she moved him closer and slid her fingers around the base of his cock. She squeezed lightly and then slipped her mouth over him with one swallow. He groaned and the sound that erupted from him gave new meaning to the word feral. She glanced up at him as she licked and sucked. A rapt expression entered his eyes as yellow flames danced in his irises. As she slid her mouth over his cock, she grabbed the base and started a new motion. Her hand slid up as her mouth did, until they worked in combination to stroke his swollen flesh. Panting, he let his head fall back as recurrent moans worked from his throat.

Warm liquid moistened the aroused flesh between her thighs, the tight, drawing sensation telling her one thing. She didn't want to give him just a blowjob. No, not at all.

She leaned away and stood. The question in his eyes barely obliterated the heat.

Without hesitation she drew off her socks and her jeans, then whipped her sweater and bra off in a flash.

"Clarissa," he said with warning in his husky voice.

She felt untamed, unable to control the rocket sled quality of her craving. She didn't want preliminaries or foreplay but a quick, unbelievable coupling right this minute, right now.

"Do it now. I'm aching with it, Ronan, and if I don't feel you inside me soon, I'll have to take care of this myself."

Oh, yeah.

She heard his mental exclamation. He'd love to watch her masturbate, she knew, but more than anything she needed him tunneling inside her wetness. She wanted to grasp his large thickness and hold on tight while he caressed her hot walls.

His eyes flared up, a red glow that would have looked sinister if she didn't know he would never hurt her. Working quickly he got rid of his clothes, then urged her to lie on the bed.

"You're pushing me too far," he said.

"Oh?"

Without explanation he dug through her suitcase.

"What are you doing?" she asked him, certain he'd lost his mind.

"Aha. Just what I needed."

He turned and held up her fleece winter scarf and a polyester scarf she'd added in her case on impulse in case she needed to dress up a blouse.

Still, she didn't know what he wanted. "What are we doing?"

He didn't give her any explanation, almost as if he didn't hear her. Still, she'd tempted him into a quick lovemaking session and realized she had remarkable power over this vampire. Heady and excited by the idea, she closed her eyes.

Ronan turned her around. "Dog style."

No other man could make those two words sound sexy. Her arousal burned deeper and higher. Oh, yes. Dog style would do fine.

"Standing." His breathing came quickly, and as he turned her around gently she felt restraint pouring from him. "Bend over and put your hands out in front of you."

Before she could blink he tied her wrists together and then lashed them to the bedpost. She gulped in surprise and pulled at her restraints. "Ronan?"

"We won't do it this way if you don't want to, but I wanted to see if you liked it." He put his arms around her and drew her close. She could feel his cock bumping against her ass cheeks. He brushed aside her hair and kissed the back of her neck.

Delicious anticipation snaked into her body. "Let's do it."

Seconds later hot, thick hardness slid deep and sure into her center.

Clarissa didn't think about the past or tomorrow. Only the smooth, slick passage of his cock meant anything. He kept his motion slow, his fingers buried in her hair, his breath rasping between his teeth. With each deep, exquisite thrust she experienced a joy that drew her straight out of the universe into unknown territory. Heady and filled with the strength of the ages, his loving made her feel precious, cared for, needed beyond everything.

Again he thrust deep, but kept his pace slow. She arched back against him and defied his desire to kept things gentle. Soon he couldn't resist her urging and she knew when he'd lost control. The scarves tightened around her wrists and Clarissa pulled back against them. She eased the tension in her arms. With one hand gripping her hips, he tangled his fingers in the long hair flowing down past her cheek and held her in place.

"Clarissa," Ronan said in what sounded like tortured voice.

He slammed into her, then paused. Slammed, then paused.

She closed her eyes. As he held high and deep inside her, her orgasm burned deep inside and burst forth in great, rolling contractions that howled through her. Suspended at the top of a glorious sensation, she savored the climax as it seemed to go on and on. As the splintering beauty faded, she gasped for breath like a swimmer just coming up for air.

"Feckin' A!" He burst inside her with a harsh groan.

His cock throbbed, and she absorbed the sensation with greediness. Quickly he pulled from her and wrapped his arms around her again, his touch possessive and incredibly loving. In a blink the bonds fell from her and landed on the floor. He gathered her into his arms and they laid on the bed for a moment in total silence. He peppered tender kiss after tender kiss on her nose, her lips, her cheeks, her forehead, her neck.

He let out a deep sigh. "I can't believe we did that again." He let out a low laugh and climbed off the bed to redress. "I need to go downstairs for awhile. Why don't you rest?"

Before he left he leaned down and kissed her forehead. "Rest easy, sweet colleen. I'll be right downstairs. If you need anything, let me know."

After Ronan left the room and headed downstairs, animal need continued to fire his libido. More than anything, even though he'd worried only moments before that he'd harmed Clarissa, he wanted her. He wanted to slide deep into her hot, wet channel and fuck her into oblivion for what would be another heated exchange of their bodies. He wanted to feel his seed shooting deep inside her and enjoy his primal need to know she was his.

And she was, whether she knew it or not. She was *his*.

When he got downstairs the group had congregated in the living room, Jared and Micky included. As they said hello, he thought he could feel an extra element of fear residing in each of them. They didn't know what the next day, next hour, next minute would bring. Everything hung in a balance.

"Is she all right?" Micky asked as she settled onto the loveseat with Jared. "Does she need to go to the doctor?"

Ronan leaned against the fireplace mantle. "I didn't detect anything life-threatening, but I'm still worried about her. I'll keep watch and if she doesn't improve, then I'll get her medical attention."

Jared cleared his throat and leaned forward. He braced his forearms on his thighs. "We've been talking about the possibility that your link with her caused the problem."

"I don't know." Ronan turned away from his friends to stare into the tall mirror above the mantle. Guilt ate at him, despite the reassurance Clarissa had given him. "It's possible."

"Aye, though I don't remember hearing anything in vampire lore that talks about women getting sick after coupling with a vampire," Lachlan said as he stood next to a window and looked into the backyard.

And never in a million years did Ronan expect to standing in a living room discussing his sex life. In this case, though, he didn't have much choice. "After she had the nausea and pain I detected an imbalance in her system."

After a pause, Erin said, "She'll be all right. I'm sure of it."

Lachlan turned away from the window and settled on the couch next to Erin.

The phone rang and Erin went to the table near the front door. When she answered she put her finger in other ear, as if she couldn't quite hear the person on the other end. "Of course. Yes, he's here."

She took the cordless phone toward Ronan. "The connection is bad but I think he said his name is Yusuf."

Ronan took the phone. Keeping his tone light he said, "Feckin' time I heard from you."

The energetic laugh on the other end assured Ronan the older man appreciated the joke. "A bright good morning to you. Now this is costing me money, vampire. So be quiet and listen. Oh, and by the way, my daughter Selima sends her salutations. Vampire, I think you made her fall in love with you."

Ronan snorted and noticed the gazes in the room locked on him. "Right."

"It's true. She moons around the house all day and she's very lazy."

"She wasn't lazy before?"

"Never."

Before he could ask Yusuf more about his daughter, Yusuf asked, "Have you found the woman you needed to couple with?"

Ronan suddenly hated that word. What he felt and experienced when he made love to Clarissa far surpassed mere coupling. "Yes. But nothing is happening. At least I don't think so."

"Explain." The man's voice snapped like a whip.

Ronan explained what had happened since Clarissa returned to Pine Forest and the subsequent experiences with criminals, fires and the corpses turning up as the ancient one killed without compunction.

"Sounds like a mess," Yusuf said. "Hmmm."

"What?"

"You say this woman, this Clarissa is ill?"

"Yes."

"Humph."

Ronan didn't know what to say, but part of him found the Moroccan's statement very interesting. "Wait a minute. Selima didn't get sick in any way after she and I coupled?"

Ronan caught Erin's raised eyebrows, but ignored her look.

"No, why?" Yusuf asked.

Ronan explained and Yusuf huffed and made noises that said he found the situation odd. "Very strange. You say she's nauseated and dizzy?"

"Yes. And she had pain in her side." Ronan paced again, his heart drumming a little quickly. "Damn it, Yusuf, if you know something just spit it out."

"Nothing. It's nothing."

Ronan rolled his gaze to the ceiling, his antagonism coming to a slow bubble. "You said if I had sex with this woman then I would receive the power I needed to defeat the ancient one. Time is running out here."

Ronan heard the depersonalization in calling Clarissa *this woman* and winced at his own callousness.

Yusuf opened up. "It is written in an ancient text that only when a great vampire finds a woman who he can impregnate, can the ancient one be destroyed."

"Impregnate?" The word shot out of Ronan's mouth like a bullet. "Are you saying I can get Clarissa pregnant?"

Ronan glanced at his friends and they all stared at him like people who'd just been jabbed by a stun gun.

Ronan's mouth came open as he stood there in stunned silence. Anger grew inside him. "You didn't tell me this earlier. Why?"

"Don't yell at me, Ronan Kieran." The line crackled with static. "I didn't know until the seer called me. Obviously she was too afraid of you to relay the answer she found in the book."

"What book are you talking about?"

"An old tome at Trinity University that's being held in secret by a professor. Apparently this guy is a bit of a vampire hunter himself."

Shocked and colder inside then he'd ever been, Ronan said, "I can't have children. No vampire can have children."

The old man grunted his dissent. "*Most* vampires cannot have children. Ninety-nine percent, actually. You, sir, may be the one percent that can."

A panic started to well inside Ronan as something occurred to him in scary black and white. "Feck me."

Yusuf chuckled. "So you see, great vampire, unless you can get your woman pregnant, there isn't much chance you can conquer the ancient one."

Furious, Ronan responded. "How the hell did I get through seven hundred years without knowing some vampires can impregnate mortals?"

"Or if there is a female vampire that is fertile, she can become pregnant by a mortal male or that rare male vampire in the one percentile."

"Interesting, but I don't care about that right now. How did I miss hearing about it?"

"You sound suspicious, vampire."

"Well, maybe I am. Emotions are running a bit high now. In case you've forgotten, we're fecked up beyond all reason here."

"All right, all right." The Moroccan sounded exasperated by the reprimand in Ronan's voice. "It makes sense you wouldn't hear about the one percent factor. You've been roaming the world hunting the ancient one forever. Also, if only one percent of all vampires can impregnate or get pregnant, how often do you think these births would be noted? There have only been three recorded vampire-caused impregnations in the seven hundred years since you've been immortal."

"What happened to those children?"

"The seer said the first was killed in Huntingdon, England. The second was long-lived before being killed in a fight with another vampire in Russia. The third lived until twenty years ago in Germany. He committed suicide."

"Suicide?"

"He arranged to fall on a silver stake."

"Shit."

Ronan walked to the fireplace mantle and looked down at a fire that Lachlan had started earlier.

"Perhaps, if nothing extraordinary has happened by now," Yusuf said, "Your virility is in question."

"You mean *fertility*," Ronan almost growled.

"That is what I meant." Yusuf cleared his throat. "If you impregnate her, it will be accelerated. She could be pregnant right now."

Clarissa, pregnant. Right this minute.

Ronan felt like someone had just hit him over the head with a sledgehammer. He sagged against the mantle.

Yusuf continued as if he hadn't dropped a bomb. "It appears to be another chemical reaction, an alteration in thinking between the vampire and his or her mate that makes the difference in whether an impregnation occurs."

"Chemical?"

"As in feeling between you. There has to be sufficient feeling between you and this Clarissa before she can conceive. You have to want a child with her. Is she in love with you?"

The question echoed in Ronan's head. *Is she in love with you?* "I...I doubt it."

"Unfortunate. You must make her love you, you must bed her and impregnate her. And the very last step..."

"Yes, go on."

"You must be in love with her. No step must be left out."

Ronan wanted to reach through the phone and strangle Yusuf. Instead he took cleansing breaths while he ruminated. He couldn't believe what he'd heard; the implication disrupted his sense of reality.

"You said the love must be in appearance only," Ronan said.

"Apparently I was wrong." A slow, soft laugh came over the phone. "Nothing is sane about vampires, so why does this surprise you?"

Closing his eyes, Ronan tried to clear his mind and think rationally. Objectivity and the cool detachment slipped between his fingers. "This is insane."

Clarissa wasn't *any* woman he'd slept with. She wasn't Selima, a virgin vampire who must be fucked or die. Clarissa had taken him into her body with his promise.

I can't have children.

"Shit, shit, shit," Ronan said.

He dared glance at his friends. Erin and Lachlan retreated into the kitchen and he thought he heard them say something about coffee and breakfast. Micky and Jared stayed on the loveseat, but their expressions said they felt a little uncomfortable, as if they'd intruded on Ronan's privacy. Oh, what the feck? They would have to know the information anyway so what difference did it make? Ronan felt like he needed another pint of blood.

Yusuf's voice came back over the line. "As I said, in order for her to become pregnant you must want a child with her and must be in love with her."

Ronan swallowed hard. "I don't believe you."

"Believe me or not, it is true. It was never just the coupling alone that would bring down the eventual downfall of the ancient one. It is the love and then the impregnation. So it would be advice, vampire, to own up to what has happened to you and learn from it."

Stunned, Ronan walked back to the kitchen and saw Lachlan and Erin had started scrambled eggs and toast. "If I impregnate her. There's no guarantee."

"No, but if you love her, the fertilization will be more certain."

He gritted the next words through his teeth. "I don't love her."

Lachlan and Erin both looked up from their work at the kitchen counter, deep frowns impressed on their faces.

Damn it all to hell and back.

"Think of it this way," Yusuf said. "If you do not get her pregnant, then you cannot defeat the ancient one."

The finality of his statement made reality seep in around Ronan's anger and surprise and the regret he felt after saying he didn't love Clarissa. "We only have a day until Halloween. You think I can get her pregnant in that amount of time and we'll be able to learn how to kill the ancient one?"

"Yes. It is written."

"It is written," Ronan said, grumbling. "Where is all this crap written all the time?"

Obviously Yusuf knew Ronan didn't expect an answer to that particular question. "The seer explained that vampire pregnancies come on fast and hard."

Incredulous, Ronan walked out of the kitchen again and wandered to the center of the living room. "So?"

"You will know, Ronan. You will know."

Closing his eyes, Ronan willed himself not to yell. Instead he moved onto the next important subject. "Maybe you can help me with something else."

He explained to Yusuf what had happened to Sorley and his fears that Sorley now had the same evil eroding him as the ancient one did.

"So you're saying that brazen little Irish vampire is now possessed by evil?"

"When we entered the mind of the ancient one to get his name something happened to Sorley. And the ancient one kept saying something about the *darkest*. The evil in the tunnels must be what he meant. The same evil that attacked Micky and took her to another dimension."

"You think the ancient one has absorbed this evil?"

"It's possible."

Silence came over the line for so long Ronan thought the connection had dropped. Finally Yusuf spoke. "When the seer and I talked earlier she mentioned that the *darkest* you speak of has been growing and feeding on the evil in the town for a century. Do you believe that?"

"It's what Clarissa believes. She found a book in the library on local history that references things happening in this town a century ago that pretty much bear out the suspicion."

"You must be very careful, Ronan. The ancient one may be a formidable foe, but this *darkest*, this ultimate evil is perhaps far worse. You must impregnate Clarissa immediately so the power will be released to you. Without it against the ancient one you are doomed. With this more powerful evil backing the ancient one, you are even more likely to fail."

Ignoring the man's reference to impregnate Clarissa, he went with his second concern. "What about Sorley? Is there anything I can do to help him?" He explained how Sorley wanted to drain the criminals they'd caught. "I've got to stop him."

A long sigh came over the phone. "If you want to stop him permanently, you know what you must do."

"No." The word came without hesitation. "No, I can't do that."

"You must consider it and keep a silver stake or bullet on hand just in case. It will not destroy the ancient one, but it will kill Sorley if the time comes."

Ronan closed his eyes and passed one hand over his face. "I can't."

"It doesn't come any clearer than that. Good luck, vampire." The line went dead.

Ronan clicked off the phone and walked to the phone table where he replaced the receiver.

Jared appeared shell-shocked. "Did I hear you say impregnate?"

Ronan leaned back against one wall. As Lachlan and Erin came out of the kitchen, Ronan explained without leaving out details, what the man had said. The others didn't stop him to ask questions, just listened while he poured the information like a faucet. When he reached the part about Sorley, they all went grave and silent. They knew, as he did, that he would give serious thought to the possibility Sorley had turned rogue forever.

He would have to hunt his friend. His crazy, funny, yet good-hearted vampire friend. An ache started in his heart and spread outward. He wanted to scream to the heavens for everything that happened the last few days. Sorley didn't deserve this, no matter how irreverent or pesky he could be.

Ronan decided he would do whatever it took to help his friend.

"Sorley will be all right," Micky said, her words doubtful.

Suddenly a smile came over Erin's face and she stood up quickly. Erin's smile broadened as she looked at Ronan. "Excuse me a minute, everyone. I believe breakfast is going to have to wait."

"Why?" Lachlan asked.

She pursed her lips and a mischievous look twinkled in her eyes. "I have something in the medicine cabinet I think we're going to need."

"What?" Ronan asked in apprehension.

"Why, a pregnancy test, silly," she said as she headed for the hallway.

"Holy shit," Jared said.

Lachlan's mouth popped open and he swallowed hard. "Aye."

Ronan's eyes widened as the implication hit him between the eyeballs like a grenade. "Oh, my God."

Chapter Seventeen

Ronan ascended the attic stairs, his heart at turns heavy and elated. He had to tell Clarissa what he knew and face the consequences if she became angry. But he'd faced the anger of the ancient one. Surely he could face the wrath of a thoroughly pissed-off mortal woman.

Huh. Maybe. He'd insisted on taking the pregnancy kit up with him in a plastic bag, unwilling to show it to her right away. This would take finesse. And maybe it would give him time to stop reeling from the very real possibility that he'd made her pregnant. He didn't know where this tale would lead, but in the meantime he could protect Clarissa and — dare he think it? — their baby.

Whether he liked it or not, whether any of them liked it, Clarissa Gaines might be pregnant with his child. Not in a week, not in a month or a year. *Now.*

At the attic door he paused. Time to face the music. The very loud, most likely inharmonious music.

When he opened the door Clarissa turned away from the dark wood mirror over the Queen Anne dresser to look at him.

"Hey," she said softly, her smile tender.

God, he loved her smile.

For what couldn't have been more than a few seconds, but felt like much more, he took in her beauty. She wore a plain coral-colored sweater over jeans. She didn't have shoes on yet. Tumbling like a thick, lustrous curtain, her hair shimmered and her smooth skin had the flush of a woman who'd been loved well.

He walked toward her with intent, his desire surging and flowing as vampire lust came to the forefront. She must have seen it in his eyes, a warning. Her gaze widened, her nostrils flaring as she stepped back. A turbulent sea raged in her eyes, then for a flicker golden sparks danced inside that ocean.

He came to a dead stop right in front of her. Her eyebrows rose, then her eyes cleared. Whatever he'd seen in her gaze disappeared as if he'd imagined it.

"What's wrong?" she asked.

"Maybe nothing," he said. "Maybe everything."

Amusement curved her lips. "What is it about you vampires always being mysterious and obtuse?"

Pulled in by her lighthearted statement, he smiled. "I can't hide the fact I'd like to toss you on the bed and make love to you again."

"Is that all you vampires think about?"

"I don't know. How many other vampires are you acquainted with?"

"Sorley and you. That's it."

He'd give her a piece of truth before he had to reveal that he'd deceived her earlier, albeit unintentionally. "The wanting to fuck you part is normal for a vampire. When a vampire finds a match it becomes difficult to keep from wanting to fuck daily. Many times daily."

She moved away from him slowly and sat on the bed. She reached for her socks and pulled them on. "Other than wanting me again, I sense there's something else you need to tell me. Several somethings."

He walked from one corner of the bedroom to the next, aware it made him appear nervous as hell. The news he must impart had never come from his lips before. He stopped pacing and sat on the bed near her.

"I've got only one piece of bad news," he said. "At least I think there's only one piece."

She smiled. "Oh, goodie. Then give it to me first."

He told her about Sorley, and her expression turned to pure concern. "Oh no. What are we going to do?"

"I'm not sure there's anything we can do now. If it comes to it…if it comes to it we'd have to…" He couldn't say it. His throat tightened.

"Kill him," she said with a soft, almost broken whisper.

"Yes."

"I'm so sorry, Ronan."

He couldn't sugarcoat the next piece of information. "I've talked to Yusuf a short while ago."

He gave her all the theories piece by piece and her gaze took on a shell-shocked quality, a woman outgunned and ready for execution.

Damn it. He'd hoped she wouldn't take things so hard. "It's not for certain. Sure, and the sickness you've experienced doesn't have to be from—"

"It isn't. It can't be."

"You have to take the pregnancy test."

She frowned, the ice in her eyes as deep and thick as a glacier. "I don't have to take anything."

Right away he'd come on too strong. *Back up a step, Ronan old boy.* "It's not only the sex between us that gives us more power to defeat the ancient one. It's the new life we make."

Clarissa stared at Ronan, what he'd revealed about a potential pregnancy sending her mind and heart into a tailspin of epic proportions. Her heart pounded, a flush heated her body. A rushing filled her ears. She turned her gaze on him and saw in his eyes something she'd viewed more and more in the last few hours.

Worry. A longing for her to understand. No matter what she felt about the startling revelations of the last few moments, she knew he cared for her. Maybe he didn't feel the soul-grinding, devastating emotions she experienced, yet she knew in her heart he would do everything in his power to keep her safe.

He straightened his spine as if making himself taller would make the information more palatable to her. "I can see your turmoil."

"Oh, it's more than that." When he walked to the bed and sat down next to her, she stood and marched to the big revolving cheval mirror near the dresser. She surveyed her body. "Are you saying that I could be manifesting signs of pregnancy already?"

His voice came soft and husky. "Most likely. The acceleration is a normal part of a vampire mating. In terms of mortal pregnancy you're probably more like three weeks along."

Instinctively she put her hand to her stomach and held it there in complete awe. Then her anger returned. "You told me vampires can't conceive."

His reflection came up behind her, and another vampire truth went down the toilet. She could see him in the mirror.

"I didn't lie."

"Huh."

His gaze held contrition. "I didn't know vampires could conceive at all until Yusuf told me. Apparently only three pregnancies have occurred during the entire time I've been immortal."

Curiosity overran her annoyance. "Are vampire children...do they need blood? Do they have fangs and live forever?"

She saw his lips twitch with humor. "Yes, yes, and yes."

She moaned softly and turned away from the mirror. She walked past him and to the window. Pulling the curtains apart to look out, she took in the winter scenery without really seeing it. She knew she perused the outdoors to avoid thinking about the now.

Reality came forward anyway. Lives depended on her and Ronan and the decisions they made. Clarissa turned back to him. "What happened to those three vampire children?" After he explained she asked, "So if even one of these children had lived, we wouldn't be having this conversation? Because they would have had the power to slay the ancient one?"

Ronan stood and walked toward her, and she tried to keep her anger fed. "Very possibly."

Close enough to touch, Ronan's face held remorse and stern determination. He would see her through to the end whether she wanted him to or not.

You got that right. You could tell me to get out of your life and I wouldn't. His silky voice filled her mind.

Become a stalker?

Sure and you would have to send the cops after me to get me to leave.

But you'd always come back.

Tenderness warmed his eyes to chocolate tinged with yellow. "That's the size of it."

He leaned in and kissed her forehead. Without thinking she reached up to touch his face and savored the warm heat beneath the stubble on his face. He clasped her hand and kissed the back. A shiver wiggled through her body straight down to her belly as his tongue touched her fingers in a quick caress. His gaze filled with a soul-wrenching tenderness that burned her antagonism to cinders.

"You're still angry with me?" he asked.

She shook her head and closed her eyes. "How could I be? You had no way of knowing it would come to this." When she opened her eyes, she looked deep into Ronan's gaze. "Let's get this done. Where's the pregnancy test?"

* * * * *

Clarissa headed down the hallway to give her friends the news. Never in a million years did she expect to be announcing something like this in front of several people at once. When she came to Pine Forest she knew strange things would happen, but never, ever like this. She didn't know what to think about the test results. At first glance at the test she'd smiled, then at second glance realism took over and she frowned. What would she do now?

When she arrived in the living room only Lachlan and Erin sat on the couch. Jared and Micky were nowhere to been seen. "Where are Jared and Micky?"

"While you and Ronan were talking we decided it was best if we all stayed together in the same house until things settle down. They're making a quick trip to the hotel, check out, and move in here," Lachlan said.

"Good idea." She smiled even though it felt false. "We'll be safer together, I hope. Where's Ronan?"

"He went outside to cool down." Lachlan gave her a reassuring smile. "I think he was about to hyperventilate. And I've never seen him do that."

Erin's gentle eyes were supportive, and she knew this newfound friend understood the emotions bobbing and weaving inside her. "Are you okay?"

"Yes. I...I'm glad you had the test on hand." As awkward as an elephant in an elevator, she stumbled for the right words. "I'll find Ronan and tell him first."

After retrieving her coat, she stepped out into the fading daylight as it skimmed across the porch. Ronan stood under the overhang, his cloak on and the hood pulled up to shield him. He turned quickly, an eager light in his eyes.

When he held his hand out to Clarissa, she put her fingers into the warm grip of his palm and allowed him to guide her down two steps.

"I did the test," she said, her mouth dry and her heart aching with unshed tears.

He didn't answer, but drew her close. She hadn't prepared for a situation like this all her life, but now that it occurred she could only hope she would know what to do next.

"Tell me," he said.

She could hardly enunciate the words. "I'm not pregnant."

His eyes narrowed, then closed. He drew in a deep breath. When he didn't speak, she cupped his face in her hands.

"What are we going to do?" she asked.

He folded his arms around her and brought her close. He buried his face in her hair and breathed a few words in Gaelic she didn't understand. She opened her mind to his stray thoughts. Instead of hearing words she saw pictures. A vision erupted in her head full-blown and in vibrant color.

Ronan walked alongside the bank of a river at twilight, his cape flapping in the breeze. His hair fluttered in the wind and he turned to look at her. In the distance she saw towering castle walls. She held a small hand in hers; a boy of about three with burnished brown hair and brown eyes that toddled along with her. Ronan smiled with joy and pride and held his hands out to them. She picked up the little boy and walked eagerly toward Ronan. Love made her ache with a happiness she couldn't have imagined long ago. When they reached him Ronan embraced them both.

The vision faded.

She drew back and looked deep into his eyes in the dimming light. "Is that what you want? Or is it what I want?"

His mouth opened and she saw moisture in his dark eyes. He drew in a shuddering breath. "While you were doing the test I was running all these scenarios through my mind. And my favorite one was the scene you just witnessed. I wanted you to be pregnant not for this town's survival, but for us. I didn't know how much I wanted this until I fantasized about what it would be like to have a family. Until today I never *expected* to have a family. It would have made me a very happy man."

A shimmering, bursting happiness settled in her heart. Tears filled her eyes again. This time she let them flow over and trickle down her cheeks. "I'm so sorry."

"Ah, sweet colleen, don't cry." Deep and husky, his voice held regret. "We'll get through this somehow. I swear to you."

Silence wrapped them as he drew her deeper into his arms and pressed her face against his shoulder. The wool cape felt rough under her cheek, but it held Ronan's scent and she breathed deeply. She sank into his comfort and for a space in time she forgot they had a real problem.

"I guess the nausea and pain was really from just screwing like a bunny," she said with a dry throat.

He laughed softly. "Probably."

He turned her face up so he could look at her, pain etched in his features. His lips brushed her forehead as he clasped her head between his palms. Teasing the delicate skin, he traced his lips slowly down to her cheek and nuzzled her. Her skin tingled in delight. He kissed his way to her chin, then to the other cheek. She quivered with longing as fresh need arose within for his affection. His attention moved to her ear and as his hot breath touched her there, she shivered again. The cold couldn't reach her here, and the bliss she felt wiped out all worry. She surrendered another piece of her heart to him.

Ronan licked her earlobe. "Sweet Ireland, you make me crazy."

She shivered as his tongue dipped into her ear, mimicking cock moving in and out of cunt. Teased beyond endurance, she arched her hips into his and felt evidence of his arousal. A maelstrom of tender emotions surged inside her.

"We're making out in the backyard," she said softly. "And we haven't discussed what this all this means."

Even under the cloak hood, Ronan looked more handsome and loveable, more delicious than any man she'd known. Her heart throbbed for him, wanted him, needed him.

He brushed his fingers over her forehead then tasted her lips. "I couldn't bear if anything happened to you."

Trembling emotion, tender and loving, swept through her soul. She knew it right then, if she hadn't been aware before. She wanted to be with this man, vampire or not, for the rest of her life.

"Ronan—"

He put his finger to her mouth. "I trust what the seer and Yusuf have told us. You must get pregnant for us to save this town. We don't have all the answers, but it's a part of the puzzle. But if you say you don't want a baby we'll find another way to conquer the evil stain."

Surrendering her fears, she told him the unqualified truth. "I did a lot of thinking waiting for the pregnancy test results. I know a baby would change everything for me and it isn't something I'd planned to do for some time, if ever. But now I do want this. For me, for you, and for this town. I want your baby."

His eyes flared, red and gold and yellow mixed in the dark irises. Without hesitation he moved in and walked her backwards until his body pinned her to the wall. His mouth covered hers, his kiss assertive and deep. He didn't ease her into passion this time, but pushed her headlong toward a soul-stirring, gut-wrenching desire to mate and mate hard. He took her breath away as his tongue brushed hers repeatedly, staking his claim. As her palms brushed over his cloak, she wished she could feel his hard chest and powerful muscles. Reaching up to his shoulders she held on for dear life, buffeted by a tide of longing and desire more swift then a waterfall. Carried away by the heady way he made her feel, she decided nothing mattered but pleasing Ronan and taking him into her body.

Shifting her away from the wall, he gripped her ass and squeezed. She moaned into his mouth as his thigh slipped between her legs and pressed up against tender, already aroused tissues.

Oh, she wished they could be naked and do it here. She allowed wanton hunger to carry her along.

We can do it here. As silken and seductive as a wet dream and building her feverish need for him, Ronan's voice smoothed into Clarissa's mind.

Without a word more he turned her around and faced her toward the wall. His big body kept her cozy warm and away from the elements. He unzipped her coat and slid his hands under her sweater. A flick of his wrist and he unhooked the clasp on the front of her bra. She gasped as he cupped her breasts. Callused but tender, the steady, plumping action of his hands warmed her entire body. He avoided her nipples but they turned hard and aching in anticipation of his touch.

Not yet, he said in her mind.

Then he reached between her body and the wall and undid her jeans. He pulled her jeans and panties down so they hung to her knees. He worked his fingers between her legs from behind so he could play with the slit that turned moist and hot with desire. Spreading her slickness over highly sensitive folds, he strummed every inch of soaked flesh. When his fingers found her clit and spread her slickness over the excited tissue, she almost groaned loudly. As he massaged, a fire grew higher and hotter, the strokes only pausing when he drew his fingers back to her cunt and slipped inside.

She bit back another moan as he dipped in first one finger, then a second. Her palms flattened against the wall as her eyes closed. She ached as he continued a maddening exploration of wet, hot, engorged territory. Just imagining the moment when he'd slip inside her and pump her full of seed sent coils of radiating heat into her lower body.

"Sweet colleen, you are so wet and hot."

He undid his jeans and shoved them down. Suddenly, he dipped his cock into her cunt, a quick little probe that made her gasp in surprised pleasure.

"Please," she whispered as his heat wrapped around her like a blanket.

Again he plunged inside, but this time he didn't withdraw or stop. He drove forward and she muffled her cry as he speared straight into her.

With unbearable slowness he withdrew, then arrowed deep. Wedging his thighs against the back of hers, he kept his movements short and rhythmic. He clenched her hips between his palms, anchoring her. Each rub of his cock caressed sensitive, exquisitely aroused tissues. The back and forth friction opened her wider, deeper as she absorbed his thrusts.

Sensation spilled over and reduced her to a mindless drive toward completion. On the edge of consciousness, she heard their primal sounds, the gasp for breath and small moans of pleasure that fired her need. Her heart pounded a new, relentless beat in time with his cadence. Eagerly she spread her legs as far as the clothing around her knees would allow. Merciless, he took the hint and stepped up the pace. Stroking now with sharp digs, he thrust hard and sure.

Her skin flushed, heated, her breath panting between parted lips. She couldn't stand the pleasure; her cunt clenched his body as his thrusts now pounded inside her slickness. Beyond speech or thought, she allowed her body to fly free.

Climax hit her hard as it rose up and stung her clit, then burst with staggering intensity in jolts of bliss. She quivered and shook as the orgasm rocked her core.

He gave one last, stabbing thrust. His cock swelled and he gasped out, "God, how I love you!"

He burst inside her and moaned low in his throat. His revelation made her shake as another climax ripped through her in small, unbelievably delicious shivers.

Tears filled her eyes and she sobbed with happiness. Immediately he slipped from her body and pulled up her panties and jeans. He rearranged his clothing. Turning her around, he kept his body against hers.

He cupped her face and his intense, worried gaze held a fiery copper. "Are you all right? Did I hurt you?"

She smiled through her tears. "I'm wonderful. Did I hear you say you loved me?"

Clarissa never thought she'd see a bashful smile on his hard face, but this time he grinned and it came across almost embarrassed. "Sure and I suppose you want to hear it again?"

"Oh yes," she said, a little breathless.

He kissed her deeply, his tongue wrapping and twining with hers in a dance seductive and loving. When he came up for air he confessed, "I love you so much I ache. I never thought I could feel like this again. Please tell me you feel the same way about me?"

He looked a little boyish and uncertain, an expression she never expected to see on his face. With a tender melting in her heart, she slipped her arms around his waist and smiled. "I love you. I love you so much."

Pressing his forehead to hers, he closed his eyes. "You don't know how much I needed to hear that."

"Then let me tell you again. I love you. You were wonderful. I thought I was going to split into a million pieces."

Low, sinful laughter filled her ears. "It's colder then a well digger's arse out here. Let's go inside where I can love you properly."

Yes, that sounds so good.

They finished fixing their clothes. Inside the house Lachlan and Erin sat close together on the couch, their arms tightly around each other as if they, too, felt the heat. They loosened their embrace, but Clarissa could see the adoration and need thrumming between the other couple. When they learned she wasn't pregnant, disappointment entered their eyes. Lachlan and Erin knew how important this had become. Micky and Jared walked in a few moments later through the utility room with their luggage. When they heard the news, resignation passed over their features.

"There must be something else we can do." Desperation tinged Micky's voice and she blushed. "We can't expect Ronan and Clarissa to just…"

Lachlan shrugged. "Aye, we'll start thinking of an alternate plan." His gaze flicked to Clarissa and Ronan. "Just in case."

The radio blasted a new report about the sporadic crime around the small city.

"I hate to ask what it's like out there," Erin said to Micky.

Jared nodded. "It's dicey. It makes me think that with this upsurge in crime the Halloween party might be cancelled anyway."

"Don't count on it," Erin said with sarcasm. "I'm not sure the people around here get it. Even if crime has gone up, it's likely the mayor is going to think the reason is something entirely different."

"Like?" Micky slumped onto the loveseat with a sign.

Erin leaned forward. "Devil worship. He's not exactly one of the most enlightened people in town. He doesn't understand the true origins of Halloween."

Clarissa felt an inherent discomfort with people like the mayor who stayed deliberately ignorant of the truth. "One of *those* people."

"Yes." Erin clasped her hands.

"Why would he allow a party if he thinks Halloween is devil worship?" Micky asked.

"Because he understands that most other people don't think of Halloween that way," Lachlan said.

Ronan's voice was out low and derisive as he said, "Political book."

Jared settled down next to Micky. "What if we could convince him that something evil was about to happen at the party?"

"How?" Erin asked.

The cop ran his hand through his hair and smiled ruefully. "Beats the shit out of me."

Lachlan laughed softly. "Thanks. You're a lot of help."

Jared tossed his friend a chagrinned expression.

"We can't worry about the mayor," Ronan said. "We can't rely on anyone but ourselves. I know you all feel like were riding this wave by our arses. The ancient one and this darkest evil will find us, one way or the other. We can meditate on what could happen tomorrow. Maybe one of us will have an inspiration."

"What about Sorley?" Micky asked. "Do you think he's beyond help?"

Clarissa saw the hurt on Ronan's face as his finely carved lips twitched in reaction. When she'd first met him she'd thought of Ronan as cool and yet hot, a man with two emotional switches. Now she'd witnessed more of his depths, it made her feelings for him grow in turn.

"No. But I don't know what we can do at this point. Maybe he'll come back on his own, and maybe he won't. We can't go after him. It could be that's just what the ancient one wants. We may have won two battles against that bastard but the war isn't over. We can't afford to let our guard down one minute." Ronan drew a hefty breath before continuing. "I don't know about the rest of you, but I've got to have some vampire beauty sleep."

Lachlan grinned. "A bit knackered, eh?"

"A bit what?" Jared asked with a puzzled frown.

Ronan looked down at Clarissa and winked. "Tired. And tomorrow is going to be one hell of a day."

Clarissa felt heat fill her face. Who needed the devil when Ronan Kieran could make saucy jokes in front of all their friends?

She didn't get a chance to retort. Lachlan said, "We'll brainstorm while you rest. Something will come to us."

Ronan tightened his arm around Clarissa's waist and led her away. As they ascended the stairs, Clarissa knew they had one last chance.

Tomorrow was Halloween.

Chapter Eighteen

Ronan dreamed again of being in a tunnel. The icy pall promised to harden his heart and his soul as it encircled his body and held him captive. He wanted to understand the message but nothing new came to him. Instead he lingered on the edge of consciousness. Then the dream changed slightly. He saw two forms in the tunnel, menacing, waiting to harm his woman. His heart beat against his chest in fear.

No, he wouldn't let them hurt Clarissa. "You can't have her. I love her."

The dark forms disappeared and he knew he'd vanquished them. Before he felt safe, the tunnels darkened.

Wearehterewearehterewearehtere.

Wearehterewearehterewearehtere.

Wewillhelpwewillhelpwewillhelp.

Once again the Shadow People wanted to reassure him; he felt no threat coming from them but uncertainty lingered.

Warm, tender hands caressed his chest, lingering in the hair over his pecs and bringing his nipples to hard, aching points.

Kin to a leprechaun. That feels way too good to be a dream.

Palms swirled over his nipples continually and then swept down his stomach and traced every ridge of muscle with teasing strokes. He shuddered as instantaneous arousal drew his cock into a tight, hard muscle. He wanted those hands all over him, but at the same time he sensed urgency in the touch. When a hot, wet mouth encompassed his cock, his eyes flew open and he looked down.

Clarissa was, in no uncertain terms, sucking him off.

When he found his voice, his accent thickened. "Mother Mary, what a beautiful, feckin' sight."

At his words her head snapped up and she smiled. She flipped her hair back from her face. She kept his flesh in her hand, firmly working him from base to tip. "Hi."

He glanced around and saw moonlight streaming from under the curtains and through the fan window. "Is it Halloween morning? Where the hell did yesterday go?"

She smirked. "It was all that lovemaking. I think we were both in a stupor by last night."

Yesterday, after he'd obtained some much needed vampire sleep, everyone had gathered in the living room to try and make plans for Halloween. Nothing new came to mind on what they should do. Disappointed, they realized the only thing they could do was arm themselves and hope for the best. They would all stay together. No one would leave the house alone. Last night Ronan and Clarissa retreated to their bedroom and spent a good chunk of the night fucking like bunnies.

He smiled. "What time is it?"

"Four in the morning, to be exact. I woke up and there you were. Irresistible." She kept the pace going, her hands slipping over him one and then the other in a sensual massage that sent jolts of electricity to every point in his body. "Besides, you were dreaming and you didn't look happy. Want to tell me about it?"

"I'll tell you if you keep doing that."

With a smile that said she appreciated what he had to say, she murmured, "Gladly."

Her mouth encompassed him, a glide and slip and stroke that put shame to any blowjob he'd every experienced. His breathing went ragged, his heart galloping as she licked the tip, then traced her tongue down his length. She then licked his balls and pressed one finger between his balls and anus. When she rubbed the spot a shiver racked his body. She tongued his balls and stroked his cock at one time and he about came unglued from the multiple sensations.

He threaded his fingers into her hair and drew his legs up to give her more room. "Holy shit. Oh God."

"I take it that means you like it?"

"Do I like it?" He about choked. "I want to be inside you."

"Not yet," she said as if putting together a casual shopping list.

Torture. She meant to torment him to within an inch of screaming.

He liked the way she'd grown bolder, more adventurous with her sexual play since he'd first taken her. He groaned as she licked him from stem to stern, her warm tongue and even hotter lips scalding him with sensations so intense he wondered if he could take the pressure without shooting seed down her throat. Clarissa slipped her mouth down over his cock and took him deep.

He gasped and his hips surged up. "Bloody hell."

Her mouth explored every texture, vein, and contour. *Feck, he'd had it. He would die right here and now.*

"Clarissa." He gasped for breath now. "Ride me."

She released his cock and slid up his body. She straddled him and when she dropped down over his cock with a plunge and gloved him in sweet, tight flesh, he about came on the spot.

Instead he said between pants, "That's it. Oh, that's feckin' it. Come on, ride me."

She did as requested as she lifted and slammed down. The sensation made him moan and he pushed his hips upwards to impale her more deeply. Silken, slick and hot, her interior held him captive. He dared open his eyes and saw her looking down at him, her lips parted and plump. Then, before his sight she became a sex goddess, a woman unleashed and swamped by ecstasy. She stopped moving and before he could protest the cessation of action, she closed her eyes and tilted her head back. Her sweet channel clasped him like a fist, then released. Clasped, then released.

"God, oh God." He couldn't keep the words out of his throat. "Yes."

Clarissa closed her eyes and pumped him, moving up and down with a quick, gyrating motion as she rotated her hips. He reached up and caught her nipples between his fingers and played. She moaned louder as he plucked at the tips. Quickening his movements he thrust upward harder as she met him with downward strokes.

He felt her hovering on the brink, bliss only seconds away. Determined to make her come now, he clasped her hips and thrust faster. Her head tilted back, her tongue coming out to lick her lips. Seconds later she burst, and the feeling of her tight cunt clutching his flesh sent him into a powerful, groaning orgasm.

She collapsed onto his chest and he cradled her close, a smile coming to his lips as he barely panted out the words, "I think she's trying to kill me."

With a sigh she subsided against him. "Mmm."

Obviously she was in no condition to talk. He heard a soft snore. Surprised, he held her in his arms and smiled. He'd fucked her into oblivion, all right. He held her close, fierce protectiveness singing through his veins.

He would keep her safe through this, even if it cost him his immortal life.

* * * * *

The ancient one watched his captives struggle for control.

Captive and helpless described the smaller, much younger vampire's hopeless situation. The spineless little immortal, once powerful in his own right had been too cocky. He lost some of his dignity as he struggled against the force field surrounding and trapping him. Nearby a newly made vampire thrashed in the force field. This one had balls. He'd give him that.

Poor vampires, struggling with your sanity and your fear and the realization you've betrayed people you love.

"Let me go!" The new vampire struggled, yanking against the hold. The man's voice was guttural and determined. "I'll tear out your throat!"

The ancient one wasn't concerned by the threat. "You will do my bidding from now on."

The new vampire's eyes glowed like hot fire, a silver and gold mixture like nothing the ancient one had ever seen. "No! I will not hurt them!"

"Yes." He walked closer to the vampires and stared down at them from a much superior height. Capturing the skinny vampire's gaze, he held him in the thrall, drawing his will from him. "There's nothing you can do but obey. Nothing. I am in your mind. The *darkest* is in your mind. There is no freedom for you. You are a slave. Open your mind wider, deeper, to the *darkest*."

"Feck you!" the skinny vampire said with a viscous snarl.

Unaffected by the inferior vampire's wrath, the ancient one snickered. "I don't think so. You're not my type."

As the ancient one bellowed another laugh, the new vampire wriggled against the invisible force field once more. "No!"

Sighing, the ancient one said, "Isn't that refrain getting a little old?" His voice went deeper, harsher, invading the other vampires' skulls with ease. "Open to me. Open!"

Grimacing, the skinny vampire appeared to resist with everything inside him. No words parted the immortal's lips, but the ancient one could read chaotic thoughts. The ancient one sensed both vampires' minds going blank, once again under his complete thrall.

The newly made vampire shifted against the cold tunnel wall, his eyes wild with anger. Certainly, the ancient one had to admire the new immortal's lack of fear, or at least the ability to hide it. "You wonder why I brought you across? Why I didn't just kill you as I have all the others? Because you have a mission to fulfill."

"I don't give a shit what you say," the new vampire rasped, his voice sounded choked and rusty.

With a hollow laugh the ancient one disengaged the force field. Both captured men slid down the tunnel wall.

The ancient one said, "You will bring Clarissa Gaines and Erin Greenway to me. When they first see you they will trust you and it will take them off guard. Bring them here and we will feast on their blood. Do you understand?"

The skinny vampire nodded and so did the new vampire. They spoke at once, "Yes."

The ancient one gestured down the tunnel. "Then go."

The vampires walked sluggishly toward the outside world, and within a couple of seconds they'd disappeared completely from the tunnels.

Amused and satisfied with his work, the ancient one laughed again, this time allowing the hearty, happy sound to bellow forth full strength. Tonight all of Pine Forest would pay for its stupidity.

Lachlan Tavish and Ronan Kieran would know special pain when the veil between worlds became most thin. After they watched him feast on their women, he would kill Tavish and Kieran and enjoy their blood as well.

* * * * *

Clarissa woke and her entire body felt achy and the mysterious nausea returned. Somewhere in the time since he'd last made love to her, they'd rolled over and faced away from each other. They'd spent all that morning making love, cherishing each other between trips to the refrigerator to gain sustenance. She'd lost count long ago how many times they'd made love. If their world was to come to an end, they would have no regrets.

The others in the house sequestered themselves in the living room listening to news reports and keeping the doors barred. To their surprise some of the violence in Pine Forest had calmed, not something they expected. Clarissa knew a growing hope in her heart that maybe she'd been totally wrong about the mayhem to come...maybe all of them had been wrong.

She could hope.

Wincing, she looked at the digital clock and noted the time read almost four-thirty in the afternoon. Night rapidly approached. Ronan would be stirring soon from his daylight slumber. She felt the need to think, to enjoy a little personal space.

She got out of bed and searched for her clothes. As she slipped into her boots and tied them up, an odd notion came to her.

She looked at the dresser and hesitated, then moved toward it with sure strides. She didn't have to fumble to find the second pregnancy kit Erin had given her. Clarissa headed for the bathroom with the idea of taking the test, but a strange intuition made her stop. A creepy feeling ran down her spine like a worm traveling with a slow and insistent pace.

Leaving the pregnancy test on the bathroom counter, she went downstairs. She saw the porch light on through the back living room curtains. Peaking between the curtains she saw Erin standing outside. Clarissa went through the dining room and opened the back door.

Erin jumped and turned swiftly. "Oh jeez, you scared the hell out of me."

Clarissa smiled and closed the door behind her. "What are you doing out here without a coat?"

"I could ask the same of you."

Clarissa's smile widened. "Touché."

Erin's expression turned serious. "I haven't been out here more than a minute. I heard...it must have been my imagination, but it scared me."

An odd premonitory sense kicked in and tickled Clarissa's psyche. She approached Erin, oblivious to the iciness for a moment. "What did you hear?"

"I was walking through the living room and I heard your voice calling to me. When I stepped out here, though, you obviously weren't here. I was just about to come back in when you startled me by showing up."

Clarissa's sense of danger increased. "Something's wrong, Erin. Come on let's get back inside and—"

Before either of them could move, two dark shadows swept out of the encroaching night from around the right side of the house. Though it could only be a few seconds, time seemed to slow down for Clarissa. She flinched but stopped short of a startled shriek. Erin seemed stunned, her eyes wide, hands going up to defend.

Clarissa moved in front of Erin, her body feeling lighter and stronger than it had in some time, as if another power gave her strength. Her defensive stance in front of her friend made Erin grab her arm from behind, but Clarissa didn't move.

"Sorley?" Erin asked, her voice choked with fright. "You scared the hell out of us. What's going on?"

Clarissa recognized the other man with him and stiffened with apprehension. Something still wasn't right. "Jim." Jim's hair was tousled and his face held two or more days' growth of beard. His down coat was torn in two places near the zipper and smudged with dirt. "Are you all right?"

"He's all right now," Sorley said, a hint of Irish wryness peeking through their startling appearance. "He wasn't before, but he's seen the truth."

Although her heart hadn't stop pounding, Clarissa said to Jim, "You've decided the paranormal is real?"

Jim's smile held an uncanny edge, and then she observed a change in Jim's eyes, a flicker of flame that matched Sorley's. "Jim, were you bitten by a vampire?"

He nodded. "You could say that."

"Enough chitchat. That's not what we're here for," Sorley said.

Sorley's clipped tone scraped over Clarissa's nerves. "Everyone's been worried about you, Sorley."

When he smiled she saw his fangs and another trickle of unease did a dance across Clarissa's skin. "Did something else happen that we don't know about?"

Jim laughed softly. "Oh, yes. And now that I know what it is, I want you to be a part of it. With me."

She glanced and Erin and her friend returned her worried look. A niggling panic worked itself into her like a slow splinter into a finger. "Jim, there is no us. I'm with Ronan Kieran."

He looked confident. "No, you're going to be mine. You were promised to me."

As Jim's lips parted she saw his fangs and then the reality hit her full force. "Oh my God. You weren't just bitten, you've been turned into a vampire."

Tears stung her eyes. She never would have wished this on Jim in a million years.

Jim and Sorley lunged toward them so fast, Clarissa didn't have time to react. Jim swooped and grabbed Clarissa around the throat. The pressure around her neck cut off her air immediately. She swung up to slash at his eyes and tried kicking him. He threw her back against the wall. Pain and shock rocked into her head as dizziness filled her head and her knees crumbled. She fell to the concrete on her right side. Disoriented, she heard Erin's struggles, and then saw Sorley lift her up and into the sky. She fought unconsciousness but as Sorley's high-pitched laugh echoed over the air, everything went black.

* * * * *

Ronan awoke with a start, his breathing coming hard and fast. In deepest sleep he'd heard strange noises somewhere outside the house. The bed felt cold. He couldn't sense Clarissa next to him.

He reached out and touched the bed and found it empty. Because he could see through the gloom without a light, he scanned the area. No sign of Clarissa. Normally it wouldn't have bothered him too much, but he felt it deep in his immortal soul that she needed him.

He opened his mind to her. *Clarissa. Where are you? Are you all right?*

He waited for an answer but nothing came. Something was horribly wrong.

"Clarissa?" Nothing. He didn't feel her in the house or anywhere. Fear snapped him like a whip. "Damn it! Shit, shit, shit!"

Using vampire speed he jumped into his clothes and then transported instantly into the living room.

Lachlan stood at the back door near the dining area, his eyes glowing like hot coals. His face looked stricken, as if he'd been kicked in the gut. "She's gone, Ronan. Erin's gone."

Ronan stiffened, his heart doing a stutter. "So is Clarissa." Ronan's mind tried to wrap around the concept a moment and failed. Then anger at himself and Lachlan exploded in his mind. "I can't believe I didn't hear anything. Son-of-a-bitch!"

Lachlan's words came strong and steady. "Aye, but there's time for recriminations later. Right now we need to find them."

Self-disgust wrenched at Ronan's insides. "I'm sorry."

Lachlan shook his head. "I don't sense them anywhere around in the neighborhood and they wouldn't leave voluntarily."

Ronan heard a sound and sensed Micky and Jared coming down the hall.

"What's going on?" Jared asked, trepidation hardening his eyes. "We both woke up at the same time and knew something was wrong."

Ronan jammed both hands through his hair in frustration. "Erin and Clarissa are gone. We've got to go after them now."

Jared grabbed his arm. "I'll go with you and so will Micky. I'm not leaving here without her."

Lachlan moved nearer his friends. "No. There's no reason to take her into harm's way."

"I want to go." Micky stood straight and her mouth had a stubborn set to it that Ronan knew didn't bode well. Her eyes glowed. "You need our help. What if the ancient one or that other dark evil has taken them into another dimension? I've been in that place before, so if they're lost there, I can bring them back."

Ronan looked at Lachlan and the Scot nodded. He also understood that Jared wouldn't be any use to them if he worried about Micky being left behind and vulnerable.

Micky's logic eased a little of Ronan's panic and she said, "We'll find them. My guess is the ancient one probably took them to the tunnels. Can we form a psychic circle and join hands to get her location?"

In the short time since Micky had become a not-quite-mortal, she'd read as much literature on the subject as she could. Ronan admired her bravery. "I think your first intuition is right. He's taken them to the tunnels."

"We could waste valuable time if we don't do a preliminary recon," Jared said.

Lachlan nodded. "He's right."

Ronan's eagerness to find his woman made him crazy with worry and he couldn't think with the logic required. He closed his eyes and took a deep breath. "Let's do it."

A few moments later, the group gathered in the center of the living room and joined hands. Ronan thanked them in his heart, grateful down to his boots he didn't have to fight this alone. As they linked minds he knew it would deplete their energies for a short time after doing the connection. They'd have to make sure they didn't stay joined for too long.

"Remember the white light, the aura around you," Ronan said. "We can't afford to be vulnerable."

They became a collective of energy more powerful than one individual. Almost right away a vivid flash of color came to his mind, disjointed and harsh. Pink ran into blue ran into red and as black spilled over his mind, he jerked out of the trance.

"Holy crap," Lachlan said, blinking rapidly. "What was that?"

Everyone broke contact and unlinked hands.

"The colors are a barrier. The ancient one knows we'll come looking for Erin and Clarissa and he put up defenses," Ronan said.

Pain flickered through his head and Ronan couldn't keep back the groan. Instinctively, he what knew what caused the pain. Anger pierced him like a sword.

Micky touched his forearm. "What's wrong?"

Ronan felt the tension rising and didn't think he could stop it. He couldn't remember the last time a vampire rage this strong had come upon him.

Yes, I can. After I was changed…and before that, after Fenella was killed.

He knew his eyes turned hell-red and that his fangs had grown. He didn't care. He wanted his woman safe and he would do anything to get her back into his arms.

Ronan stalked to the windows and looked out. His throat felt tight and raw as he spoke. "The pain in my head belongs to Clarissa."

"Oh, no," Micky said, tears swimming in her eyes. "What are we going to do?"

Ronan frowned and tried to ignore the throbbing in his temples. "We'll have to search for them the mortal way. Do you think Gilda and Tom would help?"

Micky went for the phone. "I'll call them now."

For the third time in a month they pursued the ancient one. Concern about Erin and Clarissa and even Sorley invaded his thoughts as his friends put out heavy-duty emotional thought forms. Lachlan's emotions ran higher, his concern for Erin eating away at his guts. Ronan knew the reaction too well; he couldn't wait to put his arms around Clarissa and beg her forgiveness for not protecting her.

"I suggest you drive to the Gunn Inn first while I do a quick scan of the tunnels near the crypt in the graveyard," Ronan said. "We can cover more ground that way."

"Aye," Lachlan said.

Vampire rage stirred Ronan's blood. "We *are* going to find them. Starting now."

* * * * *

Clarissa's head pounded as she opened her eyes and she tried to put her fingers to her temples. Her arms and hands wouldn't move an inch. Alarmed, she tried moving her legs and found she couldn't.

Other than turning her head from side to side, she was paralyzed. A shimmering silver essence covered her from head to foot, perhaps the same substance that kept her from moving an inch. She struggled against the force field that pinned her to the ground but it didn't help.

She heard a moan, then realized it came from her. Cold seeped into her skin like an insidious drug. She turned her head to the left and saw a broken wooden coffin tilted against a wall like a mummy's sarcophagus in a museum. Muzzy-headed and hurting to the bone, she couldn't be sure of her location. Nothing seemed quite right; her thought processes refused to run at one hundred percent.

She remembered with a jolt.

Attacked. She and Erin...they'd been attacked on the porch by two of the last people she would have expected would hurt them. *Sorley, how could you?* And Jim. She never expected Jim to hurt her.

She glanced around her prison once again. *I can see in the dark.* Horror returned.

"Oh, God. I can see in the dark and—"

Her heart started to thud, pounding in her chest. Sweat broke out over her skin despite the wintry interior. Fear swelled and threatened to overtake her good sense.

Sounds seemed to be louder. Dread crawled over her skin like spiders and she was grateful that at least she wore a thick sweater. Though she could see in the dark, the visuals didn't come as clear as day, but more like the time between sunset and complete oblivion of light. Her breath puffed out in the frosted air.

Even if the stinging pain in her neck didn't tell the truth, she would have known by other evidence. She'd probably been bitten.

No. Oh no. Tears welled up. Someone had bitten her. No, not someone. Either Sorley or Jim or the ancient one had taken her blood but they hadn't drained her to death. That meant one thing. Like her friends, she stayed trapped between the mortal world and the immortal. Her mind whirled around the idea, uncertain whether to accept the truth and move on or scream into the night. She wanted to deny the facts, imagine a nightmare took hold of her and wouldn't let go. This couldn't be real.

Evidence showed her otherwise.

As the sounds of night again intruded on her ears, a sense of wonder overcame her. This must be a little of what Ronan felt and saw as a vampire. Excitement threatened to edge out the horror that erupted like a geyser inside her. She took a deep breath. Taking action rather then reacting to what happened would be her best course. *Down the path of reaction lies death.*

Erin. How could I forget Erin?

Another chaotic thought intruded.

Since her surroundings told Clarissa she hadn't been dumped in the crypt over the tunnels, then where had they taken her? Nearby the wooden coffin lid was cracked open enough she could see inside. No one, thank God, living or dead was there. A stone stand held another coffin, this one also wood, but dark and far more expensive. Dusty and cracked, the mahogany wood looked antique.

She looked around as bewilderment wrestled with fright. She must put a noose on her emotions and concentrate on what to do. Wherever Jim and Sorley had gone, she would leave before they came back.

Ronan. She closed her eyes. *Ronan can you hear me? I need you. I'm in a crypt. Not the one I fell through, but another crypt. I'm going to try and escape.*

When she received no confirmation, when his beloved voice didn't form in her mind, she tried again. *Ronan, I love you.*

And she did love him. Thinking about how much he meant to her warmed the cold, dark place inside that feared for her life and what would come.

Ronan, please hear me.

The nagging ache in her head increased.

A soft moan caught her sensitive ears. "Erin?"

"Clarissa?"

Thank the heavens.

"We're being pinned down by something, aren't we?" Erin's testy voice assured Clarissa her friend was alive and kicking mad.

"Yes. Can you break loose?"

"I've tried. It isn't working. But if we concentrate mentally maybe we can get free."

Clarissa would try anything at this point. "How?"

"Close your eyes and try visualizing the barrier around you dissolving."

Clarissa had her doubts.

"Come on, Clarissa, I know you can do it."

"Are you reading my mind?"

"No, but I can feel your hesitation."

"All right. I'll try it."

She closed her eyes and concentrated, allowing her body to relax despite the tremendous cold. Easier than she anticipated, the barrier started to fade in her mind. As the barrier became weaker she could see through it more clearly. With a soft whoosh, the murky white stuff around Clarissa dissolved within less than four minutes.

Clarissa let out a whoop.

Erin's chuckle sounded half sincere. "Mine's gone, too. Maybe the big bad ancient one isn't so bad after all."

"Or maybe he let one of his minions help him." Clarissa remembered Sorley and Jim with disappointment.

Clarissa staggered to her feet. Her fingers gripped the rotting wood coffin on the pedestal, and she yanked her hand away in disgust. Her sense of touch seemed hyper and almost painful she could feel so much. Another deep breath stilled the frantic pace of her heart. She would regain control or fail escaping. The crypt door had a significant crack in the side of the stonework wide enough for a big man to slip through, but the door was obscured with trailing vines. Could this be the crypt the ancient one had slept in since his last encounter with Ronan and his friends?

Shoving aside those thoughts, she moved around the pedestal and coffin and found Erin lying on the ground.

Erin sat upright. "Ouch. I feel like someone has been stomping on me with a big shoe."

"I feel the same way." Clarissa gave her theory on their location and explained her attempt to connect with Ronan failed. "We're not in the crypt I fell through. But we need to get out of here before Sorley and Jim come back."

Erin's gaze, already glowing in the dark like a cat's, turned hot. She wondered if her own eyes reflected the new, more animal side she possessed. "How could they do this to us?"

"Ronan told us about the mind invasion with the ancient one. Sorley's psyche was too weak and that's how the ancient one got through."

Erin's eyes widened a little as she gazed at Clarissa. "Your throat." She reached up and touched her own puncture wounds. "They bit us."

"I'm not going to dwell on it right now or the consequences." Clarissa smiled weakly. "I'm hoping some of those supernatural powers come to me very quickly. Right now I'm just feeling weak."

Erin touched her shoulder and pressed. "You've lost blood and who knows how much."

Shivering with renewed cold and fear, Clarissa said, "Why didn't they just kill us?"

"I don't know. Maybe Sorley and Jim still have some humanity and resisted the temptation to kill or bring us across."

"Bring us across? As in turn us into full-fledged vampires?"

"Yes. Come on, let's try to connect with Lachlan and Ronan again and if we can't, we'll get out of here."

They tried and failed to connect with their men.

"The ancient one wants to use us for bait," Erin said. "He'd like nothing more than to kill Lachlan and Ronan. You know they'll come for us."

Clarissa's heart ached at the thought they'd be in danger. "We've got to find a way back to town and warn them not to come looking for us."

Erin started for the crack in the crypt. Wedging through the crack one by one, they shoved through the stiff trailing fronds of a plant that grew out of the side of the rock.

"We aren't going to survive this cold much longer." Erin rubbed her arms as they surveyed the dark landscape.

When Clarissa looked at the big crypt from the outside she could barely see it for the tangle of bushes surrounding the entrance. More than that, the crypt didn't stand alone like the one in the graveyard did. Carved straight from an enormous ridge of rock, the crypt melded with the hillside in perfect harmony. A person could walk right by this spot and never see the burial chamber at all.

"Where are we?" Clarissa asked.

Erin shook her head. "I don't know."

Their dire circumstances overwhelmed Clarissa in one horrible thought. "We're in the middle of who knows where in the freezing cold without coats. If we stay here we'll die of hypothermia. If we leave, we may die of hypothermia."

Erin's eyes flamed with a golden light, a dance of red and sun yellow that would frighten most people with one glance. "I think I'd rather die trying to find a way out of here, don't you?"

Understanding the truth when she heard it, Clarissa said, "If we keep moving, we just might stay warm enough to make it out of this alive."

A popping noise near the entrance to the tomb made them both jump. Before they could move or speak Jim appeared near the crypt entry.

Clarissa and Erin both stepped back. Clarissa's heart pumped like crazy.

Jim smiled and his pointed canines showed. He, too, stood in the cold with nothing but a sweater and jeans. She knew he didn't feel the chill of winter. If it weren't for his pointed teeth and an eerie look in his eyes, she'd never guess he'd been turned into a vampire.

"Clarissa, I see you're planning on escaping. I don't think so," he said.

Her mind raced for something to say, but her brain felt like cottage cheese. Struggling with fatigue, she leaned back against the crypt. "Why did you do this, Jim?"

"I didn't decide to do this. It was done to me." His words sounded angry, almost petulant, his smile turning into a frown.

"No, why did you hurt us and take us to this place?" Erin asked.

He continued to frown, his eyes shining with an ethereal glow like a full moon. He took a deep breath. "The old one commands it."

"Did you bite me?" Clarissa asked suddenly.

"I didn't want Sorley to do it because you're mine."

Erin asked, "What about me?"

Jim's eyes took on a confused appearance, as if he couldn't quite remember what happened. "The old one said I needed blood to survive. And I...I..."

He stopped, his voice cracking a little.

Clarissa wondered if he could see around the haze of becoming a vampire to understand what he'd done. "Yes?"

"I couldn't let the old one or Sorley take your blood." His hands went out. "They're...they would have killed you both."

Withering emotional pain made Clarissa's eyes well up with tears. "So you took our blood to save us from them."

"Of course." Jim staggered a little and leaned back against the rocks near the crypt opening. "I'm sorry I hit you. I had to make it look good. The ancient one attacked me after the last time I saw you, Clarissa. He's had me sequestered in those damned tunnels all this time. When I woke up and he explained what he'd done and what he plans to do, I couldn't let him take complete control of me. He's still inside me. I can feel him."

Jim reeled around and slammed his fist against the rock. A loud cracking noise hurt Clarissa's ears and a nine-inch gash opened in the stone.

Her heart broke for Jim, his life transformed into a new form he could never change back.

Unsure what he planned to do next, Clarissa made a decision she hoped she wouldn't regret tomorrow. "Where are Sorley and the ancient one?"

"The ancient one took Sorley with him to the community center."

Clarissa took a chance. "Help us. They're planning on the complete destruction of Pine Forest."

He shook his head. "It's already started."

Erin walked closer to him. "The people in the community center are in danger. We've got to do something to stop it."

"Those dreams I told you about in high school? Do you remember what I said about them?" Clarissa asked Jim.

He bowed his head. "You told me and I didn't believe you."

"Now's the time to believe me." Clarissa looked straight into his wary, sad gaze. "Help us, Jim."

Defeat etched his features. "How?"

"Ronan and the others are probably out looking for us. Find them and tell them what's happened to us." She turned her gaze to Erin. "We have to go to the community center."

Lines formed between Erin's eyebrows as she frowned. "How can we stop the ancient one if we go there?"

"I don't know." Clarissa shook her head. "But we must try."

Erin's acquiescence came in the form of a sigh, and Clarissa could see that despite her friend's qualms, she knew they had to stop the ancient one or die trying. "All right, let's go."

Unable to feel genuine fear of Jim anymore, Clarissa reached out and squeezed his arm. "You probably saved my life and Erin's. Now help us save Pine Forest. Find Ronan and Lachlan and tell them we're going to the community center to stop the ancient one."

Looking broken, he nodded. "I'm sorry, Clarissa. You know I never meant this to happen."

Her heart aching, she turned to look back at him. "No, I'm the one who's sorry. Despite our past, I never would have wished this on you."

He gave them directions and which way they should head to find the community center.

Erin touched Clarissa's shoulder. "Come on. We haven't got much time."

*   *   *   *   *

As Ronan searched the tunnels under the crypt in the graveyard, he tried making contact with Clarissa. There was no sign of her and he couldn't connect with her on a mental level. That worried him more than anything else. Would he know...could he stand the pain if she was dead?

"No," he said as he kept moving. He refused to believe it. "She's alive."

He inhaled and pushed back staggering pain, knowing it came from loving her and wanting her safe. It also came from the responsibility he felt for her welfare. If anything happened to her, the accountability fell on his shoulders.

Ronan. Lachlan's voice came into his head like a stab, a sharp call. *Any sign of them?*

None.

We're searching the inn. We're going into the basement now.

Be careful.

We will. Can you meet us here?

I'm halfway there already.

As Ronan continued to search he put out calls to Clarissa mentally. Though probing for her telepathically on a continuous stream could weaken him, he must keep trying until he broke through whatever miasma the ancient one had put around their ability to touch each other's minds.

He tried contacting Sorley. *Sorley, where are you? Have you taken Clarissa? Have you seen her and Erin? Speak to me.*

A tickling began in his mind, as if someone tried to touch him but couldn't reach far enough. The essence felt female, and his heart leapt with hope.

Clarissa? Please talk to me.

"Damn it, Clarissa, where are you?"

* * * * *

Clarissa tromped through the snow, grateful she wore hiking boots. Although she'd been chilled since she regained consciousness in the crypt, the activity seemed to fight the cold. That and the temperature edged above freezing tonight.

Erin cracked a smile, sad and yet genuine. "Lachlan and Ronan will find us."

While she knew Erin was a strong woman, she also knew that they couldn't rely one hundred percent on the men locating them. "We don't know if Jim is really going to find Ronan and Lachlan."

"That's true. But at least your quick thinking convinced him he'd rather do that than harm us again."

Sadness entered Clarissa in a bleak wave. "Jim didn't deserve what happened to him. I wonder if Sorley is all right."

"I'm not sure I care anymore. The little creep turned traitor."

Clarissa decided not to say that she'd already forgiven Sorley. The ancient one and the evil that joined with him could do massive damage to the psyche. How could she blame anyone for succumbing to that type of horror?

"Lachlan's going to be frantic and I know Ronan will be, too. He loves you so much," Erin said.

"And I love him." There, she'd said it into the cold night where the words became real.

Erin nodded. "Let's walk faster. I think my feet are freezing. And my hands are starting to hurt."

"Do you think you can run?"

"Can I run? Do bears do it in the woods?"

A laugh rippled out of Clarissa's throat.

"I can use those latent vampire tendencies to work at my advantage," Erin said. "And so can you. Plus, I was a bit of a track champion in high school." When Clarissa lifted a dubious eyebrow, Erin smiled. "With these short legs? I know it doesn't seem likely. But I wanted it badly enough to train for it." Erin winked. "Think you can keep up?"

Liking the cocky, refuse-to-give-up attitude they'd adopted, Clarissa said, "Probably not. But bring it on."

"I think I see a glow through those trees."

Clarissa picked up her speed, trotting along as fast as they could in the snow without slipping and falling. She felt new energy overriding all her earlier aches and pains, a sensation of freedom. Suddenly she noted the trees next to them went by at a damn fine speed, faster than a normal human could run. While she ran, at least for this moment, Clarissa felt invincible. She was half-vampire, but the benefits at present outweighed the bad.

Exhilarated, Clarissa let out a hoot. Erin grinned and kept running.

They slowed their pace as the glow of light above the tree line became clearer and Pine Creek came into view.

Erin came to a stop at the edge of the trees and Clarissa caught up to her. As Clarissa took in the scene, she felt déjà vu. Her dream of Pine Forest's destruction was well on its way.

Clarissa and Erin crouched down behind a clump of immature pine trees and looked out into the large parking lot alongside the community center. Filled to bursting, the number of people attending the function proved that despite murder and mayhem, Pine Forest had decided merrymaking on Halloween wouldn't be stopped.

"What are we going to do?" Erin said, her tone inferring that she hated not knowing what to do next.

Clarissa had an insane idea. "Maybe we should go to the party."

Erin glanced at her like she'd lost her mind. "Didn't your dream infer that we'd all be fried to a crisp in there?"

"Yes."

When Clarissa said nothing else, Erin frowned. "Yes is all you have to say?"

"Yes."

"All right then. Fire up the barbeque."

Clarissa sighed. "I'm sorry. I don't know what else to do."

"We're going to attract some attention anyway." Erin's gaze coasted over Clarissa. "Both of us have tangled hair and no costumes."

"Plus we both have these nice little marks on our necks."

"Everyone will think that's the costume."

Clarissa stood slowly. "What about the glowing eyes thing? We can't really control that when it happens, can we?"

Erin also stood. "From what I understand, that comes whenever we're angry, frightened, aroused—" she gave a humorless laugh, "—or we're ready to kick some major butt."

Incredible power rolled into Clarissa's body. "Um...are we supposed to be significantly stronger since we've been bitten?"

"Not as strong as a vampire or a man like Lachlan or Jared. But we are about as strong as two men on our own."

Clarissa gulped. "Two men?"

"At least."

They left the bushes and headed for the community center.

As they came to the double doors leading into the front of the community center, Erin looked at her watch. "Things should be in full swing for another hour before curfew. I wonder why the ancient one hasn't hit this place before now."

A scream rent the air from inside the complex and they looked at each other.

"Maybe he already has," Clarissa said.

Chapter Nineteen

Ronan met up with the others in the basement of the Gunn Inn after traversing the long tunnels that lead to the Victorian structure. He could see the growing concern on their faces.

Gilda stood close to her husband Tom, her eyes filled with worry. "Where else could they be if not in the tunnels?"

Ronan's mind raced with ideas. Before he could say anything a loud popping noise announced the presence of another vampire.

Jim Leggett appeared in the room, standing near the bottom of the stairs leading out of the basement. Instantly Ronan's anger surged forth and he saw Lachlan stiffen into a ready to fight stance.

"What the hell?" Jared asked. "When were you turned into a vampire?"

Leggett put up one hand. "No time to explain. I'm here to help you find Clarissa and Erin."

Ronan's vampire dominant traits took over and he felt his fangs growing once again. "Unless you were the asshole that took them." He stepped forward and seized Leggett by the sweater, bunching it up as he hissed in the new vampire's face, "Where are they and what did you do to them?"

Leggett didn't struggle. In fact, he seemed contrite. "I kidnapped them from the house."

Ronan removed his weapon from his leather jacket, took off the safety and jammed the piece under Leggett's chin. "Maybe I should let Jared cram a silver stake through your heart. Or Lachlan can take his silver dagger and do the job for me. Perhaps I'll put a bullet in you right now. You aren't the ancient one. It would *kill* you."

Lachlan took up position on the other side of Leggett, his expression fierce. "You piece of filth! If you've hurt them—"

"I did, but—"

Ronan lifted Leggett clean off his feet and launched him with force back against the wall. Jim grunted as he hit and landed with a thud on his ass, his breath gasping out of him.

Ronan started toward Leggett again, but Jared grabbed his arm. "Wait. We can't find out where the women are if you beat the shit out of him. Save revenge for later."

Leggett rubbed his throat. "They sent me to tell you where they're going."

Fearing a trap, Ronan said, "Bullshit. You're a feckin' liar."

Leggett laughed, no true mirth in his tone. "Go ahead. Kill me. I've been turned into a vampire. Do you think I wanted that? My life was taken away from me."

Ronan felt a pang of sympathy for Jim and put the gun back into his leather jacket. The man hadn't sought out vampirism like he had. Still, anger burned in Ronan's gut like a hot coal. "Just tell us where they are."

"Sorley and I were imprisoned in the tunnels together and ordered by the old vampire to take Clarissa and Erin to a big crypt on the east side of the forest cut into a rocky outcropping on Cold View Ridge."

"Let's go then," Tom said out-of-the-blue. "What are we waiting for?"

Leggett pulled himself into standing position but stayed against the wall. "They won't be there now. They just wanted me to tell you they're free and heading to the community center."

Fear raced through Ronan. "No."

"Oh, no. No," Micky said.

"If they're all right, why couldn't we contact them via telepathy?" Lachlan asked.

Leggett hesitated, then said in a halting voice, "Because the ancient one put a restraining force field on them when we got to the crypt. They managed to break it before I came back to the crypt."

"Then shouldn't we be able to contact them now?" Micky asked.

"They're weak," Leggett said. "I doubt they could hear you or send telepathic messages."

This time Lachlan advanced on the man, severe consequences boiling in his eyes. He came practically nose to nose with Leggett. "Why are they weak?"

Leggett again hedged, real fear in his glowing eyes. "They were bitten."

Ronan felt new anger making its way to the surface, one that included kicking this vampire's ass as soon as the confrontation with the ancient one finished. "The ancient one?"

Leggett shook his head, his Adam's apple bobbing as he swallowed hard. "I did. To keep the ancient one from killing them."

"Son-of-a-bitch!" Ronan stalked toward Leggett and this time no one tried to stop him. He pointed a finger in the man's face. "When this is over you'd better hope you run far because I'll find you."

Leggett's eyes widened, then rage replaced fear in his face. "I saved their lives! What do you want from me? I could have let the ancient one bite them and they'd be dead. Not half-vampire, not vampire. Dead!"

Ronan took a heaving breath. He couldn't see his way clear to thank the man for biting the women. "Leggett and I will go to the community center via teleportation."

"We need a coordinated plan," Tom said. "We can't go barging in there and yell at everyone to get out of the community center. That won't work."

Gilda walked toward Ronan. "Tom's right. What can we do to make sure everyone gets out of the building *and* keep the ancient one from launching an attack?"

"I'm not sure it's just the ancient one launching an attack anymore." Jim looked almost ill, his skin deathly pale. "When the ancient one attacked me I was outside my hotel room near the alley. He dragged me back into the alley and I was helpless." A visible shudder ran through his body. "When he bit me I felt a new evil inside him, and later he told me that he is now a part of that evil and it directs him."

"That makes sense," Gilda said. "He's talking about the power that took Micky captive when we went into the tunnels. It has to be the same thing."

"Great," Lachlan said with a grunt. He crossed his arms and glared. "So we have the ancient one, Sorley, and this other evil to contend with." He threw a sickened glance at Leggett. "And you."

Weareherewearehere wearehere.

The whispering made everyone glance about the room.

Micky smiled. "The shadow people."

Gilda snuggled up to Tom and he put his arm around her. "How do you know it's the so-called good shadows and not the bad?"

Micky's smile broadened. "I can feel them. They're always with me and they're here to help."

Ronan wouldn't turn away any assistance at this point. He knew that whatever happened next could be the last time he would see his friends, and he looked at each of them in turn.

He explained how one or more of them would scream fire when they got in the building. "We'll grab Clarissa and Erin and get out."

Leggett put up his hand. "I'll do it. I'll scream fire."

Ronan grabbed Leggett's collar and said, "Teleport to the community center. Now."

* * * * *

Clarissa jammed on the bar door handles at the same Erin did and they stepped into the empty vestibule. Both rooms in the separate wings of the community center held at least a hundred people milling about in costumes. The popular song *Monster Mash* filtered out of both rooms. Clarissa figured she'd see some murder or mayhem going on after that scream. Instead everything looked normal, people walking and talking, dancing and laughing.

Another screech erupted, sending chills up and down Clarissa's spine. A low groan followed. She figured it out. "It's a soundtrack. They're playing noises along with the music."

Erin sighed. "Thank goodness." She looked into one room, then the other. "Where do we go first?"

Clarissa made a command decision. "The main room with the stage is to the left. Let's go there first."

They plunged into the crowd and Clarissa felt a renewed strength simmering deep in her body until the power percolating in her system felt more intoxicating than wine. Earlier she'd been aching and feeling a little dizzy, but ever since the exhilarating run through the woods, she'd felt much better. She expected fear to make her heart operate like a jackhammer. It didn't. Fright didn't seem like an option any more. All these people depended on her and Erin whether they knew it or not.

Plowing through the throng, they bumped into people dressed like ghosts, goblins and assorted devils. On occasion a little kid costumed as an innocuous cat or bunny rabbit wandered into their path.

Clarissa's heart ached and her throat went tight when she thought of anything happening to the children. They'd made it almost all the way to the stage up at the front.

A rumbling overruled the sound system, and several people stopped dancing, looking around as if they heard the noise.

"What was that?" Erin asked.

Clarissa didn't get to answer. The lights went brighter and the stage made a strange cracking noise. Another crackle came from the speakers and a husky laugh drowned out the music.

"I don't think that was planned," Erin said.

"Definitely not. Do you know where the main plug-in point for the decorations is?"

Erin made a thumbs-up gesture. "I do. I'll unplug it."

"One less thing to catch fire. I'll get the music unplugged, too."

"While I'm at it, I'll check the circuit breakers outside."

For a second their eyes locked, their friendship cemented by mutual peril.

"Be careful," Clarissa said.

Erin managed a smile. "You, too."

Erin headed toward the area beyond the stage and the backrooms.

Within seconds the twinkling orange, yellow and brown lights around the stage and in the autumn leaves arrangements around the room stopped blinking and the last few strains of *Monster Mash* faded. Groans and mutters of surprise filled the room.

Before Clarissa could move the ancient one's cruel voice filled her head. *They must all die.*

Clarissa sent a confident message. *They don't have to. This isn't necessary.*

If it was up to me, I'd consume them when I needed, one by one over the days and months ahead. But that's not what the darkest wants. And the darkest wants you and Erin and all of Pine Forest to be shattered.

You've already turned the town into a major crime center. What else could you want?

A sinister chuckle filled her head. *The darkest must have complete domination. Chaos. Ruin.*

She didn't know if psychology would work on a creature like the ancient one, but she tried. *What about what* you *want?*

A long pause lingered until the ancient one said, *I am only the servant, not the master.*

These words, whispered with a tone filled with savory delight and resignation, formed a cold, hard pit in her stomach. She'd thought her nastiest worry would center on the vampire, but perhaps she'd been mistaken.

She recognized that to get everyone's attention she would have to make a scene. She moved to the steps leading to the stage with a preternatural speed and stood upon the stage. She started for the podium. Danger simmered in her blood, pulsed through her skin. She knew anyone who looked could see the glow radiating from her eyes. People started to notice before she reached the podium. They pointed, a combination of fear and annoyance holding them captive. Instinct took over as new strengths swelled in her body.

I have your friend. This time the putrid voice was a combination of the ancient one and something more baleful. *Cease your efforts or she dies.*

"Listen!" Clarissa called out above the noise. "Everyone needs to leave this building now. Something bad is about to happen."

Voices went up around the crowd. "What is she doing? What is going on? Who *is* that?"

A commotion at the front made people part like the Red Sea as Jared and Micky pushed their way through.

"She's telling the truth." Jared's voice carried way above the crowd. "Everyone's got to leave. It's like we said at the meeting the other night."

"Who are these fruitcakes?" a man dressed like a pinecone asked. "Is this part of the party?"

"Get down off there!" A man attired as a stereotypical vampire, white-painted face twisted with annoyance, jeered at her. "Stop scaring people!"

Blinding emotion made her say again, "Listen to me."

She noticed people bunched up at the front of the building in the foyer.

"Fire!" A male voice came from the front entrance above the restless murmurs. "Fire!"

She glanced over and saw Jim. *Jim.*

People whirled at the sound of his voice.

Everything seemed to switch to slow motion, despite the instantaneous reaction of the people.

Clarissa saw Ronan's beloved face behind Jim and heard his husky Irish tone in her head. *Clarissa, it's all right. We're here now. Leggett's trying to get everyone to move out of the building by saying there's a fire when there isn't.*

Overjoyed at seeing him, she wasn't prepared for the popping noise on stage. Screams went up as two huge hands clasped her shoulders from behind. Sharp nails and bone-hard fingers pressed into her flesh with splinter intensity pain. She saw Ronan's eyes widen before the cruel fingers spun her around to face their towering owner.

All previous description didn't prepare her for the reality of seeing the gargoyle face. Gray and hard as stone, the face held the curves and sharp cuts associated with a gargoyle's lines. With his bald head and somewhat pointed ears, the creature stood out. His lips drew back in a caricature of a smile, the canine teeth extraordinarily long and sharp. Cloaked neck to toe in a huge black cape, the gargoyle-like vampire fit in with a few of the other fake vampires wandering the room.

She heard Ronan's voice in her head. *Clarissa, do not look into his eyes!*

More voices gathered inside her, their murmurs and pleas frantic for her attention.

Look away. Jared's voice echoed in her head.

Then a voice came she didn't expect, his sharp Irish tone so different from Ronan's. *Please don't look!*

Sorley?

Two light fixtures in the high ceiling exploded. Screams went up and someone shouted again, "Fire! Get out now!"

More voices entered her head. Shadow people.

Resisthimresisthimresisthim.

Useyourpoweruseyourpoweruseyourpower.

Two more fixtures in the ceiling burst, plunging the room into semi-darkness. Glass and sparks rained down from the ceiling. People ducked and panic erupted as they poured toward the exits.

"Clarissa!" A guttural shout, filled with sharp anguish, belonged to Ronan.

Her heart pounded in her chest like a jackhammer, her breath short and punchy.

Shouting, pushing and trampling, the partygoers reacted like all typical crowds. Before she could react to the shadow people's direction for her to use her power, the ancient one's pitiless fingers clamped on her face. He jerked her head toward him and she inadvertently looked into his eyes.

Hot and fierce, the ancient one's eyes burned solid crimson. No lens, no iris. Just fiery depths of hell. Nausea swept into her stomach and her knees weakened. Her muscles felt like gelatin, her body under the monster's command.

You are mine. You will do as I bid.

No! No! She writhed in the strong hold.

Weakness threatened and she feared this might be the last chance for life.

Pushawaynowpushawaynowpushawaynow. The shadow people whispered to her.

Wewillhelpyouwewillhelpyouwewillhelpyou.

Dramatically the energies surrounding her built. Blood pumped furiously through her veins as her heart raced and her muscles cried out for action. A weird sensation, like that of a gathering storm, pierced her midsection. Instead of hurting, the feeling galvanized her into action.

With a grunt she shoved against the ancient one's chest. The creature loosened his grip and she stumbled backward. She slipped and landed on her ass on the hard, cold stage with a painful thump. Renewal of energy surged into her system and she leapt to her feet to confront the old vampire.

Fire crackled behind the stage. Smoke started to fill the room as the remaining people scrambled to leave the building. As smoke attacked her lungs she coughed and shoved aside dizziness. Fire climbed onto curtains arranged behind the makeshift stage. A blur of movement caught her attention and then Ronan stood between her and the creature.

She sensed something, an instant when time stagnated and peril held the advantage. She reached out for him with one hand as terror rocketed through her. "Ronan! No!"

"Worthless scum!" The ancient one took a swing and landed a punch to Ronan's face.

Ronan sailed backwards past her and fell from the stage. The ancient one laughed.

Her heart felt like it might stop. More anger exploded and she took action. She reached for the podium without thinking. Grabbing the top with both hands, she yanked. The podium came away from the stage floor. Spitting angry, she lifted and swung the podium just high enough to send it sailing across the floor toward the old vampire's shins. It connected, sending the ancient one flying. Triumph burst inside her, but the vampire was hardly fazed. He jumped to his feet and came toward her. With certainty she shouldn't have, Clarissa knew she could fight the ancient one.

What choice did she have?

Instinctively, she put up both hands and concentrated all her energy outward. A shimmering transparent wall formed. The ancient one slammed into it and fell back with an indignant cry.

"Take that, asshole!" She punched one fist in the air.

A hand grabbed her shoulder and she swung around, an elbow aimed to land in the person's stomach. Ronan dodged her swing. "It's me. We've got to go now!"

Relief filled her as he clasped her hand and they ran toward the south exit. Several steps later she was snatched off her feet, dangling as she kicked out in reflex.

Her scream came more as a defiant, heated shout. "No!"

Before she could scream again, lacerating pain gripped the right side of her neck. A strange crunching noise and excruciating pain told her one thing.

Stunned by the pain, her vision went white, then black and started to fade at the edges.

The ancient one had bitten her.

Unlike Jim's bite, this one would kill her.

No. Must fight.

Putting all her strength into escaping, she wriggled, twisted and writhed against the hold tightening around her waist. A revelation came a second later. Combating him like this worked like quicksand to suck her down deeper into his tangled web, exhausting her resources as he drained her blood with deep, lapping suction.

As if she'd fainted, she went limp.

Seconds later she fell, taking the ancient one off guard. She landed on her left side with a painful slap, and the pain rocketed through her head, shoulders, hips and legs. A moan of anger and hurt parted her lips. Despite the pain, she couldn't lie here and wait for him to finish her off. She struggled upright just as Ronan again stepped between her and the ancient one.

Ronan didn't take his gaze away from his mortal enemy as Clarissa struggled to her feet. She stood just to Ronan's left side, her vision fuzzy through pain, weakness and smoke.

Fighthimfighthimfighthim

Nownownow, echoed in her head as the shadow people encouraged her.

"Fight him together!" Ronan's red-hued gaze clashed and tangled with hers and she knew he heard the shadow people, too.

In that instant she saw infinite love in his eyes and it mixed with the resolve of a man who would go down fighting.

Fight him together. Fight him now. Now. Now. The voices came from all around her and suddenly she saw Gilda, Tom, Jared, Micky, Erin and Lachlan lining up near her and Ronan. Sorley and Jim appeared just behind the ancient one and grabbed him by the arms.

"Push him toward the fire!" Ronan directed them with a movement of his hands.

Sorley shouted his command. "Together!"

With a toss the vampires propelled the ancient one toward the fire raging behind the stage and climbing ever closer to their position. The old vampire growled deep in his throat as he stopped short of the conflagration.

Perhaps, with the force of the *darkest* behind him, the ancient one could resist all their powers.

The thought terrified Clarissa. Sharp and staggering the fear threatened to undetermined her courage.

Before she could resurrect confidence, Sorley withdrew a long blade about the length and appearance of a cutlass, a contrivance that gleamed in the fire like silver. He rushed the old one and swung in an arch as if he meant to chop off the vampire's head. Sorley screamed like a warrior as the blade swung around.

The ancient one put up one hand and the blade stopped midair before it could reach him. With a loud, screeching laugh the ancient one flicked his wrist, Sorley went flying backwards and the cutlass clanged to the floor.

Ronan pulled out his weapon and started to aim for the heart, but the ancient one motioned at the gun and it came away from Ronan's hands and went airborne. Breathing deeply and seemingly unaffected by the smoke, the ancient one threw back his head and laughed.

"You will all burn in here with me." He pointed to Erin. "If I can't have her, no other man will! The *darkest* commands it!"

If they left now, ran to save their own lives, Clarissa knew the town was doomed. The ancient one would come back. Tears stung her eyes, smoke and terror and sadness mixing with the abrupt knowledge of what she must do.

Sacrifice, she projected in her mind toward her friends. *We must be willing to sacrifice everything to stop him.*

Without pause her friends took up the chant. *Sacrifice. Sacrifice. Sacrifice.*

The shadow people filled her head.

Sacrificetosaveall.

Sacrificetosaveall.

Sacrificetosaveyourselves.

It was then she felt it, a strange stirring in her stomach. A blast of potency came from her solar plexus and washed outward like a shock wave as her hands pushed forward in a heaving motion.

She had maybe two seconds to register the unqualified shock spreading over the ancient one's face as her psychic force gathered up the silver blade. She motioned with her right hand to lift the blade and swung in a wide arc. With a single slicing motion the blade severed the old vampire's head. With a motion of her left hand she pushed his head and body until it sailed backwards the last few feet necessary.

To her horror, a shriek came from his disembodied head as he vanished into the consuming flames.

Clarissa didn't have time to rejoice or warn everyone to leave the building before it burned down around her ears. As Ronan turned toward her, only a few feet away, her vision went black at the corners and her knees gave way.

Ronan's anguished cry was the last thing she heard. "Clarissa!"

* * * * *

Ronan thought his immortality would end and in that lonely instant he knew he would gladly give up his existence if only Clarissa would live.

Clarissa's face had gone paper-white as she collapsed and right away he felt her distress slice with razor-sharp pain. Unadulterated terror clutched his gut as he raced with supernatural speed toward the woman he loved. No time to assess her condition in this hellhole.

He hauled Clarissa up in his arms and sped toward the nearest exit. As he burst through the door, everyone followed close on his heels.

The wail of sirens filled his ears and the throng of noise and smoke, screams and shouts went across his hypersensitive nerves like a sharp object nailed into his head.

Without waiting for medical assistance to find him, he ran into the surrounding woods with Clarissa in his arms. When he reached an area where no one could see, he realized his friends weren't far behind.

He sank to the ground with Clarissa wrapped in his arms and tears soaked his cheeks.

"Clarissa, speak to me." He leaned toward her and detected instantly something horribly wrong. "She's barely breathing."

Few seconds went by but in those increments he suffered a thousand deaths. His woman had done everything she could to kill the ancient one and succeeded.

She sacrificed her life for everyone else's.

Sorrow belted him and he gasped with the pain. He'd thought Fenella's death had lacerated him to the quick, but nothing in his life mortal or immortal reached the purgatory he felt this minute. He cupped her soot-streaked face and saw the blood drying on her neck. No sign of life, her skin cold as the grave.

Jared dropped down beside him. "I've got a little medical training. Let me see her." He tested the pulse in her neck. "Extremely faint pulse."

A sob slipped from Micky's throat. "The ancient one took too much blood. He's killed her."

Lachlan reached them and put both his hands on either side of Clarissa's head. He closed his eyes. "Ronan, concentrate with me and see if we can heal her."

Shocked out of his misery, Ronan closed his eyes and complied.

"Jesus, Mary and Joseph," he heard Sorley gasp. "Help her."

"It's not working," Lachlan said a few moments later.

Lachlan looked into Ronan's eyes and there Ronan saw a question form in his old friend's gaze. "You have to do it."

Silence passed, steady and growing. Ronan froze up. "No."

"You must," Lachlan said, his eyes blazing, his face stern. "We can't get her to a doctor in time. She's fading too fast. You have no choice."

"What?" Erin asked as tears streamed down her face. "What does he have to do?"

"Ah hell," Sorley said with a broken voice. "Bring her across. He has to bring her across."

Gilda groaned and put her hands over her eyes. Her voice came out hoarse and pained. "Make her a vampire?"

Ronan hung his head. "She doesn't deserve this."

"No, but do you want her with you?" Lachlan asked, his deep voice full of sympathy.

"Of course I feckin' want her with me," he said through his teeth, tears flowing harder down his face as a sob left his throat. "I love her. I love her more than my own life."

Without another word he stood with her in his arms and looked at his devastated friends. "I'll take her to a holy place where it will be pure."

He popped into invisibility and transported the woman in his arms to St. Bartholomew's. It didn't matter what type of holy place he went to, nor did religious affiliation. Vampires were made in many faiths and he had once been Catholic. It seemed only right to give her the light in his undead soul and the small cathedral's cleansing power.

He made sure no one lurked in the building before he proceeded with what he must do. He strode to an alcove which featured a large stained glass figure of Mary. A single bench stood in front of the window. Ronan sat down with Clarissa in his arms, and as her head flopped back on his cradling arm, he winced in mental pain. What he did next would break his heart, but if it succeeded it would also mend his torn soul.

Without further hesitation he bit into the left side of her neck and drank. As her remaining blood came into his mouth he felt the last of her life drain away.

Immediate and blinding ecstasy filled his head and temporarily obliterated his anguish. He'd forgotten the untainted bliss that came from draining a mortal of their life's blood.

As the pleasure mounted it flowed from his mind to his body, reaching his cock and making it fully engorged within seconds.

Oh, feckin' hell. Yes!

As his cock grew tighter and harder he felt her go lax in his arms and knew she would now cross over. As he removed his teeth from her neck, he lapped at the wound and it closed. Ronan bent his head and nuzzled the very neck he'd ravaged. Then he allowed the sobs to come and the horror of what he'd done enfold him.

* * * * *

Clarissa drifted in a dream engulfed with heat and flames, her world tumbled into a mix of conflicting images and physical pain. With a jolt, strength returned. As awareness also came back, she heard a plaintive sob. Worried and bewildered, she took in what she felt and heard by degrees. After Jim had bitten her and she'd awakened in the crypt, she'd understood she did possess more physical ability and heightened senses then a mere mortal.

This felt different.

Sensual overload hit her and for a moment she couldn't move, could scarcely breathe. Pain seared her neck on both sides but she couldn't make a sound. She could hear water dripping somewhere, and the cold touched her but did not. Her skin, supersensitive, prickled with corporeal wakefulness. Warm, powerful arms held her as if she might break or dissolve. More than that, a man's breathing rasped, his heart-breaking sobs searing deep into her. She couldn't bear to hear him cry this way, to hurt so much.

Her eyes popped open and she recognized Ronan's wavy, tousled hair as he nestled against her and his tears dampened her skin.

Ronan is crying? For me? Why?

As her fingers slipped into his hair, she also clutched at his trembling shoulder to give him comfort.

His head snapped up and she stared into his red-rimmed eyes, filled with a special misery reserved only for the damned.

"Clarissa," he whispered hoarsely.

As she sat up her arm slipped around his shoulder and she sat on his lap. "Ronan, what happened? What's wrong?"

At first he didn't answer her and his gaze reflected a profound joy mingled with desolation. He swallowed hard and as he explained, her heart jolted with shock.

Before she could speak he continued. "I brought you here because it is a sacred place, a holy place."

Her own tears flowed, cleansing her eyes and her heart at the same time. Deep concern still filled his eyes.

"Do you hate me?" he asked. "I couldn't let you die that way. I had to...it had to be on my terms, so that you'd come back to me. I wanted you any way I could have you." He pressed shaky kisses to her forehead, her cheeks and her lips. "I love you. I love you."

Sensing and seeing his complete misery, she knew deep in her now undead soul she wouldn't want it any other way. "As long as we're together, it doesn't matter."

"I've destroyed you, broken you in pieces—"

"No." She put her finger over his lips. "You've given me an eternity with you. I'm *complete*."

"Not quite. Two more things must happen. One, you must take blood from me." His eyes blazed, fire returning to them. "A new female vampire must mate. We must do it now."

"Yes."

As she kissed him her desire for life turned to an appetite for physical union. Vampire in her heart and body, she hungered the way he hungered, felt what he felt. His tongue rasped over hers and a hot, tight sensation seared between her legs requiring immediate and total satisfaction. He drew back from her and blood ruby stained his eyes, the passion riding high and fierce. With a single rip he tore her sweater off her body and her bra went flying. He dipped his head and captured one nipple in his mouth, sucking hard. She cried out as holy fire breached her body in one swell of ecstasy.

They tasted each other and as their breathing turned hot and fast, Ronan whispered, "We are one always."

Nothing mattered but this driving need to reaffirm their love. Clarissa could tell, with her heightened sense of hearing, that no one was within miles of the church. They wouldn't be interrupted.

"Do it now," he said. "Taste me."

She knew what he meant, and for a moment she hesitated. Then she realized the very idea of blood, of taking his blood within her, made her body ache with longing. Her stomach yearned for the fulfillment, her body needing what he could give her for nourishment. She realized her teeth had already grown longer, and in astonishment she hesitated.

All worry lost, she reached for him, her teeth going to his neck. She lapped at his skin with her tongue and he shivered. With one sharp bite she fastened to his neck and he flinched.

When she tried to pull back he held her head gently against his neck. "No, don't stop. God, don't stop."

Blood filled her mouth, and where she would have been revolted before, now the sensation, the joy it brought her and Ronan removed all doubt.

Heat rolled through her body like a new sun rising, a deep throb filling her womb, her nipples tight and aching as she shivered and quaked against him in a new sexual ecstasy. Her loins filled with need to hold him, to feel that hard cock driven over and over inside her until she screamed. She drew her lips away from his neck, then licked instinctively at the wound to close it. She must have him now.

She left his lap and helped him unfasten his pants. In seconds they were stripped naked and she straddled him. He held her at the waist, her wet, throbbing heat almost touching his erect cock.

She gazed into his fiery eyes and said, "One always."

He lowered her onto his cock with one hard, deep thrust.

She gasped, the sensation beyond description, the heat instantaneous. She whimpered.

"Easy." He groaned. "Oh, yes. Yes. Open to me. That's it. Open to me."

With love and trust she relaxed her muscles, fitting her tightness around him.

"That's it," he said softly. "That's it."

They didn't thrust against each other, the gloving of her body around his enough to start the final fire. She clasped his shoulders tightly and within a few minutes she couldn't stand it anymore. She gyrated upon him and he thrust with tiny movements designed for pure sexual torture. Hanging on a treacherous cliff she rode out the delirious feeling of his cock rubbing firmly against that place high and deep inside her that only he could reach.

"Oh, more." She said as ecstasy rose. "More."

He held on to her waist and drew her up. He slammed upwards as he brought her down, giving the vanquishing thrust.

Clarissa erupted and her scream echoed and entwined with his throaty roar as they found new life together.

Epilogue
Four days later

The small party of friends looked cozy and happy as Clarissa watched them gathering in the living room of Erin's home. The entire group, including Gilda and Tom, participated in a celebration of life and the salvation of Pine Forest.

Sorley chatted with Ronan, his old self restored after a few days recovery from the effects of the ancient one's tainted influence. Sorley sometimes looked at her with scared eyes, like she might blame him for what happened. She didn't. Besides, she'd become like him, a creature of the night. They would share this through their immortal days.

In the days since Halloween Pine Forest limped through recovery, the papers reporting the strange crime wave had subsided. People went through the day acting almost as if nothing untoward had happened, and Ronan explained this occurred wherever the ancient one had plundered. A sort of self-induced amnesia produced by the need for mortal denial of a hideous truth. Not only did Pine Forest forget the grisly details of the killings, no one except their little group remembered seeing the ancient one and the unbelievable incidents in the community center.

The entire fire incident was reported as a freak accident caused by an electrical short. Blessedly, nobody but the ancient one lost their lives in the inferno.

Earlier in the day, shaded from the depleting effects of the sun, their friends told them their plans.

Erin and Lachlan would leave Pine Forest and do some traveling. First stop, Scotland. A wedding in the Highlands was planned for the spring.

Micky would move to Denver with Jared, and a wedding would be celebrated in the fall in Denver.

Gilda and Tom and their son also planned to leave Pine Forest, though they hadn't decided where they would go yet.

No one had seen or heard from Jim after that night, but Clarissa suspected he'd left in shame and horror at what he'd done to her and Erin. She hoped wherever he'd gone he could learn to forgive himself and understand he'd played a part in saving Pine Forest that terrible Halloween night.

She would never forget her days here in Pine Forest whether she stayed or left.

Ronan smiled at her from across the room and she felt the inevitable stirring deep inside for mental and physical joining.

Holding her hand over her stomach in a protective gesture, she crossed the room and settled onto the loveseat next to her man. She gave him a mysterious smile, even though her condition hadn't been a secret for two days. On the night the ancient one was destroyed, she'd taken the second pregnancy test and discovered what she suspected. She was with child. Whether the first test missed the boat or their subsequent couplings had produced results, they would never know.

Lachlan walked out of the kitchen with Erin, champagne in hand. They started filling glasses.

Once everyone else had bubbly, Clarissa lifted her glass and said, "I have a toast to make. To a wonderful man who came into my life and changed everything. I will love you for eternity, Ronan Kieran."

A cheer went up and they clinked glasses. When they settled down, Ronan made his own toast. Clarissa's heart turned over and started to thud like crazy with excitement when he got down on one knee in front of her.

"To Clarissa, the woman I love. I could have done this in private, but I wanted to make it official in front of all my friends." He took her hand and kissed the back and pure love shone in his eyes. "Will you marry me?"

Choked with emotion she managed to say, "Yes, of course. Yes."

As they kissed, their friends clapped and cheered.

Tears rolled down Clarissa's cheeks and he brushed them away with his thumbs. "Can I talk to you in private a moment?"

He led her back to their attic hideaway, making their way in the dark. When they reached the room and closed the door, he drew her into his arms and kissed her deeply.

When he let her up for air, she asked, "Ronan do you think my special abilities on Halloween were because Jim bit me, or because I was pregnant?"

His eyebrows quirked upward. "I forgot to tell you what the seer said when she called today. She believes the power came from both situations. Yusuf told me that the love of a woman and my willingness to sacrifice would be what saved us. I think the pregnancy also gave you power. When all of us combined forces with you, it was enough to defeat the ancient one."

She nodded and snuggled deeper into his arms. She gazed out the fan shaped window at the stars. Things were winding down. "Everyone who remembers what happened this month is going away."

"Perhaps that's a good thing. All that matters to me is that you don't regret what I had to do to keep you with me."

Hastening to reassure, she kissed him. "I have forever with you. I could never regret that."

He brushed his lips across hers in a scorching prelude of what would come later when the house quieted and their passion heated. "Would you like to honeymoon in Ireland? Visit my homeland and see where I was born?"

She laughed with delight and he swung her around in his arms. After a few more torrid kisses, she said, "Ronan, do you think the *darkest* is gone? I don't want to visit Pine Forest in a few years again to…to hunt…*it*."

Ronan knew what she meant and it concerned him, too. He shook his head. "I don't think the *darkest* is ever gone. It exists in the world in many places. Here in Pine Forest it waits for the next time. It sleeps in the dark, lonely places, fragmented tonight by the power of true love."

The End

About the author:

Suspenseful, erotic, edgy, thrilling, romantic, adventurous. All these words are used to describe award-winning, best-selling novelist Denise A. Agnew's novels. Romantic Times Magazine called her romantic suspense novels DANGEROUS INTENTIONS and TREACHEROUS WISHES "top-notch romantic suspense." With paranormal, time travel, romantic comedy, contemporary, historical, erotica, and romantic suspense novels under her belt, she proves her gift for writing about a diverse range of subjects. (Writing tales that scare the reader is her ultimate thrill.)

Denise's inspiration for her novels comes from innumerable sources, but the fact she has lived in Colorado, Hawaii, and the United Kingdom has given her a lifetime of ideas. Her experiences with archaeology have crept into her work, as well as numerous travels throughout England, Ireland, Scotland, and Wales. Denise currently lives in Arizona with her real life hero, her husband.

Denise welcomes mail from readers. You can write to her c/o Ellora's Cave Publishing at 1337 Commerce Drive, Suite 13, Stow OH 44224.

Why an electronic book?

We live in the Information Age—an exciting time in the history of human civilization in which technology rules supreme and continues to progress in leaps and bounds every minute of every hour of every day. For a multitude of reasons, more and more avid literary fans are opting to purchase e-books instead of paperbacks. The question to those not yet initiated to the world of electronic reading is simply: *why?*

Price. An electronic title at Ellora's Cave Publishing runs anywhere from 40-75% less than the cover price of the exact same title in paperback format. Why? Cold mathematics. It is less expensive to publish an e-book than it is to publish a paperback, so the savings are passed along to the consumer.

Space. Running out of room to house your paperback books? That is one worry you will never have with electronic novels. For a low one-time cost, you can purchase a handheld computer designed specifically for e-reading purposes. Many e-readers are larger than the average handheld, giving you plenty of screen room. Better yet, hundreds of titles can be stored within your new library—a single microchip. (Please note that Ellora's Cave does not endorse any specific brands. You can check our website at www.ellorascave.com for customer recommendations we make available to new consumers.)

Mobility. Because your new library now consists of only a microchip, your entire cache of books can be taken with you wherever you go.

Personal preferences are accounted for. Are the words you are currently reading too small? Too large?

Too...**ANNOYING**? Paperback books cannot be modified according to personal preferences, but e-books can.

Innovation. The way you read a book is not the only advancement the Information Age has gifted the literary community with. There is also the factor of what you can read. Ellora's Cave Publishing will be introducing a new line of interactive titles that are available in e-book format only.

Instant gratification. Is it the middle of the night and all the bookstores are closed? Are you tired of waiting days — sometimes weeks — for online and offline bookstores to ship the novels you bought? Ellora's Cave Publishing sells instantaneous downloads 24 hours a day, 7 days a week, 365 days a year. Our e-book delivery system is 100% automated, meaning your order is filled as soon as you pay for it.

Those are a few of the top reasons why electronic novels are displacing paperbacks for many an avid reader. As always, Ellora's Cave Publishing welcomes your questions and comments. We invite you to email us at service@ellorascave.com or write to us directly at: 1337 Commerce Drive, Suite 13, Stow OH 44224.

Discover for yourself why readers can't get enough of the multiple award-winning publisher Ellora's Cave. Whether you prefer e-books or paperbacks, be sure to visit EC on the web at www.ellorascave.com for an erotic reading experience that will leave you breathless.

WWW.ELLORASCAVE.COM